GREAT HEX

ALSO BY ANDREW FORREST BAKER

MORE FROM THE HEX'D SERIES

HEX MAGIC : BOOK ONE

HEXUAL AWAKENING: BOOK TWO

HEX, BLOOD, & RITUAL: BOOK FOUR (COMING SOON)

NOVELS

THE HOUSE THAT WASN'T THERE

LESSER GODS & DEMONS

WHERE THE BIRDS FLY SOUTH TO (COMING SOON)

SHORT STORY COLLECTIONS

WE TREMBLE AS WE SINK

ROAST

GREAT HEX

ANDREW FORREST BAKER

Parlyaree Press
Atlanta, Georgia
www.parlyaree.com

Library of Congress Cataloging-in-Publication Data
Names: Baker, Andrew Forrest, 1980, author.
Title: GREAT HEX / Andrew Forrest Baker
Description: First Edition | Atlanta : Parlyaree Press, 2025
Identifiers: LCCN: 2024919682 | ISBN: 978-1-961206-11-3 (paperback)
Subjects: LCGFT: Novels
LC record available at https://lccn.loc.gov/2024919682

Design by Parlyaree Press

Front Cover/Title Typeface is Rosella Solid.
Interior Text Typeface is Baskerville, designed in the 1750s by John Baskerville and cut by punchcutter John Handy.
Interior Ornaments from Espiritu, LTC Flourons, & Bodoni Ornaments.

Paperback ISBN: 978-1-961206-11-3
Ebook ISBN: 978-1-961206-12-0

For those who are not afraid of the world—
even when the world fears them.

Explore it | Indulge in it
Brighten it with your magic.

ANDREW FORREST BAKER

GREAT HEX

HEX'D BOOK THREE

Spring had already sprung for the southern part of the northern hemisphere even though Ostara was still a week away. HEX was abuzz with customers—witch and human alike—scouring the newly built display tables (thanks to my wonderful boyfriend Cernun) for dried irises and lavender, amethyst and rose quartz, and pastel candles to welcome the Spring Equinox. We even had some special candles—large, thick phalluses; floral expressive vulvas; and intersex combos—to mark the new life and fertility aspects of the holiday in addition to the painted eggs and wood-carved hare statuettes our more mortal customers were used to.

I'd been worried in the month since a Defend Mankind From Magic attack had sent a good portion of my shop up in flames, but my fears had been for naught. Folks were actually flocking in—largely in spite of the DMFM—to support one of Atlanta's oldest magical establishments, here since well before magic was revealed to the world. The hexagonal shelving Cernun had added along the far wall, which I'd since stocked with leather-bound journals or tomes on ritual and intention, had drawn new groups of patrons I'd never met before. The section I'd filled with smutty romance—which was not magic per se, but held its own kind of power—was especially picked over.

Stacey winked at me from across the store as she guided a young woman through the herbal and stone concoctions that would work best in her hand-made poultice bag. It was illegal, by edict of the Moral Authority of Witches, to sell a readymade spell (unless the MAW sanctioned them for themselves to make money off or for a special event held by one of their large donors), but a little instruction—particularly to a human—was not forbidden. At least with the more mundane magics. Besides, witch or human, it was the focus and intention of the caster that determined whether the spell would work or not. Usually. Magic was a fickle thing, passed down by family and tradition, and there were several aspects of it that had been pulled and hidden from circulation by the MAW. I was just beginning to understand the full extent of their severance of our ancient ways, thanks largely to the aide of my other boyfriend, Learco, the head over the Southeastern US Division of the worldwide organization.

"Darragh?" Verne called to me from behind the cash wrap, despite the blush of the young Asian woman standing at the counter. "We got any more of those dick candles in the back? She's looking for a large veiny black one!"

Speaking of Learco, I thought and shook my head while rolling my eyes at his horrible attempt at flirting with the customer as I pushed off the floor to check the stockroom.

In the grand tradition of queer uncles, I'd inherited the place— and the apartment upstairs—from my Uncle Gardner years back when he'd decided to retire to Key West with his husband. It'd been the perfect excuse to leave the small town and farm I'd grown up on a few hours south to move to the city permanently. And, since I'd accidentally exposed magic to the world a few years ago, business was booming. The shop and apartment had been my haven within the City in the Trees for nearly a decade now. Cernun had even installed planter boxes and a greenhouse on the roof for me to retain my nature connection from the sidewalk adjacent building making it altogether the perfect place. I already had my seeds on hand and blessed for their Ostara sowing.

I was really looking forward to that first planting. And my trip the morning after to New Orleans for the Business Owners Gathering of Witches Gala. I'd been surprised to receive the invitation. It was a fairly exclusive, though extravagant, party in the Old City, and I'd never been asked to join in before. But when the letter showed up in my mailbox, I proudly took on the moniker of BOG Witch. Witches really loved their acronyms. And puns.

As I made my way back to the stockroom, Madison hopped down from atop the ash wood spelling table I kept back there and twined my ankles with a loud purr. Their electric blue fur bristled with excitement as I bent to rub the length between their forehead and tail.

"You gonna be alright while I'm in NOLA?" I asked to their scrunching nose and flicking whiskers. Sensing their concern, I added, "Cernun and Learco will both be here to feed you."

I hated that my boyfriends, my coven, weren't coming on the trip with me, but Learco couldn't get away from work, and Cernun had promised to mind the store for me while I was away. I also hated that it'd already been a month, and I had not been able to find a way to change Madison back into the person they were. The Fae-magic transfiguration spell that had saved them from the clutches of the Dark Fae leader, turning them into a cat in the process, was tricky; their time as a cat trickier. From my own brief (and mental, not spiritual) moments in the body of a hare, I knew the call of the wild, the want to succumb to the animal of it all, was strong—and would get stronger with time. But we'd bested

Balor—at least for the time being—and Madison had survived when others had not. Plus, as I stared into their deep brown eyes, I thought I could still see witch-Madison somewhere behind the instinct.

I found the backup box of cock candles and clutched it to my waist as I headed back toward the sales floor.

"Whatcha got in the box?" Cernun smirked as he descended the stairs from my apartment.

His broad, muscled frame looked fantastic beneath the tightness of his dark denim jeans and the stretch of buttoned-up flannel across his tattooed chest and arms. His mop of curly black hair was tamed beneath an army green beanie, and the rough stubble across his chin looked downright kissable.

"Oh, just some things to keep me occupied when I'm in the Crescent City all alone," I quipped as I fished one of the dongs out and brandished it toward his hearty laugh.

"I'm sure you'll find plenty of… less waxy suitors to keep you in trouble while you're there," he said. "Plus, it's only for five days."

"And four nights," I added.

I loved Cernun with all of my heart—and Learco too—and the last nearly four years with him had been a truly magical time in an already magical life, but no matter how much our coven gave to us—and by the Fae, it gave!—none of us expected to be the be all and end all for one another. Though I did have to say our little family was pretty damn close to that "everything." At least as close as I'd ever been before.

"Whatever shall you do?" Cernun mocked as he held open the swinging backroom door for me.

I slipped the box over to Verne, surprised the young woman had waited through the embarrassment of his storewide announcement, but the way she twirled her chin length black hair in her fingertips told me she was interested in more than just the candle. Maybe Verne had more game than I'd thought.

"I'm off to talk to Gloria," my boyfriend whispered, voice full of hope as he bent in to kiss the edge of my lips and a customer attempted to flag me down.

Cernun Kyteler was one resilient witch. He'd left the home of his adoptive parents—as much by force as by purpose—when he was still a teenager. Coming into his powers, and not knowing quite how to control them, had led to further alienation from his religious caretakers and to the creation of one of the most infamous—and ever-growing—anti-witch hate groups in the world. But even with Defend Mankind From Magic nipping at his heels, and decades of false starts, dead ends, and roundabouts, he was as determined as ever to find some trace of his lineage. With Learco's help, the MAW had determined he was a Kyteler. Now, Gloria Raine was helping him from within the organization to trace out any other relatives from the long-since hidden line. So far, it'd been one missed connection after another—a magical line that wanted to stay hidden rarely sparked a spell—but none of that had deterred Cernun from his mission.

"Good luck!" I smiled to his winking face as he walked out the door.

HEX was located in a once fashionable, then passé, then hip again stretch of neighborhood bars, boutique clothing stores, and specialty coffee shops just a little east of Downtown. A haven for the would've beens and never weres, the punks, the rockers, the goths, and the witches kept the streets alive whether or not the more well-to-do clientele paced the streets. I had to admit that I loved the grit the stores retained, even in the midst of the five dollar coffees from Brew (another witch-owned establishment) or the twenty dollar cuts of beef from the Butcher Block or even the two hundred dollar jeans from Madaline's Boutique. The place that always had my heart though—and where the prices never changed—was Aunt Paulina's.

A little down the block and across the street from my own shop, Aunt Paulina's had been around almost as long as HEX. Its local art and pinup girl ladened walls housed the best burger and fries combo in town, and its namesake owner Paul made one kick ass Old Fashioned. Paul had been great friends with my Uncle Gardner for decades and had taken it upon himself to watch over me when I'd inherited the shop. And, like any good Uncle, he'd brought his queer niece Katrina in for training last Autumn to one day pass the place along to her. When the time finally came, I was sure I would miss the smeared lipstick on his painted face, the errant bra strap that inevitably slipped from beneath his top, but, despite his age, I had a feeling it would be quite a while before he finally got up the nerve to retire.

"You heard anything from Mads?" Katrina asked as I saddled up to the bar to wait for my to go order of two medium rare cheeseburgers, one veggie burger, and three orders of fries. Though it was really just an excuse to slip away from the hubbub for a moment, I'd promised to treat the staff to lunch. They deserved it. Stacey and Verne were amazing workers.

"They're loving Prague," I smiled. "But we're all hoping to have them back home soon."

I hated lying to Katrina, but the fewer folks who knew the truth about Madison's transformation into a cat, the better. Still, the cover story that they were doing a semester abroad in the Czech Republic was getting harder and harder to maintain.

"I thought they'd reach out by now," Katrina frowned as she slid the Old Fashioned she'd made me across the condensation-stained bar top. "But losing their best friend and all…. I guess they will when they're ready."

Katrina and Madison had had a very rocky first date. Yet it was Katrina whom Madison turned to when Angel was brutally murdered by Balor's attempt to overtake her body. The two of them had a definite connection. I hoped they'd be able to pick up where they left off when I found a way to return Madison to their witch form.

The cocktail was good—though not as good as Paul's—and I gave her expectant stare a grinning nod as I sipped it. She'd been working on perfecting the technique for a while now. I had a feeling it was the last thing standing between her and the keys to the restaurant. Well, that and Paul's reluctance to go quietly into that good night. It amazed me that such a simple combination of whisky, sugar, and bitters could vary so much in taste depending on who concocted it. Though, I supposed the same was true for witches and their spell craft. The same potion with the same ingredients could produce wildly different outcomes contingent on the witch who stirred it.

"I'm sure they're just caught up in some magic," I lied again. Though, I supposed it was a half-truth considering their state of being. "Plus time zones and all that. And, you know, Prague is a fantastic city in the Spring."

Katrina blushed as she ran her hand over her closely shorn blonde hair.

"I ain't never even been to Europe," she said. "Hell, Atlanta's the biggest place I've been to since I left where I grew up."

Like me and a lot of the other denizens in the perimeter, Katrina was a country girl turned city dweller. The lilt of the backwoods still affected her voice, and it made me smile when she slipped into that cadence.

"Well, maybe the two of you can go together someday. I'm sure Madison misses you."

That was not a lie. On multiple occasions, I'd caught them staring their cat eyes longingly through my apartment window to watch Katrina glide her way through the tables across the street. A part of me wondered if that connection was the one thing keeping the feline from overtaking Madison completely.

"Order up!" a cook bellowed, and I downed the rest of my drink as Katrina loaded the meals into a paper bag for me to carry back. Before I crossed the road, I stopped briefly to pay homage to the dandelion pushing its way through a crack in the sidewalk. Already the jagged knives of its leaves gleamed a deep green in the afternoon light, and its petals shone to match the bright face of the sun. I always thought they were such beautiful flowers, carried up through the concrete as a reminder to the entire city that nature always found a way.

I was surprised to see Rafael Acosta waiting furtively near the cash wrap when I made it back to my shop. He'd been a MAW agent for less than a year and Learco's assistant for nearly two months which, to his credit, made him the longest running aide since Learco had been burned by Samara Byrne. Nearly literally. A jovial demeanor teetered just beneath the calm, placid countenance required by his position, and he met my eyes and nodded as I entered.

I was glad he wasn't the type to draw attention to himself.

Being MAW-sanctioned was one thing. Having MAW agents milling about while witch and human customers made their selections was quite another. It probably helped that his powder blue cashmere sweater and hunter green slacks were a sharp contrast to the military-inspired black garb of most other agents in the field. His clothing allowed him an inconspicuousness, and, along with his broad shoulders, accentuated the weight of his belly quite well. I held up the to go bag from Aunt Paulina's and motioned for him to follow me into the backroom. I supposed it didn't matter if the fries got a little cold.

"So what's the word, Raf?" I started before quickly adding "ael" when the shortened name felt funny in my mouth.

"Mister Clarke sends his regards," he said as I stopped myself from walking toward the white ash spelling table Uncle Gardner had left me and about-faced toward the new break area Cernun's renovation had allowed within the stock room. "And his regrets."

My face scrunched as I placed the bag on the counter between the new sink and mini-fridge and turned to face him. He looked apologetic as he presented a black box tied with an exquisite gold ribbon. It broke the air between us with its sweet offering of solace. When I didn't reach for it immediately, he placed it gently on the table.

"He's been called to Salem on official business," he continued. "He's not sure when he can return. He… wanted you to have this before your trip to New Orleans."

My brow furrowed further. Being called to Salem was never a good thing. Worse though, Learco did not think he'd be around to perform the rites of Ostara with us. I'd been really looking forward to celebrating the advent of Spring with the dual planting of him and Cernun. Not that that was much different than a Tuesday. I wondered what could be so important they'd call him away during one of the most significant witch holidays of the year. I knew I'd get no answers from Rafael, but it didn't hurt to ask.

"What was pressing enough to drag him away from Atlanta but leave you behind?" I goaded.

Rafael's mouth twitched into a smirk as he cleared his throat.

"Actually, you were important enough to keep me here," he smiled. "I'm to catch the next flight up after I've delivered your gift."

"Well, you've done your duty," I pouted, even though it wasn't directed at him. "Best be on your way."

I sighed as I moved to retrieve the three meals from Aunt Paulina's and place them at the ready for my warming incantation. I knew the fries were already limp and the buns were soggy. Even reheated, they wouldn't be quite the same. So much for my nice gesture. But what truly upset me was Learco's sudden absence.

"I'm to stay until you've opened it," Rafael said. "In case alterations are required."

Leave it to Learco's attention to detail to derail my desire to sulk. I frowned as I pulled the ribbon free and let it fall to the floor. From inside the box, a beautiful Spring green suit stared back at me. Even at a glance I knew its luxuriously woven fabric would feel exquisite against my skin. Though not as good as Learco would.

"He thought you could wear it to the conference. I'm to ensure it fits."

I smirked at Rafael. "Should I try it on right here in front of you?" I asked.

"I— No. That won't be necessary."

His Venezuelan accent came out a bit when he was flustered, and I grinned as I picked up the blazer. I'd only ever splurged on one outfit from the Miorai before. As the top—and most expensive—witch-owned design house in the world, their pieces, like their namesake's, were said to be created from a single thread tailored to create the whole. It was a remarkable ensemble. Learco had chosen the color of my manifested magic as its base, but I also noticed the tiny sparks of Cernun's blue and his own gold woven through to let me know my coven was always with me. Beneath the suit, a Green Man-inspired masquerade mask waited. Its leather was soft beneath my fingertips, and the embossed leaves matched the suit perfectly.

"Tell him thank you when you see him," I said.

Rafael nodded.

"Good luck in New Orleans," he said. "And have a joyous Equinox."

"Happy Ostara," I called as he made his way out the door.

I folded the fabric gently as I placed the suit back in its box and slid the lid into place to keep it safe. It truly was a remarkable gift. My mind was already tripping with ideas to thank my lover when I saw him again. Most of them required way less clothing than what he'd just given me. I moved the gift box to the stairs leading up to my apartment to pick up later, and cleared my mind to magically zap our meals back to life. My stomach growled, but I could manage the sales floor while Verne and Stacey ate. It was the least I could do after the delay. Madison purred loudly as they leapt to the table to sniff the re-awakened burgers, then slid gracefully to the stairs to settle contentedly atop the box.

"Nice duds."

I grinned slyly at Cernun's entrance as I admired myself in my floor length bedroom mirror. Learco had gotten the sizing just right. The luxe material of the blazer formed nicely over my shoulders and across my chest, tapering down to v into a pair of matching pants which were tight, but not too tight, and hugged my ass just right.

"They're a consolation prize from our boyfriend." I smirked though I couldn't hide my excitement at how well the suit fit. "He's been called away on official MAW business."

"Fuck the MAW," Cernun quipped, and Madison yowled their agreement from the living room.

Even though we were dating one of its highest ranking officers, I still held a hefty distrust of the Moral Authority of Witches. For centuries—even before real magic had been exposed to the world—the shadow organization had taken it upon itself to police witch kind, deciding what spells were sanctioned and when our powers could be exerted; then punishing those who disobeyed by flaming them at the stake. Their mantra claimed it was for our protection, but now that they were in the light, so to speak, their power-grabs had only gotten worse. Cernun, having not grown up with the boogeyman-like stories of the MAW, did not harbor the same cynicism as I had. But he knew where I stood and echoed Madison's favorite phrase accordingly.

"Wait'll you see this though," I smiled as I retrieved the mask from the box.

A card beneath it held three words in Learco's tight, practiced hand: *Ni apẹrẹ ti*. The language of the spell didn't matter, and though I usually used my family-taught Irish or Gaelic words in my own spell work, I was sure Learco's Yoruba would still function in my voice. I concentrated my intent on the meaning behind the words as I said them aloud, and the leather vibrated slightly as it formed and contoured to my face. The color of the mask made my hazel-green eyes pop, and the points of the leaves were only accented by the slight, unruly wave in my mop of reddish-brown hair.

"Well, damn," Cernun laughed as I made funny faces into

the mirror. The mask contorted to broadcast my emotions almost as well as my own skin. It was one expensive spell with just the ingredients used to cast it, let alone the fine leather stretched and carved to shape. I guessed that was why it only came with three uses.

"Did you know about this?" I asked when I caught Cernun's pleased expression in the mirror.

"I helped pick it out," he shrugged as I removed the mask and set it gently back inside the box. "We wanted you to have something of us on your trip since we can't go with you."

"I'd much rather have the two of you," I purred.

Madison's electric blue fur bristled as they stretched their way into the room and hopped onto the bed to snuggle into Cernun's lap. The engine inside their chest rumbled as they curled into a ball.

"Somebody's got to stay here to take care of our new ward," Cernun sighed. "Besides…."

Shit. In my model moment of excitement, I'd completely forgotten to ask him how his afternoon with Gloria went. I blushed as I removed the jacket and folded it neatly, raising my eyebrows expectantly at his dangling preposition. It wasn't Cernun's only dangling piece I was hoping for. I crossed my fingers that the news was good.

"We've got a real lead this time!" he grinned, breathing a sigh of relief.

"That's amazing!" I squealed and rushed to kiss him. I loved when good things happened for the people I loved.

"It's a first step," he demurred when I released his mouth. "But we both know how those have gone before. Gloria thinks this one is pretty legit though. Still…. It's going to be a process."

"If anyone can handle a long process," I told him, "it's you. And, of course, Learco and I will help with whatever you need."

Though he tried to play it cool, I could tell Cernun was excited. Growing up witch-born in a human world, he'd missed out on so much history, so much family lore, when it came to magic. He'd acclimated to our world quickly—if somewhat roguishly, which was part of his charm—but there was so much of his line yet to be discovered. He was wary of getting his hopes up which I understood. I'd seen him crushed behind that beautiful smile before. But he never stopped trying, and that was more powerful than all our magics combined.

"You should slip out of those new pants before you crease them," he winked.

Madison took their cue and stirred from his lap, wafting elegantly from the room as I closed the door behind them. Even if they were in cat form, I still didn't want them to witness what was coming. Or when I came.

Cernun watched with a wicked gleam in his eyes as I removed the new slacks and folded them along their crease. He waited for me to move the box to the top of my dresser before he leapt up to grab the hem of my underwear and pull me into his embrace.

"That's better," he growled as his lips found the space where my neck met my earlobe.

His tongue massaged my skin, quickening when I let out an uncontrollable moan. My fingers clawed his back, wishing the thick fabric of his flannel was not between us. As if reading my mind, his fingers made quick work of the buttons, and he shed the shirt like snakeskin to the floor.

My aura reached to meet his, and the warmth of our spirits undulated around us. He bit his lip seductively as he pushed me to the bed. I welcomed his weight atop me as our lips met once more.

I wasn't sure what I was going to do for five whole days and four whole nights without him when I was at the conference, but, by the Fae, I knew exactly what I was going to do with him for the next few hours.

CHAPTER 2

The honking blare of my alarm clock surprised me. Usually Madison's yowling demand for food brought me to my senses well before the hour I'd set my phone to go off. Yawning, I wiped the sleep from my eyes and stretched into the soft haze of morning wafting through my window. Cernun groaned and pulled his pillow over his face. Most times, he was up well before me, but I'd kept him busy late into the night. I wouldn't have woken up early either if I hadn't had to open the store.

The subtle tap of Madison's claws against the glass drew my attention to their perch on the windowsill. They batted the pane timidly, their concentration captured by the world beyond its polished surface. I'd often caught them enraptured by the activity of the street, their cat eyes catching way more than my witch eyes ever could. I wondered if there was a point where animal instinct and witch desire intersected, leaving the one indiscernible from the other.

"Keeping an eye out for Katrina?" I whispered, smirking at what I saw as proof of their witchly yearnings still present beneath their fur. "I know she misses you too."

Madison's soft purr rumbled into a low growl. Their whiskers twitched in agitation as they pressed the pads of their paw against the glass once more. My brow furrowed as I pulled myself from the bed and slipped into a pair of sweatpants. Watching the comings and goings of the humans and witches as they went about their days below was one thing, but I'd been fearing the day a squirrel or a pigeon on the fire escape would overtake their sensibilities. When they got there, I worried the animal would have them completely. If that happened, no amount of magic I found could turn them back.

I approached the window carefully, timing my footsteps with each twitch of Madison's tail. Their whiskers quivered as their eyes urged me to follow their gaze. Whatever was out there agitated them more than any else I'd witnessed in over a month of their animal form. My breath caught in my throat as I turned my eyes to peer through the glass.

But there was no bushy-tailed squirrel, no plump, red-breasted robin. In fact, the only difference from my normal bedroom view were the sixty or so daffodils which had sprung up around each of the poplars lining the sidewalks below. Atop each of their lean stalks, bright golden trumpets aimed toward the sky like a herald of Spring's warming beauty.

I couldn't help but laugh as the nervous energy exited my body.

The last six months or so had definitely taken a toll on my emotions. Between wanton witches attempting to steal my power to reignite their own, a string of grisly murders literally turning witch-kind inside out, and a friend taking and keeping the form of a house cat, I was seeing danger and dark magic in the wake of natural occurrences, like Fomóraiġ dancing in the corner of my eye. Learco had warned me against allowing the horrors we'd witnessed to overtake my worldview. And he would know. Working his way up through the Moral Authority to become the head of the Southeastern Division, he'd no doubt faced a thing or two better left to the forgotten folds of the mind. Though it did warm me to know that, were he here, he'd be laughing along with me. Or maybe at me at the very least.

I caught my giggle to keep from waking Cernun as Madison frowned and nestled down on the window sill, still keeping a close eye on the new spring flowers blooming below.

"*Fokki!*"

As if I'd conjured him into being, Learco's voice startled me from the other room. My brow furrowed as I followed the sound to my kitchen.

"Fuck," he sighed again, this time in English, as he stooped to wipe the remnants of yolk and broken shell from the floor. On the stovetop, bacon sizzled in a cast iron pan while a bowl of eggs and cream waited to be whisked and scrambled.

Learco pursed his lips but smiled when he saw me.

"I was hoping to surprise you two with breakfast in bed," he said. "But I guess my exclamation when I dropped this little fucker ruined that plan."

He turned to brush the egg shells into my compost bin then rinsed the dish towel in the sink. The firm, rounded orbs of his ass cheeks shone at me from the below the bow tied on his apron. The small of his back caught the overhead light like moonlight on the sea of his dark skin. He was completely nude beneath the apron. It was obvious he had more on his mind than just breakfast.

"I thought you were stuck in Salem," I said, taking a seat on one of the island stools so I had a front row view of the show. "Rafael said you wouldn't be back before the Equinox."

Learco froze for half a second then continued his swift whisking of the eggs. His bicep flexed beautifully with each twirl of his wrist.

"Turned out to be nothing," he shrugged. "Just a quick in

and out. I almost forgot I even went."

My brow furrowed for the third time this morning. It wasn't like Learco to act so obtuse when it came to MAW business. But, once again, maybe I was searching for poisonous hemlock where there was run-of-the-mill Queen Anne's lace.

"Anything you want to talk about?" I asked as he poured the eggs into a sizzling frying pan and wiggled his ass to distract me. "Or, at least, was there anything in their archive room on Balor?"

"Balor? What do you know of—"

The vacant look in his eye and the question in his voice bothered me, but I didn't have time to dwell on it as Cernun sauntered in from the bedroom. Sleep still heavy on his face, I watched the tattoos across his pecs dance as he stretched into the morning.

"Coffee, please," he mumbled before he'd even opened his eyes.

Yes! That was exactly what I needed. A morning jolt would pull me out of the worried funk I'd woken up to. Besides, I knew I should be happy. My lover was home, Spring's daffodils were already popping out to summon the sun, and Ostara's festivities were right around the corner. Whatever anxieties my encounters with the Dark Fae had summoned within me were better left locked in the other realm along with them. Plus, now that we'd bound the mental reach to our world that Aiden's summoning and our bargain had given to Balor, we had some time to figure out what to do on that front. And The Mórrígan had actually been helpful without asking for a favor in return. I guessed there was more to come from that, but it wasn't worth getting bogged down in what ifs. I had the here and now to be excited for.

Learco was already adding a dash of oat milk to the freshly poured mug of dark roast he had brewed and waiting for us. He grinned as he spun across the room to place the cup in Cernun's hands and kiss him gently on the lips.

"Oh!" Cernun smiled. "You're home early."

"I am," he purred, then waltzed back to retrieve the iced coffee he'd made for me and kept cold inside the fridge.

It was Cernun's turn to furrow his brow at me as we watched Learco's 50's homemaker dance while he dished out the scrambled eggs and bacon then pulled two darkened bagels from the toaster. I shrugged. It was odd for Learco to be so light, so airy in his movements and demeanor. But we'd only been dating since last Autumn. Maybe the advent of Spring sent him flying over the moon.

"This looks amazing," I smiled as he placed a plate in front of me, then frowned when I glanced at the clock on the oven. It was my day to open up the shop, and I was already running late.

"Not to worry," Learco said without missing a beat. "You go shower and get down to HEX. I will wrap this all up in a sandwich for you to take with you. You should have time to eat behind the counter before your adoring customers rush in for their spells."

"Perfect," I grinned again.

It felt odd—the whole morning did—but far be it from me to dampen his good mood. The man worked so hard he deserved a little frivolity. And if something really was bothering him, he'd tell us when he was ready.

I noticed Madison watching the scene intensely from the bedroom doorway as I stood to get ready. The placid expression beneath their electric blue fur was only betrayed by the gentle spasm of their tail.

"Sorry, Mads," I said, then called back to Cernun, "Can you dish out their breakfast for them?"

"I will get it," Learco sang, and Madison slunk off under the bed.

"Did you see all those flowers?" Stacey asked in awe as she entered to start her stretch shift. "Must be at least a thousand bulbs on this street alone! Think it's some promotion for the Botanical or something?"

It was a decent theory. After the case of the disappearing Silphium last Fall, it made sense for the Atlanta Botanical Gardens to go all out on some extravagant advertising campaign. Plus, the gesture was exactly the sort of mea culpa Cressida Troy, the Chairwoman of the Board, would pull to get the pocketbooks of the city's witch elite re-opened. Of course, the Garden's Winter Solstice festival was bigger than ever before, and the Ostara tours had been sold out for weeks already. Still, some beautifying floral undergrowth for the City in the Trees was a wonderful addition, no matter who had done the planting.

"Are they all over the city?" I asked as Stacey stopped by the display on the cash wrap to re-fill her handmade sachets. The natural volume of her recently dyed hair was the perfect complement to the lavender shade of her locks and only served to highlight the freckles that lined the bridge of her nose even more. Her lips thinned when he grinned, and the vibrancy of her pale green eyes seemed always to sparkle.

"From my neighborhood to here at least," she smiled. "And it's not just daffodils. There's tulips and irises too. I thought it was a bit early for the irises to bloom, but I can't even imagine the spells they have on those bulbs."

I nodded my agreement. While most witches would have been able to perform a simple incantation to urge forth the growth from a Spring-ready seed, it would have taken one hell of a spell— and a lot of witches working overtime—to coordinate that many fresh-faced flowers appearing simultaneously in full bloom.

Once upon a time, in my mind anyway, all of witch-kind would have had the ability. At least to some extent. Sure, some family lines were more powerful than others, but, as earth witches, our bread and butter was in the plants and the soil and the gifts that nature gave to us. But in order to keep us safe from the stake—humanity's, not our own; that stake was still planted firmly and waiting to burn—the Moral Authority of Witches had spent centuries redacting Books of Shadows, locking up Grimoires and other dark magic related items in their archive rooms and vaults, and keeping the most powerful potions and rituals available to the select few who could afford the sanctioning and licensing fee.

It angered me deeply when I thought about it: their self-righteous claim to know what was best for us; their deep state policing of our ways. Especially now that magic was out of the broom closet and witches were allowed to live freely. So I tried not to think about it too much. Particularly since I was becoming more and more entwined with the MAW the more and more entwined I became with Learco. Besides, seeing some of humanity's reaction to our existence being known—writing laws and forming hate groups like Defend Mankind From Magic—I had to admit that maybe their origins were justified. Or, at the very least, had begun altruistically, even if their practice edged on totalitarian.

I shook it off as a new wave of customers entered, and Stacey dipped into the backroom to pull on her work robe. While it was true that most witches had given up their ritual attire eons ago, the nonmagical patrons who came in searching for money spells and triple moon necklace charms were enamored by the flowing brown fabric cascading around our bodies. Plus the nod to our history piqued the nostalgia of the magic-inclined folks who shopped here for their supplies. Not to mention, the freedom of movement was unmatched.

The new shoppers—a trio of young witches just coming into their powers—gawked at me as they wove their way through the displays of dried plant matter and polished rocks. They probably should have been in school, but I wasn't a truancy officer. I remembered the sheer wonder of the world which came with that first spark of internal magic inside of me. While a witch's innate magic was inherited, passed down through family lines and fostered through family learning and ritual, their true power didn't appear until right around puberty. I'd been eleven when I first felt it surge within me, and all the colors of nature had taken on vivid hues. The dull red clay of my hometown dirt roads was now a rich ocher, specked through with the subtle nuances of all the lives that had decayed to form the earth. The boring white of the magnolia blossoms teemed with all the bone and pearl variances the flowers were actually dressed in. Even the mousy brown of my own tousled hair took on the reddish tint I had now come to love. Of course, I had used a tincture to keep it that way since my late thirties.

"Are you— Are you him?"

I smiled as the children approached me, pushing forward the girl who'd drawn the shortest straw to speak. The deep black of her hair had a slight frizz despite the lack of humidity in the air, and her umber skin burned darker as she blushed through her words. The rich color of her eyes reminded me of my mother's freshly baked Irish Brown Bread.

"I'm Darragh Cullen," I said, extending my hand across the counter to take hers.

"See? I told you so!" one of her companions exclaimed. His fist met the other boy's shoulder playfully as they rushed forward to accept my handshake.

"I'm Veda Chakrabarti. And this is Thomas Kim-Odessa and Marcus Jackson."

She was bolder now that the formality of names was out of the way. It always amazed me how the naming of things granted so much more power to any situation. I supposed magic worked a fair bit in that principal as well. For me at least, I'd always felt the vocal calling of the corners or the reverence given in the naming of the spell's offerings played a significant role in how well the ritual succeeded.

"Are you really the guy who exposed magic?" Marcus asked.

Stacey stifled a chuckle as she reappeared on the sales floor, and I blushed. It was a question I'd long since gotten used to in the years since I'd inadvertently revealed my power to the mortal world. It truly hadn't been intentional. I'd acted on impulse to save Cernun's life on the very same day we'd met. But the consequences had been the same as they would have been if I'd meant to do it. All of witch-kind was free to be who we were, openly and unapologetically. We even had schools and museums and businesses like HEX which catered directly to us. No more hiding in the shadows or only convening deep within the forest by the light of the full moon. I mean, we still did both of those things, but now it was by choice instead of by force.

"I guess I am," I said, not liking to take credit, but appreciating the appreciation all the same.

It was Thomas's turn to step forward, cheeks glowing and eyes brimming with excitement.

"Can you—" he stuttered. "Can you teach us some spells?"

My smile twisted to a wincing frown. It was strictly against MAW rules for a non-familial witch to teach spell craft to anyone under the age of eighteen. As a nod to tradition, they dictated that lore and ritual were to be passed down by bloodline through the matriarch or patriarch of the family. It was a bit old fashioned if you asked me. But the Moral Authority had been slowly making exceptions. A few select primary schools around the world were now opened since the successes and over-enrollment of the MAW-sanctioned collegiate campuses and programs had brought more money than expected to its coffers. But those schools were still only available to the rich and the lucky. A lot of young witches were being left behind.

It was part of why I'd been hoping to turn the area around Uncle Gardner's white ash spelling table in the backroom of HEX into a learning center... if I ever got around to begging Learco to push some approval through for me. Even though the idea of using our relationship to my advantage like that sent my stomach into somersaults, in the end, it would be a wonderful thing for the witch kids of Atlanta. Maybe it'd be worth asking him now. His cheerful mood—dancing nude in my kitchen and frying bacon— might leave him in a better spot to say yes.

"You know the MAW won't allow that," I apologized, the disappointment in their eyes matching my own.

"Tell you what," Stacey smiled, stepping forward and pointing to her handiwork on the finely carved rack. "Why don't you each pick out a sachet? I made them myself. And then we'll let you fill it with whatever you want. We can't teach you how to perform the spell that sparks the magic on it, but it'll give you a head start when your parents are ready to show you how it works. Deal?"

The kids beamed as their hands shot toward the display, riffling through to choose the one which called to them most.

"Thank you," I mouthed to Stacey, and she winked as she herded the group toward the angelica, mugwort, and other protection-centric herbs.

I startled as the store's landline rang out from beneath the counter. In the days of cell phones and an online presence, it was odd to even have a connected line, but it'd come bundled with my internet so I kept it around just in case. Still, it'd probably been over a year since I'd last heard its stifled bell buzz.

"You've reached the Herbal Emporium Xpress," I cooed into the receiver. "How can we HEX you today?"

I winced immediately as I spoke the words. They were so

overtly cheesy, but they were the same ones used back when Uncle Gardner had owned the shop. I guessed I had a thing for tradition too.

"Mister Cullen? Darragh?"

Rafael's voice was anxious as he panted through the line. He sounded out of breath, as if he'd just run up fifteen flights of stairs. He was usually so calm and reserved. It shocked me to hear Learco's assistant sound so panicked.

"You alright, Raf?" I asked, attempting to match his urgency yet calm the situation at the same time. "You sound flustered."

"Have… heard from—. Sorry… bad reception. Let me—"

The line went dead. I frowned as I returned the handle to its cradle. It was odd for Rafael Acosta to sound so rattled, stranger still for him to call my shop instead of Learco's cell. I had a feeling when he finally got through to his boss, Learco's sudden good mood would dissipate within a wash of Moral red tape and Authoritarian control. Damn it. At least the breakfast sandwich had been excellent.

The phone had barely finished its first ring before I had it once more to my ear.

"Rafael," I said. "What's going on?"

He took a few deep breaths, attempting to slow his pulse, before he spoke. I could hear wind beside him and the honking of cars that seemed a great distance away. I could tell he picked up on my worry and was trying to control his own. That was part of what made him such a stellar assistant.

"Sorry," he offered when he finally spoke. "Reception is horrible in this hotel. I had to go up to the roof to get a good signal."

So that explained the panting, but I could tell something else was teetering beneath the surface.

"Have you been in touch with Mister Clarke?" he continued.

"He didn't show at the Salem office this morning. His clothes and his cell are in his hotel room, but he hasn't been seen since last night."

I forced a response through my confusion. "He's upstairs at my place."

A sigh of relief washed through the phone, but I wasn't convinced. Between this phone call and Learco's strange countenance this morning, I knew something was off. And this time I wasn't imagining monsters in lieu of the mundane. Something had happened in Salem; I was sure of it.

"What was this trip about?" I pressed, hoping Rafael would be honest with me in the mix of his heightened emotions.

He cleared his throat.

"I'm sorry to have worried you," he said, slipping easily back into the cool, casual calm of his position. "There must have been an error in communication. Entirely my fault. I shall collect Mister Clarke's belongings and return with them on the next available flight. Thank you, Mister Cullen. And please, let this stay between us."

He hung up before I could respond, and I stood listening to the dial tone as I gathered my thoughts.

Something was definitely wrong. I could feel it in my gut, churning there like an omen from my power itself. The butterflies which had been circling within me all morning now felt like hummingbirds flapping their quick wings against my stomach. If I wanted answers, I'd have to confront Learco himself.

I did my best to smile as I told the children goodbye and let Stacey know I'd be right back. Then I huffed through the stock room and up the stairs to my apartment.

"What the Fae happened in Salem?" I belted as I pushed open my door.

I felt it best to come in hot and hard. I'd decided as much in the few seconds it took me to pound my way up the stairwell. Otherwise there was a chance I'd melt into the cool, sweet caramel of my lover's eyes. Determined and defiant were better than soft and forgiving.

Cernun stood prone in the middle of the living room, his face both befuddled and filled with awe as he turned to watch my explosive entrance. His mouth gaped, and his pale blue eyes sparkled.

"Holy shit, Darragh," he said. "You are not going to believe this!"

I followed his gaze back to my bedroom door where Learco appeared, a sheepish grin plastered across his face. He'd given up the apron and looked dapper in the slacks and sweater he'd left in his drawer of my dresser for his occasional sleepovers. He was humming as his eyes caught mine, and he stepped aside with a flourish to reveal….

"Holy shit!" I parroted Cernun's sentiment. "Madison?"

They stood in the threshold of my doorway, smiling the same bashful grin as Learco. Their electric blue locs cascaded over their fully witch shoulders. A pair of my sweatpants were tied tightly around their slim waist, and they shrugged their shoulders as they opened up their arms. I ran to embrace them.

"How?" I stuttered.

"I figured out how to turn them back," Learco cooed, then wrapped his arms around us both.

Fuck! Here I'd charged in all fire and brimstone ready to—lovingly—lambaste my lover, and Learco had managed to break the shapeshifting spell that was keeping our friend in cat form. Whatever had happened with the MAW in Salem could wait.

Right now, Madison deserved to be celebrated!

CHAPTER 3

"What do you remember?" I asked when I finally managed to loosen my embrace.

Damn! It felt great to have Madison back in witch form, even if they seemed a bit frazzled by the entire experience. That was to be expected though. From what I remembered of my own transformation into a hare—albeit mentally and not physically—the entire experience had been a jolt to my being, as if every cell inside of me was connected to an ungrounded wire. It was a lot to come back from, and the jostling swirl of freedom the animal promised alongside the agency of true form was as heady as understanding one's own being, as acknowledging the concept of existence for the first time.

"Everything is a bit fuzzy," they admitted. The usual wavering deepness of their voice still carried on it a bit of the guttural feline growl. "But I think I was happy." They read the concern of my ever-revealing facial expression as I heard their statement in opposition to "now" and quickly added, "I mean, I am happy to be back. I just— I honestly cannot really remember."

I nodded as I stood back to take them in once more. The electric blue of their tight locs seemed brighter than I remembered, even though their cat form had carried the same hue in their fur. Their brown eyes sparkled, and the deep mahogany of their skin carried on it a newfound golden glow. The tight muscles in their shoulders flexed as they shrugged, and Cernun wrapped his arms around my waist to cradle my excitement at their return.

"Your scars are gone," he smiled.

Madison's fingers pulled at their pecs as they stared at the smooth skin left where the thin lines of their top surgery had been. It made sense though. I'd theorized the shapeshifting spell would heal the wounds Balor had inflicted upon them as they moved into their animal form. It was only right for their body to take its true form as they shifted back to witch-hood.

"I feel stronger too," they rejoiced.

I could tell the stretch in their legs was still a bit animal-like. It was obvious, even through the excess fabric of my oversized sweatpants tied tight around their midsection. Learco spun in to join their movements, twirling them into a dance with the same exuberant glee he'd had while making us breakfast this morning. He had every right to be excited. Madison's return to their natural form was nothing short of miraculous. They giggled as Learco pirouetted across the living room, the two of them collapsing to the couch in boisterous laughter. I smiled as I took their joyous return as a bright omen for Ostara.

"I imagine you're probably craving a shower," Cernun suggested as he and I rounded the couch. I sat in the seat of the armchair as Cernun perched on the arm. "Why don't you go get clean while we work on finding you some better clothes until we can get you back to your dorm room?"

Madison nodded and patted Learco's knee in gratitude.

"We can also swing by Aunt Paulina's," I offered. "I know Katrina will be happy to see you!"

Madison's brow furrowed as their gaze shifted to the distance.

"Aunt Pau—," they trailed off, then smiled as they brought their eyes to mine. "I would love to see Cousin Katrina," they beamed.

I shook my head. Their stare was so intense, it hurt to break eye contact.

"Um, no," Cernun said, clasping his hand to my shoulder and bending into their eye line. "Katrina works there. The two of you were…"

"Dating," Learco finished, his voice still filled with a musical quality that exaggerated his island lilt.

"Right," Madison sighed, then shifted their mouth into a wide, toothy grin. "Sorry. Like I said, things are still a bit fuzzy."

"I am sure a bath will set you right," Learco said. "I will show you where the towels are."

"There should be some shower caps under the sink," I offered. "I don't know if your locs will fit, but worth a shot."

As the two of them left the room, Cernun's tension met my own baffled expression. He held his palms upturned in a telegraphed question as he moved to sit opposite me on the couch. I shook my head. Yes, they were acting odd, the both of them. But Madison had spent over a month in their cat form. I imagined it would take some time for them to return to normal. And I still didn't know what MAW business had sent Learco fleeing Salem in the middle of the night. But I didn't want to dwell on it. Madison's return was a happy occasion. It deserved to be celebrated. The rest of my concerns could wait.

I heard the water shift on in the bathroom as Learco glided back into the room.

"Can you believe it?!" he asked.

"I really can't."

I could hear the distress in Cernun's words, even as he tried to shift his frown to a smile. Learco paused his dance to kiss the top of Cernun's head from behind the couch, then slid around to take my hand and pull me up from the chair. His free hand clutched the small of my back as he swayed me in a two-step.

There was so much joy in his eyes, I hated to break the trance by asking the hard questions. Luckily, Cernun did it for me.

"How did you manage to turn them back?" he asked. "The shifting spell is Faerie magic."

It was true. In the months since we'd discovered that the Fomóraiġ were real—that they once roamed this plain and mixed their own magics with those of our ancestors—we'd also found that some of our own lost powers were due to the Fae being pushed from our realm. The transmogrifying spell didn't work without Fae presence. It had taken Balor, the leader the Dark Fae, attempting to take over Madison's body, and, after that, the unsolicited aide of The Mórrígan to complete the ritual in the first place. Them being expelled from our world was the reason Madison had stayed in cat form for so long to begin with. Had the Fae been present back then, Madison would have reverted back to themself at dawn's first light.

Learco shrugged but did not pause our dance. Instead, he shifted to pull Cernun from the couch and hold us both in his rocking embrace.

"Will and luck," he said. "The same thing that keeps the three of us together."

I forced a smile before it became real. It did feel great to have the three of us in one place, pulled into a dance, and feeling the warmth of our bodies pulled tight to one another's. The flowing brown of my work robe could not hide the excitement I felt as the heat passed between us. I let my smile shift to a wicked grin. We had a little bit of time before Madison emerged from their shower. If we couldn't perform the full show, we could at least start the first act. And a little foreplay to break the tension was just what the witch doctor ordered. Plus, it would keep us all on a delicate edge until we could come together to finish the job; and that, in and of itself, was sexy as hell.

I bit my lip and raised my eyebrows as I sent my aura out to my lovers. Cernun smirked as I felt his own energy wash over me. It was fierce and electric as it pulsed with the warm vigor of his life-force, and I melted a little as it fought with his usual aggression to consume me. A third aura joined the fray, but it felt different than what I was used to. Though Learco's aura push always strummed at a higher vibration than either mine or Cernun's, this time his energy felt bungled and chaotic, spasming outward in a frenetic cadence. It ground against my own aura like salt breaking a spell, and I cocked my head in question.

"Sorry," he said, still smiling as I felt him pull back from us. "I must still be a little off from shifting Madison back from their cat form. It took a lot out of me."

"Plus you've been dancing all day," Cernun huffed. I could hear the suspicion in his voice even if Learco didn't notice.

"I should be fine by tonight," he assured us. "Or, at the very least, by the Equinox."

He dropped us from his arms, but his steps still carried a syncopated rhythm as he moved to the kitchen to wipe down the counter and give us his best reassuring smile.

Cernun and I shared a worried glance as our own auras pulled back into ourselves. I didn't want to push it though. Something was definitely off. I had a feeling it had to do with whatever business had taken him to the Moral Authority headquarters in Salem. But whatever that was had also opened the path for Madison's return. I sighed as I resolved to let it go. At least for now. Learco deserved a bit of privacy—and happiness—when he needed it. The best Cernun and I could do was be there for him when he was ready to open up.

The owner and namesake of my favorite spot in town, Paul, was standing by the beer taps behind the bar when the four of us walked in. It was early enough in the day—well before the midday lunch rush and further still from the regulars who lined the bar when work ended—for his lace front wig to still be firmly attached to his head. His foundation—always a shade lighter than the rest of his skin—highlighted the rosy blush on his cheeks, the crimson red of his lips, and the purple lids of his eyes. He grinned his broad smile as he saw us enter.

"Hey, fellas!" he called, then upon seeing Madison in our midst, added, "Oh, sorry. Is 'fellas' alright with you? I may be an old dog, but I want to get it right."

Madison's eyes welled a bit in confusion. They were still bewildered by their transformation. Though the shower had done them good, and they looked spiffy in the skinny jeans I'd been too resolved to throw away but not resolved enough to fit into.

"'Folks' would work just fine," I replied for them. "Or 'y'all.'"

Despite some of the South's issues, we sure did have a way of keeping language inclusive. Even if some assholes now tried to fight even that.

"I tell you," Paul said as he rounded the bar with the laminated menus he always brought even though we all knew exactly what we'd be ordering, "Katrina's gonna shit bricks when she finds out you're back! How was Prague?"

Okay, so maybe not all southern phrases were worth keeping in the repertoire. Madison looked confused as we poured ourselves into my favorite booth in the back corner of the restaurant, Cernun beside me and Madison and Learco across from us.

"Your study abroad trip in the Czech Republic," I *reminded* them. "That's where you've been the last month."

"Oh, right!" they nodded. "It was beautiful. But I am glad to be home."

"Bet you're craving a good old fashioned American burger," Paul said as he slipped the menus in front of us. "Take a look and I'll go get started on your drinks." He winked at me and said, "I already know what you boys are having. You know what you want, Madison?"

They bit their lip as they studied the laminated page in front of them, then mumbled, "Um… Maybe just a glass of milk?"

"You know, milk sounds great. I think I will have that too," Learco said, and I smiled at his attempt to dissuade the awkwardness of the situation. I guessed the feline wasn't completely out of Madison's system yet, but it was better if Paul didn't know that.

"Alright, then," he smiled. "One Old Fashioned. One pale ale. And two glasses of our finest two percent. Coming right up."

He shook his head as he walked away, and I gave Madison my best comforting smile.

"Is Katrina here?" they asked. Their voice was slow, as if they were practicing each syllable with their mouth before the words could flow.

Cernun's knee found mine with a sharp wrap beneath the table, and his fingernails dug into my thighs.

"It doesn't seem so," I said. "But I'm assuming she'll be in for the night shift."

Relief flooded Madison's face as they smiled. Their eyes scanned the descriptions on the menu as if the words were all new to them. If I believed they'd spent the last four weeks surrounded by a different language, it wouldn't have seemed so odd. But I knew that wasn't the case. Even if I wasn't ready to fully admit to the strangeness of it all myself.

"You know," I whispered, leaning forward across the table to catch their eyes, "if this is too much for you, we can come back later. After you've had more time to adjust."

Learco cleared his throat, and Madison beamed, their brown eyes all aflutter as they met mine.

"No," they said, the hint of normalcy a promise on their voice. "I think I just need things to get back to the usual routine as quickly as possible. I am sure that is what will work best for my adjustment… my readjustment to this form."

"Well, after we eat," Cernun added, relinquishing his worry as best he could and attempting to be supportive of our friend, "we can catch a Broomer over to your dorm to get you into your own clothing. Unless the MAW agents packed it all up to make it really look like you were on a study abroad trip."

He looked expectantly to Learco who seemed as engrossed in the menu as Madison had. When he felt us staring, he shook his head and smiled.

"Right!" he exclaimed, as if only just remembering. "My agents packed your clothes…. So I can take you to the headquarters after our meal to get them for you. I can even give you a tour of the artifacts room."

The idea of heading into work seemed to excite him. Now that was the Learco I knew.

"Rafael said you left your wallet and your cell phone and your building ID in your Salem hotel room," I said. I wanted to press further, but wasn't willing to push. "We may have to wait until he's flown back down with your access card."

"I am the boss," he shrugged. "They have to let me in. This body comes with special access."

"You are the boss," I nodded. But the brush of Cernun's thigh on mine, the uneasy lines around his mouth, told me that neither of us were completely sure.

I paid for our meals while Cernun used his cell phone to summon a Broomer to take Learco and Madison to the Buckhead headquarters of the Moral Authority. I didn't like that neither of them had a way to be contacted, but I figured Rafael would probably be back in town soon, and Learco would at least be able to retrieve his own phone. Besides, once he was on MAW property, he'd have all of his agents and black sedans at his disposal. As Cernun saw them off, I promised Paul we'd be back by later to reunite Mads with Katrina.

"But they're still a bit jet lagged from their overseas flight," I warned him. "So let her know they may seem a little off?"

"A little off?" Paul laughed. "You witches always seem a little off. But I can't help but love y'all anyway."

Cernun gave me his own *we'll-talk-about-this-later* stare as he disappeared into the backseat of his own Broomer to his scheduled afternoon meeting with Gloria. Both our boyfriend and our friend were acting off right now, but I hoped his newfound leads could serve as a distraction. And I was sure they'd be back to normal in no time. The transformation—and the spell to accomplish it— had to be a lot.

The late morning chill had dissipated as I left the restaurant, and I took a moment to breathe in the warming air. The street was filling already with shoppers and walkers, all of them admiring the displays of daffodils and even sidestepping the array of dandelions that sprang up between the concrete slabs of the sidewalk instead of treating them like weeds. A wisteria vine I hadn't noticed before snaked its way around the windows of the dress shop up the street, and I couldn't help but smile at the buoyancy of nature as it revived itself from its long Winter's nap. The Botanical Gardens had really gone all out on their *Trust Us Again* display. I would have to send Cressida a thank you and congratulations card. I was sure she'd be ecstatic to hear from me.

Yet, even amongst the blooming, even basking in the spotlight of the warming sun as he made his way back around to visit our side of the equator, something felt off. My power, usually a comforting buzz in my gut as it frolicked there like connection came just as much from within me as it did externally, swirled like a horde of moths batting at a porch light on a misguided flight to the moon. I'd learned long ago to trust my intuition when my magic cycled into overdrive. Even if, as Learco put it, I sometimes saw the Fomóraig where there were just ruffled feathers. He hadn't seen The Mórrígan's shift from her crow form though. I knew feathers could be more. Much more.

Still, I told myself, daffodils were smiling up at me, the sweet scent of wisteria crested every breeze, Learco was home early from Fae-knows-what the MAW had him doing, and Madison was back on two feet instead of four paws. There was absolutely no reason to be concerned.

Maybe I was just horny. Spring did that to me. Hell, Tuesday did that to me. And the rites of Ostara were drawing near. I suppose the anticipation of Cernun's sweat-stained skin, Learco's turgid cock, and me nestled sweetly between them could leave me quivering. Both in the lead up and when it finally happened.

"Is it true that Madison is back from Europe?"

Verne hadn't even finished helping his customer when he bombarded me with his question as I entered the shop. Stacey's eyes rolled as she stepped in to take over the transaction, but I could tell from the smile on her face she was used to Verne's inherent flightiness. Well, the mercurial tendencies that appeared when he wasn't trying to hit on the customer anyway. He'd let his hair grow out a bit for the season, but it complemented his new stubble, even if the beard wasn't as fully formed as he thought it was. Still, he did well with the women at his school, and I could understand their attraction. His ego teetered just this side of affable, which was enough to keep him somewhat grounded and endearing.

"Yeah," I called. "They just got back this morning."

I appreciated the care the staff at HEX had for one another. It made us feel more like a family than coworkers. I'd always striven to create a fostering environment—at least since magic was exposed, and I'd needed staff other than myself—and it felt good to have employees who were excited to see each other come home.

"Great!" he exclaimed, half sighing in his excitement. "I'm gonna need them to cover some of my weekend shifts since they're home now. I may have missed a lab or two this semester so my Chem professor's giving me some makeup days. I assume that won't be an issue."

I couldn't help but chuckle. We were a family after all, complete with all the nonchalance that accompanied it. Of course, Verne didn't know that Madison had spent the last month in the body of a cat.

"I mean, I would have asked you, but I know you've got that party in New Orleans coming up."

It was a gathering, technically, with a party or two thrown in for good measure, but I saw his point.

"I'll ask them if they're ready to get back on the schedule," I told him. "And, if not, we'll figure out some coverage for your makeup work at school."

"Thanks, boss," Verne pandered, his eyes already locked on the quartet of young witches entering the shop. "Oh," he added, obviously wanting to offer support before Stacey could make it to the new patrons, "can I get that book back from you soon? I guess since most of the library's magic reference books went up in flames, they're being real sticklers about getting the ones they loaned out back."

"No problem," I smiled, but he was already beelining across the store.

Shit. In all the hubbub of the DMFM's flames and Balor's twisted witches, I'd completely forgotten about the book I'd borrowed from Verne. I imagined the late fee was pretty hefty already. I'd have to slip him some cash to cover it alongside the tome, once I remembered where it was.

I was about the leave the floor to head upstairs and track down that Kelly green cover when the phone rang for the second time today. It was strange, years of just sitting there, and it'd gotten more action in a four hour span that it'd seen since its installation. I shrugged off the coincidence as I breathed my greeting into the receiver.

"Mister Cullen. Darragh."

I recognized Cressida Troy's voice almost immediately. When the restrained shriek of someone's vocal cords has tried to condemn me to the stake, I have a tendency to remember their resonance. I could tell she was attempting to sound polite though, despite the begrudging undertones in her pitch.

"Cressida!" I smiled, knowing the informality at using her first name would drive her mad. I preferred it though. Honorifics, to me at least, felt dated and unnecessary, like vestiges of hierarchical language better left in the history books. Except maybe *doctor*. But even that lost its meaning outside of an office, the byline of an article, or a time traveling police box. "It really is quite lovely to hear from you. But if you're calling for donations, you should know I'm already a Botanical Gardens Platinum Member and give a good chuck of coin on a monthly basis."

I could practically hear her lips smack as she wove her viper's tongue across the surface of her teeth. For a witch who relished in her upper-class upbringing and her myriad of Board positions, it had to be difficult to turn to those she deemed "beneath her" with open palms.

"That is not why I'm calling," she said, her words measured and practiced, like she was reading a kidnapper's script and hoping I'd fork up the ransom.

"Oh?" I teased. "You couldn't be calling to apologize for suggesting I be flamed for your own lack of oversight last Fall, could you?"

It was a low blow, I knew, but she had punched much lower when Cernun and I had been witness to the displaced dirt and poor planning on her behalf at last Autumn's unveiling of the revived Silphium plant. She had been so certain it was my fault, even when Learco categorically proved her wrong and embarrassed her in front of her highest donors. It was my first chance—and probably only chance—to rub it in a little. She didn't need to know that it was actually my former employee who'd taken the plant by the roots, or that he'd given it as an offering to the Dark Fae realm where it now thrived.

"I…" she stuttered. "Yes, I'm sorry for that misunderstanding."

My face couldn't hide my surprise at her actual apology, and Stacey cocked her eyebrow at me from beside the bowl of egg-shaped ocean jasper she was showing someone to complete their Equinox offering altar. I held up a hand to let her know I was okay as Cressida continued.

"I'm actually calling to thank you."

The words ripped from her throat with more blood and bile than admitting she was wrong had even mustered. I shook my head to be sure I was hearing her right.

"Your display of Spring flowers all across the city have drummed up quite a bit of business for the Botanical Gardens. We are now booked solid with ticket sales through the end of June. So… thank you."

"*My* display?" I asked, my thoughts pouring from my mouth even as I attempted to gather them.

"Yes," she said. "I suppose you intended to keep it anonymous, but our contacts with the Moral Authority have informed us that your spell sign is all over the patches. The Board decided, at my urging of course, a thank you was in order. As well as a trio of tickets for your…. uh, coven." I supposed *lovers* was too much for her. "I'm assuming Mister Clarke can find a home for his MAW-given tickets and accompany you to the Ostara Starry Nights celebration this Thursday evening."

"I— Yes. Thank you. You can send the tickets to my shop."

I hung up before she could speak again. Why would my spell sign linger over each of the new patches of daffodils and irises lining Atlanta's streets? Unless I'd been sleep-spelling, I thought I would remember such a large undertaking of power. And even then, could I have manifested a spell so vast? I knew the MAW assumed me powerful—more powerful than I actually was—but they couldn't honestly believe me responsible for a conjuring like this.

That was definitely something else to add to my list of discussion topics when Cernun, Learco, and myself reconvened this evening. Even if they believed I was jumping at ghosts, something was definitely afoot.

CHAPTER 4

The sun was beginning to set, painting the sky in a swirling basket of tangerines and pomegranates, exciting the clouds to mimic the fruits of the earth. I liked how the colors sent the buildings into overdrive, adding depth and dimension to the man-made landscapes to make them appear more natural, more present, and more real. I took a moment before I locked up the shop to breathe in the dusk air. I mean, if my spell sign was all over the city's new flower beds, I deserved to bask in the sweetness of their aroma, right?

I couldn't help but laugh at Cressida's revelation. Spell signs were a fairly new investigative source for the Moral Authority, and I had a feeling they weren't as reliable as they should have been in assigning credit or blame in whatever way the organization deemed fit. That or, knowing how she loathed me, someone at the MAW was playing a joke on the uppity Board Chair of the Atlanta Botanical Gardens. Either way, that she had called me, broom tucked between her legs, to apologize and thank me was a brighter gold than the sun slinking off behind the skyline.

"Embracing full witch-mode, huh?" Cernun asked as he danced up the sidewalk toward me. "Cackling into the night?"

There was a lightness to his step, and I grinned as he pulled me into a waltz along the curb. His musky scent of cinnamon and pinewood smelled enticing as I nestled in close to his chest. I hadn't realized he'd changed his deodorant—he never really wore cologne—but it was certainly working for him. On instinct, my lips kissed the curve of his pec through the thick black fabric of his shirt, and my fingers snaked up to twine into his pitch dark hair. The pale blue of his eyes sparkled, and the shocking width of his smile filled me with contentment.

"I take it your meeting with Gloria and her team went well," I said, excited he was one step closer to finding his blood family to join in with our chosen one. Or, at the very least, evidence they had existed. He was a good witch, that Cernun Kyteler, no matter how his adoptive family and their Defend Mankind From Magic maniacs tried to paint him.

"Huh?" His face fell for a brief moment before the beaming grin returned and he twirled me out and back into his embrace. "Oh, I skipped that," he said, his voice still singing on the staff of the evening wind. "It is still such early stages, and I thought it would be a better use of my time to do some preparations for the Equinox. We have got quite a big night ahead of us, after all."

I chuckled. It wasn't like Cernun to blow off important meetings, especially when it came to the family he'd been actively searching out for nearly thirty years, but he was right in that the upcoming festivities would be draining. Hopefully in more ways than one. It was sexy that he wanted to do the spadework, and I sent my aura out to his as my lips found purchase on his stubbled cheek.

"Uht-uh-uh," he scolded me playfully. "For the rites to go as planned, we should probably be saving ourselves."

My lips pursed in an exaggerated pout as I pulled away, and he slapped my ass with a wink. I guessed I could handle a few days with no sex. It wasn't like I was just some horned up teenager. Or the hero of a smutty romance novel. Besides, we'd more than make up for it when the day and night equaled out on Thursday. And if my mind happened to practice a few of our moves—if my imagination played out the curve of his backside, the slow bob of his dick as he stood in anticipation—that could just be chalked up to ritual prep as well.

"Speaking of Ostara," I grinned, pulling him toward the shop door to finish locking up, "Cressida Troy called to offer us all tickets to the Botanical Garden's fête this Thursday. I figured we could do our own plantings early in the day, swing by there to catch the sunset, and be bound to your bed in Grant Park before the moon gets jealous of our absence."

"That was nice of her," he said, stepping inside as I closed the evening out. "Good ol' Cressida."

There wasn't a hint of sarcasm as he spoke, and I applauded his practice at civility for the upcoming event. It did no good to hold grudges. And now that word had spread about his Kyteler money, I knew Cressida would be on him for donations like warts on a toad.

I flipped the open sign and turned off the brighter overhead lights to leave the space warmed by the glow of flames from the spelled chandelier which remained lit. Cernun paused by the display of obsidian and mandrake root to stare at the candles. There were forty of them, placed there once upon a time by my uncle, but they'd lain dormant for decades. Cernun had helped to conjure the magics to bring the fixture back to life during his remodel, and I wasn't sure how I'd ever opened the space without the flickering glow of the contained fires on the crystals dancing above.

"It really is beautiful, isn't it?" I asked, slipping my arm around his waist and saddling up beside him to appreciate his handiwork. "You really are amazing for getting it going again."

The candles were all spelled to prevent the flames from igniting the shop—I'd already been there and done that, as had, it turned out, Uncle Gardner a few times over—and a knob by the stockroom door would ignite and extinguish them all faster than my tongue could say *adhaint* or *múchadh* forty times over. It wasn't like in the movies where a witch could set a thousand candles ablaze simultaneously as she entered a room. Each wick was a focus, each fire called an intent. But even though it felt like cheating, I chose to assume the pre-potioned trigger within the knob acknowledged the elements as it summoned the flames.

The light ricocheting off the crystals sent a prism of color across Cernun's face, and he glowed as his eyes shifted to take in every color of the spectrum. I loved the way the magic of the natural world, even beyond the power that cycled in our blood, still fascinated him. Even with everything we'd seen over the past few months, even with knowing that Fae-kind were real or that witches once had the ability to shift into animals, the wonders of the everyday remained captivating. Those were the reminders that kept our little coven intact.

"Have you heard anything from Learco since he and Madison went off earlier?" I asked, breaking both our gazes from the mystifying light.

"No," Cernun shrugged. "Is that weird?"

"I just expected them both to be back here by now," I sighed. "I was kinda looking forward to celebrating Madison's return. And I know Katrina wants to see them."

Cernun's mouth twisted as his fingers tapped against the display as if he was feeling the smooth and polished wood of his own craft for the first time. His eyes wandered the room with his thoughts.

"Madison has been through quite a change," he finally

said. "It is natural for them to want to take some time to get re-acclimated, right? And I am sure Learco is just helping them out and got sidetracked."

I supposed it made sense. It had to be jarring to walk suddenly on two legs instead of four. And Learco's avoidance of whatever had happened in Salem had rendered him a bit flighty. I'd just expected at least a phone call.

"I mean, I guess he did lose his phone," I sighed.

"Tell you what," Cernun smiled, face bright again in the neon prism. "I will head out and try to track the two of them down to make sure they are okay on my way back home."

My mouth fell into a frown, and he giggled as he kissed my forehead.

"I know. But if we are keeping our hands to ourselves the next few days, it is probably better that I not be here. Besides, the anticipation is kind of hot, is it not?"

I shrugged but gave in with a single breath.

The streetlights were already flicking on like fireflies awakening as I let Cernun out and relocked the door. A couple nights on my own wouldn't be so bad. I could watch a movie: something filled with high stakes drama and plenty of shirtless men. Or maybe get entangled in the centuries old love affair of two vampires spelled out in ornate language on browning pages.

Or try to find the book that Verne had loaned me so I didn't have to pay a heftier fine.

It was just two nights after all. Besides, with the fire-hooped jumps my mind was making, perhaps I could use a little communing with myself.

Cocooned within a plush afghan my mother had crocheted for me last Winter Solstice, I snuggled onto the couch and chose a movie that was easy to zone out to. A few stray strands of cat-Madison's electric fur shone in the light from the television, the brightness of the blue highlighting the somber, earthy tones of moss and burnt umber my mom had chosen to make the blanket feel warm and alive as it surrounded me. A second homemade Old Fashioned rested atop a coaster on the side table, and I occasionally slipped a hand out of my fort to sip the warming orange from the ice-chilled and sweating glass. It really was a lovely evening, even without my lovers there to keep me heated, and I sighed as my head sank into the cushions.

Yes. A night to clear my mind was just what the witch doctor ordered.

I had a tendency to spiral. I knew that about myself. And after a month of seeing The Mórrígan on every budding tree branch, of seeing the Fomóraiġ in every sidewalk crack, it felt nice to relax into a return to normalcy. Spring was coming, my lovers were happy, and Madison was walking on two legs again. There was absolutely no reason for me to feel on edge. Still, my power churned in my stomach like it had whole essays on its lips. But maybe that was more about the sweat v-ing down the abs of the men brandishing swords and stakes and fangs on my screen.

I did have to give it to Hollywood. Since magic had been revealed and the MAW had released its hold on "glamours for artistic purposes," the special effects departments had really upped their game. I could almost believe the actor on screen—the man with the chiseled jawline, long blond hair, and crow black stubble—was actually staring at me with his icy, quest-hardened eyes. The energy which swirled around him glowed a magnificent crimson, an eerie match to the slow drip of blood on his neck left as the lips—and the cuspids—of the one who had enthralled him slipped away. Both men were stripped bare. Their chests, carved of marble or onyx, heaved in the dim lighting, nipples hard as diamonds, while the aura of the one still living pulsed between them. I felt it reaching from the television, begging me to join them.

Damn! I missed Learco and Cernun.

I shook my head to break my trance and took another sip of my cocktail to calm my nerves.

It's just two nights, I told myself. *And, if this first one is too much, you can always rip their clothes off when you see them tomorrow!*

Or maybe I wouldn't have to wait.

The TV clicked off as the door swung open, leaving the room washed in a dim silver moonlight which slunk in through the window. Even the streetlights seemed far away as they made space for the majesty of the moon's reflected power. Learco and Cernun spun in a jitterbug, gliding with a raucous energy as they sidestepped furniture to frolic together, bare-chested and grinning from ear to ear. I could almost hear the music that moved them, carried on the faint air which jostled to a breeze with each twirl of their bodies. Cernun's hand—thick and firm—held his every ounce of comfort and seduction as it grasped the lean, taut muscles at the small of Learco's back.

"I'm so glad you're here," I smiled, but they didn't seem to hear me. They were trapped in one another's gaze, both staring deeply into the glistening green of their dance partner's eyes.

But I was entranced too. As much as I wanted to join them, to relish in their bodies, in the movement of their spell, I couldn't pull myself from the comfort of my couch. The throw clung to my body, a warm, weighted offering as I delighted in the show.

They had such beautiful green eyes. Like fields of clover pushing all the charity of the earth to the skies, promising life and renewal and eternity. Like the hardbound cover of the book they kicked open as their two-step found its way atop the coffee table. These men, I could dance with them forever, if I could manage to pull myself from my cocoon.

"To life!" Cernun exclaimed as he dipped Learco, quickly raising him to pulse the heat of their chests together.

Sweat dripped like magic down their muscles, accentuating the undulations of Learco's eight-pack abs, the mighty curve and flush of hair and ink on Cernun's pecs—all the places my tongue longed to travel—as if highlighting the course of my destiny in flesh.

"To living!" Learco replied.

The pout of his thick lower lip, always slightly chapped and kissable, hung in the air between them, making me bite my own. By the Fae, my boyfriends were sexy! I was one lucky witch. It didn't matter that I couldn't rise to join them. I was still getting one hell of a show. The way their words echoed around me— pulling life from the cold clutches of a waning Winter, the living reverberating through every atom in the atmosphere—excited me nearly as much as the sight of their bodies twisting together in unison.

Their auras exploded around them as their lips finally met, sending swaths of green energy to pulse like firefly paths across the room. I moaned as the weight of the blanket pushed me further down, restraining me as a wiling voyeur while their hands pulled at buckles and buttons, pushing the last threads of fabric away to leave them bare and turgid. A smile still on his lips and a hungry glean in his eye, Cernun's fingers wrapped the girth of Learco's cock, holding it steady between them as its head pulsed from the ecstatic flow of blood and sensuality. First, Cernun's lips found Learco's neck, then his teeth did, as he made his way from shoulder to nipple to hip, kneeling there on my coffee table while Learco howled to the moon.

I loved the way Cernun's back arched as he settled to his knees, his ass pushed out on display and calling to me though he knew I could not move. I wet my lips as Learco's member disappeared down Cernun's throat. Learco flexed his tight, toned biceps as he placed one hand behind his own head, the other behind our lover's, twining his fingers through the rich soot of Cernun's hair. Their green energy glinted from his forearm with each twist of his muscles as he guided Cernun's mouth closer and closer to his body until Cernun's eyes watered, and he pulled back quickly, gasping for air before he swallowed Learco's throbbing rod once more.

I felt my own excitement press against my sweatpants, straining for freedom, for touch, but this wasn't about me. This was about the beautiful bodies before me. Cernun's hand replaced his mouth as Learco pulled his cock free and guided their lips back together. Their kiss was powerful, bursting with the life their echoes continued to promise in ricocheting bands as their auras stretched to fill the space between us.

I could be consumed by them. I knew it. We fellow travelers set upon our path toward greatness, aligned within a flourishing forever. It wouldn't take much for me to be swallowed whole.

They knew it too. As their lips parted, Learco shifted Cernun's form between us. Still perched upon the pedestal of my coffee table, his hands traced Cernun's body from behind, sliding gingerly from the curved mounds of his chest and down his sides, accentuating the taut expanse of skin as it sharpened toward his hips. Cernun's tattoos were alive as his lungs heaved beneath them. The milestones of his past became rich with flight and fancy. His eyes, bright and vivid in their greenery, locked on mine as he arched his back slightly forward to receive our lover. The pleasured agony on his face intensified as Learco's dick pushed inside of him. His lips fell slightly ajar with a moan of ecstasy as his own stiff cock bobbed in the air between us.

A whimper of bliss tripped across my lips as the weight of their auras, the heft of my blanket, anchored down on me. I could die here, happily crushed by the pressure of their sex, ready to be re-formed, renewed, reawakened. To live. *To living. To life.*

Cernun growled as Learco exploded inside of him, his own cock dripping his desires between us. Fuck, they were hot!

A third pair of green orbs appeared and I shifted to see Madison enjoying the show from my armchair. They smiled widely as their eyes met mine, licking their lips to show off the knife-like sharpness of their feline incisors. Their neck craned as their claws worked the underside of their pectoral muscles, tripping across their nutmeg skin as blood and power oozed from their new wounds.

"I have my scars again," they snarled. "I am not changed. I am living. I am real."

"To life!" Cernun bellowed.

"To living!" Learco joined.

Blood, thick and heavy, dripped down Madison's stomach, glowing green and forceful in the moonlight, pooling at their hips like entire oceans of concentrated power. I wanted to stand, to move, to do anything, but I could not. I was trapped inside my cocoon, awaiting my own change, my own chance at new life. It was coming. It wouldn't be long now.

I gasped for air as I awoke, tossing the sweat-soaked blanket aside. My hands clutched at the cushions of the couch. My skin felt clammy as it met the air, and I did my best to slow my panting to a steady pace. The television mocked me with its *Are You Still Watching?*, and my own hazel eyes burned red within my distorted reflection from the screen.

The ice had completely melted in what was left of my drink, making it easy to down the rest of my Old Fashioned in one quick swallow.

"Well," I said aloud, as much to make it real as to calm myself, "that's the last time I fall asleep watching horned up vampires."

At least while my mind was running rampant anyway. As much as I wanted to believe everything was fine, as many times as I tried to tell myself things were normal—or, great even—deep down I knew otherwise. And my instinct, my power, would not let me forget it.

I'd had prophetic dreams before: vision awash in haze and symbolism I couldn't always grasp before the incident itself had come to pass. Images that melded with my subconscious desires until I sometimes wondered if my magic and my mind spoke the same language in the first place. This dream was no different.

It helped, at times, to pick out the real from the unreal, as tricky as that was when the entirety of the omen was fabricated.

When I blinked, I saw green. But Cernun's eyes were not green. They were blue. Pale and searing as a clear sky on a Winter's day. His power, too, manifested in a cyan explosion of warm and calming light. And Learco! He had brown eyes and a glistening golden aura that mimicked the threads which wove through his irises and glowed each time he looked at me. Madison's eyes were brown as well, flecked through with black like the shells of the pecans I would scavenge as an afternoon snack from the tree in my childhood front yard. But my vision had shown them all surrounded in green. Why? And what was it they said? The words had echoed on repeat, forming music all around me, keeping time and cadence with the show.

I tried to remember their words, but it was fading fast. I ran to my bedside table to grab a notebook. I needed to write down as much as I could remember, to conjure the vision to our plain of existence before it was gone.

I switched on the bedside lamp before I pulled open the drawer and rummaged for a pen and paper. There amongst the lube and the cock rings and the poultice-infused eye masks for the mornings after a late night of spelling or sex—or both if I was lucky—was a hardbound, kelly green book. I chuckled and shook my head. Could that whole vision really have been induced by the imperceivable stress of needing to find the damn book that Verne had loaned me? I guessed stranger things had happened. And it certainly explained the green. I even vaguely recalled my lovers kicking a strikingly similar tome open as they mounted the coffee table to mount one another.

I sighed as I pulled it from the drawer. The metallic silver embedded on the cover reflected a dim haze from the bedside lamp: *From Changelings to Succubae: The Fright of the Fae Folk in Our World*. I tossed it to my mattress as I laughed once more. All of that drama over a book about the Fomóraiġ and their kin!

In fairness, my stomach—and my magic alongside it—had been in knots since finding out they were real. And though my coven and I had managed to defeat Balor once, we still had the bargain we'd made with him to save our own asses to contend with. Plus, even though my encounter with The Mórrígan had proven helpful, the entity herself even showing benevolence as she offered the power to complete Madison's feline transformation and thus heal their mortal wounds, I knew deep down there was more to come there. And it wasn't just because I'd grown up listening to my grandmother tell boogeyman fables about all of Fae kind.

As a child, I'd always giggled at the stories, even as I listened for the parables Grandma was trying to impart. Back then, I'd seen the Faeries as stand-ins for whatever witch or human evil they embodied: vanity or wrath or devil's deals in the crossroads. It was the stories of the elusive and constrictive Moral Authority of Witches that had actually scared me. And now, as an adult, I found myself shacked up with one of my childhood monsters and in the proverbial bed with the other.

I cleared my throat as I propped my pillows against the headboard and climbed onto my bed. If my vision wanted me to find the book so damn bad, the least I could do was read a few pages before I returned it. After all, maybe there was more to that sexy turned gruesome sight than an overdue book fee from the library.

I flipped it over in my lap as I studied its front and back cover. Aside from the finely stitched cloth binding its pages, there was nothing remarkable about it. Most books of magic—like my family's Book of Shadows or even some of the informational tomes the MAW kept locked away in their Archive Rooms—gave off a faint hum of energy, almost like static electricity, when held by one who had the power. It was as if the hands of the witch who had penned them imbued the pages with a little bit of their aura, a slight trimming of their very soul. We put our very selves into the future as we wrote the words to pass down through generations, each descendant adding more until the book itself was like a living, breathing thing.

Though sometimes a book was just a book. And this one held nothing special, at least on its cover, save for the puddle of water-based lubricant it'd received from its time in my drawer. Maybe its words would hold more.

I wasn't holding my breath though as I blinked away the last vestiges of my dream and flipped through to a random page.

CHAPTER 5

The first Fae to leave our realm did so at the hands of her kin, it read. But perhaps I should start at the beginning.

"Alright," I said to the pages, smiling as my thumbs caressed the torn edges of the paper and my back shifted to settle in for the tale. "You've got my attention."

I grinned as the words jumped to life in my mind. A good book—even if it was about the Fae—would definitely help to settle me. Besides, it was "research."

When Fae and Witch were aligned, it was not uncommon for those of our ilk to become infatuated with those of theirs. Faeries, after all, are known for the beauty of their form.

It was true. Even Balor, as frightening and mad as he appeared, was sexy as hell if I looked at him for too long. Which I tried not to. He was hot even with the single, giant eye that stretched the width of his forehead and burned with the flames of purgatory! And though I was not sexually attracted to women, I'd almost gotten lost in the great majesty of The Mórrígan's vast green eyes, her iridescent black hair. I could understand why my ancestors had swooned.

I blinked my eyes to cease my distraction and concentrate on the black and white print before me instead of the more carnal fantasies of my memory.

One Fae, however, became enchanted with a Witch.

"I mean, how could you not?" I spoke aloud again, even as my brain was yelling at me to focus. I craned my neck once more, shifting my chin from side to side to stretch the remaining spasms of nervous tension from my shoulders and sighed deeply to center myself once more.

Despite the warnings of her sisters, the Fae's enchantment grew to lust as she followed the young Witch through his days. You, no doubt, need no reminder of the hubris of the Fae. From the smallest of their sprites to the mightiest of their warriors, they possess no qualms in assuming Witches their inferiors, both intellectually and magically. It is from this belief which springs their love of bargains and trickery, their subterfuge in passing their Changeling youth as our own, and the continuous demand for worship that leaves them most dangerous. The Fae thought themselves the objects of Witchkind's desire; the reverse of which they saw as asinine.

As such, the Fae who loved the Witch was punished by her kin. They summoned their powers to leave her speechless, save for the singular ability to repeat the last of the words spoken to her. Undeterred, our longing Fae, now named Echo, continued to pursue the handsome Witch with a craven fury, always remaining just out of sight, until one day when she came upon him in the wood. Magic of a magnitude which rivaled even that of the Fae swirled within him, attaching a wondrous glow to his inherent beauty. Echo watched from the underbrush as he settled beside the still-surfaced waters of a slow flowing creek to rest.

So the Fae had always been vengeful and a bit stalky. Knowing that made my interactions with them a little more manageable, even if it added no comfort. At least it solidified my instinct that there was more to come from them. It made my preparations feel a lot less pessimistic.

The young Witch, filled with the natural power of the trees and the hunger of the hunt, sensed the presence of the Fae and called out to the thicket of hawthorns:

"Who is there?"

But Echo could only repeat his words.

"Show yourself!" he called, only to then be met with the same demand.

Still Echo, as with all Fae, had a lovely voice. Melodic and soothing, enthralling and sensual, his own words sang back to him only served to excite the Witch.

He could 'show himself,' he decided.

As such, he met the command by disrobing there beside the brook. His body, muscled from the labors of the earth, throbbed in the burning sunlight which glinted down through the flitting leaves of the trees.

Yes! Now it was getting good! I mean, if even my distractions wanted to slip into some hanky panky, who was I to judge? Or turn away?

"I am here!" the young Witch, whose name was Narcissus, called.

"I am here!" replied Echo.

Yet she dare not move from her concealment, less she face the wrath of her kin. Still the young Witch Narcissus was undeterred. He was aware of his beauty and held to it with a vainful pride. Having bedded a bounty of the countryside's women—and, too, allowed the occasional worship of the men—the young Witch had developed an appetite for pleasure. He was determined that the owner of the beautiful voice be his, that she show herself to him at once.

"You must come with me!" he cried.

"Come with me!" came Echo's reply. Excitement pricked her skin as she, too, disrobed, ready to burst forth from the brush.

Okay. That settled it. The Fae were as kinky as most witches I knew. At least we had that in common. But the cruelty of punishing their own over love, the horror of taking away the agency of her voice… Well, I guess I'd experienced worse from mankind itself. And from the MAW for that matter.

As Echo emerged from the trees, Narcissus recoiled in repulsion at her visage. He had grown to so appreciate his own form, he often missed the wonder of another's, even that of the Fae. Scorned and shattered, Echo ran back to her family for comfort, recounting the reverberation of the experience to the best of her ability.

Her kin, angered by her continued betrayal of their ways through her love of the Witch, banished her from the earthly realm, leaving only her voice behind to lurk within the darkness of the caverns and caves where we still hear her call today, mournful and low and fading evermore.

Yet the Fae were not sated in their anger, and for his rejection of their sister—for how could a mere Witch ever deem one of their own unworthy?— they cursed young Narcissus to fall deeply in love with his own reflection. It was not a powerful spell, as it was one his vanity had already begun to cast upon himself.

And so there, beside the placid stream, deep within the wood, Narcissus knelt to adore his own visage. He grew there so entranced, he could not bring himself to look away. And there he withered. And there he died.

And from his body grew a beautiful flower, a harbinger of Spring, and the bearer of his name.

"Well, shit," I said, closing the book and tossing it beside me on the mattress.

That story didn't explain a thing from my vision, but it did tell me we needed to keep the Fae from our realm at all costs. Even knowing that our magics had once been intertwined, that our powers were amplified by one another, and that so many of our ancient spells were impossible without Fae presence, it was a small price to pay to keep their anger, their mischief, and their chaos from fucking up our world.

In truth, I'd heard the myth of Echo and Narcissus before as a part of the Greek Pantheon of Gods, but this author—I checked the front of the book—G. B. Moonrider placed Echo within the realm of the Fae. Learco had always been certain the Orisha he'd grown up with were no different than the Fomorians of my grandmother's tales. I'd have to let him know what I'd found, though it frightened me a bit to have the Fae world so expanded. Every region's, every culture's Powers Which Came Before had been rife with battles and jealousies, trickery and plagues during their time in our world. As they attempted to regain a footing on our land, there was no telling what could come.

I turned off the bedside lamp as I tried to push the Fae world far from my mind. Tomorrow, I'd be able to talk to Learco and Cernun about my vision, about my fears. The truth was, I needed my coven to help parse through the circus of acrobats performing death-defying feats from my synapses.

In the darkness, I padded my way to the bathroom sink and reached for my toothbrush without turning on the light. Despite the fitful "rest" of my vision, I was groggy, and the reading had only served to further strain my eyes. Still, something in the mirror was calling. My reflection was just a silhouette as I poured the paste onto the bristles, but the viridescent glow from the alarm clock beside my bed blurred the late night/early morning numbers into a hazy, familiar ball.

My eyes went wide as I dropped my toothbrush into the bowl of the sink. The blurred, ethereal haze of the alarm clock presented the same green as my lovers' power in my vision, the same green as the blood which poured from Madison's wounds. It was the same green as The Mórrígan's eyes.

Whatever was happening, I was now certain she was behind it somehow. And the last thing we needed was another Fae attempting to enter our world.

"You just had a bad dream."

Learco was smiling as he said it, yet I couldn't help but notice the angst—or was it pity?—in his eyes. When I hadn't heard from either of my lovers by noon, I'd left the store in Verne and Stacey's capable hands then caught a Broomer to Cernun's Grant Park bungalow. It was a quiet house on a quiet street, but inside was a flurry of frolic and dance. Having obviously stayed the night, Learco was in the same clothes he'd put on yesterday, and Madison was prowling through the new growth in Cernun's expansive backyard, attempting to shake off the last of their feline instincts before they were "ready to face the world." Cernun's cell phone, thick with missed calls from my own, still buzzed its reminders from the kitchen island. They'd both whined but grinned when I'd entered and turned down the music blaring from the stereo, even as they attempted to pull me into their dance.

I'd never seen two witches so invested in the rites of Spring before. The merriment aspects of it anyway. It saddened me that my rampaging worries prevented me from joining in.

"I've learned to trust my dreams," I insisted, reaching forward from my perch on the barstool to silence yet another vibration from Cernun's phone. "Hell, you've both told me to have more faith in them."

"Dreams are the land of the *Fear Dearg*," Cernun smiled. "They are nasty little Faeries intent on warping our realities. Your true visions are what you should heed."

I guessed Cernun had been reading up on his mythology as well. I frowned as I watched him wipe down a third mis-pulled shot of espresso from his fine Italian machine. He was normally a master barista, but a morning of waltzes and jigs had tired him out. I did appreciate that he was making me an iced latte though. Or at least trying to.

"I don't mean to be combative," I sighed, leaning against the kitchen island for support as I studied the eagerly dismissive faces of my boyfriends. "I'm not trying to go all Major Arcana on you here. I promise. But I've spent a hell of a lot more time inside Balor's head than you two. And I'm the only one who's actually met The Mórrígan. I may not understand everything there is to know about the Fomóraiġ, but I am damn sure of what I saw. That green… Those eyes… They were The Mórrígan's. I don't know what my vision was trying to warn me of, but I know it has something to do with her!"

Learco and Cernun exchanged a brief, exasperated glance at the mention of The Mórrígan. Or maybe it was at me pulling the trump card of direct Fae experience. At any rate, I didn't care that my face was telegraphing my desperation. If one of the Fae was again attempting to break into our world—and this time one much stronger than even the warrior king Balor—all hell would break loose. Balor's attempt had left three young witches dead and kept Madison stuck in the body of a cat for a month! I wasn't about to turn the other way if something worse was starting up again.

"Darragh," Cernun said, purring my name even as he continued to fight with his machine, "it is your time with those creatures that has you frightened. You cannot see the bridge for the trolls. But you can see us, right? We are here. We will help make things right. Besides, you have green eyes, do you not? They are not merely a sign of that woman…. Witch tits!"

I smirked at his new swear as he dumped yet another espresso puck, soggy and crumbling, into his trash can, then tried his hand again at one more shot. Maybe fifth time was the charm?

He was succeeding at making sense though, even if he wasn't so much at making my drink. My boyfriends were both my stalwarts. However strangely my fears thought they were acting, they were still right here, ready to face whatever the future brought along with me. I had to consider my perception of the two of them was being warped by my stress around the Fae too. My lips twisted as I thought it through.

"You take too much on your shoulders," Learco said, a soothing lilt making symphonies of his voice. "The bargain with Balor. The deaths of those witches. You took charge of caring for cat Madison without a second thought. And I do not think you have even yet processed the burden of being the guy who re-exposed magic to this world. That is too much for any one witch."

"No matter how sexy and strong your shoulders are," Cernun added, "you are not invincible."

"And all of that is bound to enter your dreamscape," Learco nodded. "It is simply your inner demons making you see things that are not there."

At least my shoulders had gotten a shout out. Perhaps all that reaching for boxes on the top shelves of my stockroom was finally paying off.

My mouth still held its frown, but I nodded.

"You need to forget all about it," Learco assured me, placing a palm on my knee as he peered deep into my eyes. "Focus instead on the coming Equinox. When the day and night align, the door of possibilities springs open! We have so much to look forward to!"

"I guess you're right," I sighed.

"Besides," Cernun assured me as he passed me my drink, "if anything were truly wrong, would not the Moral Authority of Witches have alerted their leader by now?"

He had a point. As much as I distrusted the organization, despite dating its local leader, they had centuries of knowhow and procedure when it came to witchly matters. And as much as Learco held his tarot cards close to his chest when he had to, he'd never shied away from bringing Cernun and me into the shuffle when shit went dire. There was no sense in raining on Ostara before the month of April arrived to nourish our seedlings.

Still my face, never quick to shy away from the questions that rampaged my brain, squinted at Learco for answers. He shrugged as I took a sip of my iced latte. The espresso was sharp and bitter, not at all like Cernun's usual shots, and even the sweetness of the milk couldn't mull the acrid taste. I swallowed hard as I forced myself to join their smiles and nodded.

"Speaking of the MAW," I said, trying my best to sound as cheerful as my lovers, "have you been able to connect with Rafael yet? I'm sure, at the very least, you want your phone back."

Learco shrugged again, bouncing the thick musculature of Cernun's forearms as they wrapped his shoulders from behind.

"It is nice not being tied to that device," he said. "I am presently viewing it as a holiday for the holiday. I will spend my time connecting with the earth and with you all instead of work and technology."

"As Ostara intended," Cernun smiled and bent to kiss Learco's temple.

Madison bounded indoors from the back deck, limbs stretching and electric blue locs a bundle of twigs and new growth. I could still see the animal in their movements, but they were becoming more and more like themself with each aching snarl of their fingers. From my brief time as a hare, I knew how much they'd loved the freedom of inhabiting their cat form, but I was sure they were happy to be back in their own skin. Their joy was plastered across their face.

"That is one heck of a garden you are gonna have out there," they moaned through their extensions. "You are one lucky... Oh, hey, Darragh. I did not know you were here."

"Just checking on my favorite folks in the world," I smiled.

Cernun and Learco were right. I needed to breathe in the season while letting go of my Fae-induced dread. Besides, their trio of grins were certainly infectious. I knew my smile was forced, but I figured I could at least attempt to fake it until I made it real.

"Hey, Mads," I said. "How do you feel about coming back to work this weekend? Verne needs a few days off for school stuff, and I'll be in New Orleans for—"

"Definitely!" they exclaimed before I'd even finished my sentence. "The quicker things get back to normal, the better, right?"

That was good. Verne would be happy. And some normalcy was what we all truly needed.

Before all of this, before I'd exposed magic to the world and way before Fae-kind had entered my worldview, things had been so much simpler. Sure, hiding in the broom closet had been rife with disadvantages. Me, and every other witch in the world, had only been able to reveal our true selves to others like us, and even then in errant gestures or jokes. Even the practice of our power, the very use of the magic that resided naturally inside of us, had been limited to the shadows, to the deepest groves of the forest, to the basking glow of the moonlight. I mean, that all still happened— who didn't love a quick bath in the glow of the stars?—but the dependence upon it for survival, the mania that even a hint of our true selves induced in humankind which had been heartbreaking, humiliating, and life-taking was now beginning to dissipate. So maybe things had been easier in a lot of ways, but they were better now, even in the moments of chaos which sometimes ensued.

Back then, the rules were set; the magic was mine; I could trust in myself in ways that didn't even seem possible now. And now, I saw mischief around every corner. But it was only me who'd allowed that dread to consume my thoughts instead of appreciating the joys I had been given. Cernun and Learco. Madison and Stacey and Verne. Hell, HEX was thriving, and Fae-dammit, so was I!

I knew the rapid-fire ricochet of my fight to convince myself was showing on my face, despite the grin I'd painted there. Learco and Cernun shared a quick, worried glance before turning back to comfort me.

"Look," Cernun sighed, "we were hoping not to tell you this—"

"We wanted it to be a surprise," Learco chimed.

"—But we have something big planned for Ostara. Something that will light your whole world in a way you have never dreamed!"

"So if we have seemed a little off," Learco added, reaching out once more to cup my knee, "it is only because we are excited for what is in store for you. For us all!"

My grin turned real as I shook my head at their revelation. Faerie farts, I was a lucky witch! They had given me so much—their love, their trust—and here I was seeing subterfuge where surprises waited. Leave it to me to try to ruin it when they had something up their sleeves. Hell, only a month ago, the two of them had gifted me a rooftop garden and greenhouse. My face flushed as I imagined what else they could have in store.

"Now," Cernun said as he padded over to kiss the crown of my head, "should you not be attending to your own preparations? If nothing else, your suitcase for your BOG Witch trip will not pack itself. You do not know that spell, after all."

I knew they were trying to distract me, but if they needed more time to plan my surprise, who was I to judge. Besides, my flight to Louisiana was scheduled fairly early on Friday, by witch standards at least, and after we'd had a rollicking night of welcoming Spring into being. My suitcase wasn't even close to being filled. The only thing I knew for sure I was taking was the new suit and mask Learco had gifted me. Damn it! There was another wondrous thing my lovers had brought me. Cernun was right. I needed to focus on my own shit instead of making worries over theirs.

I gave myself a mental swift kick in the ass as I slipped from the barstool to embrace the two most amazing witches in my life.

My face beamed pure light and energy as I emerged from the Broomer in front of my shop. There was a newfound lightness to my step, not because my boyfriends were busy planning a surprise for me, but because I was finally able to see how befuddled my suspicion was making me. Free of that, I could actually enjoy the lead up to the Equinox.

Even from outside, I could tell that HEX was busy. It was, after all, witch-kind's last full day to stock up on spelling supplies before we closed for the holiday, and most witches—like a lot of humans rummaging through toy stores on Christmas Eve—were procrastinators. I was glad I'd had the foresight to order in extra frankincense resin and dried rose buds. As far as I knew, HEX was the last place in town to have them on the shelves.

I took a moment once more to admire the daffodils shooting up from the tree beds in the sidewalk. Their trumpets looked more like crowns as they angled straight upwards toward the sun, harkening for him to take more of our days, to let us bask in his warmth.

The wisteria, too, still snaking around the dress shop doors, now carried its vines across the northern side of the street, leaping from brick to shingle, carried by power lines across the alleyways between buildings, and calling the sun forward to the equator and beyond. Thick racemes of violet flowers cascaded amidst its sprawling limbs to give the whole street a romantic air like a bit of the Old South—the parts of it we witches loved anyway—was alive and well in the modern city.

What Learco and Cernun were trying to tell me was true. Spring was coming—and she was beautiful. I did not need to get caught up in fantasy when all that was real was fantastical in its own right. Between the intoxicating aroma of the flowers and the spotlight of the noonday sun, I found it a lot easier to heed their words and breathe out the imagined agony of the last few days.

Unfortunately, my revelry was short-lived.

The tires on the sedan barely made a sound as they pulled to a stop at the curb. As covert as they thought they were, the silent treads, the obsidian black, and the ultra-tinted windows of every MAW vehicle gave them away immediately to anyone in the know. And I'd had my fair share of Moral Authority vehicles idling on the street in front of my store. I braced myself, tapping my toe against the concrete sidewalk, as the rear door opened and Rafael emerged.

"You here to drop off Learco's phone?" I asked, knowing deep down it could never be that simple.

"Hello, Mister Cullen… uh, Darragh," he said, shuffling a bit on the curb as if he couldn't find his footing. "Has Mister Clarke not told you?"

My brow furrowed while I studied the frustration creasing Rafael's temples. The buttons of his shirt strained against his heavy breath. He was always so staid and put-together, it surprised me to see him so off-balance. But what shocked me even more was seeing Leland Hyde, the resident fixer for the entirety of the Moral Authority organization, popping out of the opposite side of the vehicle.

"Oh, for Fae's sake, Acosta," Leland bellowed, "you wanna be an agent and not an assistant, you're gonna need to pick up the pace."

His glare as he turned to me was way less friendly than it had been the last time we'd met. Even in the midst of Balor's murder spree of young witches, Leland had been eager to get to know me, to include me in his investigation. Of course, he'd also wanted me to join the MAW. I'd really thought my "I'll think about" had been an obvious "no."

"Uh…" Rafael stammered, steeling himself as he willed the words to come out. "Darragh, if you wouldn't mind…"

"Shit, Acosta!" Leland howled, then turned back to me. "Cullen, Clarke's been fired. And we need you in the car. You can come willingly or by force, I don't really care which, but you're coming with us."

Well, fuck. That certainly explained a lot about Learco's strangeness since his trip to Salem. But it didn't give me a Faerie farting clue of what they could want with me. Still, where the MAW was concerned, I'd learned it best to play along, lest they suddenly conjure a bogus charge or two to flame me as an example.

Rafael shrugged, still worried and timid as he opened the back door of the sedan. I waved a quick "it's fine" to Verne who'd stopped with his customers to watch the scene unfold through the shop window, then shivered as the door slammed closed between us.

CHAPTER 6

The room was as sterile as I remembered. Tucked away on a nondescript upper floor in a nondescript Buckhead office building, the place was little more than a white on white walk-in closet. White walls, white ceiling, and white lights shone down on the white table and its joining white chairs. Even the polished chip of alabaster set in the center of the table was white, and hopefully it would remain that way. For a room nestled deep within the highest ranking witch institution and serviced by the—supposedly—highest ranking witches in the land, there was not a single hint of the earthly treasures from which our power derived. But, I supposed, that was on purpose.

The last time I was here, I'd sat across from Leland and Learco as a formality. This time, however, sitting across from Leland and Rafael was different. The charmed, power-suppression amulet that hung around my neck felt stronger than the ones I was used to, and I wondered if the MAW had engineered new ones based around my own somewhat vague descriptions of when Balor had managed to temporarily strip me of my magic. They hadn't known about the Fae aspects of the situation, but the general idea of a mental obstruction had no doubt sent their minions scurrying to find yet another way to police witch-kind.

I shifted uncomfortably in my seat, but tried my best not to show it on my face. The amulet produced a nervous tingle throughout every cell of my body, like static electricity begging to be discharged on the nearest metal doorknob, but that was nothing compared to the chair itself. Taken straight out of some shady government's interrogation how-to, the legs were shorter than those on the seats opposite me, placing my eye line a good two inches below those of the Witch Hunter and the Assistant. The seat itself angled slightly downwards, and the chair back pushed ever-so forward, making it a conscious effort for me to remain upright as my body hunched and scrambled to appear calm and collected.

"How'd you do it?" Leland asked. His gruff, gravelly voice mixed with the nasal yank of Massachusetts to create the jarring ick of nails on a chalkboard, especially in a room this small. I'd actually found the discordance kind of charming before, but that had also been before it was directed at me.

"How'd I do what?" I asked innocently. "Snag two of the hottest witches this side of Salem? Retain my boyish good looks and vaguely defined stomach despite the number of burgers and Old Fashioneds I consume? Just lucky, I guess."

I knew that pushing his buttons was tantamount to playing with fire—literally. The MAW had flamed more witches than any angry pastor or jealous schoolgirl. But if they were going to make me squirm, the least I could do was return the favor. Besides, he'd also blatantly ignored my question every time I'd asked about Learco's firing.

In fairness, Learco hadn't told me why either. Or even that he'd been let go. I guessed that was why he'd high-tailed it out of Salem, leaving everything including his phone in his hotel room. That was why his eyes glazed and his expression fell distant whenever I asked him about what went down. I sincerely hoped I hadn't been the cause of his unceremonious departure from the MAW, though judging by the looks steering Rafael and Leland's faces, I had a feeling that hope was in vain.

"Play coy all you want, Cullen," Learco snarled. "We can sit here all day."

His shoulders shuffled as he crossed his arms over the thick expanse of his belly. The soft fabric of his shirt—white with navy blue pinstripes—strained against the buttons as he leaned back in his seat. The floor length wool trench coat he thought made him look cool was draped over the chair back like an ominous, all-black aura surrounding him. He still had his usual childlike gleam in his eyes, but now, directed at me, it looked much more nefarious than mischievous.

"Please, Darragh," Rafael pleaded, "this doesn't need to be difficult."

"Oh, I see," I smirked. "You get to be Jekyll while Mister Hyde over there gets all huffy. Or are you already auditioning for your old boss's position?"

It was unnerving to see the quivers in the usual placidity of Rafael's face. He was putting up a strong front for Leland, but I could see the genuine concern for Learco in his eyes. I sighed. He had a job to do, and I couldn't hold that against him. Even if I found the entirety of the Moral Authority to be morally gray.

Rafael was definitely the cutest of all the assistants Learco had blown through since his first right hand, Samara Byrne, had spelled us all in the back with her power grab. Of course, that was still better than spelling us straight through as she'd done with Adrian Goldfinch née Gowdie and then using an illegal necromancy spell to resurrect his corpse to her bidding. Rafael had an old money meets eager air about him that spoke as much of comfort as it did of dedication. His black hair had an auburn tint to it, and the stubble he now sported after two days of, as Leland put it, "dealing with this shit" fit his round face quite well. The broadness of his shoulders helped him carry his weight with ease, but the burden of losing his boss and becoming Leland's lackey in one fail swoop had not settled as effortlessly. The pain and confusion he felt were evident, even as he made his best attempt at brave.

I almost felt sorry for him. Almost.

"Just tell us how you did it, Darragh" he begged, the accented echoes of his grandmother's tongue becoming more and more evident in his frustration.

"How. I. Did. What?"

I honestly wasn't being obtuse. I just had no idea what they were talking about. The laundry list of items the MAW could peg me for was long—and seemed to be growing all the time. But most of my rule breaking was unknown to them. Particularly my dealings with the Fomóraiġ. And I wasn't about to clue them in on their existence. The Dark Fae were bad enough on their own. I didn't even want to imagine what the MAW could do with even the mere knowledge of Fae magic.

Leland sighed heavily as his fingers played invisible piano keys on the table. His face scrunched as he considered me, exaggerating the redness of his bulbous nose before his eyes sparked and his expression calmed like a switch within him had been flipped.

"I bet you're hungry, huh?" he asked, suddenly all roses and white lace. "It's well past lunch time, right? Maybe sharing a meal will get you talking?"

I scoffed, but I was hungry. I'd skipped breakfast in my angst over the previous night's dream, and the few sips I'd taken of Cernun's iced latte had not come close to satiating my stomach. Still, I wasn't about to eat anything the Moral Authority placed in front of me. It felt too much as if they were offering me a "last meal." But that didn't mean I couldn't have some fun at their expense.

"I could eat," I shrugged, smirking through my nonchalant cadence. "I mean, since Learco's obviously lost his table at the Dove and Crow, it might be nice to have one of the best chefs in the city whip a little something up for us."

Leland scowled as he rose from his seat, but met my smirk head on.

"Done," he said.

My eyes followed his few short steps to the door. I waited until his hand was on the knob before I spoke again.

"Oh! And an Old Fashioned. But not from there, from Aunt Paulina's. And make sure Paul is the one who makes it. He's the owner and knows exactly how I like it."

Leland's exasperation was evident, but he continued to smile. So I continued to pile things on.

"And maybe a couple beignets from Café du Monde! If this pointless interrogation carries on much longer, I might miss my trip to New Orleans, and I was really looking forward to those."

I noted a small bit of admiration behind the glower as Leland excused himself from the room.

"Don't forget to tip!" I yelled as he closed the door. I leaned back in my chair and turned my palms up toward the ceiling as I squared back to Rafael.

"Now what?" I asked.

Rafael blinked, and the hard lines around his temples I hadn't even noticed before softened. He glanced nervously from the door to his hands before the brown of his eyes found me once again.

"Is Mister Clarke okay?" he asked.

So that's where his pain was coming from. Even in his dedication to his job, it was nice to see the care he possessed for his former boss. Maybe I could work that to gain my freedom.

"He's…" I started, then reset as I settled in for honesty. "He's been a bit strange, almost like he's ignoring what happened. But I guess that's to be expected when everything you've ever worked for gets ripped right out from under you by an uncaring, autocratic organization. Really, I mean, if Learco can get handed the boot, I guess no one's really safe."

Rafael squirmed in his chair. I watched his lips disappear as he swallowed hard.

"What *did* happen, by the way?" I asked, hoping maybe this time I'd get an answer.

"I'm actually not sure," Rafael sighed. "I never saw him in Salem. And when I informed Mister Hyde of Learco's disappearance from the hotel, he blew a gasket. Told me not to bother with tracking him down, that he'd take the lead from there, and to rest assured he could make 'Clarke's life miserable.' Those were his words, not mine."

It was my turn to frown. But at least I knew this little inquisition was retaliation against Learco and not directly about me. I just hoped that whatever had gotten him fired in the first place didn't fall on my lap. That was one circle I did not want to close.

"You'll make sure he's okay, won't you?" Rafael asked. The pleading in his eyes was almost too much to take.

"The best I can," I promised. And I meant it with every fiber of my being.

Despite my reservations surrounding the organization he'd been a leader in, my infatuation with Learco had been nearly immediate. The calmness of his demeanor, the way he held himself with such power and assuredness, and the fairness in his convictions had actually given me hope for a new era in the Moral Authority's methods. I mean, it also helped that he was sexy as fuck. Compact and toned, with an irresistible pout to his lower lip and eight pack abs descending toward his massive cock, I'd become infatuated with him before I even knew who he was. It hadn't taken much for that attraction to move into desire or for desire to progress to love.

"Can you at least tell me what Leland thinks he has on me?" I asked. "I really have no clue. I actually thought he liked me. But, then again, I thought he liked Learco too, and we both see how that turned out."

So what if I added that last part to pick away at the unraveling threads in Rafael's dedication to the MAW? A little distrust of totalitarian bodies was healthy. Plus, I could tell I was getting through to him.

Just as Rafael was about to speak, the door swung open, and Leland pushed his way back to his seat. He carried with him a familiar, blood red folder and huffed as he tossed it in front of his chair. The MAW used a colored coding system for each of their cases, with a muted green for the most minor of offenses and the muddied crimson I saw before me for the most heinous. The last time I'd seen a folder like this, it had held photographs of the magically manipulated and mutilated corpses of Madison's best friend, Angel. Damn. Whatever Leland thought I'd done must have been horrific.

I suddenly felt much less self-assured than I had a few seconds prior.

"Food's en route," Leland hissed. "You ready for brass tacks while we wait?"

I stifled a gulp as I eyed the red folder. I wracked my brain for anything I could have done—anything the MAW could have *thought* I'd done—but was still unable to figure out what it contained. I did know I could probably use some help though.

"If you're not going to tell me what I did or why Learco was fired," I said, clearing my throat as I wished the angst residing there away, "can you at least let me call him? If I'm standing trial,

I want somebody who knows your ways here to help me."

The smile that spread across Leland's face scared me more than whatever that folder contained. The way his lips peeled away from his yellowing teeth, slicks of saliva dancing in the overhead light, was downright terrifying.

"This isn't a trial, Cullen," he purred. "This is just a conversation. But if you want to drag your boyfriend into this— and Fae knows associating with you has dragged him into worse— then who am I to stop you?"

His smile didn't falter as he fished the phone he'd confiscated from me out of his pocket and slid it across the table. I sighed as I picked it up. I did not want to bring Learco any more into this than he had to be, but maybe he would at least be able to tell me what the MAW thought I'd done. If nothing else, letting my boyfriends know where I was before I was flamed at the stake and never heard from again would be nice. I breathed deeply to calm myself as I pressed the call button and held the phone to my ear. As the line connected, I heard an answering chime from Rafael's pocket.

"Shit," I said, hanging up quickly as Leland snatched my phone away from me. "I forgot."

Rafael winced as he removed Learco's cell from his jacket pocket and placed it next to the folder for Leland to quickly grab and stow next to mine.

"If you're done with your games," he said, shoving the folder forward and nodding for me to take a look, "how 'bout we talk about this."

I wet my lips as I cautiously flipped open the cover expecting nothing less than the worst. Bodies turned inside out by a magic so dark it craved destruction over creation. Souls disemboweled and picked through like they were nothing more than gardens growing ingredients for potions no modern witch dreamed to use. But the pictures staring back at me were benign, beautiful landscapes.

I couldn't help but laugh.

"This is what you brought me in for?" I asked when I finally caught my breath. "Seriously?"

"Tell us how you did it," Leland demanded.

I shook my head as I eyed the city streets, dandelions and crocuses and irises and daffodils bursting buoyantly from the sidewalks. It truly was a charming sight, seeing neighborhood after neighborhood, street after avenue of Atlanta burning bright with petals and welcoming Spring. Cressida's assertion that the MAW believed my spell sign was accompanying the blooms hadn't been a joke.

"Darragh, your spell sign is coating every bulb," Rafael sighed, recomposed and doing his best attempt at a friendly face as he tried to coax information from me. "Can you at least explain that?"

I rolled my eyes as I continued to flip through the contents of the folder. A map of Atlanta showed nearly the entirety of the perimeter, stretching all the way out to 285 as it circled the city, marked as "infected" by the flowers.

"First off," I said, bolder now that the absurdity of the situation was evident, "I didn't do this. Second, I get that you're really trying to make spell signs work, Leland, but—"

"Mister Hyde," he interrupted.

"—Leland," I continued, eyes squinted but still smirking. "They are untested and circumstantial at best. Downright wrong at worst. I mean, only a month ago your spell signs pointed you toward my friend Madison Ridge as a murderer when they were actually a victim. They're back from Prague, by the way. Thanks for asking…. And third, even if I had the power to do this—which how could one witch raise... what is it? A million? Two million plants from bulb to blossom in a single night?—what are you gonna charge me with? Gardening?"

I leaned back in my chair and crossed my arms over my chest, not caring that the incline of the seat made the gesture even more awkward to look at than it was to do. Rafael bit his lip as Leland scowled and pulled the folder with its contents away from me.

"So the witch who lifted a barreling SUV along with the four human passengers inside ten feet off the ground and placed them gently back down on a whim expects me to believe he's incapable of this?"

Leland was nearly growling now, his words sputtering out with as much spit as sound, as he stared me down from across the table. I sighed deeply as his years of rage echoed through the room. I'd always expected that moment to haunt me. Yes, I'd managed that magic—and exposed witch-kind to the human world in the process—but I'd only done so out of necessity and adrenaline in order to save Cernun's life. Yes, I supposed that meant that a somewhat higher level of power was within me. But I hadn't been able to recreate it. Not that I'd tried. Not that I'd tell them if I had.

Whatever had prevented the MAW from flaming me right then and there for exposing magic—most likely their unsuccessful desire to recruit me and use me for their cause—was no longer keeping me safe, and it was obvious that Leland was determined to take me out of commission. I was actually scared, but—for once—my face didn't show it.

"I didn't do this," I said calmly, wincing as my voice cracked through the vowels. "But I kind of wish I had. You have to admit, it's gorgeous."

"It's an illegal use of magic, is what it is," Leland barked. "And your spell sign—"

"You forget my lover was on the inside," I interrupted, knowing full well I was pressing his buttons again. But I was also hoping if I pushed hard enough, the preposterousness of the whole affair would shine through. "That new witch-fingerprinting system may be your baby, but the higher ups aren't sure you can carry it to term. It's so unreliable, it hasn't been approved as grounds for conviction."

The rage slipped suddenly from Leland's face, the blood flushing his cheeks red replaced quickly with an icy pallor as he smacked his lips and inhaled sharply. He cocked his head as he blinked at me in the cold white light of the room. Emboldened, I continued.

"I don't think your bosses will let you flame me for some daffodils. Especially when you have no real proof it was me. Which, again, for the record, it was not."

The sound of Leland sucking on his teeth was nearly as jarring as the calm study which had replaced his anger. I was grateful for the distraction of a knock on the door. The Witch Hunter witch held up a single finger to halt the entrance of whomever was out there and cocked his head at me with an ever-so-slight pity.

"You may have fooled Clarke with your Fae-may-care attitude," he said, almost a whisper now as the words hissed from his throat, "but I don't swing that way. And trust me. I can do way worse to you than flaming you at the stake. So, go right on ahead, Cullen. Try me."

The way he was smiling chilled me to my bones. Even Rafael shivered, and he wasn't even on the receiving end. He lowered his finger, and the door swung inward. I felt the breath forced out of me only for it to be sucked right back into my lungs in a quickened shock. My mouth gaped. I felt my heart go crazy as the legs of my chair scratched against the floor until my back met the corner, every cell in my body scrambling to retreat as far away as possible.

Sure of step but still timid as she entered, the young woman smiled as she placed the bag of to-go containers on the table. Her green eyes, strung through with golden stardust, looked distant and glazed as they passed over me and around the room to Leland. The freckles that danced across the bridge of her nose were the same color as the orange-red hair she had cut into a sharp bob just below her chin.

She was exactly as I remembered her.

Her clothing was different though. No longer sporting the wonderfully tailored tweed of her skirt-suits or the pointed stilettos of her former position, she now appeared pale within the sharp, unadorned black of the MAW agent's uniform. But her scars—the twisted gnarl of puckered skin which traveled from her palms down her forearms from years of hatred manifested into her magic—were as obvious as they'd been the day she tried to kill me.

Yet there was no glint of recognition in her gaze. Hell, there wasn't even a bit of agency.

"Will that be all, sir?" she asked.

Her voice was demure, hollow and worn through like she knew she had been broken but could not remember what had tamed her. Or, I guessed, who.

Leland held a self-righteous glow as he watched me watch Samara Byrne bent to his will. He licked his lips in smug pleasure as he spoke, like a salivating dog who was way too proud of his kill.

"Just one more thing, girl," he said, laying it on thick as he kept me trapped in his stare. "There's a slight chill in the air today, and we wouldn't want Cullen to suffer a cold meal. How's about a little reheating spell to warm this all up?"

Samara's face fell even lower—which I hadn't believed possible—as her hands clasped behind her back and her chin met her clavicle. Her words were barely audible as they cut through the hair hanging in her face.

"I am from a nonmagical line, sir," she whispered, the self-flagellation evident in every syllable. "As such, I am unable to perform the task you require."

Leland smirked, his eyes still burning holes in my own as he shooed her away.

"That will be all then," he hissed.

My face was a flurry of shock and terror and disbelief. Before she'd partnered with the Gowdies to try to usurp Learco and then kill Cernun and me to boot, I'd actually held a bit of admiration for Samara. She was a strong, sassy, and self-assured witch who, despite her short stature and lithe limbs, commanded every room she entered. Now, there wasn't a trace of that power left in her. Or, apparently, even a bit of the magic or the memory of who she was before.

"Spell signatures may not be enough for the High Council just yet, Cullen," Leland snarled, "but a witch brandishing that much power… Well, they're bound to see them as a threat. And threats have a pretty expedient deal by date. This ain't the olden times. Flames let a witch off easy. I don't think you'll be as lucky as you say you are if they decide to throw the Book of Shadows your way."

The sudden dryness in my mouth was inching its way down my throat. Shit! He really thought I'd used my own magic to cover the city in daffodils. I could see the blatant jealousy in his eyes even as he relished in his ability to strip me of my power. Even Rafael, sitting as quietly as possible beside him, was quivering in his khakis as Leland relished in his upper-hand.

"Now," he continued, "how about you eat and open up. Depending on what you say, we can figure out how tonight will go."

"I—I'm not hungry," I stuttered, the words straining to push from my lungs.

I wasn't sure if I would ever eat again. The violence in Leland's eyes, the vitriol in his voice, tied my stomach into knots. Or maybe it was the anti-magic amulet finally working its nervous tension all the way to my gut. It was probably both. And it was definitely not good.

"You don't want to eat?" he asked, the feigned sympathy in his voice almost as aggressive as his hatred. "Fine. Acosta, take him to holding. Maybe some time there will loosen up that famous tongue of his."

Leland swooped out the door, the bag of food from the Dove and Crow in one hand, the red folder under his arm, and an evilly playful wiggle of the fingers on his free hand.

Rafael winced an apology as he rose from his chair, and I sighed as I surrendered to him. None of this was his fault, and the last thing I wanted to do was add the young witch to Leland's shit list if I didn't play along. I kept my head low but my eyes searching as he led me to my cell.

CHAPTER 7

Rafael was kind, even though he didn't speak, as he led me through the twisting labyrinth of MAW hallways. Each fluorescent lit passageway appeared exactly like the last, with black-framed, unmarked doors and speckled marble flooring that echoed ominously with every purposeful step we took toward my doom. I could understand why Rafael was silent. My own voice quivered at the bottom of my throat, aching to be released but not daring to face the ire it could awake within the building. At least he'd removed the anti-magic amulet from around my neck. He knew that, like my voice, I wouldn't dare attempt to use my power. But it was a relief to feel connected to it once more, and the slow buzz of absence was beginning to quietly resign from my body.

The holding cells weren't much, but they looked slightly better than the interrogation room. I immediately sensed the fossilized mixture of wormwood, vetivert, and mugwort—the same potion used at the Magical Artifacts & Antiquities Museum— flecked within the coal black paint which adorned the walls. The abundance of the mixture of herbs would leave one hell of a sting if I even tried to conjure the corners, so my magic was still out of reach, but it was better than being cut off from it completely. A small, straw-stuffed cot was shoved against the far wall, no doubt to remind us miscreant witches of how easily we could burn, and the iron bars on the door offered yet another dead zone for any magical manifestation.

"I know you can't phone Learco," Rafael sighed as he locked the gate between us, "but you do actually get a phone call if you'd like."

A cawing laugh burst forth from deep in my stomach, as much a relief from the breath I'd been holding onto during my long perp walk as it was at the absurdity of the Moral Authority of Witches adopting the customs of their human counterpart. The idea that a ceremonious lifeline made their policing, their restrictions of freedom, any more moral was asinine, and Rafael winced as I finished my chuckle.

Still, I supposed I should let someone know where I was.

Even though I was sure he wouldn't answer, I could have left a message on Cernun's voicemail. But, with the way my boyfriends had been acting, I had no idea when he'd actually check to see I'd called. And letting Stacey or Verne know at HEX would have spread the news through all of Atlanta before I'd even hung up. Too, I didn't want to worry my parents. The idea of them hopping in Dad's pickup with more torches and pitchforks than they could carry alone to storm the MAW's castle only to rain more trouble on us all was as palpable as the imminent sting of fire from the potion-painted walls. Besides, I knew Leland was trying to break me, but I also knew I had no hand in what he was accusing me of and figured I'd be out by dinner. I just needed someone to know I was here in case something went wrong.

Sighing, I dictated a number to Rafael, happy I still remembered it without the screen of my cell phone reminding me of the digits. He dialed it for me on the landline mounted outside my cage and passed the corded receiver through the bars. The third ring ceased abruptly as the line connected.

"Who's calling?"

"Hey, Uncle Gardner. It's me. Darragh."

My uncle answered every single call from a number he didn't recognize in the same gruff voice. I'd told him over and over he could just let the answering machine do its job, but I think he got a kick out of messing with the unrelenting telemarketers preying on the older generations, turning the tables on their sales- and scam-pitches with his own long-winded, made-up stories when he could.

"I'm in a MAW holding cell," I continued, my voice warning him that the call was no doubt being monitored and not to say anything that could land another witch in their crosshairs.

"Welp," he guffawed, "it's finally happened. I knew it was bound to sooner or later. Or is this some BDSM sex game you and Learco are playing?"

I could always count on Uncle Gardner to make me smile. I'd inherited more than just my shop from that witch. I felt lucky to have his snarky sense of humor as well.

"It's all just a misunderstanding," I said, trying my best to sound sure and calm in my convictions.

"I know it is, boy," he assured me. "What do they say you did?"

"Planted some flowers."

His laughter started powerfully but became distant as I heard the phone slip from his hands in his amusement. In the background, I listened to his husband Bill rush forward, his concern turning to confusion before settling into gaiety as Gardner recounted the situation. I rolled my eyes and tapped my toe against the concrete floor as my uncle picked back up his phone. He sighed deeply to stifle the last few whoops of laughter in his chest.

"Since I know they're listening," he said when he'd regained his composure, "I'll just say this: most of those MAW fucks are able to decide good from evil as well as they can tell their asses from their elbows. They got too much shit on their sleeves to tell the difference."

I supposed I got my distrust of the organization from him too.

"You need anything from me?" he asked, his voice suddenly serious and low across the line. "Want me to call my sister?"

"Nah." I hoped my nonchalance was coming through to assure him I was okay. Or, at least, I thought I was okay. "I don't want to worry them. I figure I'll be out of here before the candle can light. But I wanted someone in the family to know where I was in case things change. So if you don't hear from me by Ostara...."

"Got it!" I could hear Uncle Gardner's smile through the phone. He'd always been so confident in me. I was glad he'd been my one phone call. I needed that reassurance. "Remember, Darragh," he continued. "I know I've told you this time and again, but you're a stronger witch than you know. Trust what comes your way. It all has purpose."

I sighed as I hung up the phone. Uncle Gardner was a pretty powerful witch himself. His particular magic had always centered around omniscience, though, like most Seers, he kept the revelations of his visions purposefully vague. He believed that telling someone their destiny was far less impactful than them learning it the hard way. So I guessed I had to take my knocks. Still, it was comforting to hear his words.

Rafael winced again as I passed the phone back through the gate.

"I will try to let Mister Clarke know you're here," he said as his lips trembled through a slight frown. "I'm supposed to track him down for him to clear his personal items from his condo by the end of the week."

I nodded. I hadn't even considered that. But it made sense. Part of the compensation for his position had included a beautiful high rise apartment a few blocks away from the MAW HQ. I hadn't spent much time there, preferring the small comforts of my inherited home and the close proximity to my shop and the soil to the august and expansive quarters high above the earth. But, damn, I would miss that view!

"Thanks," I said, hoping he saw that I truly meant it.

We stood in a moment of unease, the bars between us distinguishing the power at play in the situation. Any other time, I might relish in the inherent seduction of the situation, but Rafael's face was even more overwrought than my own.

"I'm supposed to turn off the light when I leave," he said, apology thick on his words. "No windows, no light, mugwort in the walls… it's meant to stew folks into confession."

"I'd expect nothing less than psychological warfare from the *Moral* Authority," I shrugged, stressing the irony in the first word of their moniker. "I won't hold it against you personally."

If Cernun was here, I was sure I'd be laughing at the implied *unless you want me to.* But he wasn't here. I was alone. And I had a feeling I would be for quite some time.

I sat on the edge of the cot and nodded my understanding of the circumstances as they settled into my mind. Not that it mattered. It wasn't as if I actually had any choices in the matter.

The bed was as uncomfortable as it looked. Straw shifted and lumped beneath me, but it was still better than the floor. And it wasn't like I had any other option. I closed my eyes as Rafael clicked off the light, laying back as I listened to the sound of his heels clicking off into the distance.

Solitude and darkness were far more disturbing than I'd expected the pairing to be. In the city, a light was always shining; a soul or spirit or breath always hovered nearby. Even growing up on the farm two hours south of anywhere, I'd never been truly isolated, never lost in the pitch. The night sky had its starlight. The canopy filtered moonlight onto the wooded paths. The breath of the birds wove magic on the wind, offering to carry me through to comfort. But here, locked in the MAW's holding cell, cut off from the outside world without so much as a flicker of ambient light across the dull black walls, for the first time I felt utterly alone.

Or worse: not alone.

I wasn't sure how much time had passed, but my imagination had begun its descent into invention. Unseen motions twisted my head against the sharpened hay of the mattress. The thumps of my heart displaced to convince me of footsteps near the gate. I was no longer sure if my eyes were opened or closed. My mind conjured visions upon the screen either way. As Rafael had promised, it was enough to drive a witch mad.

I wondered what Cernun and Learco would say when they found out about my arrest. If I could even call it an arrest. I supposed "incarceration in lieu of evidence" was more appropriate. I could already hear them laughing about it. In my imagination, I was laughing too, so that was something. I just hoped my own internal giggling wasn't a sign of my growing insanity.

But it was good to focus on something funny—or something that would be funny when given enough space. Otherwise, I kept getting stuck on trying to figure out why Learco hadn't told us about his dismissal. Deep down, I understood why he would need a little time to process things on his own—and I certainly didn't mind watching him scramble eggs and dance in the nude as he ignored his loss to focus on us—but Cernun and I were his partners, and we could distract him in any way he wanted. Hell, inside this blinding blackness, trapped deep inside a forbidden place, I'd already concocted a few new positions to twist our bodies into. Fuck, I was horny.

I still remembered my contract with Cernun to wait until our Ostara rights, but these were extenuating circumstances. Besides, a little bit of self-pleasure never hurt anyone. Unless they wanted it to. And my body did crave distraction.

My lips parted as I pushed against my chest through my sweater. I knew the symphony I was conducting, but in the darkness it was easy to believe my hands were not my own. My aura warmed me from within. I didn't dare to send it outward. The zap from the herbal ingredients spelled into the wall would be intense. But it could also be extremely pleasurable if I timed it right.

I quivered as the cotton rose and fingers found my stomach, pushing up to my navel before massaging their way beneath the fabric to tweak my already stiffened nipple. Heavy breath—which must have been mine—sounded dense in my ear, intensifying the sensation as hardened hands groped my body. My sweater slipped over my head, cradling my neck while the tension pulled my arms into bondage. My mouth watered for myself.

I felt the vibration of my spirit within me urging me onward as my hands slipped down toward my cock. Already erect and throbbing, it forced its way past the waistline of my trousers, dripping in anticipation, knowing and ready for what was to come. Two fingers swirled through the wet spot on my stomach, and I brought them to my lips to taste the salt I held within. It was like I was tasting someone else. I smiled as my hands massaged my face, then down my throat and torso to undo the button of my pants.

My dick leapt into the darkness, and I pushed the waistband of my boxer briefs down beneath my balls to cradle the best of me on full display. Plus, I liked the way the pressure against my perineum felt like another forceful touch from another wayward soul.

Even knowing it was coming, I gasped as my hand clutched the bulk of my shaft, fingers wrapping to massage the strained expanse of skin. A guttural moan slipped from my throat and intensified as the walls threw it back to surround me in my own ecstasy. I shuddered as my neck arched. My crown bore into the mattress. Even the roughness of the straw was rapture now. All of it—the depth of the darkness, the isolation, my touch—wove through my body as a singular, hedonistic desire, pulling me out of myself even as I ground further and further to my core.

A chorus of growls escaped my throat as I neared my climax. A small shaft of green light shone through my slitted eyes. Within the intensity of my excitement, I had not even realized I'd sent my aura out to manifest. But I didn't care about the shock. It would only amplify the pleasure of my ejaculation.

My hands worked tight against my body, moving through the darkness with such vigor it felt like there were four, then six, then eight palms thrust upon me. Fingers clutched tight to my muscles; claws threatened to break the skin of my neck.

I was just about to cum when I was pulled from the mattress. Hands that were not mine shoved me toward the sliver of green light. I had no control over myself, over my movements.

My body seized.

I felt it pop.

My palms clutched at craggy soil. Sharp stone bore into my knees. I arched my back as my lungs heaved a heavy breath into my ears, nearly drowning out the sharp ringing tone that permeated the air. There was darkness still, but as my eyes adjusted I recognized the murky haze of light shifting in from above.

What the fuck had happened? Where the hell was I? I had not intended any real use of power, but if I'd somehow shifted out of the Moral Authority's holding cell—*could I even do that?*—my own cells were as good as toast in the MAW's flames. Or maybe they'd splice me beneath the microscope to figure out how I worked. At least then *someone* would know.

My eyes were half-opened as the pounding in my chest began to subside, slowing toward the regular beat which accentuated my days. The haze around my brain was dissipating too. Except for the low, vibrating rumble and the somehow familiar electric blue haze batting against my face, I was almost feeling normal.

First a yowl and then my name echoed around me, both calling me to full consciousness. My brain still felt heavy, surrounded, as I fell back into myself, but I was alert now. Or, at least as alert as I could be without knowing what the hell was going on.

"Madison?" I asked.

I was shocked to see them, in their cat form, sitting a few feet in front of me as I rose to my knees. Their tail twitched around them as I quickly pulled my sweater back over my head and buttoned my pants. Their eyes squinted a thank you before my name sounded again and their head craned upwards.

I allowed my own gaze to follow suit. An opening, maybe twenty feet above me, framed a turquoise sky and a familiar silhouette.

"Cernun?" I called.

My voice bounced along the cliffs surrounding me as it

ricocheted toward the figure peering down at me. Deep black stone sparkled in the descending light. How had I ended up in a cavern? What the hell was going on?

"It's really you!" he cheered. "Follow Madison. They can show you the path."

I must have been dreaming again. Or maybe I'd finally lost it. Still, everything felt so real. Yes, there was the joyful improbability of seeing my boyfriend in a somewhat impossible situation, but the rocks that had pressed against my palms had left marks. I could still feel the twinge of pressure where they had been. The air had a sour aroma, like blackness turned to rot, but above that there was sweetness. All of my senses were invigorated. My power, in my stomach, turned somersaults.

I swallowed hard as I remembered my last vision had ended dark and bloody. The thin crags of jutted rock were primed to promise more pain. But it was only a dream. If I fell, I'd surely wake up, nestled uncomfortably on the holding cell cot, before my back broke against the ground.

I nodded my agreement to Madison. Their claws kneaded the soil at their feet as they readied themself for the climb. A quick mew I took to mean follow me poured from their throat as they slunk against the wall of stone. They took the first few holds quickly, stopping atop the fourth to meet my gaze and blink. Each small overhang was narrow, barely enough for their paws to get a foothold when aligned in a row, but I sighed my understanding and tried to breathe in some courage. Two footholds. Two handholds. I knew where to start.

I'd attempted the beginner's rock wall a time or two at the gym with Cernun. I'd actually enjoyed it, but I'd also been wearing a helmet and gloves and kneepads. Not to mention the bungee cord attached to the harness around my waist that would catch me if I lost my grip. This was true bouldering, on smooth rock with sharp edges and twice the height with no softened mats on the floor.

I clung tight to the stone, pressing my cheek against its cool surface as I eyed Madison's next two leaps. *Reach and clutch,* I told myself. *Reach and clutch.* A slip of my foot a quarter of the way up quickly added *And don't look down!* to my mantra.

The whole of the climb, I could feel my power churning inside of me like so many bats in a cave all their own. My magic felt different in my dream—like there was more of it somehow; as if the spells I knew were out of reach and distant, distorted but still accessible if I could bridge the gap. But it was also mixed with something new—some part of myself I'd yet to discover. I wondered what Uncle Gardner would have interpreted from that.

My biceps strained as I bridged another gap, feet on tiptoe now as I stretched every inch of me to find the next horizontal break in the stone. We were about two thirds of the way up to the blue-green sky and the golden-red sun. Freedom was close. I appreciated the new warmth on my skin. I heard Cernun's voice more clearly now, not distorted by its echo, as he encouraged me from above.

"Just a few more feet," he promised. "You've got this!"

The sweat which wet my brow stung when it met my eyes, and I winced as I blinked it away.

"Grip and pull," he called. "Grip and pull!"

I raised my eyes to watch for Madison's next leap, gasping as the short ledge crumbled beneath their paws. Rock and dust plummeted quickly as their claws scrambled for purchase in the hard stone. I coughed as I inhaled the dirt, shifting my head downward to prevent any more from entering my eyes. But I couldn't let Madison fall, even if it was a dream.

I reached quickly to grab their body, but they were more cat than witch, more instinct than animal. Their claws were barbed wire, burrowing deep into my forearm as they clung to me for survival. Pain seized through me with a sudden convulsion. I felt it spasm throughout my limbs. I lost my grip. I pushed back from the rock and pulled Madison tight against my stomach. They may have landed on their feet, but I surely wouldn't. I just hoped I'd wake before I crashed.

I closed my eyes, and then…. Nothing.

No screaming. No impact. No broken bones.

I exhaled softly as I looked around. My aura was soothing, gentle as it surrounded me—Madison still clutched against me—in the bold green of Springtime ivy. It held us suspended in air—just as it had held that car when I'd saved Cernun all those years before. I'd never been able to replicate it until now. Maybe adrenaline—or dreaming—was the key.

Silently, I willed us upward, grinning sheepishly as we crested the cave door and Madison leapt from my arms to the soft, chartreuse grass.

"How the hell did you do that?" Cernun asked, a look of amazed admiration in his eyes as he reached to take my hand.

His palm felt warm on mine, rough and strong and right. I let him pull me to solid ground and smiled as my aura faded from view. I shrugged, not wanting to release his touch.

"We're always stronger in dreams, right?" I asked. If this vision was going to be lucid, I figured I may as well have fun with it.

"This… isn't a dream," he said.

I watched the astonishment turn to concern, even as he pulled me into his embrace. Damn, it felt good to hold him. The piney, musky scent he usually carried filled my senses as I buried my face in his shoulder. Madison twined our feet, pressing their body lovingly against our ankles.

"You're always in my dreams," I sighed.

I felt the absence immediately as Cernun broke our embraced and held me at arm's length to look me in the eye. The slight curl of his jet black hair was wild and unruly. Dark bags plagued the iced blue of his eyes.

"I'm serious, Darragh. This is real."

His face was earnest, begging for an understanding amidst everything that was still unknown. I furrowed my brow as I turned to take in our surroundings.

The blackness of the caves below seemed almost comical against the brightness of the landscape. Fields of neon grass, strung through with pockets of the radiant wildflowers which speckled the ground like dabs of paint, spread toward groves of trees whose branches twisted in ways I had never seen. A turquoise sky carried pockets of clouds—lavender and rose-colored—above us. Everything, every single thing, carried a glow about it that amplified its existence, its presence, as if it was screaming *I'm here! I'm here! I'm here!* The electric blue of Madison's fur was right at home in the punched-up color of the land.

"Come with me," he continued, taking my hand as he led me toward the forest. "Learco's made a shelter down by the stream."

My brow was still crumpled as I followed him through the trees. I had no idea what this vision was trying to tell me, but it felt good to be touching my lover once more. I certainly didn't want to reawaken in my cell.

I heard the rush of water before I saw the river. I saw his lustrous smile before I felt the bright press of his lips on mine. By the Fae, he felt so real! The soft, ever-comforting strength of Learco's lips tasted of wine and pomegranate as his kiss overwhelmed my senses.

Now this was the type of dream I loved.

"Mads was right," I heard Cernun tell Learco as his arms wrapped around us both. "Someone else was in the cave. He thinks he's dreaming though."

Learco smiled as he let me go, wincing as he looked me in the eye.

"We both felt this was fantasy when we arrived too," he said. "I spent days in that cavern waiting to wake up before Madison arrived and figured out the path to the surface. The whole time I kept waiting for the vision to end."

Days? What was he talking about? Whatever message this vision was trying to tell me was even more vague and complex than usual. It was going to be a doozy to decipher.

"Darragh," Cernun said, the seriousness of the situation taking over the joy of our reunion, "the last thing Learco remembers is checking into his hotel room in Salem. Whoever came home from that…. Whoever we were with, that wasn't him."

I nearly laughed. Yes, Learco had been acting strange the past few days, but of course the witch who'd been dancing in my kitchen was him. My mind was really pulling out all the stops for this vision.

"You were acting funny all morning too, Cernun," I chuckled, rolling my eyes. "That doesn't mean you aren't you. Plus, Madison's a witch again. And yes, they've also been off since transforming back from their cat form, but that's bound to be a jarring experience, so the strangeness is understandable. The fact that they're still twitching their whiskers here proves I'm dreaming…. Doesn't it?"

"Look," Learco sighed, the down-to-business persona of his MAW training kicking in. "I don't know what's happening, but something big is at play. The last thing I remember is checking into that hotel room before I woke up in that cavern. Then Madison popped out of a sliver of green light. As for Cernun, he stopped by his house on the way to meet Gloria to follow up on a lead about his parents before he ended up here. No idea how or why. And now you….”

My breath caught in my throat. Maybe this wasn't another dream. My face fell as realization took over.

"Where are we?" I asked.

"Wherever we are, our magic doesn't work here," Learco sighed, looking around in hopes that something would spark familiarity. "Not like it usually does, anyway."

"Darragh's does," Cernun announced.

Learco's eyes landed on me in disquiet before he shook his head and laughed.

"Why am I not surprised?" he asked.

Madison yowled at our feet as the weight of the situation landed squarely on my chest. I shook my head as I started to pace.

"No!" I demanded, following a path between my lovers to the bank of the stream and back. "You two are at Cernun's house planning some big surprise for Ostara. Madison is back in their witch form exploring the backyard as the remnants of cat escape from their paws. My mind is playing tricks on me because Leland Hyde locked me up in a Moral Authority holding cell because he thinks I've been doing too much gardening. This is all just some fantasy the isolation has concocted to…"

I stopped short. A pair of familiar green eyes shone up at me through the water. I recognized them almost immediately. Faerie fuck! I knew she would come back to haunt me.

A slender arm stretched from the flowing waters. Fingers twined to clutch the collar of my sweater. I barely had time to inhale before she pulled me in.

CHAPTER 8

"What the actual fuck? Where the actual hell? How in the actual shit?!?"

My words bellowed from my throat without pause, bolstered by the static shock of the journey as I found myself dry, breathless, and sitting on the curved shelf of a tree-carved chair. If this wasn't a dream, it was Fae-magic, and I was in deeper trouble than I'd realized. I was dizzy, and my head ached; but the expulsion of my thoughts actually helped to ground me.

"Were those actual questions, Darragh Cullen? Or simply more of your witchy potty-talk phrasing?"

Yep. I was right. Fae-magic was at play.

The Mórrígan stood before me, her head cocked to the side—much like I'd seen it angled in her crow form—as she studied me. A glimmer of amusement tickled her crimson lips, carrying the sparkle to her deep, emerald eyes. Her hair, an iridescent black which pulsed in unseen beams of light, seemed always to sway on an unfelt breeze. I trembled slightly as I fully took her in, and she appeared to be pleased by my reaction.

I had to admit she was beautiful. Tall and lithe beneath her flowing coal robe, her skin would pale against the whitest of moons.

Sharp cheekbones carried visions to safety, and her smile consisted of pure joy. However, she did look different than I remembered her. More solid and less ethereal, there was a toughness to her stature that could only form from eons of existence, of knowledge. Like water flowing swiftly over land, cutting canyons and smoothing rock until the very earth bent to its course. Both the thing that formed and the thing that was formed, she carried an all-ness that was ever more present in her corporeal state.

When I'd met her before, torn, as she put it, into triplicate—my body in our world, my mind in Balor's, and my heart in hers—she had actually been kind, if a bit enigmatic. But Faeries, according to every tale I'd ever been told, always had ulterior motives. A kindness given was a favor earned even if no bargain had been made. I braced myself for what she had in store.

"Where am I?" I asked, calmer now, more careful in my words, even though I feared I knew the answer. "Where are Learco and Cernun?"

"Still with the questions," The Mórrígan giggled. "But at least you're now polite. Shall I answer them in order?"

She moved like a skater on ice, like a bird on the wind, like green grown across the pasture of late Spring as she spread her arms before me. Her hands turned up toward the same turquoise sky, though it seemed grayer here against the brightness of the clover at our feet.

"This is our world; what you would call the Faerie Realm," she said, confirming my fears with a smile stretching her lips. "Or is it *Mag Mell*? Or *Tir na nÓg* or *Olympus* or *Nirvana* or *Òrún*? You earth-bound creatures always give so many different names to one thing. Typically so you can fight over who is correct on the matter. Though, I suppose it true that my kind, too, create battles of our own over words. As for your lovers and the feline, I imagine them to be exactly where you left them, as things left behind often are."

She spoke with the musicality of wind chimes, a jazzy syncopation carried by nature, both rhythmic and absurd, patterned and broken. Or maybe that was simply the air around her, moving at her will, at her pleasure, within her control. I wondered what of my grandmother's legends on her were true. The bloodstained hands at battles? The foretelling of fates? I should have read up on the Phantom Queen in that darn book. Damn, we really did like giving out multiple names to those who piqued our interest with their power, with their mere state of existence. Particularly when we couldn't touch them.

But even my fascination with her could not quell the rupturing excitement—or was it nausea?—in my stomach at being within the Faerie Realm. The glow I'd seen surrounding everything was fading, but it was still present if I caught it from the corner of my eye. The skewed hue of the sky made more sense to me now. But where I'd expected fields of light, misty watercolors of unbridled magic, and imps frolicking upon the highest branches where the vast canopy of treetops met the clouds, this realm was more natural, more earth-like than I'd imagined it would be.

"Don't worry. The imps won't take your lovers. They tend to prefer softer meats," she said.

I wasn't sure if she was reading my mind or the mystified expression on my face. I also wasn't sure if she was joking. I guessed it didn't matter.

"This doesn't look like it did," I stuttered, and she grinned.

"Are you let down?" she asked. "You've never actually been to our realm before now. Yet here you are, in the flesh. When we met before—and, too, in your encounters with Balor—you were in a space between, accessible by your spirit and mine, and constructed by the magic of our kind. This is something real, not imagined. Something I hope you find… exciting."

I nodded, taking in her words as I considered my own.

"How did I— How did we get here?"

It was dangerous to ask the Fae too many questions. It was too easy to be tricked into a bargain. Plus, the more they talked, the easier it was to get wrapped up in their double speak.

"At least now you're asking wiser questions," she smirked. "Follow me."

She turned to glide away as I scrambled to my feet. At least with her back turned, I had a moment to catch my breath. It felt intense, existing in her eyeline. Like I was the only thing in the world that mattered, like I was a lightning bug closed inside a jar, waiting for her to poke air holes through the thin metal of the lid. Even still, with her back to me, I could not help but feel dimmed somehow. Lost. Which, technically, I was.

The Mórrígan stopped between two elm trees—or whatever the Fae equivalent was. The light wood of the trunks, nearly as gray as they were brown, looked like vases beneath the great forked branches which reached out to twine together, forming a soft handshake above our heads. She turned her face slightly and winked at me.

"Watch this," she sang.

A warbling whistle sprang from her throat, coating the air as the leaves rustled in her breeze. I felt like I could see the staffs of her music: thin, iridescent lines spreading out to carry the notes of her song through the air like her voice was tapped directly into the invisible of the natural world. It took me too long to realize they were real, but when I noticed the tiny sprites dropping from the cover of the trees to spin webbing between the bases, I couldn't turn away.

The sprites were majestic. Tiny, ruby creatures that appeared as a cross between a spider and a praying mantis. Their dragonfly wings flapped so quickly they were nearly invisible, making them appear like aerialists weaving skeins of yarn to keep them afloat as they moved. Their eyes were large for their bodies, black and shining in a trance-like state as The Mórrígan finished her melody, and the sprites scurried back to their hidden sanctuary high above. A rustle of the leaves would have left anyone passing by to assume they were simply berries on the branches, not magical beings in their own right.

The web they left behind glowed as The Mórrígan neared, undulating like waves on the ocean's surface as her fingers brought it to life. I stepped to her side as images began to form. I blushed when I saw myself masturbating inside the MAW holding cell, but she didn't seem to mind. Honestly, I didn't either. I wondered if I could get a copy of the vision recorded for posterity. It'd make a fun little gift for Cernun and Learco. If we made it out of here by Ostara.

I leaned in closer to the Fae version of a crystal ball, hoping the proverbial flaw in the orb would bring clarity. And there it was! The faint green line I'd thought was my aura spread vertically a few feet from my cot. Hovering there in the darkness, it looked like a rip in space, a solid beam of green energy scarred across the thin folds of mesh which kept our worlds intact. I gasped as a pair of hands that looked identical to my own pushed their way through the crack, followed by my head, my face, my body. When all of me had emerged, I moved silently to myself—the me on the cot, the oblivious me, the real me. It all happened so fast. The not me grabbing the me me. The not me pushing me through the magical line. The vision ending.

"So that's that then," The Mórrígan smiled, wiping her hands as the webbing faded from existence as if it had never been there to begin with.

"That's what then?" I asked, exasperated. "What the hell just happened?"

The Mórrígan turned to me with a smirk twisted across her

lips. The gleeful excitement in her eyes was palpable and chilled me to my center.

"It would seem, Darragh Cullen, that your travels have carried with them consequences," she grinned. "Your excursions into our world, though until now only in spirit, have created cracks. Nothing too large—yet—though obviously enough to let some lesser beings through."

That didn't explain anything. And worse, I could feel her delirium over the so-called cracks taking her over. It pulsed from her body in the same frequency as her power. I did not want to imagine what those cracks could mean.

"That... thing... looked just like me," I said, hoping the confused furrow of my brow would urge her story onward.

"Changeling," she laughed. "I expect they went for your lovers and your feline as well, seeing as you've all recently spent time in the space between our realms."

Okay. So that was starting to put rhyme to reason. At least it accounted for the odd behavior I'd been noticing in Learco and Cernun. And why Learco's aura had felt so different when I'd tried to touch it. Fae dammit! All the signs were there, and I let myself reason them away.

"I thought Changelings were injured or elder Faeries. Sent to replace children when your kind didn't want to care for them any longer."

Again, The Mórrígan laughed.

"You silly witches and your lore," she smiled. "Creative though you may be, you get so much wrong. Changelings are the children of our dear Echo. We cursed her once for loving one of your kind. As she faded, Changelings were her way of seeking revenge on the witch who spurned her. Like Echo, they are mimics, able to copy traits in a believable enough manner for those who do not look too closely. But, as I said, they are lesser creatures and carry with them very little magic."

The past few days conjured like a potion bubbling in its cauldron as the last few ingredients plopped into place. I kicked myself for not remembering sooner. Daffodils were also called Narcissus. They were the flower the witch was turned to by the Fae. Those buds suddenly springing up all over Atlanta were a harbinger of the Changeling's cross through to our world. My vision of their green and altered eyes. Their blood. Hell, even the story on the exact and random page my instinct had opened that book to. All the signs were there, and I'd missed every single one.

I could see The Mórrígan beginning to lose interest in me, the rip between our worlds becoming a greater call than the existence of a witch in her land. That didn't bode well. Cracks had a tendency to stretch the more they were prodded.

"How do I stop them?" I asked. "How do I get my life back?"

"Hmm? Oh. Changelings are simple nothings. They fade away like voices on a rushing river. All you need to do is exist in place simultaneously and look them directly in the eye."

Nothing with the Fae was ever as simple as it sounded. Plus, I'd have to get the four of us back to our world. Shit. I was going to have to ask The Mórrígan for help. Which meant I would owe her. Big time. At least it would draw her attention back to me.

"Okay, then," I said, sounding suitably trepidatious and enamored enough to draw her into my fear and worship, "send me back—to my coven and to our world—so we can be done with this."

The Mórrígan turned, squinting her emerald eyes at me as a smile spread over her lips.

"Did you just ask me for a favor, Darragh Cullen?" she purred, something akin to glee swimming on her words. "I thought you more clever than that."

"You brought me to you, unannounced and against my will,"

I asserted, hoping my logic was sound. Though I wasn't sure logic even held court in the Fae Realm. "Asking to be sent back to where I was is not a favor. It's simply an about turn."

The Mórrígan sighed as she considered it, apparently accepting it as true.

"It does not matter either way," she said. "You and I have been intimate, you see. You having inserted your spirit into my mind. I felt your aura the moment you entered our realm. That knowledge, that understanding alone is what enabled me to pull you here. I know not where you were or who you were with. So I cannot send you back. Although a deal with you would be quite delicious, you'll have to find your lovers on your own."

My face fell. Did she really expect me to wander aimlessly throughout the whole of the Faerie Realm? No knowledge? No compass? No sure destination? It was a Sisyphean task, doomed for failure before I'd even started. Not to mention, I had no idea what kind of creatures I would come in contact with. And what if I stumbled upon Balor? Even with our bargain in place, after binding his mind to this world to prevent him from killing any more witches in his attempts to break into ours, he would squash me on the spot. And that was in the best of circumstances.

"Fine," The Mórrígan hissed, something akin to pity on her features as she studied my expression. "I forget your earth magic doesn't work here, and I hate to see any charge at a disadvantage. If your coven were all taken by Changelings, they will still be near to Echo's home. I can, at least, point you in the right direction."

I nodded solemnly, keeping my face placid as I took in her words. My magic had worked, at least under duress. Maybe there were more than mere cracks between our lands. But I couldn't let her know that. The rip she knew of was bad enough.

She mistook my silence for fear, pulling her dark robes around her as she considered my face. It was good that she liked me. Even better that she—like all Fae, apparently—considered witches to be amongst the "lesser beings" they liked to overlook. I could use that to my advantage.

"Okay, Darragh Cullen," she said, a quick resolve filling the voids of her sharp features. "I suppose we can make a bargain after all. Once you've reunited with your own, I will ensure your safe return to your realm. *If* you complete a task for me."

My play at striking a bargain deteriorated into terror as it began to realize. I hoped I knew what I was getting myself into. I tried to remind myself that The Mórrígan had actually been helpful in the past. That had to count for something, right?

"I need three items," she smiled. "You witches enjoy your threes, is that not so? A *cochaillín draíchta* of the *murúch* of the stream; A single scale of the *Ollphéist*. Those two should be easy to acquire as the river shall guide your journey."

My heart sank, but I nodded. I didn't think the transformative cap of a mer-creature or a scale from the body of a sea serpent would be as easy to snag as she was making it out to be. But I would have to try.

"For the last item, I require a jug of wine from the *clobhair-ceann*. Full. And… red. Be careful not to sip of that nectar, Darragh Cullen. No matter how enticing it may be. Collect those items, and I will return you, your feline, and your lovers to your land. Fail and… well, that's a bargain broken, is it not?"

The lust in her eyes as she made our pact was nearly as great as I'd noticed when she thought about the rips between our worlds. But I couldn't think about the consequences that would no doubt come from our agreement—satiated or not. I couldn't even consider failure. I needed to find Cernun, Learco, and Madison. I had to get us home.

"You will find a stream fifty clicks ahead," she said, pointing between the trees she had used to show me the vision of my capture. "Walk steady through the unclaimed lands, careful not to disrupt the homes of my kin or their offspring. Follow the waters downstream, and you will find your coven. Though be certain to collect that which I require along your way."

Alright. Fifty clicks. If I remembered my math right, that was roughly thirty miles, assuming Fae measurements were equal to those of our world. And for a Fae so fond of the battlefield, it made sense The Mórrígan would use a military term. I just hoped it didn't foretell warfare along my journey.

"I will warn you though," she continued, taking on the stature of the Old Crone of Destiny, even as she retained her youthful glow, "time works differently here. One hour in your world could be a month within ours. A blink of your eye here could see three years pass there."

My jaw dropped open.

"So those Changelings could be living our lives for years?" I asked. "Doing Fae-knows-what in our world?"

She grinned at the expression that had slipped from my mouth, and I blushed.

"Think nothing of it," she said. "Best not to get weighed down in regret when the world itself remains unimagined. Still, do not let it stretch to years. If the Changelings manage to survive your realm through a power shift, their lives there will become permanent."

"Ostara is tomorrow," I gasped.

If anything was a power shift, the sleep of Winter giving way to the life of Spring certainly was. That must have been the surprise the Changeling versions of Learco and Cernun were planning for me. Shit! That didn't leave a lot of time.

"You should be on your way then, Darragh Cullen," The Mórrígan smiled. "And may good fortune bless your adventure."

She seemed perturbed as she studied my still anguished face.

The nervous energy permeating the whole of the situation was heavy, but I was trying not to let myself spiral. I could do this. I had to do this.

"Fine," she sighed, misreading my expression as directed at her. "Your silence drives a remarkably hard bargain. As I did assist your friend in becoming the feline, I have an intimate knowledge of their aura as well. I will bring you your companion for the journey. As a kindness."

I startled as the green of The Mórrígan's eyes went gray. Her fingers wove the air around her, both in spell and in searching, as she picked through the fibers of her reality. Her beauty intensified as the magic worked through her, glittering across her skin like the power in every children's cartoon classic. It was literally spellbinding.

My breath caught in my throat as her fingers snapped together. Her arm pulled back as Madison's electric blue fur slipped through the ether. They yowled as The Mórrígan clutched the scruff of their neck, shifting their brown eyes from me to the Faerie as they adjusted to their new locale.

"What the Fae-loving fuck?!"

Holy shit. It was amazing to hear Madison's voice emanating from their feline vocal cords. The sound rushed like relief through my body. After so much time not hearing it, I was beginning to fear they'd never speak again.

"Hmmm," The Mórrígan moaned as she released Madison's electric fur. "They have their voice back. I assume that will make their companionship much more enjoyable on your journey."

Madison landed on their paws and swiftly pounced to my side, circling my legs before sitting firmly beside me.

"Journey?" they asked. "Where are we?"

"You, little witch," The Mórrígan purred, "are in the Faerie Realm. And Darragh Cullen has just entered into a bargain to get you home. I know, I know. I thought him more wise as well, but perhaps your company along the path will bring back the clever witch I believed I'd found in him."

I swallowed hard. I thought I had been rather brave, all things considered. Here I was, trapped in a foreign, mystical land, separated from my lovers who had no freaking clue what the hell was going on, and face to face with the physical, fleshy form of a real life Faerie. So what if I wasn't as feisty as I usually was? There was a lot to take in and process.

Still, I rallied to gather my cunning. I had a feeling I was going to need it as I attempted to fulfill my end of the Faerie bargain. I was glad to have Madison with me though, and ecstatic they could speak again. Perhaps, since we were in the realm where Faerie magic resided, we'd have an actual shot at changing them back to their witch form. We'd just need to find a way for them to access their own magic while we were here. According to The Mórrígan, that was impossible. But my magic was intact, even if it was slightly skewed to adjust for the variations in this world's natural order. If I could figure out how and why my own power worked—without revealing that it did to any of the Fae here in the process so I didn't wind up a test subject for their own magical marvels—perhaps I could ascertain how Madison could access theirs. It was a long shot, but well worthy of adding to my checklist, right after Learco and Cernun, the hat, the scale, and the wine.

Fuck, this was not going to be easy.

"Fifty clicks," the Fae queen repeated. "The Merrow and the Serpent make their home near or in those waters. Move downstream toward your lovers, and do not forget the wine. Here."

A flourish of her hand produced an amulet in mine. I gasped as I studied the stone, the same brightness of her eyes, inlaid in knotted gold which clasped to a leather-like strap. It was beautiful.

"A bit gaudy, don't you think?" I smirked. "I wasn't really planning a drag show on the journey."

"There he is," she smiled. "There's the witch I believed I was dealing with. Keep the necklace safe. Others may want it for its power. You may use it only once to call to me when you are in need. Be wise in its usage, Darragh Cullen. Be fleet of foot, and do not give your name. As you know, a name holds power as good as any currency. And you, Madison Ridge. Keep your instincts and your reflexes about you. Our world is not particularly kind when your species is discovered in our lands. You'd be wise to keep one another safe and your true natures concealed."

With that, The Mórrígan turned, raising her arm to point in the general direction we should travel. Her face was somber, but I could tell her mind was miles away already. Whether she was thinking about the split between our lands or the items she'd enticed me to steal, I wasn't sure. But I figured neither would lead to anything good.

Madison purred their encouragement as they brushed against my leg. The fur on their back bristled a steadfast resolve. My eyes scanned the path ahead, stretching out between the elm-like trees she'd used to conjure the vision of my capture. We had one day in our world to complete the bargain and get back home, but no way of knowing what that same amount of time would look like here. Still, I couldn't get bogged down in the details—or the fears. The main thing was finding my boyfriends. And I would go to the ends of any realm to do that.

I nodded to Madison as my fingers wrapped to fists at my side. Their whiskers twitched as their claws kneaded the earth. We could do this. We *had* to.

"What?" I asked as I stepped beside The Mórrígan and steeled myself for the distance. "No yellow brick road?"

CHAPTER 9

I placed one foot sternly in front of the other, attempting a sense of purpose and assuredness even as my mind rambled through a myriad of frightful possibilities. I didn't know if we should walk through the clearing where we were visible but also able to see the horizon or through the woods where danger could lurk behind every behemoth of a tree trunk but at least we'd be concealed. I didn't know if the minutes of my journey collided with seconds at home or if the Spring Equinox had passed and our souls were trapped with the Faeries forever. But I did know we had to reach Learco and Cernun. That even if we were stuck here, at least we'd be stuck here together.

The Mórrígan was gone by the time I turned back toward her dwelling. A thin, misty haze cascaded between the elms of the clearing. A murder of crows perched on the branches of the trees, heads cocked as they eyed me with a stubborn curiosity. She could have been any one of them. Hell, she could have been all of them.

The amulet she had given me excited my skin as it pressed against my chest beneath my sweater. I could feel the power within it reaching out to find my own, as if the necklace itself contained an aura that was searching for others like it. Fae magic really was different than witch magic. We witches, we could shift the elements, working in tandem with the natural world to produce light or fire or wind. We could draw forth water or bring the spiritual properties of plants and stones toward a purpose. But those magics were inherent within the elements. We spoke with them, sure, and we guided them, but our craft was a conversation—a communion with the natural world which relied on our intent and our reverence to bring forth something that was already there.

Fae magic was something else entirely.

I'd known it was the difference in Fae magic that had enabled our ancestors to shift into animal forms, likely leading to the idea of witches having familiars which still permeated our mythology today. Madison, pacing along beside me, was living proof of that. But The Mórrígan had locked onto my aura from Fae knows how far away and brought me to her instantly—through a river!—without so much as a drop of water in my hair. She'd sorted the atmosphere like threads to pull Madison through as if she was choosing a sweater from a rack in her closet. She had shown me a vision of my own kidnapping that was as clear as a high definition film—not the hazy, figure-it-out-for-yourself mirages of the dreamers or the seers or the tarot readers of our world. She had produced an amulet from thin air with just the wave of her hand! Hell, even the Changelings which she repeatedly reminded me were lesser beings had taken our forms, cut through the realms, and taken our places in Atlanta. It was frightening to consider what we could come up against while stuck in their land, especially if my magic wasn't supposed to work here. My gut told me I couldn't get caught using it. If the Fae knew a witch could use magic in their world, I'd be under their proverbial microscope faster than the MAW had shoved me into a holding cell.

I pushed the cuffs of my sweater up my forearms, and my skin met the air with a bristle of comfort. It was warmer here than it'd been in Atlanta where I'd dressed for the early Spring. Still, a pulsing breeze, like the breaths of too many onlookers watching, swept over me with each new step. At least that was something. The air felt always to be moving, like the atmosphere itself was a living thing.

"So, uh," Madison purred as we both kept our eyes locked on the distance, "how've you been?"

"Locked in a MAW holding cell," I laughed at their attempt at small talk.

Damn, it felt good to laugh. I hadn't realized how much I'd needed that.

"Fuck the MAW," Madison growled. "Except Learco. He's actually kind of cool."

"How've you been?" I asked. I couldn't believe they could speak again. That definitely gave my hope.

"Cat."

There was my laugh again. It seemed to hang on the heavier air of the Faerie atmosphere. It reverberated like a woodpecker's call around us.

"Thanks for taking care of me," they said. "A lot of that time is just instinct and napping in my mind. But I do remember you. And Cernun. And Learco…. And Katrina too, but she seems so far away."

"You watched her from the fire escape while she was clearing tables at Aunt Paulina's," I sighed.

A guttural purr broke from their throat.

"Damn, I could use one of those burgers," they said.

"She asks about you," I said. "Katrina does. Every single day."

If a cat with electric blue fur could blush, Madison would have. I filled them in on the cover story and the time that had elapsed since their transformation. I tried to be gentle, to not show my worry, about the time that had passed.

"I did try to change back that night," they said. "Once Balor was gone and bound, I tried. But the magic wouldn't work."

"Because it needed both your magic and Faerie magic to function," I sighed.

"That's what I thought. And I was okay with that. With letting the cat take over. I figured eventually you would find a way to turn me back."

I winced. I hated that it'd been so long.

"That wasn't a jab," they assured me. "These things take time. And we're on the right path. Besides, it was kind of awesome taking naps in the afternoon sun. Having these muscles, these reflexes. You know, jumping from the floor to your countertop would be like you leaping to the roof of a high-rise from the sidewalk. That's some Super Witch shit. Pretty fucking cool if you ask me. Plus, I'm the first witch in how many years to physically transform like this? They're gonna give me my own exhibit at MA'AM."

I chuckled as I pictured it: graphics—or better yet, statues—depicting the stages of transition from a bright blue feline to a fully-fledged witch, like the human evolutionary chart, and wall text proclaiming the heroism of Madison Ridge and their shift to take down the Atlanta Witch Killer. The Magical Artifacts & Antiquities Museum didn't need to know the full story—or at last the parts about the Fae—to enshrine Madison's glory.

We kept a steady pace, quick but not too quick, purposeful but with a touch of wandering. It was the same step I'd adopted the first few times I'd visited Atlanta from the farm. One that said *I'm casual; I'm cool; I belong here.* One that broadcast the words *I'm not a target.* A coping mechanism of being young and queer, of being a witch in a human world, I'd realized that sometimes one foot in front of the other was the best way of claiming space and safety simultaneously. Of course I'd wanted to gasp at the infrastructure: buildings taller than the pines on the far side of the property I'd grown up on, and just as thin as those trunks as they stretched toward the low-lying clouds; streets wider than any of the dirt roads back home, teeming with SUVs and pickup trucks larger than even my father's tractor; and people, so many people—witch and human alike—bustling about the concrete sidewalks which stretched like front porch extensions from the shops and the bars and the apartment buildings, waving or nodding or mumbling hellos to the passersby without even the aid or comfort of a row of rocking chairs.

It was the same in this foreign land. I wanted to gawk— maybe that was why The Mórrígan had insisted we travel by foot even though I was certain she could have sent us closer to our destination—but I needed to appear as if I belonged. A slack jaw and a meandering eye only screamed *I'm different!* to the world. All the work I'd done at accepting myself, and here I was, pulled right back into the terror of nonconformity. But these were extenuating circumstances.

Still, I managed to take in as much as I could. The Faerie Realm bore a lot of similarities to my world. Not the Atlanta of it all, but to the primary elements, all the Things That Were before hands built tools to build a new creation on top of the one we'd been given. The colors were different—brighter, somehow, and skewed slightly to the left of what I was used to—but the hills rolled, the trees stretched toward the sky, and the ground beneath my feet felt solid. Flowers I didn't recognize reached like open mouths, biting crimson or cerulean petals at the turquoise above, hungry. The clover compressed beneath each step I made all consisted of four-leaved clusters, making me wonder if the luck we associated with the mutation in our world had originated here. Faerie magic would certainly feel like luck to someone accustomed to the natural order we knew.

In the distance, I could hear the gentle gurgle of the stream, carried on the soft wind to lure me forward. Too, even above the clusters of the epic trees, a row of purple mountains majesty ached to pierce the sky. It was as if everything I could attribute to the natural beauty of my own world was manifested here for the pleasure of the Fae. A floral fragrance, delicate and sweet like that of apple blossoms, wove the high notes of the atmosphere with the spicy duress of cinnamon grounding it to the soil. Beneath all that was a faint hint of decay, barely noticeable to anyone not looking for it, like the loamy fullness of soil opening to welcome death toward renewal to keep the whole of the cycle going.

What really stuck out, though, were the divisions of the land. A soft haze, like translucent fog, marked clear delineations between this side and that. It was the same blur I'd noticed around The Mórrígan's cove when we'd departed. It reminded me even more of back home, of the various fields we plowed to contain diverse crops for the table or the market: thick, silk-like stalks of corn here, straight and powerful and reaching ever taller; the twining brambles of tomatoes, yellow and red and purple, with fuzz on the stem that tickled my palms when I went in for the harvest; or soil mounded up in rows, the small stems above the earth only a whisper of the tubers growing below.

I wondered if every Faerie held court in their own little slice of the realm. It would make sense. All the lore I knew pitted them as wholly against one another, a few alliances aside, as they were against us. And we did it too. Formed lines to say this is my property, my city, my state, my country. But even in all our xenophobia, we also reached across those lines. That didn't seem to be happening here. Perhaps that was why the Fae were so desperate to re-enter our world. Centuries or minutes of existence here, if time really worked the way The Mórrígan said, would have to become at least a little boring, if not utterly lonely. It almost made me feel sorry for them. Almost.

The land itself was beautiful though. Surreal in its intensity, yet somehow gentle as it swayed in the constant breeze like it was listening to music. It would be so easy to get lost in it all.

I held my feet firm in the straightest line I could muster.

"You're new."

The voice sounded all around us. Deep and high and lilting, it cascaded over me like the leaves of Autumn, like the seeds of dandelions blown askew by the flapping wings of ladybugs. The fur on Madison's back stood high, and their tail twitched as we stopped in our tracks.

My head spun, but I couldn't identify the source.

"Are you a steward or a swindler?" the voice asked, androgyny thick upon its chords. The words sounded like they hissed over a forked tongue that wanted to make a meal of us.

My breath caught in my throat, unable to will itself from my tongue. I was in enough trouble already, having caught the attention of two of the major Fae, having fallen prey to the children of another. The last thing I needed was the curiosity of another Faerie piqued. I held out my fingers to keep Madison calm, to keep them from pouncing toward the swiftly moving words.

Damn it! I really should have studied that freaking book I borrowed from Verne. I mean, I'd added a whole "Fantasy" book section to HEX to prepare witch-kind for this particular outcome. Well, maybe not *this* situation. My wildest dreams had never taken me physically into the Faerie Realm, but my fear of them entering mine had been palpable. Even if some of the facts were wrong on those pages, at least I'd feel better prepared.

"Malignancy, be gone!"

A new voice rose to join the fray before I could regain my composure.

"You are not welcome here."

The first voice howled as it withered, but I still couldn't ascertain its source. It fizzled like air escaping a bonfire, burning hot as it faded into nothingness until a slight pop in the air—nestled within the haze of delineation—settled the space around us.

I swallowed hard, not daring to move as a shimmer of orange light waved before me along the path. Madison growled as they raised their back and tail, bracing their claws against the ground between me and the light.

Like it or not, other Fae had found us. I felt the pulse of The Mórrígan's amulet against my skin as the orange wave began to take form.

He was magnificent. Compact, lean muscle accentuated his well-defined torso. Freckled constellations—the same orange as his fiery hair—swept across his sun-drenched shoulders. Eyes the hue of crocuses beamed at me, pistol yellow slits focused in a means that should have been unnerving yet was altogether seductive. Even the horns twisting through his hair became alluring as he tilted his head to the side to take me in. The fur on his legs was a softer, brownish color—that of a newborn faun—but his steady hooves told me he had been well-traveled. My eyes fell to his generous endowment—he was all man there!—and I blushed.

He had not spoken since the orange wave of magic had revealed his form a few feet in front of us. Instead, his muscles flexed as he eyed me up and down, attempting to figure me out, daring me to introduce myself. As he squinted his goat eyes, the violet of his irises pulsed darker beside his elongated lemon pupils; and he let them dance across my features as he began to circle my stance. I twisted my neck to keep him in my eyeline, only breaking my gaze once as he passed my back and I swiveled my head to the other side.

He was roughly two feet shorter than me—only one, perhaps, when he straightened the joints of his cervine legs. Despite his small stature, his features—both masculine and severe—were carved from the stone of the greatest of gods. A three-day scruff accentuated the sharp incline of his cheekbones, and the bridge of his nose mocked the extensions of collarbone holding up his heaving pecs. He smelled of rut and wild things. I had to be careful. Even to look at him was intoxicating.

"Do they not have manners where you reside?" he asked, his gravelly voice bellowing like a herd of howling beasts from within his chest. "Or perhaps the view of my great organ is caught in your throat."

I blushed once more. My mouth gaped as a response rumbled through my chest, tempered by The Mórrígan's warning: *Do not give your name.* My lips snapped shut with a sigh as a bleating giggle rose from the satyr's mouth. The Fae and their laughter. Damn, it was intoxicating.

The satyr smirked as he moved his fingers through the air between us, tips touching out a rhythm between each other and his palms. A new faint gust of wind rose, twinkling orange beneath the turquoise sky, as a pair of brown shorts materialized on his body. They fit snugly to his thighs, accenting the line of his package, and, when he turned, I noticed a small stitched opening which let his tail hang freely.

"Still no words," he huffed. "Are you mute?"

His nostrils flared like butterfly wings as he sniffed the air around me.

"You reek of The Mórrígan," he huffed. "Has she been filling your head with lies about me as is her wont? Or do you simply not recognize your Great Horned King when you see him?"

So this was Cernunnos. The nature Fae my boyfriend had chosen his name after. The guy the Greeks called Pan with his eponymous flute. The Green Man. The great Saint Ciarán. I thought he'd be taller.

"You don't have to bow," he smirked. "Unless you want to. And you can call me Síl."

And yet another name. I'd always assumed the variations in monikers for the Fae were based on different cultures, different dialects, different accents. Now, with The Mórrígan's warning ringing in my ears, I wondered if the Fae themselves were responsible for all the designations as they kept their true calling hidden to prevent anyone from having power over them. I guessed that wasn't all that uncommon with mythical creatures. I mean, even humans had grown up with the tale of Rumpelstiltskin. And two could play at that game.

"I'm Dan."

I figured a name that at least started with the same sound as mine would be easier to keep track of. I wasn't as adept as the Fae were at answering to a myriad of disparate words. Except in the bedroom.

"So he does speak," Síl laughed, twisting his lips into a gnarly smile that was as endearing as it was frightening. As wolves in sheep's clothing, the Fae had truly mastered the art of beauty meeting terror. "A voice is a good thing to have on a lonely road in the Thresh. You may thank me now—Dan, was it?—for coming to your aid."

My heart fluttered in my chest, but I did my best to keep the nerves from showing on my face. My eyes squinted as my lips pursed to meet his smirk. The worst thing I could do was show weakness or fear in the face of a Faerie. And thanking him, Horned God or not, would be the equivalent of admitting to a debt. Still, he seemed unfazed.

"Salamanders truly are heinous little fire demons," he hissed, spitting at the ground as his hooves tore at the clover to reveal the dirt beneath. "Always looking for something new to slither inside and burn up from within. You're quite lucky I happened to cross your path when I did."

"I really should be one my way," I replied.

"And who is this?" he asked, bending effortlessly at the waist to look Madison in the eye.

They knew better than to speak or strike, yet raised a claw-extended paw in warning.

Síl grinned as he rose back to a standing position, and Madison retracted their claws. The glint in his eyes told me he enjoyed the game he was attempting to catch us in but was equally pleased we'd been able to keep our wits about us. The longer we stayed free, the longer he could play. He blinked slowly as he nodded, stepping aside with an elaborate bow as he urged us forward on the path. My irises followed his as I stepped forward proudly. He shimmered away in an orange glow as I passed, and a sigh of relief flooded from my lungs.

As much of a morbid fascination—morbidity was definitely a serving option—as I had with my new Fae experiences, as much as I wanted to explore this new world—one, I assumed, no witch had set foot in for thousands of years—I needed to stay focused on Cernun and Learco. I had to find them and set things right. And while I knew they were smart witches, wise enough to avoid any of their own Fae encounters, I didn't like knowing they were trapped without access to their magic. Even the Great Horned King couldn't keep me from them.

"So where are we going? You look like you're on a mission."

I turned to see Síl in lockstep beside me.

Damn. He wasn't giving up. But I supposed I was a novelty in this realm. And he had hunger in his eyes.

"Fuck," Madison growled, and Síl's eyes livened.

"Oh! The cat speaks too!" he exclaimed. "How fun!"

"Dan and Mason. Mason and Dan," Síl sang, pouring rhythm into the fake names we'd given him as he pranced along beside us.

I felt kind of bad for lying about who we were, but The Mórrígan's warning had been resolute. Besides, I had a feeling Síl—or any of the other names he'd spouted off for himself—didn't come close to the moniker he held in his heart. They were all just words after all, nouns we used to make calling one another easier. And they served their purpose. But the identities we held inside, the words that we attached to our hearts, to who we were: those were where the real power resided.

"It's been so long since we've had travelers," Síl beamed. "And, as I am positive you know, I serve faithfully as a guide to all such souls. This is exciting, is it not?"

"We don't want any more bargains," Madison called.

I winced at the "more" in their words, but, thankfully, Síl chose to ignore it. He'd already smelled The Mórrígan on us, and any Fae worth their wings—well, those that had wings anyway— would realize we'd been indebted to her in one way or another. But Madison was right. We couldn't afford any other pacts. The two I'd already gotten myself into were hard enough.

"No bargain," Síl grinned. "Just a kindness. From the goodness and benevolence of your Great Horned King. Though, should you at some point feel an urge to grant a kindness to me, I dare not say I'd be opposed to such a prospect."

Of course he wouldn't. I rolled my eyes, and Madison's low purr edged on the razor of a growl as we continued to trudge forward.

"So where is it we are going?" Síl asked again. "For what do we search?"

Shit. He wasn't going to let us carry on alone, and he'd definitely see what we were up to once we got to the stream and tried collecting The Mórrígan's items. I wondered if I should just tell him the truth. Not the truth of our names, but facts of our task. Time was limited, and Síl, with his Faerie magic, would definitely give us an advantage. Though, if he didn't like what The Mórrígan had us searching for, or wanted to prevent her from acquiring them, he could fuck us over royally. No, it was better to keep that part of our journey a secret.

"My lovers are somewhere in this world," I finally conceded. "We are on a mission to find them."

No names, no locations. That should have retained their safety, right?

"If it's lovers you are looking for, we are not too far from the hills of the nymphs. Or, perhaps the stiff wood of the dryads is more your style." He looked me up and down, a lascivious smile spreading like wildfire across his lips. "I could also be convinced to consider offering my services if the moon shines rightly."

He licked his lips as the thick bulge in his new shorts protruded with his steps.

Though I had two amazing lovers, we did have an understanding when it came to sex. And a roll in the hay with Fae kind was bound to be exhilarating. Dammit! That little pact to keep it in our pants until Ostara—the one I now realized had not been with my boyfriends but their replacements—had left me so horny even a suggestive wink could leave me aroused.

Madison's hiss brought me back to the present. I shook away the fantasy, worried at how quickly it had clouded my brain.

"Tempting," I said as the last lustful clouds of passion slipped away, stopping briefly in my dick as they left my body. "But we really should be on our way."

"So be it, then," Síl exclaimed. "Let us go, travelers Dan and Mason. Who knows what this adventure together will bring?"

Madison leapt a few paces ahead, twisting their feline form with the grace of a lion as they turned and sat, tail twitching around them, to stop us in our tracks. The bright blue of their fur rustled as they shifted their claws into the clover.

"We don't need a guide," they hissed. "We are not looking for company. We just want to find our friends and go home."

I wasn't surprised by their aggression. They had always been blunt. And I imagined there was a lot of pent up frustration after months of not having their voice. Besides, they were right. The last thing we needed was another Faerie interested in us.

Síl, on the other hand, radiated an exaggerated array of emotions, cycling between shock, hurt, and bewilderment as if he were trying them all on for the first time to see what best suited his face. Which, as a Fae king, he may have very well been.

"I understand," he finally stuttered, a remote dejection to his voice that made him all the more alluring. "I can just be on my way. Alone. Though I dare say night is nearing, and you two would do well to find shelter. The beings of the darkness are not nearly as courteous as those of the light."

Síl's form began to fade into an orange mist as I noticed the color begin to quickly fade from the sky. The Mórrígan wasn't lying about time in this realm. Sunset happened in seconds, clouds overtaking the turquoise of the atmosphere in wavering phantoms of black and navy and violet. Stars formed constellations I had never before seen, telling mythic stories I would probably never know. It would be mere moments until we were left in a murky pitch.

Madison's eyes widened as they prowled back to my side. Worry weighed on their haunches. We could be brave—we needed to be brave. But unsheltered darkness in a foreign land promised more upset if we were not careful.

"Síl, wait!" I called.

The orange of his disappearance stagnated, but he didn't materialize. Instead, his voice called from all around us, bouncing off the solidity of the night closing in.

"Yes?"

I sighed. Dammit. I didn't need to be indentured to a third Faerie leader. But he had offered his help without catch. Supposedly anyway.

"Where can we find shelter?" I asked.

He chuckled. "So, you need my help then?"

"Yes," I sighed. Then added, "Please."

A moment of contemplation sat between us as the stars I had noticed began to dance, switching positions in an array of synchronized motions like the mating waltzes of the fireflies from back home.

"I need to hear it from the cat."

A growl hummed from deep within Madison's chest. Their words pushed against the bars of their fangs, as rich with animosity as they were with pleading.

"Help us find shelter, Síl. Please. But be gone by morning."

Even though they'd mumbled the last part under their breath, I was sure Síl heard. Still, he wore a mischievous grin as he reappeared.

"Right this way," he winked, then marched, and we followed close behind.

CHAPTER 10

The darkest black I had ever known—except for maybe Cernun's hair—wove like ink around us, thick and viscous and pressing upon our skin as we pushed our way through the night. Even the stars above, still caught in their frolic of self-entertainment, added little visibility as they twinkled through the pitch. Madison, I thought, was probably faring better than me, the irises of their cat eyes better suited to the lack of light, but that didn't add much comfort. Still, I felt them keeping close to my ankles, twining through my footsteps with care and guidance.

I hoped Síl wasn't leading us too far off track—or worse yet, toward danger. Though, with us being witches in a Faerie world, I wasn't certain there was any direction *not* toward danger. I hoped Cernun and Learco had been able to complete the make-shift lean to they were working on before The Mórrígan had whisked me and then Madison away. I made a silent wish to the shooting stars above that they would know I was safe, as safe as I could be, and that I was coming for them. I had no idea if stars worked the same way in this realm as they did in our world, but hope could be a powerful enough magic on its own, and I was glad I still had that in spades. Despite the insanity of the last year—even in coming face to face with the creatures who had haunted the nightmares of generations of witch's fables—I had held onto the bulk of my optimism. So what if I spiraled from time to time while working things out? That was just… a part of my process.

"What if he's leading us into a trap?" Madison whispered, the dry sandpaper of their tongue crisp in the cooling air.

Hearing my own fears spoken aloud sent a shiver up my spine. Before I could speak, Síl's head swiveled on his shoulders, a bright, waning moon grin showcasing the sharpened pikes of his teeth.

"What good would it do to trap you?" he asked, words thick with a Faerie logic that still eluded me, as if he were, now that the task had been suggested, simultaneously considering the good and the bad of it, the possibilities in doing or not doing. I had to give that to the Fae I had met: they were nothing if not thorough in their thinking.

His steps never faltered as he continued to grin, neck still craned nearly backwards as he waited for an answer.

"No good," I confirmed. "It's just so… dark. We have no means of knowing where we're going but to trust in you."

"Of course!" His eyes lit as his lips twisted into a laugh. "I forget you do not have my eyes. Let me help with that."

I stopped in my tracks as Síl's hands began to swim around him, forming the intricate dance of a Fae magic ritual. Dammit! I did not want to re-enter my own world with the rectangular iris of Síl's animal eyes. I winced as my head instinctively pulled away from him. And then…

A crisp ginger glow pulsed before me, starting tight then stretching out to illuminate a five foot circle around the three of us. The lantern Síl now held aloft looked like an antique with its brass trims and polished glass and intricate latches and levers. The light it provided pulsed and throbbed from within the cage of the lamp, but I couldn't look straight at it without straining. Even in the newfound brightness, the three of us cast no shadows into the night.

"There," Síl smiled. "That is much better. A light for travelers to see by is, indeed, the most basic of necessities. Please do forgive me, my charges. As I told you before, it has been so long since I have been tasked with such purpose."

His bow appeared both extravagant and foolish, as if he meant every curve of his spine yet was mocking us all at once. Madison's whiskers twitched as they locked their sights on the light.

"Who's in the cage?" they growled.

"What?" Síl stuttered as he rose back to a standing position, tsking the air as he glanced between the lantern and Madison. "I forget you have your feline wits about you. They are merely pixies. Nasty creatures, their lot. War-filled, angry little dragons. Yet pixie light is the best source for the darker of nights. And these two have been indebted to me for quite some time now. They will illuminate our path to the Wayward Inn. As long as they fail to kill one another before we get there. Let us be off."

I grimaced as the Fae king turned, holding the lantern out before him as he marched forward without checking to see if we followed. Madison yowled their disapproval, but we were both quick to match Síl's pace as the light began to shift past us. Whatever the night held seemed more terrifying than the demon we knew. For whatever that was worth.

Síl steered us clear of the ethereal mists I was sure delineated the particular domains of the various Fae leaders. There were so many different lands breaking up the world. But, I guessed, according to the stories my grandmother loved, there were an awful lot of Fae. Kings and Queens and Sovereigns, the lot of them, according to the lore that passed down through us witches at least. But it wasn't too far-fetched to believe that was how they saw themselves too. Their supposed hierarchy was certainly obvious in the way The Mórrígan had talked about the Changelings and the sprites, the way Síl spoke of the salamanders and the pixies…. Hell, even the way Balor used the words "clever witch" when addressing me had an air of superiority in it, as if our kind was and would always be beneath him. Yet for all their bravado, they had broken their world apart from one another, and even these brave "greater beings" looked to avoid the territories claimed by the others. Not that I minded not meeting them all at once as I was led through the darkest night.

I stumbled as Síl stopped suddenly, turning toward us with a wicked grin, and hanging the lantern on a thorny, twisted branch of a Winter-bare hawthorn tree. I watched in awe as within the fading pixie light, the branches of the tree were set abuzz with the buds of leaves, all spreading quickly to welcome the white-pink blush of blossoms. The thick scent of gangrene and semen filled the air—the hawthorn flower's thrilling combination of sex and death—even as the petals fell away to the lush red of berries, and the leaves browned and dropped away. A full cycle, a full year of being for the tree, dispatched in just a moment before our eyes.

As the season rounded back to Winter, an exasperated voice called out: "Species and duration."

It was Síl's turn to grimace.

"Do you dare to not recognize your Great Horned King?" he bellowed.

"Great Horned—?" the voice started.

Only then did I notice the red-clad gnome within the twisted branches of the tree. Her features were as gnarled as the tree limbs, but they softened as she looked from Síl to Madison and me. Her smirk stretched to a smile as she spoke again.

"My apologies, sir," she demurred. "I didn't realize. Right this way."

Her hand gestured downward toward the trunk, and Síl glowed as he stepped toward the wood and disappeared. Madison growled as they looked to me, neither of us sure what to do in the fading lamplight. One of the pixies was definitely gone, and the other seemed to have mortal wounds. We would soon be alone in the darkness, our guide gone, and only a very disinterested gnome to keep us company.

Síl's head re-emerged from the trunk. He looked at us questioningly.

"You coming?" he asked.

Before we could answer, he reached out and grabbed my wrist, pulling me into the wood. Madison leapt in after me, keeping close to my heels.

There was a pop—like silence spreading over a too-excited world—followed by the cacophonous rush of revelry. Music and cheers, musical in their own right, bellowed throughout the cavernous room as forty or so Fae folk of various shapes and sizes danced and drank and dined. I could hear the Uilleann piping, the Bodhrán, and the harps always so vivid on my grandfather's records, but didn't see a single instrument spread amongst the crowd. It was as if the movements of the creatures themselves were creating the song: the clutch of a beer-filled stein raising the high whine up an octave; the stomp of a cobbled shoe to the hardwood floor adding the downbeat; the flutter of butterfly-like wings or the shaking out of a strawberry blonde braid emulating the plucking cadence of the strings. Every movement was timed and coordinated to create the notion that this place, this Inn inside this tree, was the very birthplace of the rhythm that was magic.

A fire pit formed a pentacle in the dead center of the room, gently boiling the contents of a massive iron cauldron. I breathed deeply to take in the aroma of sweet honey and bright ginger as they carried the notes of rosemary, heather, and elderflower to my nose. The brewmaster—a jolly fellow with large rounded ears, a protruding chin, and a poppy red blush to his cheeks—scrunched his nose and grinned happily when he saw me sniffing the intoxicating scent. I heard Madison's lips smack in anticipation, and I opened my arms for them to jump up so as not to get trampled by the carousing of the other patrons.

Síl winked at us both as we took in the sight.

"You two should go find us a table," he purred. "I will speak to the keep to inquire on rooms."

We barely had time to blink before he'd danced his way off through the crowd.

"I thought we were headed into a viper's pit," Madison whispered into my ear as they stretched their upper paws to my shoulder. "But maybe they're all just too drunk to care."

It was true. Not a single one of the Fae present inside the Wayward Inn seemed the least bit concerned by our presence. To them, we were not the rare witches of old, the targets of centuries of pent-up exile. We were simply fellow travelers escaping the black of night. Whatever hierarchies and schemes existed beyond the confines of the Wayward Inn had no bearing on the goings-on inside.

I sighed as a tension I had not even realized I was carrying evaporated from my spine. Maybe Fae kind were not as scary as I'd thought. Or maybe Síl's promise of protection was sound. Whatever it was, it gave me and Madison both the opportunity to truly marvel at, to truly appreciate the wonders of the realm. Or at least this portion of it.

"Where do you want to sit?" I asked.

A series of long communal tables were set up in expanding circles around the central fire, creating a sense of safety and movement as we pushed further into the space. The spiraling path gave us a chance to explore the whole of the floor, to see what each table offered. I felt a bit like I was back in middle school, hoping the cool kids would let me sit at their table, wishing they wouldn't realize just how different I was. Each expanse of stilted wood was covered in food and drink—fruity wines, frothy ales, steaming cups of the honeyed meade the brewmaster doled out all sipped to the quick to intensify the merrymaking. I was a bit concerned by the slabs of mutton, the hearty chunks of flesh which bobbed in carved bowls of stew, but they did make my mouth water. So what if I hadn't seen a single full animal—other than The Mórrígan's crows—in all of the Faerie Realm? That didn't mean they weren't there. Somewhere.

We found an empty corner at one of the tables, and I slipped carefully onto the bench as Madison tested the wood with their paws before slipping to sit at attention before me. Their eyes scanned back and forth over the crowd. Their whiskers twitched, but their expression remained calm.

"Don't worry," I whispered. "First light, and we're back on the road to find C and L."

I used their initials purposefully. Even beneath all the noise pervading the space, I couldn't risk any of the Fae folk knowing my lovers' names. I still believed The Mórrígan on that point at least. Although, she *had* been dismissive about my journey, and Síl had offered more guidance and safety in a single evening than she'd been willing to give.

"Best seats in the house," Síl smiled as he sat across from me, timidly reaching to pet Madison between us before thinking better of it. "Our rooms are comped for the night. The innkeeper owes me a favor."

"I suppose a free room is a better payback than fighting it out inside a lantern," Madison growled.

The Faerie king chuckled a hearty, bleating rumble as he winked at me.

"Your *cat sí* certainly does have claws, do they not?" he laughed. "You must tell me how you managed to domesticate them. Usually such feral creatures, they are. Tormenting the teats of livestock. Stealing the souls of poor *sidhé* infants. Tell me, is it to do with the sickly color of their hide? Were they cast out by their kind when they grew agate mold in place of the regal black fur of their species? Did they have no choice but to bend to your will for survival? Those types—the desperate and the needy—do make the best companions."

Madison hissed, but I could tell from their half-smile, half-scowl that they were enjoying the banter. I wasn't sure if Síl actually believed them to be one of the Faerie cats of Highlands lore, but it was as good a cover as any. And so much better than him knowing we were witches. It did make me wonder what he thought I was though. But, by the way he periodically licked his lips when looking at me, I supposed the answer was "sexy." I'd take that any day.

"Ahh, the drinks! Thank you, Val."

Síl shooed Madison from the tabletop as a pale, beautiful woman appeared with a tray. Tall and thin in flowing black robes, I had to do a double-take to ensure she wasn't The Mórrígan. But this woman's eyes were hollow, her lips thin, and her boney, talon-tipped fingers looked gaunt and frightening. She didn't say a word as she placed the drinks—two mugs of the honeyed meade that must have been the house specialty and a bowl of thick, off-white milk—between us, then floated off into the crowd.

"Banshees," Síl said. "Not too big on the speaking since they can't do more than shrill, but they make one heck of a server. And as there's not much death since the realms were closed, they do need something to pass the time. I can even forgive them for being The Mórrígan's haints when they bring me a good stiff one. Plus, Valkyrie there is a warrior in the hay."

He pulled a mug his way before shifting the other toward me and the milk toward Madison. I would have magicked up a love spell for every lonely soul in Atlanta—even if it broke every MAW law on the books—for one of Aunt Paulina's Old Fashioneds, but I had to admit the herbal-infused sweet wine looked as tasty as it smelled. I brought it to my nose and smiled.

"Wait!" Síl bellowed, snatching the stein from my hands before I could sip and switching our glasses. "There you go."

My brow furrowed as I looked at the identical drink before me, frozen as I tried to figure out what had just happened. Síl stared at me intensely for a too-long moment before breaking out into a laugh.

"I'm just at play with you," he said, switching the mugs back and taking a heavy swallow. "You don't really believe I would try to poison you, do you? No, I must keep my travelers alive."

I tried to chuckle along, but the laugh was obviously forced. Still, the attempt at a joke did help to put me at ease. I warily took a sip and let the warmed honey coat my throat. Damn, it was delicious. I could get used to the woodsy pepper of the rosemary, the bitter bite of the heather. It could never be a permanent replacement for Paul's imbibes, but if it had to be—that is, if we got stuck here—I would manage.

I swallowed another gulp and nodded my approval to Madison who took a timid lap of their milk. Síl glowed in our acceptance of his good-host offering as he chugged another portion of his own meade, a thick tongue licking away the rivers which spread from his mouth.

"Lay of the land," he said. "Of course the *Ceanns* are everywhere. The only ones of our lot who took merchantry from that other place. Mining ore and metals; stockpiling shoes none of us really wear; brewing ales and wines. But the Inn is nice, and the meade is nicer. The family split centuries ago so it would not appear they have a monopoly, but you cannot tell me the *Leiprea-Ceann* and the *Clobhair-Ceann* don't sit back at their gatherings and laugh at all their bargaining chips while thinking they shall reign when the worlds merge once more."

My ears perked at the mention of the *Clobhair-Ceann*. Maybe the overnight layover would actually be useful. If I could manage to procure a bottle of their wine, at least I'd have one of The Mórrígan's items checked off of my list. I raised my cup to the brewmaster and smiled to show my appreciation of his work. I'd rather get in his good graces than have to steal from him. Though I was not above the latter if it got me and my coven home safely.

"The *Leannán sídhe* and the *Gean Cánach*," Síl continued, "all keep to the edges of the room, practicing their seductions on one another before they pounce on the folks heading up the stairs to their beds. If I am to be honest, I have bedded a few of them, and the resulting days of itch are but a small price for the hours of rut."

Even Madison's eyes followed mine to check out the incubi and succubi of the Fae world. In all the stories my grandmother had told me, every single Faerie was a hedonistic creature, ready to pounce upon the loins of any witch they could not otherwise trick. Of course, as I got older, she said the same thing about me, so maybe she had a bit more of that puritanical distrust always so evident in humans than she liked to believe.

I had to admit, the *Leannán sídhe* and the *Gean Cánach* were beautiful though. Their bodies—varied in size and shape as if their very existence broadcast "something for everyone"—shifted in slow, sinewy motions which exemplified the animalistic elegance they promised. A faint glow highlighted their facial features, amplified and excited by each purse of their lips, each slow wink of their eyes. When they spoke, their voice carried swaths of synesthetic color to gently caress the cheek of their targets before it penetrated their ear to entice the universal sex organ of all kind—witch, Fae, or human. If I was remembering my translations correctly, the female-presenting "Faerie Lovers" and the male-presenting and nonbinary "Love Talkers" certainly lived up to their names.

Síl's eyes squinted with pleasure as he watched me watching them.

"The *Fear Dearg* stay mostly in the kitchen, carving up the meats and plopping them into the stews," he said. "But it is always good to have a butcher at the door during the blackest of nights to keep the Boggarts, the Salamanders, and the *Dullahan* at bay."

Síl's breath hissed around the names of the three outcast clans, and I shuddered as I considered what a Fae lord would find so repulsive. In the stories, Boggarts were nuisances with a penchant for firewood and trickery, but didn't seem too bad. Though, as a witch, the thought of the fire Fae Salamanders luring me to the stake—or the headless horseman *Dullahan* galloping upon me in the darkness—did give me chills. My mind flashed to the gnome-like creature who had let us inside, and I suddenly realized the red of her clothing had not been a pigment. She was so small, but the deep blood of her garments showed she was formidable.

"With the Boggarts kept out, their kinder cousins are able to enjoy the evening indoors for themselves. Though, the *Bean-tighe* often end up abandoning their drinks to wipe the tables or clear away dishes. But I suppose it's hard for anyone to overcome their nature, even when the night calls for revelry. Which brings me around to you, traveler Dan and your *cat sí* Mason. What is your true nature?"

My mouth gaped as Síl's eyes swam over me from across the table, and I shrugged as I pulled the stein up to my mouth. If I couldn't even reveal our true names, I couldn't exactly tell him that Madison and I were witches, no matter how helpful he had been to us thus far. Revealing our kind in the Fae Realm would only send more of their kind in search of the cracks between our worlds. I couldn't let that happen.

"Just travelers," I sighed. "Tasked, as you surmised, with an endeavor for The Mórrígan."

Even though Síl held an obvious dislike for her, I had to assume her position in the Fae hierarchy still held some sort of weight amongst the others. I hoped her name would continue to keep us safe, though I did notice a burning on my chest from her amulet at the mention of it.

"Hmm, yes," Síl muttered, his voice low and distant as he studied me through slitted eyes. "I have told you I smelled her upon you. So, we now establish that you are but a lackey for her gilded green eyes, and—"

"We ain't nobody's lackeys," Madison growled, milk dripping from the fur beneath their mouth. "Especially not some self-absorbed Fae who looks like a drag queen?"

Síl's eyes focused on Madison as he considered their words.

"Drag queen?" he asked. "I suppose, yes, she is a queen, at least in her mind. And she does enjoy quartering and dragging her foes. Though I'm sure such a fate is beyond you, correct? Unless something were to cause you to fail."

Madison's tail flicked, and I placed a hand near their paw to calm them. They really didn't trust the Fae. After all, one had killed their best friend and tried to murder them, and another had left them to live in the form of a cat. There wasn't much there to be trusted.

Síl grinned as he shot his eyes back to me.

"And we come once again to the question," he purred. "What *are* you? You do not directly resemble any of the Fae or any of the Fae children whom I have encountered. In fact, you look remarkably like the witches of old. And yet, any of those poor souls brought here through failed bargains or unmet demands are but fragile slaves, holding no power and forced to toil for their masters. At least until their weak, mortal bodies give out. And yet, *you* have magic. I can sense it, fluttering inside of you like the tree leaves shake when the pixies start fucking. So what. Does that. Make. You?"

He asked his question in a staccato pace as his eyes lit from my gut to my neck to my lips to my eyes. My breath hung in my throat as I tried to figure out what to say. The piping music slowed as my pulse quickened, and I felt the eyes of all the other patrons glance my way as they continued their conversations but listened for my answer.

"Why the hell are you so concerned with labels?" Madison yowled, hopping from the bench to sit before me on the table. Their tail twitched as they stared Síl down. "You got some fetish you need to fulfill? Or are you so insecure about your little deer legs you feel the need to make sure anyone you come across 'knows their place'?"

Síl's thick hand hesitantly reached for Madison, but stopped short when they brandished their claws. The curious anger and suspicion in his face faltered for a moment as his eyes darted between the two of us. I didn't think we were going to get away without giving him an honest answer. Or at least an answer that would get him off our backs for the time being. Determination clung to his features like gristle stuck in the teeth of the other patrons who were now openly watching us, their sharp fangs bared as they awaited the outcome of our standoff. Shit. As much as I welcomed the meade and the place to stay for the night, we never should have followed yet another Fae.

A throat cleared and the crowd parted as a grotesque creature hopped his way toward us. When I caught sight of his singular eye from the corner of mine, fear nearly made my heart leap from my chest. But it wasn't Balor. This creature wasn't nearly as tall or menacing as the Fomóraiġ King. He did have his Balor's wicked eye though. A single arm with one thick hand protruded from the center of his torso, and he hopped on a singular but sturdy leg as he saddled up beside our table. It was as if he had all the features of Balor cut in half. A gruff, billy goat of a beard hung across his neck, and his ears came to rapier points two inches above his bald head. I almost felt sorry for him. Perhaps I would have felt sorry for him if it weren't for the thick stream of saliva glistening like hungry violence across his teeth as he smiled.

"Is there a problem here?" he asked, his voice as hoarse as his demeanor.

"No problem, Fachan," Síl assured him, laying on the same sweet casualness he'd used to lure me in before. "Just having a conversation with my traveler friends here."

It sounded like bees swarming around a metal spoon in a garbage disposal when Fachan laughed. It held in it no joy, no mirth, and served to silence the entire room.

"Are you pretending to be Cernunnos again to ensnare lost souls?" he asked, a certain admiration in his voice even as Síl made a grandiose show of feigning innocence. "Just be the Púca you are, Síl. As if your hooves don't give you away."

Síl's face fell. So that was why he didn't look at all like I'd imagined the Great Horned King to appear. He wasn't him in the first place. I should have known. Or at least been smart enough to figure it out. But, in fairness, my high school adaptation of Shakespeare had not equipped me for meeting a Faerie King or a Puck in real life.

I froze as Fachan turned to me, and Madison jumped to sit behind me on the bench as we shivered in his gaze.

"And who are these poor souls you are duping?" he asked.

I swallowed hard and tried to look away as his eye went wide in recognition.

"Darragh Cullen," he bellowed. "I know all that my father knows. And, as it was you who bound him, I will receive a great reward for turning you in to him."

Fuck. So much for a nice quiet night waiting out the blackness. So much for a chance at gathering the first of The Mórrígan's items. Hell, if he was bringing me to Balor, so much for ever seeing my lovers again.

The Mórrígan's amulet burned hot against my chest, as I sat, wide-eyed and slowly lifting my hand to summon her help. She wouldn't be happy that I'd not yet fulfilled my end of our bargain, but this was life or death. I took a deep breath. My fingers felt the heat of the stone beneath the fabric of my shirt. All I had to do was call her name.

Suddenly, a hoof kicked out from under the table, slamming Fachan in the side and quickly knocking him to the floor.

"Run!" Síl yelled.

I scooped Madison into my arms and did as I was told.

CHAPTER 11

"Well, that was a fucking riot!"

The blackness of the night was so deep I could not get my bearings. The erratic drumbeat of the Bodhrán as forty—or maybe it was just one—Fae adversaries chased me, the wheeze and wallow of a pulsing wind was all I could hear. But I felt the clover spread between my fingers, the soft brush of Madison's electric fur against my arms. We had made it outside at least, stumbling from the trunk of the hawthorn tree as it expelled us from the Inn it kept hidden inside. The hooked thorns of its branches had clawed me on our exit, ripping the fabric of my clothing and snatching a trickle of dark blood from my skin. I felt it smear across my side like war paint, sensed the scratch like Fachan's talons finding purchase still.

My heartbeat and my panting—was that what I was hearing?—began to subside as I pulled myself to my knees. I heard the too-near babble of a river as my senses returned, felt its spray waft upon the night to meet my face.

"Fucking Balor!" Madison spoke again. Their shiver of disgust as they remembered his co-optation of their body when he'd last attempted to break into our realm buzzed against my own. "He's worse than the fucking MAW!"

It was nice to hear that Madison was unscathed. And that they had their fighting spirit back. I had a feeling we were going to need it to get through all the Fae had in store for us.

"Can you tell where we are?" I asked. "I can hear the water. Which means we aren't where we entered the Wayward Inn."

At least the night was warm, or maybe that was just The Mórrígan's amulet heating me from my sternum. I felt a faint breeze tickle the newly exposed skin from my tattered sweater, but other than the rush of water, the area seemed relatively still. I sighed heavily. No Fae were chasing us. At least not yet.

"I honestly can't see much," Madison replied. "Probably a little better than you. But ever since I got my voice back, I can feel the animal slipping away as the witch takes over. My reflexes aren't as sharp. I can only make out some outlines when I squint. But, hey. At least I'm not still fascinated by balls of yarn or scurrying field mice. For now anyway. It's a constant struggle to keep the cat from taking over again. But I don't mind the trade-off to have my mind back."

I wasn't sure if they could see my nod, but I understood completely. In my brief, mental excursion as a hare, the call of the wild had been fierce. I respected their strength in keeping it at bay even as they retained their feline form. It couldn't have been easy. Feeling the rawness of instinct, the seductive ease of movement, the strength of realigned muscles and bones all fading away would be hard fought against the burdens of mind, the understanding of emotion. But fear and worry were a small price to pay for a voice. A reduced spectrum of sight was nothing compared to comprehending what was seen.

"It doesn't seem like Fachan was able to follow us though," they offered.

I nodded again. The whole of our escape from the Wayward

Inn had been a blur of wings and limbs floundering about. *Ceanns* hiding beneath tables or taking the opportunity to dip their cups into the brewmaster's unguarded cauldron. Pixies I hadn't seen before ascending high into the rafters. Val and the other Banshee waitstaff grinning from the outer rim of the room, excited for the chance to finally get to scream once again. I could hear Síl's baying grunts as he fought to keep Fachan pinned to the floor. Had he actually helped us? Whether his instinctual directive to help travelers had taken over or he just wanted us for himself, I wasn't sure. Whatever the case, I would have to thank him if I ever saw him again. If we made it through the night.

"Should… Should you try using your light?"

My mouth twisted as I considered Madison's suggestion. I *did* have my power, and that secret was out. I wasn't sure it was ever even a secret to begin with. If a Puck like Síl had been able to sense it within me, then surely The Mórrígan had too. Why she'd let that tidbit be was beyond me, but whatever her reasons were made me anxious.

Plus my magic was changed here. I could feel it, I could access it, but I couldn't quite control it. It was like I was a kid again, just coming into my own—waking up one morning at the start of puberty with an erection and a rumble deep inside me, unsure of what to do with either. But it had all been instinct then. Maybe it would be now.

"Everything is so left of center here," I sighed. "I'm afraid I won't be able to control it. What if I reach for the light and shoot a homing beacon straight into the sky for Balor to find us?"

"I've got a theory on that," Madison purred. I felt their paw press against my knee for comfort. "All this time as a cat, I could *feel* my magic. It was still there, inside of me, but I just couldn't access it. In my feline brain, the synapses fired differently. I didn't have the language. I didn't have the thoughts to focus it."

A witch's earth magic relied so much on their focus. The words—hell, even the ritual—were all a means to direct their intent through the innate ebb and flow of the elements. Practice made us understand those elements. Focus let us control them.

"But Fae magic isn't based on thought," Madison continued. "Not directly anyway. It's based on movement. We use our minds to connect to the natural world, to guide the elements. It's a gentle nudge. For non Dark Witches, it's symbiotic. But I think the Fae…. I think they are actually… picking through the fibers of the universe. The strands that hold it all together."

My eyes went wide. It made perfect sense. That's how The Mórrígan and Balor had been able to pull objects from out of nowhere, to produce something from nothing. A witch needed a seed to make a plant grow. The Fae dug through the fabric of space and time to pull that plant from somewhere else. That was why a witch needed Fae magic to shift into their animal form. The body did not want to be realigned, but if the threads of reality were shifted, then the body would too.

"Well, shit," I gasped. "I think you're right."

Still, it would take eons to learn how to do that properly. And I wasn't even sure a witch's internal power would meet the task in the same way as a Fae's. Hell, three other witches—that I knew of—were inside the Fae Realm, and they couldn't even access the magic inside of them. So why could I?

I closed my eyes, exhaling a slow and calming breath as I eased my body into the detached state of focus necessary for the larger magics. In our world, a simple ball of light would be a thought that barely met the tongue, a sigh swept through a hurricane of wind. But this was new, and I needed to be sure my intent was firm and controlled.

The tensions in my shoulders eased, and I kept them still as I breathed in the Fae air, willing my lungs to take note of the distinctions between what I knew and what I was experiencing. The variations would be the key to getting the spell right. Another deep breath, and I could just begin to see it: a faint glow of power in the distance of my mind's eye, too far away to touch, but close enough to give me hope.

I left my eyes closed, retained my focus on the brightness, and lifted my arms before me. My fingers clutched and twisted as they pulled at the veils between me and the light. Being careful not to dishevel any more than I needed to in order to reach my goal, a swivel of my wrist wound through a layer; a slight touch, a gentle shift of my fingers separated the in-between to form a path from where I was to where I wanted to reach. I could almost touch it. I could almost feel its heat. It called toward my fingertips just as I beckoned for it.

And then… nothing.

I crumpled over my knees, exhausted as my body snapped back into reality. I felt Madison brush against the crown of my head.

"I almost had it," I panted. "It felt so close."

I pulled myself up to try again, reaching for my magic as a sharp whine pierced through my ears. My power smoldered with cellular smoke in my gut. I was burnt out.

"It's okay," Madison purred. "Maybe a light is not what we need right now anyway. How about we just try to get some rest? We can sleep in shifts. I can take the first watch."

I tried to protest, but my sigh sounded more like a whimper. I swallowed hard to wet the dryness in my throat and agreed.

"Wake me up when you get tired," I said, shifting my body to lay in a fetal position on the dew-damp grass.

I didn't think I'd actually be able to sleep, but a chance to lie down was definitely a good thing. We were both going to need our strength to outrun Balor and find Learco and Cernun before it was too late to take our lives back from the Changelings. Rest, even a sleepless rest, would be worth it when the day returned.

The ground was remarkably soft as it met the curve of my cheek. I listened to the rustle of the nearby flow of water, the hum of the wind, the rumble of Madison's chest as they nestled at alert next to mine. I closed my eyes.

I knew I was dreaming. Still, it didn't make my grandmother's house any less real.

I awoke to the smell of bacon, heard it sizzling in the cast iron pan on the kitchen stove from all the way in the guest room. I knew Granny would still have her muck boots on from raiding the chicken coop for the morning's haul, dropping her signature scratch mix throughout the run on her way in then filling up her basket with the speckled brown of the hen's eggs. Her favorite cornflower blue apron, darkened and stained by decades of blood and grease even her best magics couldn't get out, would be tied around her waist, the hand-sewn frills along the hem arching and aching for a taste of the massive breakfast she was preparing. Her hair would be perfectly coiffed, pulled back and high behind her ears in loose curls which mimicked the roiling sea. Her lips would be washed in the near nude wax she never let anyone except my grandfather see her without.

The guest room—my home away from home for three weeks every summer—was the largest in their tiny house in their one horse borough of ex-farmers looking for community rather than expanse. And yet, there was barely room for the twin mattress which lumped and creaked beneath my young body due to the reams of fabric stacked floor to ceiling along the far wall, the folding table cut stations littered with the scraps of half-finished projects and patterns, the behemoth of a sewing machine with its greenwashed iron foot treadle. The room was a kaleidoscope of color, exploded through in a prism met and mirrored by countless bobbins and buttons and batting. It was Granny's home within her home on the days I wasn't there, and she prided herself on the coveralls she made for Paps, the quilts she sent out for Solstice, and the dolls she constructed for the grandchildren of all of her friends.

I heard the screen door slam and then the whoosh of cold air as she opened up the reach in freezer on the screened-in back porch to pull out the white pudding that would finish off the feast she was creating. I only had a few minutes until she hollered at me to get my *butt out of bed!*

Planting my feet on the short pile of beige carpeting that covered every inch of the house except the kitchen and the bathroom, I wiggled my toes and stretched into the morning. The pajama set I was wearing felt at once old-timey and newly kitschy. Four large, wooden buttons clasped the collared top loosely around my torso, but the elastic of the pants bore into my hips from last Summer's measurements. Still, the whimsical depictions of domesticated animals—cats and dogs and canaries and roosters—domesticating the land with their tills and their baskets of carrots and their watering cans didn't make me feel any less dapper.

I smiled. I was seven, maybe eight years old, and life was simple and uncomplicated. No Fae were breathing down my neck. No shadow organizations were using their time in the light to inch me closer and closer to the flame. No darkness was waiting behind closed doors. The doors all creaked on their hinges amidst the thick humidity of the South, but it was a comforting sound, an announcement of the solidity of space.

Breakfast was laid out across the formica dining room table— pan-fried eggs, thick slabs of fatty bacon, a small pot of baked beans, salted and grilled tomatoes and mushrooms, and the freshly boiled white pudding Granny'd pulled from the freezer after making the batch the week before. It was a lot of food, but I was a "growing boy," and a good portion of it was already being packed away into a Tupperware bin for Paps to carry with him down to the Boat Basin. He'd spend most of the day there, holding onto the thick end of a fishing pole and laughing along with the "fish as big as a boat" or the "turnip the size of a tractor" stories of the friends who'd pass through the folding chair next to him on the dock.

"How'd you sleep?" Granny asked, and I smiled my approval of the bed that would have left me bent and sore if my spine had reached my thirties. "Eat up! We've got a big day today."

I grabbed the tempered glass of my plate and sighed contentedly at the familiarity of the brown decorative floral pattern that circled the rim. Serving spoons and spatulas, all a polished silver and heavy with baroque handles, were tucked into each of the dishes, and I piled the food high onto my plate. It was more than I could possibly eat, but that didn't matter. It was a dream. And even if it wasn't, Granny always grinned at a healthy appetite.

I sat down to eat, and, in a flash, the meal was gone.

"What color thread do you want?"

My mouth twisted into a pout as I looked at the array of needles spread out on the table before me. From the thick and dangerous edge of the tapestry needle to the delicate sharpness of the millinery point, their open eyes all stared back at me with a gaping indifference. Granny had traded her kitchen apron for the patchwork one she preferred to use in her sewing room. Bits of our family's history were stitched throughout its expanse, including the newest square of clover-colored fabric she'd sewn in over her heart. It was from my baby blanket, and I still felt warmth and comfort when I saw it.

"Any color you want," she urged.

"Paps spent three hours yesterday making me tie treble hooks into fishing line," I huffed. "Why do I gotta do this today?"

"It's important, Darragh," she smiled, always the bastion of patience, as she pulled an assortment of green spools from her supply. "You may not have your power—yet. And you may not realize how right away, but trust me when I tell you these lessons will be helpful to you one day. Now, thread the needle."

I held the needle between my thumb and index finger, closing my left eye and squinting through my right as I guided the blunt edge of the thread to the hole. The thread bunched as it hit metal instead of air, and I sighed as I dropped both before me.

"Again," Granny said.

"I don't understand why I can't just use that wire thingy that looks like a nickel," I groaned. "Isn't this what it's for?"

"And what happens when you don't have a threader handy?" she asked. "What do you do when the tools you need aren't at the ready?"

"So I won't have a threader, but I'll have a needle and thread?"

She smirked at my sarcasm, and gestured for me to pick them up once more.

"The needle and thread are metaphors. Go again."

I inhaled slowly, centering my vision as I brought the items before me. I steadied my hands, twisting my fingers slightly as I brought them closer together, willing them to intertwine, for the space between to be filled until the separate objects became one instrument. The thread slipped the eye, and I reached quickly to grab hold and pull it through, smiling as the spool twirled and bobbed against the table. I held it aloft to Granny with a shit-eating grin of triumph plastered to my face.

"Now, we're going to learn the pick stitch."

"I still don't see why this is important," I whined, my fourteen-year-old voice cracking with the changes of puberty. "I've had my power for a couple years now and have never had to use this."

"Earth magic is not the only power there is, Darragh. There are magics beyond what you know. Energies which, like this stitch, connect the future to the past. Threads which hold together what would otherwise be ripped apart. You are stronger than you know."

Like Uncle Gardner, Granny was a seer. And she'd reminded me time and again it was better to believe her than not.

I still did not know what that made me, but I pushed the needle firmly through the fabrics, counting the fibers carefully as I went, sure to leave only the bits I wanted seen showing, particular in the placement of that which was to remain hidden.

"Good," Granny smiled. "Now remember this moment when the threads of space seem tangled. Hold this pattern for when you need to pull yourself through."

My grandmother's words echoed through my head as I came to. A soft, yellow light was just beginning to break, and I wiped my eyes as I pulled myself from the grass. Madison had fallen asleep, curled into a ball in the crook where my chest had been, and I rubbed them gently to wake them.

"Shit," they growled, suddenly alert and on their feet. "I didn't mean to—"

"It's fine," I assured them. "We both needed the rest. And we're both still here."

The Wayward Inn had spat us out in a relatively safe place, as far as those existed in the Faerie Realm. Nestled beneath the curtain of branches from a willow tree near the river we were headed for, I wondered if my will—my thoughts and wants— as we hurdled through the doors had had something to do with our ending location. If Madison was right about how Fae magic worked, if places like the Wayward Inn existed in between the fibers, then I supposed the entrances and exits were more varied than those of our world. And perhaps I was more adept at Fae magic than I'd believed.

Or maybe I was giving myself too much credit.

But from the shelter of the tree, we were hidden, and the flow of the river meant we were getting closer to finding Learco and Cernun and getting ourselves home. There was no sense staring a gift Fae in the ass. No matter how nice the ass was.

The hum of a sea shanty like the ones my father liked to sing pulled my thoughts back to the present. Madison followed as I crawled to where the branches bent to meet the earth, closing one eye and shifting my perspective just as I had with the needle in my dream, until I could make out the landscape beyond the fluttering leaves. A shoal of Fae meandered a path toward a dock set deep into the wide river, laughing and dancing and singing as they moved. I would have almost thought them human—clad in their green rubber boots and coveralls, their plaid and tartan button- ups, and with grime-covered skin—but the high points to their ears and the slight webbing of their fingers told me otherwise. Too, their hair—long and flowing through a delicate salt-washed curl regardless of what sex they presented—seemed to undulate through the air as if not controlled by the laws of nature. Like all the other Fae I'd seen—good or bad; Fomóraiġ or Tuath Dé—they were beautiful. Even Fachan, in all his grotesqueness, had possessed a gilded lure within him. That was part of what made them all so dangerous.

"We shouldn't move until they've cleared the area," I whispered, shifting back toward the trunk of the willow and pulling my knees up in front of me to wait.

My trousers had a few snags but had mostly survived the ragged snarls of the hawthorn. My sweater had not been so lucky. Rips spread across the sleeves and my torso, and I could feel the bark of the tree against my back. The remaining weave of tightly knitted cashmere threatened to pull and disappear at the slightest breeze. At least the scratches on my skin had healed over, and the remaining marks were kind of sexy, like the hard wrought remnants of a too passionate night. The shirt was kind of sexy too in a late 70s punk rock sort of way. But it did little to hide my skin or the amulet The Mórrígan had given me for emergencies.

I chuckled as I thought about Granny's lessons.

"Maybe this was what she was preparing me for," I whispered to myself. Deep down, I knew I was right, but it had nothing to do with my clothing.

I pulled the sweater off and used it to fashion a pouch for the amulet, tying it tight to the belt loop at my side. At least that way the charm would stay hidden and there'd be one less visible reason for any other Fae to come after us. Not that I was certain they'd even need a reason.

"I was going to make a joke about gay men and their disdain for shirts," Madison purred, "but honestly, after I got my top surgery, I don't think I wore one for a whole month."

I smiled. It was good to hear the sarcasm, the fight back in Madison's voice. The sleep had done us both well.

"While we wait for the literal coast to clear," I whispered, "I'm going to try my hand at that Fae craft again. I was so close last night I could feel the heat from the light."

As Madison nodded, their ear pricked and turned to focus on the noise beyond our canopy.

"Just keep an eye on me, okay? Make sure I don't get lost."

They nodded, and I steadied myself for the ritual.

Pulling a manifested object into being was difficult, even in earth magic. I had set the bar a bit too high for my first try. But reaching—sending my thoughts, my voice out into the ether—that had to be a little easier. Plus, after remembering what my grandmother had taught me, I had to try.

I closed my eyes as I tried to remember anything I could about the cavern I'd encountered when I'd been kidnapped. The black of the rock. The way the light cascaded along the jagged handholds of the lift as I pulled myself upwards. The exact turquoise of the sky.

I imagined the grass, its near chartreuse hue, as it waved in an unfelt breeze when I reached the surface. I tried to see each blade individually, to picture as many details as I could deep within my mind's eye. I needed to be as accurate as possible as I locked onto the specifics of place.

My arms rose as I pushed my mental form through the field toward the grove beside the river, my fingers moving instinctively to pull the landscape to me, to push myself through it. I saw the flowers which I couldn't name, heard the rush of water in the nearby stream. It was different than the flow where I actually sat: slower, calmer, shallower. As I heard the change, I knew I was getting close.

"Darragh?"

The sound of Cernun's voice—as haggard and gruff with worry as it was—filled me with instant warmth. I grinned as he scrambled to his feet and Learco emerged from within the lean-to he'd been constructing. Their clothes were filthy, but the remnants of fruits, fish, and a fire told me they weren't starving.

"Holy shit," Learco laughed as he stared into my eyes.

"Hey, fellas," I blushed.

It was a task, concentrating on keeping the veils pulled open and trying to speak at the same time, but seeing them there—beautiful and real and mine—gave me strength.

"Leave it to Darragh Cullen to figure out how to do something like this," Cernun smiled.

He reached out to embrace me, but his hands pushed straight through my vision.

"It's Fae magic," I said. "We're in the Faerie Realm."

"I thought as much," Learco groaned. "Everything here is a little… off. It didn't seem possible for this to be of our world."

"How did you—? How are you using Faerie magic?" Cernun stuttered, aghast, but I could tell he was proud.

Damn, I missed those men. I wanted more than anything to push myself through the folds, to land there, physically beside them, to feel my lips on their bodies.

"I have no idea," I confessed. "I also don't know how long I can keep this going. I just— I wanted to tell you that I love you. And that I'm on my way back to you. And not to trust anyone you come across."

"I was a scout for a hot minute before I got my powers," Cernun laughed. Fuck, it was good to hear his laugh again. "First rule of being lost in the wilderness is to stay where you are until you're found. Especially if you're by a river."

"It feels shitty to do nothing though," Learco added. "How did we get here?"

"The Mórrígan says we were kidnapped by Changelings. Our time in Balor's mind left us susceptible."

"And you believe her?"

I shrugged. I didn't know what to believe. I just knew I had to find them and get us home.

I could feel the folds of reality strain against my magic, pushing at my chest to constrict the air. I didn't have much time.

"We'll be there as soon as we can," I told them. "I have Madison. And we're coming for you."

Cernun and Learco nodded as the gravity of the situation took hold. They were strong witches who didn't like sitting on their laurels when faced with adversity, but they were willing to wait for me if that was what was best.

"I love you," I said. "Both."

"To the stars and back," Cernun smiled.

Half a laugh escaped my throat. We were certainly finding out—in real time—exactly how far our love would travel.

I closed my eyes as the threads of the Faerie Realm slipped back into place. A sharp breath pushed from my lungs.

It took a lot out me, pushing through reality like that. My pulse pounded at my temples, and an urgent burn radiated from my torso. But it was worth it to see them.

"You *have* me?" Madison asked, eyes squinted as I brought mine to theirs. "I may be in the body of a pet, but I'm all witch. The inside is what counts, not the physical form."

"Sorry," I blushed. "Habit."

"Uh huh," they pouted, but they twitched their whiskers to let me know they were joking. "Well, while you were making googly eyes at your boyfriends, I was watching the river. Those fishermen we saw heading down? They each grabbed a little feather cap from that barrel by the dock and went full-on Hans Christian Andersen when their bodies hit the water."

Well, that was certainly one way to man the river. And it also meant that one of the items on The Mórrígan's wish list might actually be closer at hand than I'd thought.

CHAPTER 12

Madison stayed low as they crept across the small expanse from the willow to the dock, shoulders high as their torso dipped to brush the ground. Despite the electric blue of their fur—or maybe because the sky itself held its own turquoise luster—they were nearly invisible as they made their way through the taller grasses which exploded from the nearby source of water.

The river itself was wide—wider than any I'd ever seen in my world—and mimicked the choppy pull of an ocean moreso than a babbling brook. Still, even through the rise and fall of its currents, the water held a peaceful tranquility, as if the river itself were singing a gentle hymn, a siren song meant to lure sailors to its depths. I had a feeling it was as deep as it was wide, especially since I had yet to see even one of the nine or so fishermen we'd seen heading towards the dock surface from beneath its meniscus.

So those were the murúch, I thought to myself as I stepped timidly from the shelter of the willow branches. I was glad I'd been able to work the spell to speak with Cernun and Learco, but it would have been amazing to see the merfolk transform as they donned their red caps and met the water. I hoped there would be another *cochaillín draíochta* waiting inside the barrel when Madison reached the dock. It would be great to have at least one of The Mórrígan's wants taken care of so we could focus on home versus bargains.

The air was warm on my bare chest, but a slight chill from the river's breeze sent my nipples to points and tightened the muscles in my stomach. That was fine though. My vanity would have induced the same reaction as I stepped from my hiding place anyway. I took a few brief steps to ensure the makeshift pouch I'd tied from my sweater was secure at my hip and The Mórrígan's amulet was not at risk of falling out.

Madison frowned as they peered into the wooden barrel at the base of the dock, and I scurried forth to join them.

"Nada," they growled as I got nearer. "Unless it takes some kind of magic eye to see them."

I shrugged. It wasn't beyond the realm of possibilities. The Fae did seem to like hiding things in plain sight, shifting the cords of the universe to pull their belongings to them when they wanted. But I had a feeling it wouldn't have been that easy. If it was, The Mórrígan could have just sifted through space to grab the items herself. Still, I did my best to see what wasn't there, pulling up a second sight that was becoming much easier to control, as I squinted down into the container. Only wet wood and a few rusted bolts stared back.

"Well, shit," Madison purred. "Do we just wait here until they resurface?"

"I don't think we have a choice."

As much as I wanted to continue our journey, we'd need The Mórrígan's help to get back to our world, and she would just ignore us if I didn't complete my end of our bargain. Or worse. Damn it! The fucking Fae were fucked up with their bartering systems. And I'd been trapped into two of them already, so I supposed I was fucked too.

"We could try to find some grub," Madison suggested. "I

don't guess old crow eyes gave you any for the road."

My stomach churned with the hunger pangs I'd been trying to ignore. My meade and Madison's milk had been a welcomed sustenance the night before, but we'd had to leave before any meals were served. Some food would be nice.

"We could try fishing," I winced. I didn't like the idea of offending—or worse yet, snagging—the *murúch* while they swam the waters below, but we stood a better chance of seizing fish from the stream than attempting a daylight hunt away from the waters. "I'll grab a willow branch to use as a pole. Check those tarps over there to see if you can find some sort of line or string. Or maybe bait."

Madison's feline face filled with a mixture of excitement and determination which I understood all too well. Since arriving in the Fae Realm, I'd felt lost and overwhelmed, tossed and pushed about like a dandelion seed on an errant breeze. Fashioning a fishing rod was a task we could accomplish; a simple, self-reliant measure which gave us purpose and agency, however brief it was.

The willow bowed as I approached, its yellow-green leaves fluttering like eager eyes all turned on me at once. I raised my hand to touch them gently with my fingertips. Mentally, like any good witch, I asked forgiveness for taking while simultaneously thanking the plant for its offering. An earth witch was trained to utilize what nature contained for their magic. The good ones appreciated the renewal inherent in the cycle. The best ones revered the sacrifice of each clipping.

I selected a branch that seemed adequate—thick and solid at the base and tapered down to a fine point—ensuring it was older and already showing signs of dieback as newer offshoots jockeyed for light and water.

"May I?" I asked aloud this time then closed my eyes to listen for the answer. A feeling of surrendered peace washed over me, and I smiled as I snapped the branch in two as cleanly as I could without my tools. It stiffened in my palm, hardening almost immediately as its leaves fell away and it straightened to my will. One piece down.

"No luck on any line," Madison called as I made it back to the dock, "but I did find some bones we could probably use as a hook. I think they're from a fish. Maybe."

The rib bones were hardened and bleached by the sun. They were a far cry from the metal hooks—the ones fashioned with bright colored bobs and trickling feathers—my grandfather used to entice the redeye bass, the white and blue catfish, and the common carp onto his line, but they would have to do.

I sat down on the dock and pulled the thin end of my pole toward me then went to work pulling the laces from my boots. I used the knots Paps had taught me and the closures from Granny to secure the bone hook to the laces, the laces to each other, and the far end of the line to the rod. It made a serviceable, if makeshift, pole. I just hoped nothing happened before I could get my shoes back together. If Fachan, or worse, Balor, showed up, I'd hate to end up as the bare chested, bare footed yokel running through the woods of most of my favorite southern novels. But my growling stomach said it was a chance I'd have to take.

We didn't have any bait, but we couldn't let that stop us. I stepped to the end of the dock and sat. The water calmed when my feet touched it as if welcoming our presence, and I dipped the hook into it, willing it to sink as deep below the surface as my shoe laces would allow.

The water felt cool and refreshing as it pulsed against my feet, and I couldn't help but give a quick sniff at my shoulder.

"Yeah," Madison purred. "You really could use a bath. But, you know, given where we are, I didn't want to say anything."

I blushed. If we survived this—if we all made it back home

and in one piece—I was going to spend three whole days beneath the rainfall shower Cernun had installed in my bathroom. I didn't care if I had to constantly spell to keep the water heater bubbling. It would be worth it. Maybe I could also entice Learco and Cernun to wallow in there with me.

"So sorry I can't just lick myself," I countered.

"Bet you wish you could."

As I laughed, the water sloshed around my feet, accenting the rhythm of my chuckle. Damn, it felt good to laugh. Even Madison was light as they let their anarchist-youth-filled guard subside for a moment. My Paps, always armed with a one-liner, had told me laughter was as good for the soul as any lavender-scented spell and that keeping the air light above the water would help the fish break the tension of the surface. I always thought he was just more interested in telling jokes than catching fish—we rarely did seem to bring any home with us, and the ones we caught we always thanked and threw back—but my impromptu pole with the shoelace line was certainly highlighted by my feet in the water and the vibration in my throat.

I watched the circles ripple out and dissipate from our center at the docks, basking in the quick serenity of it all; the calm agitation of nature. If we could avoid Balor, maybe the Fae Realm wouldn't be so bad.

I smiled as our laughter subsided. The waves of the river met our undulations head on, cresting the blue water with white crowns. I jostled the fishing pole in hopes the light would catch the shiny end of my shoelace and entice the fish to bite. Humor may have lifted our spirits, but it did little to suppress our hunger. Madison's eyes squinted as they perched at the edge of the dock, claws at the ready for anything they saw swim too close to the surface. But all we could do was wait.

"Uh… Darragh?"

I noticed their electric blue fur stood high on their backs and turned my gaze to view what had spooked them. The river, already as restless as the sea on a full mooned night, churned with a greater ferocity than it had only moments before. The water changed course, a whirlpool forcing downstream up, the push toward land inward. So much for any tranquility when it came to anything Fae.

I gasped as I pulled the line from the water and stepped back onto the dock, Madison rounding my wet ankles in an internal fight between protector and protected. Instinctively, I reached inside to grab hold of my power, recoiling as the new, off feel of it spindled inside my gut. I breathed deeply and adjusted my pull, letting the changed vibrations feel their way from my center into my mind. It was so close to what I knew—powerful and natural—yet as it connected me to this new world, it made everything strange. I hoped if I had to use it quickly, my intent would still be enough to guide it toward my goal.

"Should we run?" Madison asked as we both froze in place, eyes fixed on the fizzing whirlpool as it cratered into a black as deep as Cernun's hair a few yards away.

I eyed my boots still sitting at the shore end of the dock, the laces still tied to the willow branch I'd dropped behind us on the planks. Whatever was rising would be on us before I could stoop to put them on. Besides, I didn't want to turn my back on what was happening, even if it would mean putting some distance between us and it.

A shining, crimson expanse emerged from within the whirlpool, breaking the water with a ferocious, swordlike strike. It looked more like the petals of a dahlia than a fin, sharp and plentiful, as it rose and submerged, only to reappear once more, further up the vortex. As the maelstrom intensified, the fins reached further into the air, showing the green scaled form to which they were attached.

Like all things in the Faerie Realm, the sea monster was a beautiful as it was horrifying, as violent as it was majestic. The very water of the river itself leapt in spasms from its scales of variegated green as if repelled by the power the creature held, as if making room for its effortless glide. It wasn't the raw force of the dragon that kept me frozen though. It was the screams.

Wails like the siren calls of a thousand lost souls filled the air in wafting, discordant song, drowning out the gurgling churn of the river. It was unnerving, and I willed the noise to stop as it pulsed in torrents against the sky.

"I don't think that's coming from the serpent."

I squinted as I tried to focus on the vortex, to make sense of the speed of its swirl. Madison was right. Gills and fins and faces were trapped within the whirlpool, jostled by the current even as they scrambled to be set free. Some of the faces, despite the greenish hue beneath their pale skin, looked utterly Fae, but the others, even with features that were more like those of carp, held all the fear and agony of expression the others had succumbed to. Whether it had intended to or not, the *Ollphéist* had captured the *murúch* in its eddy. I had a feeling it was intentional, and that the creature wanted Madison and me in there as well.

I had to help. And judging by the anguished bellows still lifting to the air, I had to do it fast.

"Get back to the willow," I told Madison, barely shifting my eyeline to take in their crouching stance. I couldn't afford to let the monster out of my sight. It knew we were here, and any noticed inattention would give it opportunity to strike.

"I'm not leaving your side," Madison growled.

I knew they'd go down tooth and nail on the "great worm," but they'd still go down. I couldn't risk their life, not when just knowing me had gotten them into so much trouble already.

"If I don't make it out of this, I need you to carry on to Cernun and Learco," I pleaded, hoping my voice sounded as strong as I wanted it to despite its wavering crack. "You need to get the three of you home. Or, at the very least, let them know what happened."

The vortex was picking up in speed, the wails of the merrow along with it. Water sprayed against our bodies as the *Ollphéist* rose, splashing buckets at our feet, creating a storm of both the river and the air above us. Madison's hiss at the creature was nearly drowned out by the screams.

"Please, Mads," I tried again. "My magic is different here. I'm not sure how it'll strike when I unleash it."

Groaning in acquiescence, Madison twined my ankles before padding back toward the safety of the shore.

I touched the power clawing through my gut, pulling more of it into my consciousness. The longer I held it, the more it started to make sense to me. At least, I hoped that's what was happening. The vibrations were equalizing with my new place in this new world, steadying the more I accepted the change. As long as my magic followed my intent, I stood a fighting chance. Which was good because I definitely was in for a battle.

I focused on the violent swirl before me, attempting to find the pattern in its madness. I doubted I'd get more than one chance to hit the monster where it would hurt, and I needed to ensure as little collateral damage of the mer-folk I was trying to save as I could. If I was lucky, maybe I'd dislodge a scale or two from the creature for The Mórrígan's bargain before my magic sent it scurrying away, but that was the least of my current concerns.

Slowly, I raised my arm up, pulling it back like a pitcher, my fingers clutching the empty space where my yet-to-be-manifested orb would form. Power pulsed from my stomach to my mind before cascading through the veins in my arm. My fingers tingled. My head ached. My vision began to blur. I had to release the magic before it fried me from within. I just needed to figure out the *Ollphéist's* pattern, its rhythm, the way it moved to create the maelstrom.

The crimson of its fins bobbed and sank—at six and three; at nine and twelve—around the circle, punctuating the speed of its coil as it steadied the whirlpool's destructive pull. Okay. There it was. The push and pull, the swift and slow it needed to keep the *murúch* trained to its wake. Those Fae though, they were the random factor in the equation. Webbed fingers or toes or fins poked from the eddy at random as they struggled to free themselves. Distraught faces, throats still screaming from their gills, met the air as quickly as they were buried by the flood. If the sea dragon's intent was to discombobulate them, to play with its food before it tired them out so it could snack, it was certainly winning.

Trust yourself, Darragh. I heard my grandmother's words as clearly as if she had been there on the dock with me. *It's not your power. It's not your vision. It's you. When you thread the needle, you just need to trust that the yarn will go where it should.*

I could taste the blood as I bit my tongue, reeling back to throw the power from my grip. My magic manifested from my palm—virescent and ferocious—as I heaved the energy toward the monster. It struck the scales in a callous blast, just behind a florid expanse of the fins at its neck, and I exhaled from the force as a new screech joined with the merfolk's song. I heard my mind scream *more!* as a new wave of power traveled up from my gut. I wasn't sure if I had directed it or my magic was acting on its own, but I steeled myself as another push manifested from my palms to pelt the *Ollphéist* again.

This time the whirlpool wavered. I could see its walls becoming weak as the monster's movements reacted to my spell. Even if I couldn't kill it—I didn't want to kill it, did I?—I could at least break its hold to give the *murúch* a chance at survival. I braced myself for one more bolt as green lightning slid from my fingertips. My aim was true, and the vortex collapsed in a thunderous cascade as water rushed to fill the space it knew it belonged, to right its flow downstream.

I fell to my knees on the dock, my hands sore and spent against the rough, wet wood. Electricity still fizzled around me, and I could see every molecule of the air in neon yellow, swimming the sky before my eyes. I heaved as much air into my lungs as I could, gasping between each breath, as I attempted to equalize the force sent and the emptiness received by my body. A silence louder than the screams of the *murúch* filled my ears. The river fought to regain its autonomy. As did I.

"Darragh?" Madison's voice was low and far away, even as the blue of their fur singed into my line of sight.

"I'm okay," I panted.

The sound of my own voice helped to bring me back into myself, and I swallowed hard as I rose to my knees. Madison beamed as they sat before me, tail still twitching with excitement.

"That was fucking—" they started, eyes dancing as they studied me. "I've seen a lot of shit since I met you last year that I didn't think was real, but I ain't never seen something like that."

I'd never felt anything like it either. The Faerie Realm and Fae magic aside, before my battle with Samara Byrne, I'd never even considered a power manifestation of that caliber. And still this was something entirely different. Instead of pushing the power from me, it was as if the whole of my being was being pulled from inside of my veins, ready to do my will by whatever means necessary. It would have been intoxicating if it wasn't so damn exhausting. I could feel myself already wanting to recapture that feeling while simultaneously struggling to understand it.

But whatever it was, it worked. The river had smoothed and was beginning to undulate, its sea-like waves gaining traction as they rushed to meet the safety of the shore. It seemed so tranquil again, as if I hadn't tapped the recesses of my magic to battle a sea dragon only moments before.

I gasped as the water rose near the bank, pulling up to form a body before the thick tension of the water surface broke to reveal the elongated shape, the telescopic eyes of a fish head atop the broad shoulders and chiseled chest of a man. His arms stretched as the gills on either side of his neck flexed in the open air. Scarred over gashes from knife fights or boat rudders glistened—at once both paler and darker—across his skin to let him claim a rugged, weathered sexiness as he made his way to shore.

A second figure joined him, this one female presenting. Her flowing red hair and oval green eyes would have made her look like a witch if it weren't for the pointed elongation of her ears flecked with opalescent scales protruding above her high cheek bones. Her breasts were small and uncovered as she glided from the water, and the fish tail which started at her waist matched the green-purple-pink scaling of her ears.

As they reached the shore, their hands removed red, feathered caps from their heads which only became visible when they parted from their brows.

Madison and I were frozen as more and more of the *murúch* left the water, silent as they returned to their land-dwelling form and climbed the bank toward the dock. There were seven of them in total, but I was nearly certain I'd counted nine when they'd made their trek toward the water at first light. They did not speak, but I could feel their eyes on us as they tossed their caps into the barrel waiting at the land-side of the wharf and climbed back into the same grimy clothing they'd worn to work that morning. The minutes felt like an eternity as they dressed, blocking our access to the land, and I knew even the water at our backs would not be adequate for escape.

Shit. I hadn't really thought this through.

Finally, one of the merfolk stepped forward, and I scrambled to my feet.

"So 'twas you who fought the dragon kind, and shook the waters frightly."

As she spoke, a humming musicality built upon the air. The river quieted to her words.

"To save thine kin not at your side, before the beast could smite thee."

It was a song. Her brethren provided harmonies from the shore as she stepped along the wooden planks toward me. Of course the sirens would sing while they spoke. Their sea shanty jaunt to the shore made so much more sense now. I just hoped they didn't expect me to carry a note in return. As much as I loved to belt out an Aoife O'Connell song in the shower, I'd never been one to carry a tune. At least not well.

"It was the least we could do," I demurred.

"Great power held is magic told, though rivers swell and rivers fold, your triumph 'twas there to behold. You came upon us rightly."

Her body shimmered in the daylight, balancing her writhing limbs with a beautiful glimmer as she welcomed us. Her mates—the friendly kind, not the sexual kind, though I had no clue what they got up to at home—stayed back though, the joy of the gratitude in their song brimming under with a dirge for those they'd lost. It felt weird being serenaded, but I smiled and tried to nod along to their beat. It was a good thing my father loved to hum old sea songs when he worked the fields back home. Those memories provided a good basis for their rhythm.

"I'm glad I could help," I said, nearly picking up their lilt, but not wanting to throw them with my atonal tendencies. I considered using the opportunity of their praise to ask for one of their caps—it would have been nice to have at least one of The Mórrígan's items checked off my list—but decided it was better if they offered one as thanks so as not to introduce any possibilities of a bargain. Even though I'd saved their lives, I didn't trust the Fae to not leap at any chance to turn the tables. Besides, I could already hear it in my mind: *So what, fine soldier, fair and true may we the* murúch *give to you?* Or something like that.

As I mused, the lead mermaid's face paled. Her song stopped suddenly, the music of the ether with it, and the gasps of her accompaniment crescendoed even as they backed away on the shore. A shadow crept over the docks from behind me, casting out the warmth of the day like the wet wind of Winter, like an eclipse come to forever block the sun.

At my feet, Madison growled even as they wound my legs for protection, and I slowly turned back toward the water. The *Ollphéist* rose from just beyond the dock, towering into the air as the water leapt from its sides.

It was massive.

It was angry.

It was looking straight at me.

CHAPTER 13

When Death was staring me in the eye, it was really quite beautiful. There was a peace which came in its knowing, a brief moment of acceptance where lifetimes of doubt and uncertainty melted away and only that moment, that great state of power was left to entertain. In less than a year, I'd faced Death more times than I could count on my fingers, yet I'd always out-maneuvered it. I'd always managed some trick, some spell just this side of the witching hour that saved me, or at least bought me a little more time. This time, I didn't think I'd be so lucky.

The *Ollphéist* was enormous. Its muzzle spanned the sky above me, as wide as the downtown connector, with flaring nostrils keeping tempo as its red fins splayed around its head. Anger teetered just this side of hunger as its yellow eyes bore down upon me, sizing me up as the minnow I was in its gaze. The scales where its darker underbelly gave way to the brilliant green of its body were nearly the size of my hand; those along its back, the size of my torso. The river water cascading off of it seemed as anxious to get away from its power as I was. Everything was in slow motion.

"Well, shit," I heard Madison growl from my ankles.

The silence left as the *murúch* ceased their song was almost as ominous as the wheezing hiss of the *Ollphéist's* breath. I reached inside of myself to try to grab hold of any sliver of power I had left. It was sparse, but it was something. Still, I knew it wasn't nearly enough.

"Get back to the shore," I whispered, urging Madison to dry land. There was no sense in both of us dying for my inability to not get involved.

I trembled as the monster opened its mouth. Baleen, like those of a blue whale, hung like bristles from the ridges of its jaw. At least they weren't the sharpened fangs I'd been expecting. Though I assumed they would be just as dangerous.

The Mórrígan's amulet pulsed at my hip, and I let my hand drop to the tattered sweater that was holding it there. *One use,* she'd warned me. Staring down the gullet of a sea dragon seemed like one hell of an opportune time. But if Balor found me later, the torment he'd have in store for me for managing to escape him thrice would be unbearable. No, the amulet was a last ditch effort. I'd have to survive this on my own.

The *Ollphéist* hissed as it arched forward, slamming its gaping maw toward the dock. I tumbled backwards just in time to escape, clinging to the planks of wood as the end of the dock splintered and went under with the beast. I huffed away the inner cries of *what the fuck are you doing?!?* as my brain once again tried to reprimand my instinct. Instinct was what was going to get me through this. Instinct and magic.

Drawing a deep breath and holding it, I dove into the water. My power may have been mostly spent, but at least I had adrenaline going for me. Plus the element of surprise if I managed to attack before the beast could rear its ugly head once more.

The water was cold, yet surprisingly clear, and the rush of the dragon's body created an undercurrent which pulled me toward it. Grasping securely to one of its red fins, I planted my feet firmly against its back.

Just like riding a horse, I told myself. *A wild, bucking, no way to tame, trying to throw me from its back horse. Oh, and underwater. No big deal.*

I could only hope it stayed in the general vicinity instead of hauling me off to Fae-knows-where within the river. But it had set its sights on me and the *murúch*, so I figured it wouldn't take off until it was full, dead, or wounded. Whichever came first.

My palms burned against the monster's fin, and I realized the red I was seeing wasn't just its flare, but my own blood. Shit! I'd chummed the water. But that also gave me an idea. I picked a singular spot behind the fin and twisted with my feet. It probably would have been easier if I were still wearing my boots, but I had to work with what I had. And I had to work fast. I wouldn't be able to hold my breath forever. My chest burned as I directed all my force through my legs, willing just one scale—which, to be fair, was the size of a knight's shield—to be freed from the creature. If it was half as sharp as the fin I was clinging on to, I'd at least have some means of attack, and perhaps the perfect place to strike.

My blood in the water sent the great worm into a frenzy, and I nearly lost my grip as it whipped back and forth to find the source. The scale was loosening though. I could feel it. I just needed to…

The *Ollphéist* rose from the water once more, and I took the opportunity to catch my breath. Madison's brown eyes were wide as they watched me from the shore, huddled at the feet of the remaining merfolk who had miraculously not fled. When I was done with this, I was still going to need a hat from them.

"Darragh? What the fuck?" they bellowed.

I must have been a thing to behold: clenching my fists to the creature as blood streamed down my arms, my feet dancing against its back to gain purchase as it rose into the air.

"I've got this," I called. "I think."

That was the wrong thing to do. Before it heard my voice, I was just some debris, some barnacle clinging to its scaly surface. Now, it knew where I was. And it wasn't happy to have a traveler on board.

Instead of lurching forward as I'd expected, the *Ollphéist* shook, coiling through its body to slam backwards to the water's surface in hopes of knocking me off. With the mass of its body though, the shift could not occur quickly, which gave me enough time to take a leap of faith.

As we fell, I released the fin, palms aching as air met the gashes there, and clasped hold of the scale my feet had loosened. It was as keen as I'd expected, and the new cuts joined the old in a pain that was as sharp as it was dull. But it worked! The weight of my body was enough to free the scale from the *Ollphéist*, and I held it above me as I plummeted to the river.

My feet hit the water first, kicking hard to escape the expanse where the creature would fall. I held the scale before me at arm's length, using it to cut through the water and trying not to let it cut me any more than it already had. Ten feet is a lot of water to tread when the swimmer is unsure where they're going. When they can't use their arms, and the currents of the river are just as confused as them. But instinct had taken over completely, and there was still enough magic in me to beg the water for guidance.

I heard it before I felt it: the boom of the monster crashing to the surface followed by the great rush of flood waters that plunged me in its wake. I waited for the waters to equalize before I thrust my way toward the surface. I couldn't believe it had worked! I couldn't believe I still had the scale! Now all I needed to do was make it to shore before the scale's owner had me.

I gasped as my head broke water, so happy to see the sky, even if it was turquoise, and I was still trapped in the Faerie Realm. I spun my head to find the shore. Fuck. I'd gotten turned around during my plummet and swam the wrong way in my escape. But my head was above water, and the water was quiet. Hopefully, the beast had retreated like a wounded puppy, and I'd be able to dog paddle my way to the bank with one of The Mórrígan's quest items in tow.

I winced as I tucked the scale beneath my arm, keeping it tight against my side and angled like a dorsal fin to slice the water as my right arm pulled me across the surface. I was tired and bleeding, but it could have been so much worse. I was certain I'd think differently when the adrenaline wore off and my mind could actually process the pain, but I was just happy that something had actually gone my way for once in this Fae-forsaken land.

It was no wonder every Fae I'd met was so desperate for a way back into our world. If this was the wildlife they had to contend with, even the terrors of the Moral Authority of Witches with their cells and their flames didn't hold a candle. Of course, with their trickery and the bargains, a lot of witches would say that the Fae had brought their fates onto themselves. But then again, a lot of humans said the same thing about the rage against witch-kind.

I was halfway to shore when I felt it, a sudden shift in the water's directionality, a cloying warmth beneath the cold. The sky went dark, the water darker. My legs pushed hard against the stream. My free hand clawed at the water, begging for grip as I pulled myself forward. I closed my eyes as I realized it was not a change in the weather that had darkened the world but the *Ollphéist*. It skimmed the water, its great maw opened and bearing down on me.

And then there was silence.

It was dark and wet and hollow inside the *Ollphéist's* mouth, but I was grateful I'd managed to snag hold of one of the keratin bristles of its baleen as it attempted to swallow me whole. Even with its mouth closed, I was able to stand upright, and I tried not to move so it wouldn't notice me atop its fleshy, bumpy tongue. The swishing of its gills a few yards back created a soothing, trancelike tone, but this was no time to relax. One wrong move and I'd be engulfed by the acid of its belly. One direction held certain death, the other the baleen bars of a jail cell. But I'd escaped a cell before. Okay, maybe not willingly or of my own accord, but the Changeling's kidnapping of me from the MAW's holding cell had definitely shown me one thing: sometimes we had to make our own way out.

I remembered my grandmother's stories of the Fae of old, of the warriors and the hunters and the Christian co-opted saints who'd traveled the lakes and rivers of Ireland to rid them of their snakes. They'd used their swords or their pipes or their prayers to work from the inside out. There was no reason I couldn't do so too.

Timidly, I released my hold on the bristle and clutched the scale I'd procured firmly with both hands. I felt its edges carefully, finding the sharpened point of it, and angled it down. If I was lucky, the impact of the cut would make the creature spit me out. If I wasn't, the sudden spasm of its tongue would send me toward the roof of its mouth, and I'd have no choice but to work my way out by moving up. I wished for the first option, but had a feeling it was going to be the second.

The scale pierced the meaty mound of its tongue cleanly, and a sudden waft of pain and bile filled the air around me. Its tongue, thick and solid, rose toward the offending object, and I quickly pulled the scale free and flipped it above my head. As I'd hoped, it broke through the roof of its mouth, tearing flesh and bone in its wake. Gagging, I pulled myself through behind it, calling on the last bit of my power to save me, willing some of it was still there to be accessed. Blood and flaky muscle cascaded around me as its cut tongue continued to reach upwards in an attempt to rid its body of the parasite I'd become. I held my breath and closed my eyes while I pressed through the sinew and bone. I didn't think I'd ever be able to eat sushi again.

Suddenly, I felt a warmth that wasn't blood upon my face, and I opened my eyes to find my torso pushed through to the top of the *Ollphéist's* muzzle. Its yellow eyes crossed when it saw me, anger overcoming the agony of me boring through its mouth with its own scale. Its blood was black against my skin and pooled across its snout in waves. It gushed like a waterfall toward the river below us. I felt the wavering lilt as blood loss overtook bloodlust in the creature, and we wobbled back toward its sanctuary beneath the surface.

I refused to let go of the scale as I pulled myself free of its body and found my footing on its snout. We were near the surface now. There was a chance it would swim away to nurse its wounds, but I could tell as I looked into the frightened terror of its eyes that it was not one to simply slip away.

"I'm sorry," I said, and I honestly meant it as I charged forward, ramming the scale between the folds of two others at the center of its eyes.

Its roar cut short as I pierced through to its brain, and its eyes glazed over when I pulled the scale free, using it to stay afloat as the *Ollphéist* sank beneath me. The water turned a crimson red all around me, batting its unnatural darkness against the turquoise sky.

But it was calm once more. As dead as the great worm sinking to its depths.

"Ho-Ly-Shit!"

Madison's awe carried through the staccato cadence of their words as I pulled myself ashore, tossing the *Ollphéist* scale a few feet away and collapsing onto the clover. My lungs heaved to bring in the clean air of the land, and I felt grateful for as many points of contact with the earth as I could have.

"You killed it," they said.

"I did," I winced.

The first rule of witchcraft, at least the first rule of *my* witchcraft was "and it harm none." I mean, sure, I enjoyed a good burger from Aunt Paulina's, but I really tried to live by that principle. It felt strange—willfully taking a life. But it had been the creature's or mine. That had to count for something, right?

"The *Ollphéist* can't be killed, brave sir…"

I opened my eyes at the *murúch's* words to find her and all her kin staring down at me.

"The water heals its wounds, to regenerate just as it were, and swell with the monsoon."

Again with the singing. But at least I hadn't actually taken a life. That was something. Still, if it was healing, we needed to get the hell out of dodge before it came back!

Exhausted but with a new surge of adrenaline, I scrambled to my feet, reaching for the scale and standing at the ready. The merfolk chuckled, their laughter a harmony of chords that was as enchanting as it was rattling.

"The time moves slow where water flows, and months and years move by, where we'll find freedoms in the sea all safely by and by."

I relaxed a bit and let the scale fall back to the ground. Interpreting their songs was a little much when I just wanted directness. But in my experience, none of the Fae were that great at being direct. At least my first boyfriend in high school had fancied himself a poet so I'd had a lot of practice in discerning meaning from too many florid words.

"Does everything have to be a sea shanty?" I asked, and the *murúch* erupted in another cacophonous symphony of laughter.

"I guess we're living in a musical," Madison grinned. "I mean, I suppose it kind of makes sense for this world."

I smiled. At least the merfolk were beautiful to look at. Up close, their skin sparked with iridescence as the sun created prisms of their faint, barely noticeable scales. Lean muscles carved their forms, and the flames of their hair licked at the sky as if they were still suspended in water. Too, their eyes! Wide as a lighthouse beam, they reflected all the serenity, all the sharp danger, all the life of a coral reef within a pearlescent sheen. I could easily become hypnotized my them. It was no wonder the stories of them from our world had sailors routing their ships into rocks just to get close to their grace.

Their leader pursed her lips as she looked me over, and I grimaced as I clasped my palms together. I was a mess compared to them, even on a good day when I hadn't been battling a mythic beast. But at least my trek to the shore had washed the bulk of the monster's innards away. My touch burned with the flow of blood still streaming from the gashes left by the *Ollphéist's* scale. Where my hair wasn't matted to my forehead, it was sticking out and wild in the wind. Dried blood, both my own and the sea monster's, clung to my bare torso which was not nearly as defined as any of the merfolk's. My pants had ripped during the battle, probably snagged on the sharp edge of one of the creature's shattered bones as I pulled myself through the roof of its mouth, and the remaining fabric flopped lazily beneath my knee. I was sure my face was gaunt, my eyes hollow—from hunger or the expulsion of power I'd used—and my smile crooked and forced. My bare toes fidgeted nervously against the clover.

The mer-leader grinned broadly as she hummed—a soaring, jubilant tune that tickled the air around my ears—and one of her brethren stepped forward. Like her, he was ever more handsome the closer he got, and he bowed his head slightly as he reached out for my hands. His fingers were strong, and the webbing between them pulsed with light as he touched me, opening my palms and laying his firmly on mine. His song joined his leader's, and my eyes fell to the flex of his pecs as a magic pooled there, traveling down the bulge of his biceps and forearms to meet my wounds. My nipples went hard, perking to attention as he moved his power over me. Though that was probably the wind slipping off the cool waters of the river and not the touch of a gorgeous Fae.

"The healing waters of thy river," he sang, "guided by the ebb and flow, shall cleanse the wounds of thy, the giver of the vanquishment of mine own foe."

Damn, his voice was sultry. Maybe being serenaded wasn't actually all that bad.

My palms tingled in his grip, and, when he pulled away, not even a scar remained where my heart lines and head lines had been wounded. Now that was a power I wouldn't mind having. But, even if my magic somehow worked in the Faerie Realm, I had a feeling this use was something unique to the *murúch*, guided by their sole connection to and understanding of the waters that flowed through the land.

Between their healing powers and the *Ollphéist's*—albeit beleaguered—rejuvenation abilities, I was a bit concerned by what The Mórrígan wanted with their cap and scale. But that, like all things Fae, was a problem for another day.

"Thank you," I smiled.

"Now, let us feast!" he cried.

Of course, there was more to it than that. But that's what the verses whittled down to. And both my and Madison's hunger stopped us from really hearing anything beyond the offer of food.

Madison and I watched in wonder as the merfolk went to work, singing and dancing as they moved. Their bodies as if choreographed—a few of them working to build a fire pit on the shoreline as others donned their caps to dive into the river to find our meal. It sure beat fishing with a shoestring. Seeing the way their bodies transformed as their skin met the already clear water, gliding effortlessly from Fae to fish, was astonishing. I could feel the freedom of it in the air. It was the same freedom I'd felt using old Fae magic to transform into a hare—the same magic that had transformed Madison into a feline. My face fell as I looked at them, watching the scene intently from beside me.

"It's okay," they purred, sensing the heartbreak that had overcome me. "I'll get back to my witch self someday. For now, I just hope they have something like salmon and not dead *Ollphéist* meat."

I laughed. I could always count on Madison to bright side things. Despite their anarchist rebellion, a hopeful gleam lived beneath their electric blue fur. Or maybe it was because of their rebellious spirit that their hope for a better future stayed close to their heart.

I blushed as two of the male *murúch* approached and took my hands. Fuck, they were sexy! The fire roaring on the shore, they now tasked themselves with me, leading me to the water to cleanse the dried blood and bits of sea worm from my hair. I shuddered as their hands caressed my skin, feeling almost holy as their webbed fingers carried fresh water to my head and torso. My face fell back, and a slight moan escaped my lips, but they didn't seem to mind. They worked slowly, meticulously covering every curve of my body. Their breaths warmed the water before they made me new. The song of it—flowing from the current to their lips and then to me—gave the whole of the ritual an erotic, spiritual charge. That was another feeling I could get used to. Maybe the Fae Realm wasn't so bad after all.

I kicked myself for even thinking that. Every single time I had during my stay in that strange world, something had appeared to prove me wrong. Hell, for all I knew, they were preparing me for their stew. But the *murúch* smiled, returned me to the shore, and left me watching on with Madison as they carefully stacked the smoothed rocks of the river bed above the fire to create a natural grill.

When the others returned from the depths, they fed us fish that they splayed with only their hands, grilled ever so slightly atop the fire. We slurped down raw oysters they shucked with a twist of their wrists. And the slightly charred kelp they insisted we try had a lemony zest beneath its brine.

Damn, it felt good to have something in my stomach, to have a moment not preoccupied by watching my back. It almost felt like a celebration—or at least a party of some sort—but I had a feeling this was how they'd have entertained themselves even if Madison and I had not been their guests. There was a frivolity behind their eyes as wild as the ocean's depths. We laughed, and they sang. And, once we'd had our fill, I thanked them for their generosity, but they demurred.

"A warrior come from lands afar, with magics unknown by the sea. And though we don't know who thou are, we cherish our time with thee."

There it was again, that strange insistence that I was something different and unknown since my witch magic worked in the realm. I didn't think I was the first witch to ever have power here. But it had probably been centuries since another of our kind had come through these lands. So if an epic sea shanty was in order, sang and passed down through generations of merfolk, then who was I to judge? We witches had made the Fae into the heroes and villains of many an epic tale. I figured a witch deserved one too. At least one where they weren't luring kids into ovens or stealing babies for a sacrifice. I was flattered to hear them making one about me.

A part of me wanted to stay there forever, on that shore, listening to their music as the troubles of land were smoothed and rounded by the sea. The sun was getting low, though, and if night came on as quickly as it had the day before, Madison and I needed to get moving before it hit. The *murúch* had been so kind, but from what my grandmother had told me of the sirens, it was too easy to lose track of time with them. We had my boyfriends—and our lives back in our world—to save.

I puttered along the edges of our circle as I tried to rally myself for goodbyes. It felt a bit like leaving a party before the birthday candles had even been lit, but time was ticking and bargains wouldn't fulfill themselves. Or maybe my anxiety was because I still needed something.

I hated to ask for more from them, but I still had to obtain one of their red feathered caps to fulfill my bargain with The Mórrígan. I didn't even know if it was possible to get one. Those things only appeared while in their grip, vanished when they placed them atop their heads, and disappeared once again when they dropped them into their barrel for safekeeping. That was certainly a foolproof way to prevent them from falling into the wrong hands. I bit my lip as I thought about how to even ask for one.

"Uh… Darragh?" Madison called from my side as I hemmed and hawed over what to say. "Where's the amulet?"

My hand clutched to my thigh. Shit! The amulet was gone, my tattered sweater with it. It must have come untied when I was fighting the *Ollphéist*. Which meant that it, along with our one get out of jail free card, was resting on the riverbed with the worm's regenerating corpse. And that was the best case scenario. Otherwise, it was somewhere along the worm's digestive tract.

Fuck! How could I have been so stupid?

"That which thou lost lies underneath, where treasures often go," the *murúch* leader sang, walking to the barrel at the dock and pulling forth a red feathered cap. "The magics here shall help you breathe and mind the water's flow."

My jaw gaped. She was offering me one of their hats! Perhaps my luck was changing after all. Though I was not excited about swimming to the bottom of the river, I now had two of the three items The Mórrígan had requested. Not bad for a day's work.

"Uh… Can I use it?"

My brow furrowed as I turned to Madison, softening as I took in the hopeful tremor in their eyes.

"I mean, even if I'm just a catfish for a minute, it could be enough to re-trigger some of the cells in my body toward change. You know, when the powers align and all that."

I raised my eyebrow to the mermaid, and she smiled as she nodded. As she knelt, the cap resized itself in her hands to fit atop Madison's feline head. Its cardinal red looked exquisite against their electric blue fur. They purred happily as they padded to the broken end of the dock, stopping there to turn and blink their eyes at me.

"Wait!" Madison's paws trembled beneath them, the feline aversion to the water heavy in their limbs. "Is there a spell or something to recite?"

The *murúch* leader's laughter crashed like gentle rain against the sea, filling the air with the stunning frivolity of more.

"Thou holds to beauty in thine mind," she cooed, "and sing the waters to thy side."

Madison blinked as they looked to me for encouragement. I saw the action behind their eyes as they tried to capture what was beautiful. I smiled and nodded as they leapt into the river, letting out a breath I had not even realized I was holding.

"Take care, brave warrior," the murúch leader smiled, touching my arm and speaking instead of singing for the first time. "I pray that you and your companion find what you are searching for."

The merfolk departed quickly, traveling back the way we'd seen them come this morning, chanting a more mournful version of the sea songs they'd traveled in with. I watched them leave for a moment, my heart breaking for those they'd lost—for those I could not save—before turning back to face the water. I was determined not to lose any of my loved ones to the Fae Realm, no matter what it had in store for me. I'd fought a sea beast and survived! I was certain I could get us home.

CHAPTER 14

The vermilion orb of the sun looked especially peaceful as it made its way across the turquoise sky toward the horizon. I sat beside the dwindling fire left behind by the *murúch*, my stomach finally full, watching the calm dips of the river for any sign of Madison. The *Ollphéist* scale made a great seat against the rocky sand, and I pulled my knees close to my chin as I did my best to breathe away the battle of the day. My magic was still a bit spiky inside me, but I could feel it beginning to recover from the blasts I'd sent forth. Even in my own world, impulse magic was funny that way. Sure, there was always intent behind the power—that's what made it work—but without at least a little bit of forethought, the parameters of the spell were always tinged with the fire of too much gone too soon. It was always risky; always painful. But the sea monster had called for it. And it had worked!

"I figured I would find you here. Where's your *cat si*?"

I leapt to my feet, pulling the scale up with me, and brandishing it before me like a shield. Luckily, its time detached from the body had made the edges less cutting. That or the *murúch's* healing magic was still working.

"What do you want, Síl?" I asked, my energy suddenly alert

and prickling my extremities. "Here to lie to me again? Or lead me to Balor to collect whatever reward he's put on my head for yourself?"

Síl chuckled as he crossed his arms over his chest. His cloven feet pawed at the clover, but he didn't venture toward the pebbles of the small shore beach. I imagined they'd be hell on his hooves. That gave me some ground at least, though I was sure he'd trod the rocks if he had to.

"Are we speaking of lies?" he smirked. "Tell me, Darragh Cullen, witch of the other world, how we should approach untruths? Or do you still prefer 'Dan'? Even 'witch' may be a stretch, though I will give you that as you know no better."

He paced the clover a few feet from me, hands clasped behind his back, his fuzzy pecs jumping to punctuate each word. He was still wearing pants, thankfully, but had traded the brown tweed of the pair he'd materialized before for an oak leaf green that looked amazing beside the brownish red of his pelt. His little billy goat beard curled across his chin, and the horns of his upper forehead appeared more prominent than before. He may not have been the Great Horned King, but he was one sexy satyr. And that would have been astonishing enough for me at our first meet.

I pushed aside the innate carnality of his being to train my mind on the present. He was right that we'd both fibbed a bit, but I still wasn't ready to trust him.

"You can drop your weapon," he said, stopping suddenly to look me in the eye and holding his hands up in surrender. "I mean you no harm. In truth, this time on my honor, I never would have taken you to the Wayward Inn had I known who you were. The Fomóraiġ give all our kind a bad reputation, Balor worst of all. But we are not each of us quite so... demented as he. Or his offspring."

I shivered as I recalled Fachan, the monstrosity of his form. He had held a beauty like the one inherent in all Fae, but the large, singular eye he'd inherited from his father held all the madness and anger of his sire. Though, I supposed I'd have been vexed as well if my only arm jumped from the center of my chest. And I did have to give it Síl. The moment Fachan made me, he'd encouraged me to run, tripped my pursuer, and created enough of a diversion to allow Madison and I to escape.

I lowered the scale but not my guard, keeping them both in a fist at my side.

"So, Darragh Cullen." He said my name with the same sense of savoring all the Fae who knew it did. It was kind of unnerving, though it also made me feel special. Important. Maybe that's why they did it. "Where is your companion?"

"They, uh… They've gone for a swim."

Síl smiled, nodding as he peered across the undulation of the water. There was a longing within him I hadn't noticed before. It made him almost endearing.

"I suppose we will have to wait for them then," he said, crossing his legs beneath him and gliding seamlessly to the ground. "You may stay where you are if you still fear my presence."

My mouth twisted as my brow furrowed, my face ever unable to hide the thoughts that paraded through my mind. I sighed as I made my way to the greenery, sitting a few paces to Síl's right, and keeping the *Ollphéist* scale on mine. Darkness was beginning to crow its way across the sky, though it seemed to approach more slowly than the night before, and I wet my lips as I returned my gaze to the water. I hoped Madison would return soon, amulet in paw, and we could set off to cover. Then to Cernun and Learco.

"I see you lost your shirt and half your pant leg," Síl said casually. "Is this an attempt to emulate my style?"

I laughed. It came harder and faster than I expected—I guessed I needed it after the day I'd had—and Síl's chuckle twined with it to ease the air around us.

"So I am not Cernunnos, and you are not Dan. I suppose that also means your companion is not Mason," he said. "What shall I call them upon their return?"

"Their name is theirs to tell," I smirked. "But yes, you can call me Darragh."

Síl nodded, a wicked gleam in his eye at being caught, but enough humility there to show me he didn't mean any harm. At least, not in that moment.

"How did a witch who is not really a witch named Darragh Cullen wind up in the Faerie Realm?"

"Changeling," I shrugged, and Síl nodded. "Why do you keep insisting I'm not really a witch?"

He pursed his lips as he looked at me, eyes swimming over my flesh as if he were considering every cell individually, trying to ascertain the whole of my parts. It was both uncomfortable and strangely erotic, and I fought the urge to shift away from his stare.

"Perhaps the better phrase would be not *merely* a witch," he said.

It was my turn to scrunch my lips. I wanted to follow up, but I didn't think I'd get anything else out of him. Besides, the way his attention turned to the water told me the conversation had met its end.

I let my eyes follow, though still kept him like a ghost in the corner of my eye. I felt easier with him, perhaps because he'd stopped putting on airs, but I wasn't about to be blindsided by another Faerie. The waves were calmer now, jutting ever so slightly, as the dusk took hold to show the river its true course.

In my world, the moon would have heightened the water's activity, calling the nocturnal dwellers forth to splash in the cooling currents, bringing the waves higher in their reach to touch its power. Maybe the waters weren't as affected by the moon here as they were in our world. Or perhaps, with the merfolk returned to their earthly dwellings, their hold on the river was dissipating.

It was peaceful though. Living in Atlanta, despite all its trees, the real rivers were interstates and highways, teeming with SUVs and the MAWs black sedans instead of fish and barnacles. It felt nice to be somewhere so wholly natural, even in its unnaturalness compared to what I was used to. I felt like I was hiking in Sweetwater National Park, stopping by the old mill ruins to appreciate the shallow waters. Or maybe taking that long dreamed of and too often not pursued trip up to the Blue Ridge Mountains, cuddling on the big porch of some OccultList B&B, and watching the parts of nature that hadn't co-opted to human life just yet. I wished Cernun and Learco were with me. I hoped they were noticing the beauty as well as they waited for me from their vantage point downstream.

The water broke about fifteen feet from the shore, splashing out to reveal Madison's smiling face. Their electric blue dreadlocks billowed like a crown, and the ruddy black of their skin glistened in the burnt ginger of the setting sun. Damn, it was good to see their face again! Their real face, not the Changeling one.

From what I could see, the *murúch's* red feathered cap had transformed them from feline to witch once more. Their large, brown eyes gleamed with excitement. Their joyful grin danced beneath the flattened bulb of their nose. They raised their eyebrows as they caught sight of the satyr sitting beside me. I shrugged, and they shook their head before they began to pull themselves toward the shore.

"You and your strays," they gasped between strokes as they swam closer.

Síl gave an exaggerated grumble, but the amusement in his eyes told me he wasn't upset. In truth, Madison had been a stray themself, even before their feline form. When we met, they had fan-theyed out over me—one of the supposed perks, according to Cernun at least, of being the witch who exposed magic to the human world—and their bold energy alongside the sense of queer otherness we shared had pulled them into my orbit and shop. Plus, now that Angel was gone, brutally murdered by Balor's last attempt to enter our world, they were more a stray than ever.

Cernun had been a stray too, so to speak. He'd told me time and again how being with me was the first time he'd ever truly felt family.

Even Learco, despite his wealthy upbringing and being the leader of the Fae-damned Southeastern Division of the Moral Authority of Witches—well, former leader—didn't quite fit in with his fellow agents—well, former agents—and often felt out of place. Except with us. Though the pull between his duty and his love had caused its fair share of discordance too. Maybe that was a bright side of the Changeling ruining his career.

Madison paused as the water shallowed, tossing the amulet to me, and frowning at the shore.

"So I found the amulet," they said. "Real gross job you did on that dragon, by the way. I'm also not a cat anymore, so there's that too. I don't suppose you brought any extra clothes with you on our little journey, did you?"

"I wouldn't be half naked if I had," I sighed. Then added, "Okay, maybe I would," to their raised eyebrows.

"I might be able to help with that," Síl smiled, scrambling to his feet as the orange glow of his magic began to move around him. He had conjured his own shorts out of nowhere. And maybe a little bit of help from him after the trap he'd led us into would be a good thing.

Madison's brow furrowed as a sudden realization crept across their face. They'd have to take the cap off when they came ashore. And there was no guarantee they wouldn't immediately revert back to their feline form. I understood it as soon as they did, and it crushed me.

"Do you… do you feel any of your power?" I asked, stepping closer to the waterline and leaving the scale and amulet behind next to Síl. He was trying hard to make amends. I was sure he wouldn't abscond with them. "If you're like me, if something's there, then you may have the right combination of witch and Fae magic needed to make the transition permanent. "

"No," they sighed, shaking their head as they watched their reflection in the water. "My magic's not there. I mean, it is, I just can't access it. Not like you can."

I frowned, tapping the edge of the water with my toe as I searched my mind for any way to make things better for them. I'd been doing research—both me and Learco had—but all the transmogrification spells we could find required both witch power and a "lost" magic we now knew was that of the Fae. It was ironic that we had one or the other. Worse still that we'd have to find a way to un-banish all of their kind in order to have both.

"Keep the hat," I said.

Madison shook their head. "You need it for The Mórrígan's bargain. Besides, it's mermaid magic. It only works when I'm in the water anyway."

"I know," I insisted. "But you can swim downstream to Cernun and Learco. And that'll give you a bit more time as yourself. I don't need the hat until we're all reunited anyway."

I hated the idea of losing my companion for the trip through the Fae Realm, but I hated the idea of Madison losing their body again even more. At least with the *Ollphéist* gone—for now anyway—they'd be safer in the water than they were on land. And with Balor looking for me, I didn't want the soul he'd tried to take that had necessitated their feline transformation in the first place to get caught in the crossfire.

"I'll keep him safe," Síl promised Madison, still unwilling to let his hooves hit the rocky sand.

We both turned to him in question.

"I think it's much more likely that Darragh will keep you safe," Madison snapped. Then, to me, they added softly, "You sure about this?"

I nodded firmly, even though my face told a different story. It would be good to give Madison some more time to kick their legs. And I could handle Síl. I wasn't so sure about what else the Faerie world had in store for me, but my power was slowly beginning to bristle inside my belly once again. I'd figure it out. I always did. Somehow.

I walked back to the clover to retrieve the amulet and the scale, then waded slowly into the water to present them both to my friend.

"Take these with you," I said. "If I don't make it, you'll have the amulet to call The Mórrígan to you. And two of the items for my bargain. That may be enough to convince her to get the three of you back into our world. I think the third was just to odd the evens anyway."

They started to protest, but stopped as I shook my head firmly. The amulet sparkled against their chest, and they nodded as they slipped the scale beneath their arm.

"You're going to make it," they said, wrapping their free arm around my neck and pulling me tight against them. "You're Darragh Cullen, dammit. The guy who exposed magic, the MAW be damned. The *Ollphéist* slayer. The witch who already saved my life from a mad fucking Faerie. We'll wait for you. Just get there fast."

I smiled as I pulled back from their embrace, watching in awe as they shifted their form and dove into the deeper waters. They'd made it sixty feet in a flash, and rose as a silhouette against the darkening sky to wave before disappearing once more.

It would be night soon, and I hoped Síl had something other than the Wayward Inn in mind to keep us both safe from the *Dullahan* and the other Creatures of the Night. The daylight dwellers were hard enough to deal with.

"So you really slayed the *Ollphéist*, huh?" Síl asked as I sloshed back to shore. "Not merely a witch indeed."

I felt lighter without The Mórrígan's amulet. Not that it was particularly heavy. I mean, it was garish, and weighted, and definitely not my style; but despite the safety net it offered of getting her to my side in aide, the thought of it on its way to keep Learco, Cernun, and Madison safe made me feel a hundred times better. Especially since I was the only one of my coven with magic in this realm.

Síl had manifested a pair of laces to replace the ones I'd lost during my fishing adventure for my boots, but hadn't offered to pull a shirt out of the ether for me. I thought he liked that our outfits matched as we trudged along in the darkness. Plus, the air was remarkably warm, even in the absence of light, and he'd assured me we "wouldn't need shirts" where we were going. I kept pace beside him through the scent of him—natural, and foul, but still strangely alluring—and my eyes slowly began to adjust to the blackness. He hadn't summoned another lantern, and I didn't want to ask for one. Somehow, not being able to see where we were going made me feel safer.

"So," I started, making small talk in hopes of easing some on the tension in the air, "what happened after we left the Wayward

Inn?"

Síl grunted, but did not break his step. I felt his eyes on me, but could not make out his face.

"I mean," I tried again, "did Fachan give you any trouble?"

"The Fachan," Síl corrected me. "It's his name, and his race. Both. They're all called Fachan, and they're all Fachans. Sad little existence. Anyway, he tried. But rule number one of the Wayward Inn is that the obligations and duties of our leaders are left at the coat check. So he really didn't have a leg to stand on."

"Especially after you kicked it out from under him."

Síl laughed at my joke, a hearty, rumbling noise that filled the air in echoes even after it subsided. I wasn't sure why he had taken a liking to me, or even why he'd come back to find me, but—now that we were both being ourselves, or at least a truer version thereof—I was starting to feel a sort of kinship with him. Or, at the very least, a bit of trust.

"Well, I should thank you for helping us escape," I said when his laughter trailed away.

"Oh, you will."

I could hear the smirk in his voice, and I stiffened, even as his palm reached out to clasp my arm and make me shiver. His cadence and caress made it seem he was joking, but I wasn't so sure. I was never sure of anything when it came to the Faeries.

"The Fae leaders. They pretty much control everything here, huh?" I asked, still trying to sound casual as I pried him for information. "I mean, the Fachan are beholden to Balor. The Changelings are the charges of Echo. I'm certain every crow I see reports back to The Mórrígan. And, I suppose, you do the will of Cernunnos."

"I do the will of no god," Síl snapped. "But you are mostly correct in your observations. The Fae leaders—the Tuath Dé and the Fomóraig—the good and the bad, although, if you ask me, put them in a pot and stir and no one can tell the difference—control these lands, divided as they are, to their own purposes. Most Fae you come across are the children of those leaders, born to do the bidding of their bearers in some form or other. As for me and my allegiances, let us just say, when it came to Cernunnos, I had an issue with authority and leave it at that."

I nodded, assuming he could see my reaction despite my obliviousness to his own. But I understood now, both about the Fae Realm and about the camaraderie I felt with the satyr. I had a great relationship with my family, but I knew I was lucky in that respect. And I had developed a healthy mistrust of absolute authority at a very early age. Politicians, preachers, and Moral Authority agents all fell squarely onto that list. Growing up in the South, that had sometimes made me feel like an outsider. Adding queerness and witchcraft to the mix had doubled down on it. Síl's ostracization from his family, whether self-imposed or having been cast out, must've have been what was lowering my guard and drawing me to him. Hell, it was what had drawn me to both Cernun and Learco too. Me "and my strays."

"I guess the Fae elders are as popular with the rest of you as they are with the witches," I laughed.

"Depends on the faction," Síl shrugged, turning suddenly and leaving me scrambling to follow his voice.

It was obvious he was done with our conversation, but I wasn't finished pressing.

"I just—," I said, settling in beside him once more, "I figure if I'm going to be stuck in this strange new world, I should know something about how it works."

Síl stopped, turning to face me, the orange rage of his magic swirling in his eyes. Despite his fury, not at me but at something long ago, there was a sorrow tinged within the swirl of his power. It hung there, embroidered to the edges of his being, like it was the only thing he had left to replace something majestic he had lost. I felt its sadness—the only overwhelming light in that blackness of night—like it was a spell in and of itself.

"You want to make sense of the Fae Realm?" he growled. "Of the hierarchy of souls settled here? As if that will grant you some foothold the rest of us could never accomplish? You have witnessed the lines of demarcation between their so-called kingdoms. You have enjoyed the company of those left to abide within the Thresh. You have fought the Great Worm and escaped the clawed clutched of both Balor and The Mórrígan. I believe that is everything you need to know. Except for what I'm about to show you."

The light in his eyes dimmed as he retracted his power and smirked. I marveled at his turn in character—from haughty to kind; from telling to obtuse; from demure to powerful. Like everyone, witch or human alike, it seemed the Fae contained multitudes. Síl could flit through each state during the course of a single conversation or subtle soliloquy. I supposed it was necessary for his survival as a castaway within his own lands. The Fae were never the straight-forward type anyway.

I followed him blindly into the night, listening as his hooves crunched solidly against the ground. The gentle rustle of the river, made both heavy and peaceful by the pull of the night, had quieted as we moved farther from the water. I hoped Madison was enjoying the time they had to kick their witch legs, even if Fae magic and river currents were needed for that to happen. And I hoped they'd make it back to Cernun and Learco soon.

I had no idea how far downstream my lovers were waiting. I had no idea how far off course Síl was taking me. But listening to the motion of the water—sending out subtle tendrils of my power to ensure we were still traveling *with* its flow—at least I knew we were moving in the general direction of home. That was something.

It concerned me that we were well into my second night inside the Faerie Realm. The Mórrígan had warned me of the time disparity between our lands, but even that was as obtuse as the rest of the Fae's omens. I hoped the two days I'd lived through here were moving faster than the one day my world had until Ostara. But for all I knew months could have passed there. Or, maybe, years would pass here. Even if home were no longer an option, I still had to make it to my lovers. In the end, that was all that really mattered anyway.

Síl cleared his throat to pull me from the circumlocution of my mind. I stopped walking as I brought my attention back to the present. Even in the thick obsidian of the night, I could make out the wavering mist of a Fae demarcation border. I swallowed hard to fight it, but I was sure Síl had seen me tremble.

I was safe in the Thresh. Well, *safer* anyway. I could feel it in my gut. The Thresh was a no man's land where no single Fae reigned. It connected the kingdoms and, judging by the river, provided sustenance and life that no Fae could seize control over. Even the Wayward Inn had existed beyond those folds. But were I to step inside the confines of one Fae's sovereignty, that Fae could know me, could know I was here, could send me straight to Balor if they were not keen to keep me for themself.

Fuck! Síl had led me straight into a trap. He'd pretended to be my friend, kept me just enough on the edge of trust and suspicion to not become too skeptical of him, and I'd followed him straight toward my capture.

Was the reward on my head that fucking high? I'd certainly pissed Balor off enough for it to be. Or what if it was Balor himself waiting behind that mist?

My power was mostly back—I could feel it inside of me—but I still wasn't quite certain on how to use it. And there was no way

I'd be a match for Balor's magic on Balor's terms on Balor's turf. Fuckity, fuck, fuck, fuck!

"Are you quite done with your little mental breakdown?" Síl asked, laughter coating every word as he cocked his head in front of me. "You needn't worry. Neither Balor nor the Fachan are welcomed beyond this line. I am almost offended you believe I would lead you to them. At least for the petty pittance currently offered for your hide. The fur on my legs is worth more than that alone."

I sighed as I tried to steady myself. My boyfriends always told me I had a tendency to fatalize situations. But that distrust was part of what kept me safe.

Maybe Síl could be trusted… a little. That didn't mean whoever ruled the roost in there wouldn't turn me in to gain favor with the Dark King.

Síl groaned.

"It's wise to trust no one," he said, "but I promise you the leader of this kingdom has more important things on their mind than the introduction of some witch who is not a witch to their world. It is *Fleadh conricim*, after all. As such, you and they and me will all be otherwise occupied."

His rough hand clasped mine as he pulled me forward. I barely had time to take a breath in protest before I was inside the line.

CHAPTER 15

Where the Thresh had been lush but barren—save for the *murúch*, and Síl, and the ever-present crows—the land inside the barrier was teeming with life. Loud and boisterous, Fae were everywhere. *Púca*, like Síl, with their bare chests and haunches; *Sídhe Draoi* who, like the Dryads of Greek myth—though I guessed they were one in the same—sported flowing locks of tendriled hair which appeared more like vines of wisteria and jasmine or moss than what I was accustomed to; and *Leannán sídhe* and the *Gean Cánach* like the ones I'd seen in the Wayward Inn, though these creatures seemed somehow more beautiful than those who had gone to live in the Thresh in ways I had not deemed possible. All genders and shapes and sizes. All glorious and gliding and graceful.

And busy. They moved with an effortless charm as they worked toward ritual. Even when a few of them stopped, pausing briefly to look Síl and me up and down as we paused just within the edge of the wood, they held an ethereal serenity. It was utterly amazing. I'd had no clue that just beyond those borders so many Fae—so much life!—abounded.

"Close your mouth," Síl whispered, smiling at my slack jaw

as I took in the wonder. "There'll be plenty to keep it open soon."

"I had no idea…" I started.

Síl grinned once more, wider this time as he twisted his arm out as if he were offering it all to me.

"Forest for the trees," he said. "Or some other Earthbound witch phrase that is more appropriate these days."

This was the brighter side of Faerie lore which always fluttered within the edges of my grandmother's cautionary tales. This was what we witches—the ones of us who practiced through the spirits of the Earth and had not traversed our power to the darker sides of blood or death or humanity—aspired toward. All of these creatures, each so connected to the life of the woods, the giving of the ground, the majesty of the air, all of them working in tandem with the forest to honor it, to mold it toward greatness, to revel in its significance. I felt myself enamored with them—all of them—immediately. This was the part of Fae kind the world actually needed. This would be worth opening a door between our Realms for.

"Be careful not to fall in love, traveler," Síl warned, snapping me out of my reverie and bringing me back into myself. "These woods, particularly at the start of *Fleadh conricim*, have a tendency to captivate one unprepared for such energies. Captivation is but another form of control. Even if unintended. This is but a stop for the night. A safe haven beyond the reach of the Salamanders or the Headless Riders or Balor and his ilk. Though it is safe, should you fall within its spell, years may pass before you remember your travels and the lovers whom you so desperately seek."

I sighed heavily as I nodded, clutching onto a mental image of Learco and Cernun to ground myself. I wished I had a rubber band bound around my wrist to snap or a watch to keep me mindful of the passing of time. I could definitely feel the pull of becoming lost here. It was all just so enchanting.

"Although, should you so desire, there are plenty of loves to be made here."

Síl's words snapped me back to the present once more, and I twisted my mouth into a wry smile as I looked at him. Even he was more beautiful within these woods, as if the proximity to the power of all this nature was washing through him, raising his rut to full display. My eyes traced the sharp jut of his jaw, the bold, broad mounds of his pecs, the gentle curl of hair that led downwards toward the pants he no longer wore. His cock, thick and solid and firm, jumped a bit when my eyes fell upon it. I darted my gaze back to his.

"There you are, Darragh," he purred. "There is no problem with promiscuity. It is nature's way, after all. But you must keep your wits about you so as not to become spellbound within it."

It was good advice, even had I not been surrounded in the teeming pulse of nature's wooded orgy. Cernun, Learco, and I all had an understanding when it came to sex and sexual attraction. We were safe, and we were full, and we were not jealous. At least in as far as our time together had taken us. Besides, any of our extracurricular activities—the telling of them, the demonstrations thereof—nearly always led to much hotter activities amongst the three of us.

"Though, I dare say," Síl continued, "at least your mind is in the proper place. I believe your kind call it 'the gutter.' Yet you are a bit overdressed."

His orange magic engulfed me for a moment, and, when it cleared, I looked down to find my pants and boots gone. He eyed me with approval, biting his lip as he winked. My sudden lack of clothing did nothing to hide my building excitement.

"Yes," he purred. "You are now ready for *Fleadh conricim*."

I smirked. I may have been nude—and semi-erect—but at least it helped me keep my wits about me. Somewhat, anyway. At the very least, I was much more aware of myself.

"What is *Fleadh conricim*?" I asked, pronouncing the words carefully as I worked my mouth around them. "I mean, I know '*fleadh*' means festival, but…"

"*Conricim* means coming together. In both the literal and figurative sense of the words," he grinned.

So I was right. Síl had brought me to an orgy. I bit my lip as I looked to the Fae around me, seeing now that their movements, their preening and pawing over the lushness of the wood, was in preparation of platforms, of soft places to lay, of hard surfaces to gain purchase. There were secluded stations, hidden by the brush or the leaves of the great trees. There were circles built like stages for a performance. There was nectar and water and honey and oils. And there was meat—so much meat!—in case the party-goers got hungry.

"Do not think you must participate," Síl said, his hand gently brushing my dick between us as if on accident as he gestured. "There are viewing centers should you just want to watch. Yet the festival is much more enjoyable when you play along instead of playing alone."

My body was definitely reacting to the provocation—and we did need to wait out the night somewhere safe—but my mind was aflurry with thoughts of Cernun and Learco. I hated the idea of them lingering around in anticipation, almost as much as I hated the idea of them missing this. Plus, we were on a time crunch, assuming there was still time left to crunch before Ostara in our world, to supplant the Changelings who had wreaked havoc on our lives. I could not afford to get lost in a fantasy. Any more than I already was anyway.

The night bugs—crickets and cicadas and katydids by the sound of it—were beginning their nocturnal symphony, tuning up their violins to strum chords with their powerful hind legs.

The sound echoed from the canopy in a joyous crescendo as it welcomed more and more Fae into the wood. All of them nude. All of them ready.

Síl tilted his head and raised an eyebrow at me, but didn't push forward to join his kin. Perhaps he was waiting for my answer, but it seemed there was something more going on behind the sheepish grin he had plastered on his face. With the Fae, there was always something more going on.

"You must come to the *Fleadh conricim* freely," he said. "As in, you must verbally give your consent."

"What?" I asked. "I don't just drop my keys in a bowl and pick a hole?"

He scoffed, turning to face me full on and shaking his head.

"This is a sacred event," he scolded. "We may not know what you are beyond your witch ancestry, but I believe you may have a bit of Fae in you."

The growl in his voice was intense yet gentle as he looked me over. His eyes squinted as they traced the lines of my body. His stance demanded I take him seriously. It was not a question; it was a requirement. I felt my breath freeze in my lungs at his sudden sternness. I had not meant to disparage his ritual.

"And if you don't," he added, "you soon will."

His laughter broke the tension he'd created. He seemed to enjoy playing with me. I could tell he wanted to. At least it quelled the knot that had formed in my throat at his suggestion I might be something Fae-akin instead of pure witch. That was not an option I was interested in entertaining. The MAW already wanted me behind bars or flamed at the stake, and that was, by far, better than becoming a lab rat for them. Síl's joke on the subject, however, could be something I would entertain.

His hoof tapped the forest floor as he watched me, my face no doubt contouring with each consideration that passed through my brain. I let my eyes shift beyond him to the scene unfolding just beyond the twining underbrush before us. Preparations set, the nature Fae—now nearly fifty of them with their numbers consistently growing as more flooded into the wood—moved in concentric circles, dancing seductively as they preened to show off the beauty of their varied bodies. The movements appeared at once rehearsed and spontaneous, fluid and practiced as they twisted in reverence of the earth, the plants, themselves. Yet, even as the music of the night grew louder with their calls, not one of them touched another. It was as if they were waiting for something—some cue, some signal, some insurmountable level of erotica to break open and begin the *Fleadh conricim*. This was the foreplay. The tension before a main event I could tell they were desperate to begin.

Síl was too. He grunted impatiently to draw my gaze back to him.

"What do I have to say?" I asked.

I hoped my sigh sounded more resolved than broken down, but I honestly wasn't sure which countenance had asked the question.

"It is quite simple," Síl grinned, the corners of his lips thinning with his eyes as he looked me over. "Follow my hands, and repeat the words: 'I give myself to Nature, in and of my own accord, that Nature may inhabit my body as the vessel for which it was intended, through which all things flow, and within my vessel we shall come together.' Now, Darragh. Say it quickly!"

My mouth gaped, pausing as I tried to ensure I had the phrasing right within me. The password for this speakeasy sounded an awful lot like a spell, and I knew full well what could go wrong if a Fae spell were spoken incorrectly. I liked that about witchcraft. The words were less important than the intent. They were there to focus a calling. Fae magic seemed to be a bit more inhabited by ceremony, in that it was the words and the weaving of hands which moved the power, rather than a request for the power to move. I didn't want to get things wrong.

"Say it now!" Síl demanded.

Before I could speak, a shrill wave of excitement flooded through the participants before us. Each Fae fell to their knees, heads tilted downward in deference, in prayer. Síl's expression changed from powerful to anxious. The urgency in his voice stung as he urged me to "Say the fucking words!"

I froze. No sound would come from my throat even if I wanted it to. Every instinct I had was fighting for control, campaigning to get me away from the festival. Or, at the very least, from whatever had led the participants to genuflect in servitude. I'd bent the knee a time or two in my life, but I truly wasn't one for bowing.

"Say it isn't so," a voice called from the ether, rattling the entire forest like a gust of wind, trilling the leaves, and shaking its inhabitants to their cores. "The great and powerful seed of my loins, he who thought himself far more worthy than this humble wood, has returned!"

The "fuck" which emanated from Síl's throat sounded more guttural, more animalistic than anything I'd ever heard. He trembled with the rest of the trees, glancing at me with a sorrowful worry.

"Why couldn't you just say the words?" he whispered as he bowed, taking a knee and shivering as he tried to calm his body.

The brush before us parted, stretching like the adornments of a shrine as a massive figure began to materialize from the ground up. His feet, bare but covered in the caked on ruddy brown of dried dirt, stretched like roots against the forest floor. The thick tree trunks of his legs were muscled and firm with pulsing veins that appeared like vines ready to sprout leaves, hungry to climb, to consume anything or anyone nearby. They stretched through his groin, across the undulation of his abs, to his broad pecs and even broader shoulders. His head craned atop his neck, angled slightly sideways as he peered down at us from his nearly seven foot stature. His face was beautiful—like the rest of him—with green-spun eyes and features that angled sharply like the leaves of a magnolia tree, that threatened the pain of thorns. Wild black hair spun from his head like dark-leaved elder blowing in an unfelt wind. Jutting horns that looked far more like gnarling elm branches than bone rose from just behind his hairline. The way his veins formed branches across his skin in certain lights reminded me a lot of Cernun's tattoos. Hell, the whole of him reminded me of Cernun.

"What say you, Síl?" he smiled. "Have you returned, tail between your legs, to face the fate of your disobedience?"

I shuddered. The nonchalant rage which dripped from his words was definitely not like Cernun. It hung in the air around him like storm clouds clinging to stardust for their lightning to form. It threatened tornadoes waiting to take out everything in their path. I could understand Síl's fear. I had a healthy dose of it myself.

"I'm waiting," the Fae said, his eyes squinting as he focused solely on the satyr. "Or has your time in the Thresh denied you the ability of speech."

The similarity in phrasing to when Síl had first appeared to me and Madison sent a cold chill down my spine. At the time, Síl was pretending to be the Great Horned King. Which meant this was the green man Cernunnos.

My breath caught in my throat at the presence of yet another Fae leader. The last thing I needed were three of them on my back. Four if I counted Echo, though I was still hoping it was only her children that had tagged me.

"I am back for the *Fleadh conricim*," Síl announced a little louder than I thought he'd expected to. His voice was firm, but I could still hear the waver he was trying to hide within it. I was certain Cernunnos could hear it too. "And… I've brought an offering."

My brow furrowed as the satyr raised his hands. I watched for the orange haze of his magic to conjure something suitable for a Fae who thought himself god, hoping it was something living and not a sacrificial bull or baby or virgin. And yet, his magic didn't materialize. Instead, he flourished his open palms toward me.

Shit. *I* was the offering.

My heart pounded as Cernunnos turned his eyes to me for the first time. Eons of power raged within them like thickets of brambles twining upon themselves to create something solid and firm and dangerous. He wet his lips seductively as he took me in, his face as unable as my own to hide the thoughts rampaging behind his features. It was the first time since middle school gym class my nudity had left me feeling so exposed. My stomach trembled as I tried to subtly grasp hold of the foreign power within me. I knew it was no match for his, but it was something.

Cernunnos smirked, endearing and terrifying, as he sensed me tap it. His lips pushed into an exaggerated pout as he moved his gaze back to Síl.

"Yet even so," he hummed, "you could not convince your offering to proclaim the words of consumption. He retains his will. Any offering of himself made now would be of his own accord, not yours. Besides, an unclaimed witch, even in their rarity, cannot purchase much within the abundance of my wood. So, Síl,"—the satyr's name slithered like serpents off his perfect lips—"what else do you possess that may bring you home?"

Síl rose slowly to his feet as his tongue fumbled over his lips. He fought to find the words to quell the rising anger—both that of Cernunnos and the budding rage in me at his attempt to trap me after all. His eyes met mine in angst that was more for himself than for me. Still, I could tell he regretted luring me to the festival. But, again, I figured that remorse to be for himself. He had obviously departed on poor terms, and his return could see his king snap him to oblivion without batting an eye. He'd imagined me as his ticket to freedom, that fucker. If he so much as thought of announcing Balor's bounty on my head, I'd snap him in two myself. If I had the chance before Cernunnos snapped me.

"He's more than a witch!" Síl exclaimed, and my shoulders slumped at the satyr's newfound courage. "He holds his power, even in our realm. He has faced Balor and The Mórrígan, and yet he still walks freely. He has slain the *Ollphéist*; been celebrated by the *murúch* without becoming lost in their song; and he has stood before you, the Great Horned King, without bowing, without fear."

That last part was a bit of a stretch. There was plenty of fear swimming through my veins, exciting every nerve-ending in my body. Still, I was proud I'd managed to maintain a calm exterior. Most likely because I was frozen in place. But all strung together like that, I did sound pretty impressive. I hoped that was a good thing and not taken as a threat.

"I've heard tale of a coven found their way here," Cernunnos sighed, feigning disinterest yet still watching me intensely with his slightly diverted eyes. "Is this the Cullen, the Clarke, or the Kyteler?"

"The Cullen," flew from my mouth with such a force of breath it surprised me. The question had been directed to Síl, but I was glad to have found my voice. I adjusted my posture, pulling my spine straighter as I raised my chin defiantly to meet the Horned King's eyes. For his part, despite all the airs of punishment and boredom he was putting on, behind it all, he seemed greatly amused. I supposed I was a novelty, particularly at the start of his

Festival of Flesh.

I did not dare to move my eyes from his, but my ears perked to the chittering noise that was raising behind him. The murmurs amongst the party-goers had shifted from their surprise at Síl's return to the wonder of my presence. The delicate, wind-like whisper of the *Sídhe Draoi* joined the whistles of the Love Talkers and Fae Lovers to highlight the rutting grunts of the satyrs. All of them had abandoned their prep work and were crowding behind their leader to take me in once more. Síl looked boastful as he continued to wave his arms, showcasing me before them like a prized pig headed for the slaughter once all the blue ribbons were won.

I wondered, for a moment, what would happen should I move a few steps backwards, back through the barrier to the Thresh we had entered. I doubted it was that simple though. Besides, all those eyes on me, all the pomp and circumstance that surrounded the meeting, the sharp green eyes of the Great Horned King… I was beginning to get excited, and it showed.

Cernunnos let his eyes fall to my cock, and he licked his lips.

"Your company will do, Síl," he said, as if he had only just decided and the last several minutes weren't merely about building tension. "However, the Cullen witch is not an offering as such. So, dear satyr, what more do you have to give?"

A wicked grin swam across Síl's cheeks. His muscles flexed as he stretched his haunches.

"Only that which I would give willingly," he cried.

And with that, he bent to take Cernunnos's great horn into his mouth, swallowing deep and holding it there in his throat before pulling back to reveal the saliva-slicked pulse of the king's cock.

The other Fae whooped as the *Fleadh conricim* commenced. It took a moment of stunned silence for me to understand the whole of their exchange had been but a show, a power play of dominance and submission—of dominance upon dominance—to send the energies of the festival coursing in the right direction, to peak the anticipation and the blood flow. It was kind of hot. And it had certainly done what it intended. All that pent up nervousness and energy was aching for release.

A mist of prismatic power rose through the wood like golden pollen on a spring day in Georgia, billowing about in an orgiastic pursuit of stamens and pistils, pulse and satisfaction. It was beautiful. It was intense. It was captivating. The magics of all the Fae present manifested in a rainbow of their inner selves. If a witch's aura push was visible, this was what it would look like. But where ours was concentrated and controlled, targeted with intent, the Fae's push was wild and untamed. I felt it all around me, prickling against my skin and calling me forward to the center of their movement. I knew I had a choice, but I also felt some primal, novel part of my power screaming its consent. The deepest depths of me wanted to be a part of it, to join in the revelry and experience a return to where it had originated.

I felt myself blushing, and I was surprised there was any blood left for my cheeks as my erection raged at the sight. Síl's eyes darted to mine, and a sly smile curved his mouth as he pulled his lips away from Cernunnos's cock.

"It truly is more exciting if you participate," he said, wiping his spit-covered chin with the back of his hand. "Besides, we're here until dawn regardless."

I quivered where I stood. Despite every urge within me to push forward, to push in, I could not bring myself to move.

"Perhaps the Cullen witch simply prefers to watch," Cernunnos suggested. "Let's give him a better view."

His hand was soft yet firm as he wrapped it around my dick and pulled, guiding me forward through the mass of writhing bodies. I'd spent plenty of time in the backrooms of various gay bars, but none of that had ever come close to the scene which spread out before me. Bodies twisted like vines around one another, pulsing, throbbing, dancing to the natural beat of the universe.

"What do you think?"

My jaw gaped as I considered how to answer the Horned King's question. So many phrases were bouncing through my brain, and none of them felt adequate. Why was I having such a hard time speaking around this Fae?

"Scratch that," he continued, tightening his grip on my cock. "I can tell exactly what you think. I can feel it inside you, that elemental twinge at the base of your power connecting you to the natural, to the building blocks of this and every other world. It is remarkable, by the way, that you hold that within you. For most magical creatures—witch or Fae alike—that primeval element of the source of our powers disappeared eons ago. Not even all Fae leaders still possess it. But you do somehow. That is what enables you to access your magic in our lands."

He looked very serious as he watched me take in his words, even with the ripples of ecstasy billowing across his skin. As he spoke, I realized he was speaking only to me. The other Fae, even if they had not been distracted by the feast before them, could not hear his words. And I didn't need to speak aloud either, simply to center my thoughts on his.

"So what does that mean?" I asked mentally. "Síl insists I'm more than a witch. Could that be true?"

"I am not sure, Darragh Cullen," Cernunnos responded. "Though I would venture the concept that we, all of us, are always more should we allow ourselves to be. Isn't that what nature teaches us through evolution and adaptation? That when pushed to our limits, we become more than what we once believed ourselves to be."

He smiled as he folded at his waist, stopping a few inches from my face and locking his deeply alluring eyes on mine.

"What do you believe yourself to be?" he asked. "What can I do to push your limits?"

His lips met mine in a rush of flowing energy. My body ached, my power calling to his, as I arched into his embrace. In that moment, I was no longer sure who I was or what I had been. I had no concept of tomorrow tugging strings of a past through to the future. There was only what was happening. There was only his kiss. And I succumbed.

CHAPTER 16

Soft sunlight ricocheted across the dew-soaked leaves of the forest, nuzzling me gently to bring me to my senses. The night before felt like a dream; a feeling urged onwards by my waking up alone.

"Síl?" I called as I pulled myself into a seated position and cleared my throat of the strain from a night of grunts and moans. "Great Horny King?"

The glen was abandoned. Still wet and washed by the night's festivities, it glowed with life renewed, life experienced. Flashes of the tryst pulsed through my brain with the same flurry of intensity as all the skin I'd felt against mine, all the magic which had swirled with wild abandon. I could still hear Cernunnos's words echo through my ears: *You have somehow retained a piece of the wild within you, Cullen witch. Foster it like a seed. Ensure it grows.* If that were true—which, despite the merrymaking, I still had trouble taking anything any Fae said as fact, or, at the very least, straight-forward—it opened vast new worlds of thought on how I approached magic. And not just my own, but power in general.

But what else was new? In the aftermath of my exposing magic to the human world, I'd undergone quite a transformation in my understanding of how things worked and my place within it all. Growing up, my grandmother had filled my head with fables of the Fae—those dangerous and conniving sprites who would leap upon any chance to help or harm for a hefty price. I'd imagined those imps as warnings, as parables of the natural world personified into a being which could be named and called to, blamed and shrugged away. Back then, the Fae of my mind had been no different than the many—or singular—gods of human religion. Something meant to explain the unexplained, to help us all feel seen when things went well for us, to look to for meaning when life went poorly. *That* made sense in my brain. My power, after all, was based in elemental energies, in the ebb and flow of the natural world as it spun its varied web around all of us. We witches were lucky enough to be tapped into that magic, like a heightened version of a green thumb or an empath or a dandelion rooted through the cracks in the sidewalk.

And then I'd met Balor.

Perhaps "met" is too soft a word. Balor had been thrust upon me through a dark and forgotten ritual attempted by my old protégé—that slimy little fuck—and suddenly those imagined entities of fable were real. Aiden had used our bloodlines—mine, Cernun's, and Learco's—to call forth the Fae leader eons after their kind had been shunned from our world and sealed back into their own. If what Cernunnos said was true, that something in me was connected to the oldest of olds, it was probably my blood that had enabled the connection, that had powered his call to break through the folds between our worlds.

But I couldn't dwell on that. At least not with the tasks at hand growing evermore urgent.

Now that I knew the Fae were real, that all of those stories, all of those gods of the past, were manifest and actualized and aching to return to our lands, I was finally beginning to understand a bit more about our magic. About its source. At least I thought I was figuring it out.

For a while, I'd started to believe that our magics—the powers of all the witches remaining in the other realm—were connected to the Fae. Sure, our magics were different. We were the Children of the Earth, and they were the Beings of the Other. But I'd imagined our witch magics had come from the Fae directly. Like how Echo's children—the Changelings—possessed an abbreviated version of their mother's powers and were able to mimic their victims on the surface, I'd wondered if the magic of witch kind had evolved somehow through us being the children of ancient Fae-folk breeding with the humans of our world. None of that had ever felt right though, despite the easy blue bow I was looking to tie around it all.

Now, Cernunnos's suggestion of the wild which had birthed us opened a firmament of vast possibility. It meant there was something beyond us both—the witches and the Fae—which had given rise to our kind. Something common and primal and still reaching out through us all. My thirst for understanding—twined with my comfort of the unknown—grinned at the potentialities.

If I had that power still mixed within me, did that mean I could perform Fae magic on my own? It certainly would explain how the MAW had mistaken the Changeling magic that blessed Atlanta with an early Spring for mine. My supposed spell sign would have been the closest match in their databases.

Could I have the potential to reach through to discover the source of all magical beings?

Still, that was an exploration for another day. My quest to find Cernun, Learco, and Madison—to set things right in the world in which we belonged—was the only thing that mattered.

I stretched into the kind morning light and marveled at the bright song of day in comparison to the intense symphony of night.

Birds paid their homage to the sun, quickly swooping to hunt out any of the nocturnal insects who'd stayed up past their bedtime. Squirrels—or whatever version of them this world had—chittered as they darted along branches of the canopy, chasing one another to stretch their muscles within the flow of warmth. And behind all of that, the river which had offered its undercurrent as a base beat to the night's *Fleadh conricim* intensified its melody to celebrate the light.

My pants, hemmed now into a pair of knee-length shorts with a twine that matched the orange shade of Síl's magic, were hung, pressed and folded, upon a nearby branch with my boots laced and tucked beneath them. They'd also left me a braided bottle of wine as a parting gift, so not so bad for a one night stand. I assumed it to be the work of the *clobhair-ceann*, meaning I now had all three of The Mórrígan's requests squared away. That was something at least.

I dressed quickly, listening to the distant trickle of water to plot my course back into the Thresh and to my lovers. Two nights had passed in the Faerie Realm, and though the second had been fun, I couldn't afford to face a third. I had no way of knowing if Ostara had come and gone in our world, making the Changeling's transition to our lives permanent, but as far as I was concerned, that didn't matter. The most important thing was reuniting with my friends. Beyond that, I was certain we'd be able to overcome anything the Changelings had done, regardless of how much time had passed or whatever Faerie customs were triggered into place. I just had to get to them first.

I breathed in the silky air of the wood as I centered myself for the journey. I was close. I could feel it. Plus, my power was completely restored after my encounter with the *Ollphéist*. I could feel it, rejuvenated by the energy of the Green Man's festival, as it twisted inside of me, ready and waiting for my will. Even the agitated rub I had felt within it since I'd entered the Fae Realm was gone, replaced with an ecstatic rumbling of connection. Of source. Like something greater than witch or Fae was deep within me, ready to talk if I could just figure out how to hear it. It was wild and untamed and instinctual and powerful. And I knew things now: the lay of the land; how my powers could work in tandem once I knew the right ways to access both; that the wild was ready to lead me to my coven.

I'd definitely need to track that down someday, the source of the wild within me. But for now it was an added comfort as I pushed through the barrier of the wood and out into the open lands.

The Mórrígan's crows kept their distance, but I could still feel them watching me as I walked. Not that it mattered. For all the eyes her spies had left upon me, she hadn't felt it the least bit necessary to intervene, even as I faced near certain death from the serpent. I wasn't sure if I should be honored that she felt me capable or concerned by her nonchalance in whether I lived or died. Whatever the case, as soon as I reached Echo's caves—and reunited with my boyfriends—I'd still need her help to get us all home.

I marked my journey a few yards in from the river, equidistant between its shores and the treeline. I felt exposed, but at least I had a clear line of sight. That was better than whatever paws may reach for me from behind some Fae's barrier or from beneath the surface of the water. Plus, the heavy jug of wine I carried would make an excellent weapon if it came down to it. And my magic was turning somersaults in my stomach, so I had that too.

I was tired, and I was hungry as the day wore on, but determination kept my feet marching forward.

The clover beneath my boots grew sparser as I traveled, replaced by the chartreuse blades of grass that pushed from the rockier land. Trees gave way to hills and cliffs and caverns. Wildflowers in a spectacular array of colors pulsed in the cooler highland breeze.

I knew I was close. I could feel it. My magic burned within me like a beacon, a homing signal, a compass driving me forward. This had to be Echo's land.

I rushed forward, nearly missing the wavering mist of delineation as I pushed into her world. It popped behind my ears and drew my attention to the vast expanse before me. Mountains rose like buildings against the turquoise of the sky. Cavities dug through the earth, ready to swallow me with one false move. The river twisted, turned, and circled back upon itself as it sought the path of least resistance.

Shit. I had no idea how large her lands were. But I did know my coven's camp was near the water so at least that would steady my aim.

"Cernun!" I called. "Learco!"

My voice circled back upon me, trilling against my eardrums. It was strange to hear my own voice mocking me. But I supposed it was to be expected in this part of the Fae Realm.

"Madison!"

My call bellowed back, repeating their name again and again as a ghost-like wind rushed against my face. The force was both solid and ephemeral, knocking me back and spinning me where I stood.

The wild parts of my power churned inside of me, jockeying

for position as it twined through my body with one simple message: Echo was near.

I gasped as I realized my mistake, the sound bouncing off her unseen form to fill my throat with my own stifled breath, threatening to slice and suffocate me with my word words. My yells had summoned her directly to me. And she was not happy I'd returned to her lands. She was protecting her children.

At least I knew Ostara hadn't happened yet. If I'd learned anything about the children of Fae, they existed in service to their creators. The Changelings who had replaced Learco, Cernun, Madison, and me were doing so at the behest of their mother. Echo was the Ostara surprise they'd promised. I knew it in my gut. They were planning to use the magic of the Equinox to give her passage through, to grant her form. That she was still here meant I still had time to get my life back.

"Echo," I pleaded, "I mean you no harm. I just want to find my lovers."

The word slammed back into my face, sharp and cutting and tinged with a razor's edge of irony as I considered what had led her to become the formless mimic of denigrated desire.

But it was just me giving her substance. Maybe, if I didn't speak, if I held my breath, she would not be able to attack.

I centered myself against the force of her wind, holding my breath as I imagined the gusts as Fae fists lashing out in a toddler's temper tantrum, pushing to free themself of the world that wronged them, clasping hard at anything near to pull themselves into agency. It was actually quite sad, what the Fae had done to their sister for her love of a witch who did not love her back. I'd felt many an unrequited love myself, and though at times they'd left me empty, I'd been fortunate enough to never be ripped from myself. I truly could understand Echo's anger. I just didn't want it directed at me.

A crows' caw reverberated through the cliffs, filling Echo, and slashing across my cheek like a swift right hook.

My silence was of no use. She could mimic any of the inherent sounds of the world, pulling upon the flow of the river, the rustle of the leaves to slam against the sympathy on my face that had only served to entice her further. Violent and cutting, the ever-fading calls of nature ripped like talons against my skin.

"Please," I begged as quietly as I could muster against the onslaught of air forcing its silence upon my throat. "I mean you no harm. I just want my life back!"

"I just want my life back!" Echo mocked, and I realized the utter truth in those words.

The statement knocked me hard in the center of my chest, pushing me backwards to the ground and rolling the jug of wine away. At least it hadn't broken. I grimaced at the barrage of air, traveling quickly as it bounced from the nearby cliffs to continue the assault. She wasn't letting up, and I could not fight the intangible wind.

I felt my power growl within me and looked down to shield my watering eyes from the blitz. My stomach, tense as I lay prone holding myself up with my arms behind me, wavered against the vibrations of her force. Shit. She was trying to force her way inside me, to rearrange my internal organs, or—worse yet—splice me apart to mimic her own invisibility. I had to act. I had to think of something.

"Cease!" I yelled, this time keeping my attention firm to count the seconds it took before my word bounced and rushed against my skin.

Three seconds before the first viscous blow. That wasn't a lot of time. But it would have to do.

I breathed deeply as I tugged on my power, pulling at what was wild and new in the hopes that a bit of the primordial Faerie dust that wove within me would work to manifest solidity. All I had going for me was that light was faster than sound.

"*Solas!*" I called, bringing my hands up before me to manifest a sparkling green orb of my power in the same way I'd seen Samara Byrne bring to life her burning. My circle floated inches from my nose, small, translucent, and brimming with the color of my aura.

It had worked! A part of me hated that it had, but it had! My spelling word had not slammed back upon me. I squinted to see Echo—well, the force of her anyway—slamming against the interior of the sphere, pushing hard to break my magic.

It took most of my concentration to hold the circle intact as I scooted to reach for the *clobhair-ceann's* bottle. Keeping one hand trained on holding my spell, I used my teeth to yank the cork from the jug, emptying the wine into the thirsty soil.

"Apologies to The Mórrígan," I huffed as the wine spilled out, then, sadder, "And to you, Echo."

Holding the bottle in my free hand, I sent whatever tendrils of my mind were not focused on keeping Echo contained to the makeup of the glass. The black glaze of it was thick and solid, free of imperfections, and a true testament to the crafter who'd blown it. I hoped it would work.

"*Gan fuaim,*" I whispered into the bottle, begging to mute its walls to the forces of sound.

I sighed as I poured the manifestation of my magic into the jug, taking the trapped Echo with it, and plugged the neck tight with the cork. I felt horrible, trapping another living being like that—even a Faerie who was trying to kill me—but even in that pain, I spelled for it to hold. I was one item down on The Mórrígan's list, but maybe a Faerie in a bottle would be an adequate trade.

The tension in my body swept out and sent me to my back against the dirt, heaving as I took in the sudden stillness of the air.

"Darragh? Is that you?"

My eyes shot open. A clear, turquoise sky stared back at me, throbbing with an unsettled stillness. I must have fallen asleep. That spell took a lot out of me.

"Holy shit, it is you! You made it back to us!"

I pulled myself into a seated position, the bottle containing Echo still clutched against my chest, as my eyes adjusted to take in the figure ambling toward me.

"And you brought wine!" he called.

"Cernun?" I asked, my throat dry and parched as I wished some of the liquid in the jar had not been sacrificed to the ground. "Is that you?"

I leapt to my feet as he reached me, smiling as I took in the blackness of his hair, the colorful expanse of his tattoos. His arms felt warm as they embraced me, and my lips found purchase on his neck. I breathed in the memory of his scent, wild and musky after days in the Faerie wilderness, and pulled his body tighter against my own. I did not want to let him go.

"Fuck, I missed you," I cried, burying my face against the gentle sparring of his chest hair.

His thick, calloused hands were comforting as his fingers ran through the untamed flurry of my hair. I could hear his heart beating rapidly within his ribcage. I knew its excitement matched my own. Finally, I pulled back to take in the radiant light of his smile.

"I see you are ready to celebrate," he laughed, nodding to indicate the bottle in my grasp once again.

"Oh this?" I said coyly. "It's not at all what you think."

"With you, it never is," he smiled.

Damn, it was good to see him again, to feel the safety his presence provided. Together was always better than apart, especially when it came to my coven of lovers. Together, I felt stronger; I felt sure. My magic tickled inside of me as it rose to meet my energy. The whole of me ached for him.

"I love you," I blurted, and his grin told me all I needed to know.

"I love you too," he purred.

I bit my lip, not wanting to take my eyes off of him, but knowing I had to.

"Where are Learco and Madison?" I asked. "I think it's way past time we kiss this plane goodbye."

"They are close," he promised. "But how about a quick drink? Steel ourselves for the road ahead."

His eyes swam the black glass of the bottle with the same salaciousness they'd caressed over me.

"Don't you think we should wait until we're all reunited?"

His lips scrunched before they met my forehead. They were forceful and chapped, and they scratched a little as he pulled away.

"I suppose you are right," he conceded. "Let me take you to them."

He reached for my free hand and turned to take the lead. I kept the jug tight in the other, my fingers pulsing along its neck. My eyes scanned the craggy horizon as he moved us toward the cliffs.

"I thought you set up camp near the river," I noted as we moved away from the water.

"We pushed further inland," he said, clearing his throat as he picked up our pace. "Too worried about the *Ollphéist* and the other creatures of the depths."

"Makes sense," I smiled.

His hand felt so good in mine. I never wanted to let it go.

Too bad it wasn't Cernun's hand.

"How much farther are they?" I asked, and he squinted as he looked my way with averted eyes. "I'm just excited to see everyone.

It's been a long three days."

"Not much farther," he promised. "You will see them soon."

I nodded as we walked on, trying to appear calm as I considered what to do. The bottle in my grip would make a great weapon for bludgeoning Changelings, but then I risked letting Echo out and having to deal with one extra pissed off Faerie queen. And if I tried to pull even a small bit of my power through, I had no doubt he would sense it, and I needed the element of surprise. The best I could do was play along. To not let him know I was onto him.

His fingers kneaded the back of my hands. I let him pull me into the jutting cliffs that leapt from the ground in angry, jagged shifts. My eyes darted to note the many caves, the opened mouths of caverns littering the landscape. I loosened my grip, and he tightened his.

"How did you know?" he asked, head forward as he continued to pull me toward his trap.

"How did I know what?"

I feigned innocence, but I knew he wasn't buying it. So much for the element of surprise.

"I would really like to know," he said, his grin stretching further than it should have as he walked me toward my doom. "We take great pride, you see, in our ability to copy those as simple as your kind. That a witch like you could see through me so quickly… Well, that just should not be."

"I'm more than just a witch," I said, echoing Síl's words as I sent a jolt of burning power through my palm.

The Changeling squealed as he released me, turning sharply on his feet to snarl with Cernun's beautiful features. The contortion of them made him savage.

"And we are more than just our skin," I told him, spreading my legs to hold my stance for the coming fight.

He craned his neck as his mouth dropped open, the teeth within it growing long and sharp. His eyes turned yellow, slitted and snakelike, as his lips peeled back and his nose grew long and upturned. Cernun's glorious black hair shed from his body and his ears turned long and pointed like a bat's. His skin caked to a muddy grey, dry and cracking like that one lump of charcoal that just refuses to burn.

So that was what the Changelings looked like before they took someone else's form. I could see why they were so desperate to impersonate others.

In a blink, he shifted once more, and I found myself staring into a mirror.

I looked tired, and dirty, and I could not tell if the confidence which spread across my face was mine or his own. My auburn hair, always redder than I remembered it when I saw it reflected back to me, was tangled and unruly. The dust and debris of my days spent walking gave an iridescent shine to my skin. But I looked damn sexy. And three days of no burgers from Aunt Paulina's had done wonders for my abs.

The Changeling balled his fists as he leaped towards the bottle still in my grasp. He moved with an unearthly speed, yet I managed to sidestep just in time, watching him tuck and roll. He was on his feet again before I could turn completely around.

"Give me my mother!" he demanded.

His sharp tongue licked his lips as his voice rumbled through the cliffs around his, shifting stone and rock to threaten an avalanche upon us. I pushed a thought of magic toward him, siphoning from my power to give him a taste of what a simple witch like me could offer. But he was too fast. The reverberations of sound which made him were too quick for the physical force of my power. The green blast of my magic blew past him to explode on a cliffside, sending more rocks hurtling toward the ground. But it gave me an idea. If I couldn't best him with speed or physical power, I'd have to rely on something else. I hoped this new magic of mine was up to the task.

I turned on my heels and ran, darting in a zig zag formation like a Florida alligator was chasing me. I scanned the rising mounds, noting their proximity to the caverns sunk beneath them. He growled in pursuit. Without looking, I could feel him closing in. He stopped in his tracks as I spun, rearing back with the bottle held tight behind me.

"You want your mother so bad?" I asked, attempting to match his snarl as my brain worked to focus its spell. "Go get her!"

I used every bit of force my arm could muster to throw the braided black jug high into the air. It sailed across the sky, catching the light of the vermilion sun as it angled perfectly toward the cavern I'd chosen, disappearing beneath the surface of its abyss.

The Changeling didn't think twice about following it. His body changed from mine to his own as he ran. Long, clawed arms brushed the ground as he bounded toward the cave and leapt, headfirst, inside. I gasped as a new force of magic erupted from within me, blasting the cliff to send it barreling atop the sunken hole. The Changeling screeched as he was buried alive, pummeled by the sharp stone of his own lands.

I doubled over as I fought to catch my breath. Damn, that had been a lot of magic, but at least my mirage of the bottle had been enough to fool him. I placed the real bottle on the ground between my feet, finally willing to let go of it, as I stretched my fingers and listened for any rumbling of his escape, any advancement of another of Echo's children.

If there were any, they didn't dare approach. The only sound that met my ears was the distant trickle of the river. I exhaled sharply as my heart slowed back to its normal pace. I prayed to whatever wild there was before the witches and the Fae to let me reach my lovers with no more villains in my path.

It was a lot to ask, particularly in the Faerie Realm. But one foot in front of the other went a long way in the evolution of the untamed.

CHAPTER 17

I froze when I saw the encampment ahead. The shelter Learco had constructed of leaves and fronds—a skill I would definitely have to ask him about later—was destroyed, mangled and spread along the riverbank. The trees were broken too. Branches hung splintered from their trunks, attached now only by thin strips of bark still struggling to hold them together. The trampled undergrowth was spotted with the unholy red of smashed wildflowers and berries. Whatever struggle had occurred, it had not been pretty.

I glared at the bottle in my hand, but quickly realized this wasn't Echo's fault. Although her tornado of winds could have easily bashed the space to pieces, we were no longer in her domain. Now that I knew what to look for, I'd felt the gentle pop of her barrier as I'd passed from the cliffs to the forest. I was in the Thresh, and without having corporeal form, I doubted Echo would have been willing to leave her designated territory within the Faerie Realm.

As much as I wanted to rush in to survey the damage, to find wherever Cernun, Learco, and Madison were hiding, I forced myself to tread carefully. Whoever had done this could still be nearby, and the last thing I wanted was another fight. Although I was certain I was going to get one.

My mouth went arid as I got close enough to realize the splashes of red weren't berries but blood. And it was fresh. Shit. It didn't make any difference anymore if I was quiet. All that mattered was finding my lovers. And by the still-wet sheen of crimson coating the clover—hopefully more from their assailants than them—they could still be near.

"Learco!" I yelled. "Cernun! Mads!"

No one answered, not even the murder of crows who had flown in as soon as I'd re-entered the Thresh. Or maybe they did. My heart was so loud on my eardrums, it could have drowned them out entirely. My mind flashed to the memory of the Changeling's sharpened talons, black and glistening and extruding like daggers from the charcoal tips of its fingers. I saw it dressed as me, luring my coven into complacency, before lashing out in capture and control.

Or maybe some child of the *Ollphéist*—smaller but a serpent all the same—rising from the river to seek vengeance for its slain yet resurrecting parent.

I saw a million pixies, all of them as angry and violent as Síl had sworn them to be, flying in with their stinger-like swords drawn and at the ready, swarming and slashing until they carried off the broken and bruised bodies of my loved ones, dripping from the bevy of paper cut gashes of those tiny, viscous creatures.

I tried to focus, to calm the what ifs spiraling through my mind, so I could fully survey the scene. If I could make sense of the broken limbs and crushed leaves, I would be able to tell which way the assailants—and my coven with them—had gone. Same as I'd done back home on the farm when the swine had broken free of their pens to rampage through the cornfields, or an errant fox had made its way in and out of the henhouse.

It was a mess. The entirety of the shelter had collapsed. Only the dryer crunch of the leaves Learco had used proved it had ever been there to begin with. Sticks and stones, stained red where they had punctured skin, held memories of a battle that would dry and fade and return to the soil. They were weapons forged of the earth rather than the tools of magic. But at least I knew my coven had put up a fight. That in and of itself gave me hope.

A gasping splash at the riverbank pulled my attention to the water.

Shit! It was a monster. Smaller than the *Ollphéist*, but a beast all the same. Its great gills shuddered against the open air, and I reared back my free hand to pull my power to it. It may have been little, but the Fae had taught me size really did not matter. I had no time to waste.

"Wait!"

Madison's voice rumbled from behind the creature's mouth, and I paused my spell just in time.

If it had consumed my coven, I couldn't risk blowing them apart as well.

"It's me. Madison."

Confused, my brow furrowed as the creature wafted with sea-colored light. Its features, flat yet bulbous, large-eyed and large-lipped, morphed into those of my friend before my eyes.

"I'm nonbinary," they said, shivering as the last bits of magic washed through them. "I can take both of the *murúch* forms when I've got the cap. Don't fire!"

Madison trembled as they pulled themselves to the shore. Any other time, I'd have wanted to admire the scaled lower half of their body, shimmering an aquamarine wave between green and blue, as it angled down to the nearly transparent lunate caudal fin they kept submerged within the river. They looked tired and beat down but so beautifully handsome. My heart leapt as I saw them.

"When I first thought of beauty, I thought of her—their leader. So that's the form I took. But I realized, just like in my own skin, I'm not forced to be either," they wheezed, holding their torso aloft with the palms of their hands against the clover still thriving as if it didn't care my world had been turned upside down again and again over the past few days. "Is it really you?"

"It's me," I promised as I dropped to my knees beside them. "What the fuck happened? Where're Cernun and Learco?"

"Fachan," Madison winced. "Like ten Fachans. They rampaged in at first light this morning. You'd be surprised how dexterous they are, especially working in tandem. They fought— Learco and Cernun—really hard, but there were just too many Fae. And I—" Their voice cracked as they looked at me with red, watery eyes. "—I just swam away."

The pain in their eyes begged for forgiveness while simultaneously denying it to themself. They winced as my hand clasped their shoulder.

"You did the right thing," I assured them. "My boyfriends are pretty fucking strong, even without their magics. They're going to be okay. And you being here to tell me who took them, that means we can follow to join the fight."

They didn't look convinced, but they almost smiled.

"Do you know where Balor's at?"

"No," I frowned. "But I know who does. I'll just use the amulet to summon The Mórrígan. This is definitely the appropriate one-time emergency use."

Madison winced again, biting their lip as they shook their head.

"Learco was wearing it when they attacked. So, unless it came off during the fight, it's not here."

They looked like they wanted to cry, but I was proud of them for holding it together. They'd been through so much these last few months, largely because of their relation to me, but they had not let it phase them. Or at least they hadn't let it make them give up.

"I've obviously still got the cap though. And…" Their eyes went wide as they threw themself back into the water, rising a few seconds later with the *Ollphéist* scale in their grip. "… This!"

"You did good, kid," I beamed.

At least we had the three items for the bargain. Sort of. That would get us somewhere even if it didn't get us home. I squinted as I turned my gaze to the crows still idling in the nearby trees.

"Please inform your mistress, if she's not hidden amongst you, that Darragh Cullen requests her presence," I called.

A few heads cocked, a few feathers ruffled, but none of the birds flew. The blacks of their eyes bore down as they watched me as if they were reveling in my desperation. I'd been certain The Mórrígan had sent them to surveil me. My mouth scrunched as I looked back to Madison. Maybe I'd been wrong. Or maybe I needed the magic words. Madison shrugged before an idea washed over their face.

"Give me a minute," they grinned and disappeared into the river.

It was good to see a smile back on their face, though I was sure the trauma—for all of us—would rear its head again once we made it back to our world. If we made it back to our world. This morning I'd been so certain of our success, but now I wasn't so sure. Of course, this morning I thought I'd be back in my lovers' arms by lunchtime. As much as I was prone to spiraling, I couldn't let a setback deter me. And that's all this was. A setback. It had to be. It wasn't allowed to be more.

Madison's electric blue dreads flipped as they broke the surface.

"Ask again," they told me.

I turned back to the crows with pleading eyes.

"Will you please tell The Mórrígan we need her?"

Madison tossed a school of tiny fish—minnows by the looks of it, or whatever the Fae equivalent was—to the shore. The murder glided down from their perches, devouring the flopping bodies in single gulps before bowing to Madison, then me, and taking flight.

"How long do you think we'll have to—" Madison started, but before they could finish, The Mórrígan materialized before me.

Her black robes, lilting always in an unfelt wind, shone against the backdrop of the trees. Her red lips smirked to highlight the ever-present amusement in her emerald green eyes.

"You made good time in the Thresh, Darragh Cullen," she grinned. "Despite your various excursions. And I see the cat is back to their witch form! Well, mostly anyway."

Her crows returned to perch as she surveyed the damage littered around her and shrugged. She squinted at the remnants of the battle as she paced. Even though she retained her regal posture, I could tell she felt uncertain in existing outside of her designated realm. As powerful as she was—as all the Fae leaders were—it was strange to see her discomfort in the supposedly "free" land of the between. I supposed that was what had led to their barriers in the first place. Her uneasiness kept her mouth moving like a nervous bank teller trying hard to finish the transaction as quickly as possible as the robber's gun was trained on her through his jacket pocket. I had not yet been given an opportunity to speak.

"And I see you've held up your end of our bargain," she continued, swiping the *Ollphéist* scale from the ground and admiring her reflection in it before it disappeared with a wave of her hand.

"I believe this hat is mine as well," she said, snatching the invisible cap from Madison's head before either of us could protest.

I froze as the departing swirl of *murúch* magic left Madison's body, shimmering around their legs as the power that had given them form moved off with the feathered hat. I was so glad they'd gotten the opportunity to be—mostly—themself again. I had hoped their return to feline would be allowed a little more ceremony. But The Mórrígan did not seem to care.

Like a cat allergic to water, Madison quickly bent their knees and used their arms to pull them away from the currents of the river, making it to shore just as the luminescent swirl of power started to fade. And then…

Nothing. They were Madison again. Two arms, two legs, and a witch from head to toe. They scrambled awkwardly to their feet, wobbly and unsure on their legs, as they stood with gaped jaw to take in their returned form. Unlike the Changeling that had stolen their form, Madison's scars from their top surgery were faint but present. I was glad. Madison had told me once they considered them as mile markers in their becoming of themself. Also unlike the Changeling that had taken their form, the real Madison was completely nude.

I wanted to embrace them—not because they were naked, because they were back!—but The Mórrígan was not about to give us time for an adequate reunion.

"And it appears that you, Darragh Cullen, hold the final item," she said, centering in on me.

Her hand swooped toward the jug I still held, but I managed to keep it away.

"It's not exactly the wine I promised you," I said when my quick detraction left her finally confused and speechless. "And we've got bigger problems."

"Your problems are your own, witch," she smirked. "We had a bargain. One which you have failed your part in. As such, I shall be on my way."

"Wait!" I yelled.

As hard as she was trying to hide it, The Mórrígan was terrified to be so exposed. And now I needed her to not only get home, but to lead me into whatever viper's den Balor called home. I needed to keep her attention. Maybe my revelation would convince her she was safe. Or safer anyway. At least in this part of the Thresh.

"The bottle doesn't have wine," I continued. "But it does contain your sister."

Madison's eyes were wide as they walked to stand beside me, but not nearly as wide as The Mórrígan's. Still, she hadn't disappeared, and the slight release of tension in her shoulders proved Echo's... departure... from her nearby queendom made this area of the Thresh somewhat safer in Fae terms.

"You have your magic," she realized, licking her lips as she regained the composure I was used to. "And you've used it to imprison another of my kind. That is quite the bold move, Darragh Cullen. Perhaps our bargain may be rekindled after all."

Her hand reached out expectantly, and I bit my lip at the sight of her palm. I gulped as I glanced to the bottle in my hand, a sudden dread washing through me and freezing me in my tracks. Madison jostled my shoulder, and I swallowed hard. I had a feeling giving up the bottle would somehow come back to haunt me. But I couldn't think about that. I needed The Mórrígan to help me save my lovers.

She smiled as the braided bottle touched her hand, running her fingers across the black tempered glass and scrunching her nose as if she could see Echo fuming within. It disappeared as she licked her lips, carried off by her magic to wherever it was the Fae queen kept her treasures.

"That's settled then. Darragh Cullen, Madison Ridge..." she

smirked, then glanced around. "Where are the other two?"

Finally!

"Balor has them!" Madison blurted, and my eyes scanned the Fae's face for any signs of sympathy. Or fear. Or anger. Anything to let me know what I was getting myself into. But with our bargain restored and Echo trapped, The Mórrígan had fallen back into her usual air of amused superiority.

"Look at you," she said to Madison, taking a moment to appreciate their form. "Just as cunning and handsome in your witch form as you were as a feline. And with nearly as much fire in you as your hero here. It's a shame neither of you could save your coven from the clutches of that insane tyrant. Oh well. I suppose it's just passage home for two."

The green of her magic swirled from her hands as her fingers began to enact her spell. It spun quickly, arching out in tendrils as it made its way towards us. I dove out of the way just in time, pulling Madison with me and crying for her to stop.

"I'm not going anywhere without Cernun and Learco," I insisted. "I need you to take us to Balor's lands."

"You would want this instead of a return to your realm?" she asked incredulously, though I could also hear a tinge of admiration in her words. I wondered how long it had been since The Mórrígan had cared for anyone so intensely she would give up her own safety. I wondered how long it had been since anyone had cared for her like that. But I wasn't leaving without my boyfriends.

"I want that *and* a return home," I stated firmly, standing quickly to look her in the eye.

Her laughter threw me off guard.

"Do I sense another bargain?" she smirked.

"No bargains. I gave you your items. And Echo in a fucking jar. It's the least you can do for us."

Her lips curled as she considered my words. Her fingers

tapped against her robes. My breath caught in my throat.

"Fine," she finally agreed. "I will take you to the barricade between the Thresh and Balor's region. But that is as far as I will go. Should you be victorious in your escape, I will see you and your coven home."

I sighed in gratitude as she spoke, but I did not nod. I needed more from her. I didn't care if I was pushing my luck.

"You will come with us into his lands," I said, attempting to sound certain and bold but hearing the obvious waver in my voice. "And you will help us escape."

She laughed once more, the musicality of it harsh and violent as it met my ears.

"And why should I do that?" she asked. "I do like you, Darragh Cullen. I like the wild within you. But I have no bones in your dog fight with the Mad King. What should make me—?"

"He has your amulet," Madison interrupted and winced as The Mórrígan's angry eyes met theirs. "The Fachans took it when they took our friends."

The Mórrígan shook her head, a flurry of emotion clouding her face as she considered all the possibilities of our request—of approving or denying it.

"Very well," she sighed. "But you shall enter first to attempt to quell the situation on your own. You are a capable witch. It is a great request to have one Fae leader enter the lands of another. The system of our lands has retained peace for eons. I shall not break that lightly. Or at least without ensured domination at play. I am certain this will satisfy you."

I nodded, then glancing to Madison, cleared my throat.

"One more thing," I said to her growing annoyance. "Could you maybe manifest Madison some clothes?"

The snap of The Mórrígan's transportation spell made me

dizzy, even though I was expecting it this time, and I clung to the wooden railing before me for balance. We'd materialized halfway across a bridge along the river. The rush of water beneath us was doing nothing for my stability. I closed my eyes to find my center.

Seeing The Mórrígan perform her spell—watching her fingers swim the air before her, pulling through the threads of existence to arrange them to her will—showed me I had a lot to learn about the new aspects of my power. It had taken all my concentration and left me exhausted when I'd simply tried to open a portal for communication, and here she was, punching a hole in the Fae Realm large enough for three whole beings to pass through with barely a few flicks of her wrists. Seeing that made me more worried about what Balor may have in store for us. Well, that alongside The Mórrígan's obvious fear of his lands. But I couldn't let that burden me. We had to save Learco and Cernun. If they were still alive to save.

"Oh, your lovers are alive," the Fae queen said, ever able to read my face as if I were speaking.

"How do you know?" I asked when the spinning stopped and I could finally open my eyes again. "Can you sense them?"

The Mórrígan was beautiful against the turquoise backdrop of the sky, floating slightly above the wood of the bridge but not allowing her feet to touch. Without the usual green with which she surrounded herself, the black of her hair, the gemstones of her eyes were even more striking. But I could see she was nervous despite the attempts she made to hide it.

"No, I do not sense them," she replied. "But immediate death is not in Balor's purview. He prefers the torture or the battle as a precursor to his slaughter. To him, it makes the loss of life more honorable."

"So he's a moral sadist," Madison smirked, obviously doing better with the transportation spell than I was. But they were younger. And, I supposed, the numerous physical transitions their body had undergone in the past few days had made them a bit more accustomed to those aspects of Fae magic than me.

The Mórrígan had provided us both with loose knit tunics that hung soft around our torsos. It felt like cashmere against my skin, but my fingers told me the fibers were from plants, not wool. I'd been hoping for some armor, but the soft tan of our new shirts was better than going in bare. She'd also given Madison a matching pair of slacks and some boots which looked eerily similar to my own.

"Morality is not something Balor is burdened with," the Fae grinned. "Though he does possess his own form of integrity. As do we all. But yes. Sadism is quite an appropriate word."

"Is that why you're so frightened of going in with us?" I asked.

I knew I was ruffling her feathers, but I didn't care. I needed her on our side if we were going to defeat Balor and get my boyfriends back, and if goading her to action was the only way to get her through the barrier, so be it.

"I am not afraid, witch!" she snapped, her hand darting a vine of her power to slither around my throat. "Do not mistake my adherence to the rulings of this land—this land you know nothing of in your millisecond of existence here—as fear. The fact that you managed to somehow survive does not prove your import. It simply shows you less worthy than a gnat at being crushed."

The intensity of her glare, made ever more intense by the beauty of her features, would have frightened me if I'd been able to breathe.

"A millennium has passed since the Tuath Dé and the Fomóraiġ agreed to these borders," she continued. "I do not take disturbing this alliance lightly. Nor should you."

I gasped as her magic released me, leaning back against the railing for stability as I massaged the skin of my neck. She *was* afraid, however she wanted to frame it. But as powerful as she was, I could not figure out why. I was afraid too—of Balor; of her—but I knew that showing it would get me nowhere. Especially with the Fae queen.

"You helped me with Balor before," I said. "You helped us. You pulled me from his mind to show me how to defeat him. And you saved Madison's life when you assisted in their shift. How is this any different?"

"That was in your world," The Mórrígan sighed, turning her attention to the river island at the end of the bridgeway. "Or at least in the piece of it your mind allowed my mind to enter. Balor had overstepped his boundaries, and I was merely setting things right. Plus, he did not know of my involvement."

I followed her gaze to take in Balor's island fortress. The barrier was more obvious as it surrounded his lands, reflecting the shimmering waters of the passing river currents and giving the whole of it a more solid, impenetrable effect. Behind it, the shoreline was littered with a thick grove of Rowan trees, heavy with berries of crimson and white. Beyond that, rock formations emulated the thick towers of a castle. I'd learned enough in my three days of travel to know that the lands beyond the Thresh were not always what they seemed through the haze of their delineated magics, but I had a feeling Balor's was showing a bit more of the truth. Almost like an invitation to try him. Or a threat.

"It is true," The Mórrígan continued, "that Balor and I have a bit more—how would you say it?—'beef' with one another than some of our other kin. When we were still able to roam between the worlds, Balor led a mighty crusade within the upper islands of your realm. Naturally, my children are drawn to such fields of play. He was not as mad then. Or at least, not in the ways he is now. When he was defeated in battle, he blamed the cries of my Banshees for both his loss and the wailing which still permeates his ears, still rattles within his skull."

I had witnessed the physical manifestation of that wailing when I was inside Balor's head. But I had a feeling his insanity had been present long before that.

"That's why his island is besotted with bird-catchers," she spat, pointing to the abundance of berried trees on the shore.

My witch friends had always referred to Rowans as portal or traveler's trees, but I did remember my great grandmother calling them bird-catchers as our winged friends were unable to resist those fruits.

"He is certain my crows or my Banshees or my self have been planning his demise. If... *When* I pass through his barrier, it will only serve to justify his madness. Another potentiality I do not take lightly."

I nodded solemnly. I understood I was asking a lot of her. But she'd been the one insistent on taking me under her wing. This was the prize knowing me seemed to come with.

"Why's it such a big deal?" Madison asked. "To him or to you. I thought y'all Fae-types couldn't die."

"Oh, we can die. We just have a tendency to return. Yet our deaths, when we face them, are still excruciating. Too, the passing of time is variable before our rebirths, enabling quite a bit of restructuring to occur in our absence. With every death, there lies the chance that a return is not possible. It has only occurred twice before. But it has happened."

"So it is possible to kill him?" I asked. "Balor, I mean."

"Is that what you took from my tale?" The Mórrígan seemed almost offended as she looked me up and down. "I thought better of you than that, Darragh Cullen. Perhaps sending you to slay the *Ollphéist* was a mistake. At any rate, the quicker we get you back to your world, the sooner this piece of wild that slithers within you may stop overwhelming your brain. So you must go. Find your lovers. Find my amulet. Attempt this on your own, but I shall be there when you need me."

I nodded. If The Mórrígan was going to disrupt centuries of Fae rule for me, I needed to at least try to level the playing field for her first. Her palm reached to caress my stubbled cheek, stopping short as the wild within me lurched to meet her there.

Her eyes went black as she cocked her head to consider me as if for the first time once again. She rose into the air, transforming swiftly into the crow form I'd first met her in. She flew to the safe side of the bridge, watching closely as Madison and I made our way to the other.

CHAPTER 18

I gripped the guardrail and pulled my weight up to the first rung, examining the waves and the shoreline beneath. The tide was low—or whatever the river equivalent of that was; whatever the Fae Realm equivalent of that was—which allowed for about three feet of rocky sand below the bridge between the water and the actual barrier Balor had raised around his lands. If we managed our jumps properly, we could avoid getting wet or penetrating the border before we were ready.

I nodded to Madison, then grunted as my feet hit the ground, bending my knees to help absorb the shock of the drop, and stepped quickly aside to give them room to land.

"This was a lot easier when I was a cat," they quipped, and I was happy one of us still had our sense of mirth about us. My smile helped cut the dread rampaging over my lungs. A little humor always made the horrible more bearable. They smiled with me. "Let's go get our boys."

"You know you don't have to do this, right?"

My voice was blunt, but firm. I was grateful to have them by my side—a true illustration of bravery, especially considering they didn't have their magic—but the chaos that awaited us just beyond that barrier would be intense if not deadly.

"I mean, you don't have to put yourself in harm's way," I continued. "That derangement when Balor was in your head and you were in his, that's just what's bubbling beneath the surface. This will be the Fae in the flesh."

Madison's eyes glazed as they remembered his assault, all the fear they'd felt rushing through their limbs to send goosebumps crawling on their skin. They squinted as they shook the memory away.

"Honestly, the dude's insane," they smirked in a way that was nearly believable. "If he's running around like a chicken with its head cut off like he was in that brain of his, we might be able to get in and get out without him even noticing."

"That's just it," I sighed. "The inside of his head, that's all rage and madness. But his physical self… Well, it's all that anger plus a calculated, cold, and careless calm. I really don't know which side of him is more unnerving."

"I think I can handle it," they smiled, but I could hear the uncertainty in their voice. "Besides, all you guys went to bat for me when I needed it. It's the least I can do to stand up in return."

I nodded, cupping my hand over their shoulder to help quell their shiver. And my own. I was glad to have so many amazing witches in my life. If we got out of this, I'd have to be sure to tell them more often just how lucky I knew I was.

The pop of the barrier sang like carbonation in my ear as we passed through it a good fifteen feet from the bridge, but it was the smell that filled me more so. An odor—like corpses piled high and decaying—permeated the whole of the atmosphere. Rank and heavy, it sat on the air like a freshly smothered flame. I hoped it was just the thick mass of Rowan trees we were hiding within—their flowers were well known to emit such an aroma— but with Balor, I couldn't be sure. At least the buzzing bristle of bees provided a faint, honeyed scent beneath it all. Though it did little to mask the rot, their noise gave us a bit of cover.

Madison gasped, digging their fingers into my wrist, as they directed my attention toward a pair of Fachans patrolling the interior barrier. They were surprisingly agile, hopping along on their sole bottom limbs as their singular eyes scanned the area. The sharpened spear they carried from the one arm protruding from their chests doubled as a walking stick for stability. We were as quiet as we could be as I ushered Madison deeper into the brush. We crouched low to stay hidden.

"It was most likely just another bird," one of the Fachans said, his voice a gurgling grinder which melted into the sounds of the bees. "More of The Mórrígan's torments laid upon father."

"Could be," the other huffed, his own voice indistinguishable from his brother's. "Yet we feel the pain of our lord, so our duty must be done."

Damn. Balor certainly had a fucked up system of leadership and control. In actuality, all of the Fae did. At least the crows and the Banshees held lives of their own, separate from The Mórrígan's eye. Síl was enabled to take his many walkabouts from within the clutches of Cernunnos's woods. Even the Changelings honor for their mother Echo had appeared to be of their own free will. That Balor kept such a mental hold on his monsters was horrific. It also showed how powerful he truly was.

"So we must," the first Fachan agreed, but I could hear the reluctance in his voice.

Grunting, the two Fachans hopped to face one another. Their eyes locked as their hands reached out to clasp hard on each other's around their spears. Their fingers twitched, their talon-like nails threatening to break the other's skin as they ticked out the motions of a Fae spell.

A faint wall of magic sprung between them. It was weak, sort of like a seer's first spell, and appeared inconsequential until I noticed the slight difference in the way the clouds rested inside their prism. Shit. They were watching the last few moments of time tied to their location. If they moved a few paces to the west, they wouldn't need to see us hiding in order to know we'd come through.

"Does dear old father not trust his prowess or his tower?" the first Fachan complained, causing a flicker to wash through their spell as it broke between them. "Those two witches don't have a spit of magic between them. And Ethniu, who does, has been locked in that place for centuries. They shall not escape."

I stifled the sigh of relief that rushed from my chest. Cernun and Learco were alive. That meant we still had a chance.

"Those witches are but bait for the Cullen one," the other Fachan scolded. "He will come, and father must know when he arrives. Now concentrate."

The Fachans hopped a step closer to our entry point and conjured their spell once more. I tapped the ground softly for Madison's attention, then pulled my legs slowly beneath me, still staying low to the ground, but ready to run when the moment called. Once they had the vision of our burst through the barrier, we would only have a few seconds to attempt our escape. We needed a distraction. Or a miracle.

I heard the twang before I saw the spear, dyed the berry-red of the Rowans and true in aim as it flew past the Fachans to pierce the distant curve of the island's shore. Their spell broke as their hands unclasped, the first hopping toward where the spear had landed before the second caught him and hurdled them both rolling along the shore before they found their footing again. Although they were strong, the Fachans truly were dense. Maybe we could use that to our advantage.

"Stop chasing snipes," one of them growled. I really couldn't tell which was which anymore. "It's just Cethlenn out hunting again."

Madison and I remained still as their growls hummed at one another, each Fachan staring the other down in a battle of wit and might neither could win.

"Who's Cethlenn?" Madison whispered.

The vibrations of the bees accelerated as a voice surrounded us, "I am!" ringing in our ears as the wood went dark.

The darkness lifted to surprisingly quaint surroundings. We were in someone's home. From my crouched position on the floor, I could tell it was circular, just as the Wayward Inn had been. I saw the lifelines of a Rowan tree along the surface of the floor, lighter at the edges and spiraling inward to the deep brown at the center where she made her hearth. A couch, which I assumed doubled as a bed, was upholstered in the same brown fabric as her dress and had only a small amount of the straw and other stuffing pushing through the fibers. Its pillows were woven with stitched depictions of plants that matched in skill and thread the embroidered array of battle-clad pictures tacked to the wall behind them. A collection of crystals hung from hooks in the ceiling. The far wall showcased an assortment of spears—all matching the one used to distract the Fachans in color—of varying lengths and barbed endings. A sweet smelling stew bubbled in the cauldron above the fire. Also like the Wayward Inn, there were no windows to the outside world, but the entire space held a pleasant, ethereal glow.

A Fae woman stood smirking a few feet away. Her skin, the

color of burnt amber, held an iridescent glow which was accented perfectly by the soft, hay-brown of the dress which clung to her rotund frame. Firm, muscular arms crossed over her large breasts, and, when she cocked her head to the side, her braided mahogany hair swung like a noose behind her.

"That should keep those idiots busy for a while," she sang.

Her voice was deep and hoarse, like water pushing through a geyser, and blended with the pulsing of the bees which swarmed around her head. They must have followed us through her transportation spell. I wondered if they felt as dizzy as I did.

"You're Cethlenn?" Madison asked, voice trembling as we both rose to our feet.

"Oh, I've had many names," the Fae woman shrugged. She busied herself as she spoke, picking the swarming bees from the air around her and plopping them into glass jars where they batted the clear edges in hopes of escape. I wondered if we'd be next.

"Queen, Empress, Caít, Lenda," she hummed. "Wife, Mother, Seer, Enchantress. Spearer of the Dagda. Murderer of Gods."

It was so similar to The Mórrígan's welcome speech when I'd first met her, I wondered if they'd collaborated on a script.

"But yes, the two of you may call me Cethlenn. And I assume one of you to be the Cullen witch who has brought this island to a tizzy."

I nodded, trying hard not to focus on the brown, crooked lines of her teeth. Though she did not seem embarrassed by them. Truthfully, the juxtaposition of her mouth's rocky visage only served to enhance her inherent Fae beauty.

"Very well," she smiled. "We have much to discuss. Please, take a seat." When Madison looked to me in hesitation, Cethlenn added, "Unless you would prefer I send you back to test your luck with Balor's henchmen. Would you like some stew?"

My stomach growled, but I was still wary of accepting food from the Fae. Unless I'd seen it prepared, who knew what it could contain.

"Why did you save us?" I blurted. "What do you want from us?"

Cethlenn laughed. It was a hearty laugh, and her crystals clinked to accent it as they swayed around her head.

"I had nearly forgotten you witch types and your penchant for questions," she said, sitting in her chair and gesturing for us to take the couch. "Always wanting to know the what and the why and the how instead of just accepting things for what they are and taking the necessary action. It's what made your kind so very delicious when striking our bargains. That constant need to know more. Very well. Let us get down to it."

The couch was shockingly comfortable. Or maybe it had just been so long since I'd had a soft surface beneath me that made it feel lush. I still couldn't relax though. I wouldn't be able to until Cernun and Learco were back by my side.

"You have arrived upon my island home," she said, "the valiant warrior come to rescue his fair princes from the clutches of my mad husband."

I hoped my shock wasn't audible. Damn it! Had we walked straight into a ambush? Or worse, a lover's quarrel.

"I have no intention of entering into any other bargains with any Fae," I interrupted. I needed to be firm. My witchly quid pro quo with nature was one thing, but the conniving essence of the Fae made the deals with them more like a trap. And I was already plenty caged.

Cethlenn's laugh was joyful, its depths heightened by the crystals clanking around the room like twinkling starlight.

"You are smarter than you look," she said. "No bargain. But I do ask of you a favor."

My lips pursed. Of course when a Faerie wanted something, it would be a favor. The irony that any witch or mortal asking the Fae for something equated to a bargain and not goodwill was not lost on me. Nor, by the look in her eyes, was it on Cethlenn.

"You will reach your lovers in the tower," she continued when her laughter died down to a giggle. "You will free them. I have seen it as so. My request of you is that you also free my daughter."

I furrowed my brow and tilted my head, jutting my chin at the sudden solemnity in her voice. I could feel her pain upon the air as easily as I had felt her joviality before.

"My dear, sweet Ethniu, my only daughter, has been locked within my husband's stronghold for centuries. I… I just want to see her again."

"Why was she locked away?" Madison asked the question I was thinking, and we were met with the crocodile tears of Cethlenn's wail.

"I am the one to blame for my daughter's internment," she gasped between sobs. "For I am cursed with the sight and, too, with a love for my betrothed. I told him of my vision: that his grandson would lead to his death. I spoke to him in love, and he turned that kindness to terror. He locked our child away to prevent her from ever becoming pregnant so that no offspring could threaten his reign."

Madison's brow scrunched as they looked to me incredulously. I was certain my expression was similar. Cethlenn's histrionics aside, the whole tale seemed a bit far-fetched. Not that in-fighting and backstabbing amongst the Fae wasn't commonplace. I just felt like she wasn't telling us the full story, and the parts the Fae left out could have horrific repercussions.

"I didn't think the Fae could be killed," I said, trying to sound as sympathetic as possible.

Cethlenn's tears dried as quickly as they'd come on.

"We die; we come back," she said. "Usually. Yet a death that has been preordained is a final death. We all have them. Nothing lives forever. In its current form at least. My marriage is proof of that."

My lips twisted as I considered her words. Balor was a menace, even to his own kin, and his final demise would free me and my lovers of our bargain with him. And save our world in the process. If he wasn't around, Learco, Cernun, and I wouldn't have to figure out a way to give him access to our realm. And countless lives—countless witches—would be saved a terrible future. Ethnui's freedom could produce a child to make that a reality. And it was not like she was asking me to kill him myself. Still, as a conscious decision, it weighed on me.

Madison could read the turmoil on my face.

"You did slay the *Ollphéist*," they said, their whisper an attempt to assuage the guilt that was bustling up inside of me.

They were right. I had slain the serpent without knowing it would regenerate. But I had done so to save the lives of the *murúch*. And, though it had a consciousness, it wasn't quite the same. Was it? I had grown up on a farm. I knew creatures—animals—died in the balance of nature. And I did enjoy way too many hamburgers at Aunt Paulina's. But as animalistic as Balor was, this felt different.

"His death will occur, should you help me or not," Cethlenn assured me. "Your actions here would only enable a mother to reunite with her child. I will always love my husband. Yet a mother's love for her child goes beyond anything any of the worlds may offer."

"Is that why you're living in the woods?" Madison asked.

Cethlenn's laugh startled us both as she switched from ecstatic to woeful and back again like she was trying on hats to see what best suited her shape. I supposed centuries of life made all of the Fae adept at emotional compartmentalization. Time—and feeling—would be as present as it was inconsequential, absorbing them fully then gone in the blink of an eye. At least Cethlenn made me think so. But there was still the very real chance she was playing us.

"I live within the Rowans due to my husband's obsessions and the madness which has overcome him through his pursuits. He is determined to be the first of the High Fae to return to the Earthly Realm. To bring triumph over the Tuath Dé for the Fomóraiġ. But such a lofty goal, alongside your binding of his mind, has amplified that drive, which I admit once drew me to him, into lunacy."

The way she stressed the "your" was subtle, but I heard the implication of the guilt-trip she intended. I was no more responsible for Balor's madness than I was for the sudden early Spring of daffodils growing rampantly all over Atlanta, even if my supposed spell sign was attached to them. People—witch, Fae, or human—made their own decisions. And I needed to make mine. I needed to find my lovers and get all of us the hell out of there.

"I will attempt to rescue Ethniu as I rescue my coven," I said. "But no bargains. And no promises."

"I knew you would," Cethlenn smiled, suddenly the gracious, homemaker host once more. "I saw you in a vision…. Don't worry. I have been in these woods for quite some time now. I have not told my husband of your coming. Though his Fachans probably took care of that."

"Two questions," Madison piped up. "First, how are the Fachan his children and not yours? And second, if you saw our coming, can you tell us how this ends up?"

Cethlenn giggled as she rose from her chair, walking gracefully to her cauldron to stir her simmering stew like every witch in every engraving I'd ever seen. Maybe we weren't so different after all.

"Fae children may be begotten in two ways. The fun, carnal way which all species share and all species enjoy. Or they may be children of the mind, of the singular flesh. The latter are dependent upon the amount of oneself one is willing to give."

That made sense. It helped define the line between child and minion the Fae seemed to have blurred. But that was why Síl, a child of Cernunnos and whomever had been his mother, was so different than Fachan or the Changelings. Why the Banshees had their agency beyond The Mórrígan. The Children of the Mind were yet another wrung on the ladder. The Fae certainly loved their hierarchies.

"As for your second question," Cethlenn continued, now spooning her soup into broad wooden bowls, "there are many outcomes with many variables, all of which are dependent on you. I cannot know your future precisely, only many futures which may be. What happens next is entirely in your hands."

She carried the stews to us and placed them on our laps.

"Now, eat up. You will need your strength for the battle ahead. It is quite a journey to the top floor cells of my husband's tower."

I stared at the mixture in the bowl as Cethlenn stared down at us. I wasn't surprised to see the Rowan berries, whole and macerated and turning the entire concoction the red of a fresh wound. I wondered if the bitter sweet taste of the fruits would complement the chunks of what I believed to be fish that floated amongst the various vegetables in the stock. From the determined squint on Cethlenn's face, I was about to find out.

I raised the bowl slowly to my lips, and Madison followed my lead.

She wants something from you, I told myself to force my lips apart. *It's not like she's going to poison you when she needs your help.*

The first sip barely met my tongue before it warmed my gullet. No immediate reaction. That was something. Cethlenn's gesture encouraged me further.

It tasted exotic and strange, yet it filled me with the comfort of a home cooked meal. It felt good to have something in my stomach. I wondered if Cernun and Learco had eaten anything since they'd been captured. Or hell, since they'd been here. I worried what I would find when I found them. Maybe I could convince Cethlenn to pack up a few containers of the delicious stew so we could bring my lovers some food.

The sounds of the crystals clanking from the ceiling filled my ears as the room grew darker. My eyes felt heavy. The gems began to shine like stars.

"Come on, Darragh! You need to wake up!"

The sun was bright. I could see it through my closed eyelids, red and orange and vehemently burning, as I pulled my consciousness from the ethereal kaleidoscope of my dreams. Trails of the night's visions were blurring already into obscurity, but I didn't want to open my eyes. There was something sweet I was supposed to be holding onto, even if I couldn't remember what it was.

"You don't want to be late!" A second voice joined the first, and I felt four hands pulling at my arms from either side, gently jostling me back and forth like a baby in a cradle. "It's not every day you get an audience with the benevolent Lord Balor."

Balor?!? Oh, shit! I was supposed to be…. I needed to save…. I couldn't remember.

My eyelashes fluttered with the sticky sand of sleep as I pulled myself to a seated position, craning my neck away from the brightness of the sun and allowing my eyes to focus on my surroundings. To my right, Learco held an amused smirk that accentuated the seductive glimmer of his dark brown eyes. The two-week shadow of his beard highlighted the sharpness of his cheekbones, and I licked my lips as my vision trailed down his naked torso to the barely there fabric of his waist wrapped skirt. Cernun, to my left, had the same excited glow to his face, and the brightened colors of his tattoos bounced with every tic of his muscles. There was so much love in their eyes. I just wanted to stay there forever, and I told them as much.

They laughed in unison as they rose from the wood-framed cot we shared, standing together at the foot of the bed with their hands on their hips and heads swaying back and forth in a synchronized dance.

"You fellas look like you're straight out of some old sitcom," I laughed.

"Sitcom?" Cernun asked, furrowing his brow in an exaggeration question even as his smile kept plastered to his lips. "That's a funny word."

Learco's mouth swallowed the syllables as he repeated them over and over between giggles. It was a funny word. I felt like it used to mean something—that it was a portmanteau of two words that once required defining, that had become so prevalent an abbreviation had been required—but I couldn't place it anywhere in my memory. It didn't matter. The past, as it were, was inconsequential within the brightened fire of the new world.

I pulled myself from our cot and smiled down at the indentions of our bodies in the cotton-wrapped straw. It was small, but we fit together on it perfectly. Just as Lord Balor, in his infinite wisdom, had intended. That he wanted to see me—a lowly sand-raker—was astonishing. I spent my days tilling the gritty, acidic earth for any signs of the metals Lord Balor had so graciously removed when he cleansed the world of our chains and enabled our freedom. I had not found a single shaving of iron or rust in the six months since our great awakening. Still, that he wanted to see me felt special.

"You should come with me," I smiled to my lovers, the curve of my lips extending high into my cheeks. By Balor, it felt good to always smile.

"Just to the gates," Cernun cooed, and his widespread lips touched the upturned space where my smile ended on my left.

"This is your day, after all," Learco added and pressed his lips upon my right

I could see the apex of Balor's tower well before we reached the walls of Atlanta. It rose, bright and glimmering in the sun, as a beacon to all who would seek to see the truth. Lord Balor had forged every last speck of metal particulate to form its reach to the heavens: a reminder of a past when we used bars and fetters and weapons as bondage; a lighthouse to the god who had set us free. We were lucky to exist in its light. The hot red fires of the sun reflected from its polish to ensure no one would face the shadows of the dark ever again. The heat had rid the world of the hideous green that once plagued the tree tops, leaving them tall and proud and brown and stretching their limbs in veneration of the sky. Under his light, we were the true children of earth and air and fire, without the obscuration of the shade which had kept our visions hindered as they once were.

"Darragh Cullen," I announced when we reached the gate,

bowing to the benevolent Fachan guard there in attendance.

He closed his great, singular eye in communion with our Lord before his hand extended to welcome me within. Learco and Cernun released their grips on my arms and urged me forward before the Fachan blinked and grinned.

"Lord Balor shall see you, too," he purred. "Darragh Cullen, Cernun Kyteler, Learco Clarke; you may all enter to his majesty."

Oh, that we had been born Fachan. That we could have the direct connection to our god that those with bi-ocular vision did not possess. Yet we were given a different lot in life. Still, we were grateful, and we were glorious; and we were called to meet him all the same.

Two more Fachans appeared to guide us to our Lord. I kept one eye trained on them, careful not to miss a step, while the other swam the vast, metallic sheen of the tower before us. I supposed that was one benefit of being split-eyed. Though I'd been told the monocular Balor and the single-eyed Fachan saw far more, far swifter than us dual-eyed creatures ever could.

The tower was even more beautiful close up. The way the metals plied together, twisting and swirling in bands of silver and gold and copper and brass, shiny and matte, bonded and reinforced as they stretched skyward was said to be only rivaled in splendor by the refining crucible of Lord Balor's eye. That he turned our past bonds into something so enchanting was phenomenal; that my lovers and I were getting to see it up close was even more glorious. I almost felt sad to walk inside.

Though I needn't have been worried. The interior was just as elaborate as the exterior, which made sense as the tower served also as Lord Balor's palace. Gracious king that he was, he surrounded himself in our bonds so that we were no longer subjugated by them.

A cold chill swept through me as we entered the throne room, but it did nothing to wither my smile. To be chosen to meet with Lord Balor was an honor. That my lovers were with me made it even better.

The Fachan ushered us to the center of the room, nodded for us to genuflect, and departed. I smoothed the fabric of my skirt as I dropped to my knees, bowing my head and lowering my eyes to wait. I could feel the heat as Lord Balor entered though I did not dare to look upon him until he called for my attention. I felt the rapture of his presence move past us as he took his seat upon his throne.

"You may rise," he called.

Cernun, Learco, and I scrambled swiftly to our feet. My eyes, not daring to look directly upon his until I was asked, shifted over the marvels of the room, of his royal seat, of his body. Fuck, he was beautiful. His thick, muscled legs spread as he planted the soles of his feet against the hard, metallic ground. The sarong around his waist did even less to cover the bulk of him than my lovers' threadbare fabrics, and his torso rippled with the pulsing muscles of the god he truly was. Behind him, his golden throne shone like a million suns with pointed rays radiating to reach every last inch of our world. The ray pointing directly upward behind him was the most refined and engrossing red I had ever seen or ever would see. Until I was called to look upon his eye.

"Be you too afraid to speak?" he snarled, and I wondered how anyone in his vicinity could ever suffer fear. "The three of you are usually such chatty, clever witches."

What did he mean? I had never had the honor of his presence before, never the glory to speak with him. And to call us witches? Well, that was downright absurd. No one but the Fae held any power, and no one but Lord Balor knew how to wield it. He must have been mistaken, though how could he be? It was impossible for Lord Balor to ever be wrong.

Perhaps he was testing us, tempting our faith with his wisdom and words. My smile refused to waver. And the slight raise in his cheek as I looked upon his lips told me he was smiling too.

"I shall deal with the Kyteler and the Clarke first," he said, and, as if by magic, my lovers were pushed before me. "Look upon my eye," he continued. "Know all that I know. And burn."

They were beautiful as they embraced each other, a smoking haze licking at their skin as flames began to caress their bodies with the might of Balor's love. Their smiles were even more beautiful as they widened, their skin melting away to reveal their souls, to welcome them into the heart of Balor's iris where his warmth and his light and his power would forever preserve them in his bright dignity.

I hoped Lord Balor would allow me to follow. I held my breath to be called. Smiling. Trembling. Eyes focused on the glorious red ray of his sun throne as he turned his smiling eye toward the sky.

CHAPTER 19

"Come on, Darragh! You need to wake up!"

Madison's voice was faint as it whispered through the periphery of my thoughts. Anxious and distant, it was the opposite of everything I wanted. I didn't want to move. I didn't want to go anywhere. The flames were so warm, so comforting as they engulfed me. Their promises of forever could never be extinguished.

"What did you do to him?" they demanded.

I wiped my eyes as my body left the safety of my dream, the security of the fire. My breath was shallow as I pulled it into my chest, but the air helped me come to. The worry on Madison's face wavered, but it was still there.

"I was unaware this one held onto his power," Cethlenn protested, though I could tell she was lying. "The fruit of the Rowan can bring on visions to those with magics."

My head pounded as I pulled myself to a seated position, glancing to the bowls of discarded stew strewn before us on the floor. Cethlenn's face still held her jovial, wicked smile, and Madison busied themself with checking my pulse as I wrenched my body back into being.

"Was that—was that the future?" I asked. My voice was smoky and dry, and I swallowed hard to wet the ash in my throat.

"Perhaps," Cethlenn shrugged. "Or perhaps it was one potential outcome. Visions are often obtuse. Ask any seer. And I, despite my many magics, have no way of knowing what you saw. Still, experience has taught me this: what your vision chooses to present to you will be prescient in your coming fight. Should you interpret it properly and in time, that is."

I had no idea how that dream was supposed to help me at all beyond reminding me to fear the fuck out of Balor. It also didn't help that a bit of that joy and reverence which clung to his name within that dystopian paradise was still lingering inside of me. I had to hope that whatever I was meant to learn from it would reveal itself to me when the time was right, if there was such a thing as a "right" time anymore. Everything was all fucked up. But I had a mission, and that would have to carry me through.

I stumbled a bit as I rose to my feet, and Madison leapt up to brace my arm.

"I'm fine," I told them, and it was starting to feel true. The further the feelings evoked in my fantasy slipped from me, the stronger I felt. "We need to get going if we're going to rescue Learco and Cernun. We need to do it now!"

Cethlenn cleared her throat, and I nodded.

"And Ethniu," I promised. "We will free your daughter too."

The smile returned to our host's face as she took my hand in hers.

"I shall lead you to the tower," she said. "The rest is up to you."

Balor's tower was stationed on a cliffside at the far side of the island with only one way in which meant only one way out. Unless we wanted to dive into the rocky waters beyond it. I had to admit I was impressed by the structure *and* the magic he'd woven through his barrier to make it appear as a rock formation from the far shore of the river. As far as glamours went, the hiding-in-plain-sight plus the imposing terror of it all were remarkable. But maybe that was just residual bliss still lingering from my vision.

"I don't see any guards," Madison whispered from our cover within the underbrush at the edge of the wood. "Maybe they're all stationed over by the bridge waiting for us to arrive."

"Or maybe he's just not worried about us," I groaned.

I would almost feel better to have to fight my way through a horde of angry Fachans. At least that would mean Balor was somewhat concerned instead of just wanting me in his tower dungeon too. That the tower was left unguarded meant either Balor was already smug in his defeat of our little faction or the whole thing was a trap. I hoped it was the previous. History had taught me the self-satisfied and arrogant fell hard, even if I was still waiting for that tumble from the MAW. That was something I could work with. The latter would be trickier.

"Alright, boss," Madison smiled, slapping their fist against their palm in anticipation. "Are we gonna Rapunzel up this bitch or go knock on the door? I'm down for either."

"I need you to stay here," I sighed, knowing it was the last thing they wanted to hear. "I don't know what we're walking into in there. And I need to know you're safe. Ish. Plus, if I…. *When* I get Learco and Cernun out, I need you here to lead them back through the woods while I take care of Balor once and for all."

"Dude," Madison growled. "I've been a cat for months. And then a fucking fish. This battle is ours. I need to stretch my fucking legs."

"You don't have your magic," I protested.

"But I have you."

The way they said it made it final. I still didn't like it, but I nodded in acquiescence.

"Plus. And I hope this is not the case. But, depending on what state we find them in, you may need help getting Learco and Cernun down the what I'm assuming are spiral stairs and out."

They had a point. Even if it wasn't an image I wanted to face. And it would be good to have someone watching my back. I just knew I would never forgive myself if they didn't make it back to our world, with or without the rest of us.

"Okay," I conceded. "I guess it's not like I could stop you anyway."

"You really couldn't."

"Stick to the Fachans if we're ambushed," I told them. "They're strong, but wobbly. And if that little display by the barrier was any indication, they don't have much magic either. I think it takes two of them to conjure anything, so don't let them clasp hands."

"Seems simple enough."

"We just need to remember that when they see us, Balor does too. Which means once we're spotted, he could pop up fucking anywhere. So we need to be as covert as we can be."

Madison shivered. Even having not seen Balor in the flesh, they'd had a front row seat to his power. I was glad they understood the gravity of the situation. And honored they'd insisted on pushing forward.

"Alright," they nodded, cataloging our goals in their head. "Attack the Fachans but stay hidden. Climb the tower to an unknown location. Rescue your boyfriends and the princess. Then slide down the flagpole to victory."

When my face fell at their assessment, they quickly added,

"I know it's not a video game. We don't get to regenerate like the Fae."

"Which gives them the ultimate advantage," I sighed.

I turned my attention back to the tower, surveying the periphery for any sign of movement, any sign of Fachans in wait. I tried to convince myself it was good they weren't around. It actually worked in our favor, even if the nagging voice in my mind was trying to convince me it meant there was a neon sign above the door flashing "Step Into My Parlor."

But if Balor was so sure he could best us, maybe we could actually slip in and out without being noticed. Growing up gay in the South in the 80s had taught me a thing or two about stealth. Plus, Madison had their months as a feline to draw from. Maybe we really could pull this off.

"What did your vision show you?" Madison whispered, pulling me from the circus of my fears and back to our hiding space.

I trembled.

"A world we can't let happen."

"Then we won't."

Madison's resolve was encouraging, and I pulled a tiny tendril of the wild magic I'd inherited into my consciousness. Using it still felt unpredictable, but I knew I needed it close at hand. I just hoped I hadn't called enough force to reveal our location to the Fae as we traveled.

That the tower door was unlocked only lent credence to my "it's a trap" theory, but we had no choice but to push forward. I motioned for Madison to hold while I scanned the interior for any signs of trouble. The Fae certainly enjoyed their circular structures. I supposed it made sense. No dark corners to hide in meant no surprise visitors from the shadows. Plus, I guessed it was a little more of a natural shape than the squares and rectangles I was used to.

Unlike Cethlenn's place or what I'd seen of the first floor of the Wayward Inn, Balor's tower was divided internally. The design still kept a curve to the walls, but it also meant arched doorways leading to Fae knew what. It looked a little like it had in my dream except all that was metallic, sleek, and shiny there was cobbled stone, mud, and muck in this reality. If my vision had been correct, the doorway to our right led to what Balor called his throne room. So that meant the curved expanse to our left hid the staircase which spiraled toward the cells.

The ground floor was eerily quiet, but we could not afford to lower our guard. I nodded toward the left, my eyes urging Madison to follow my lead, but they held up a finger to stop me. Wetting their lips, they lowered themself to the floor and scooped a handful of the dry and cracking clay floor into their palms. My brow furrowed, head cocking as I watched them spit repeatedly to douse the clay in saliva. It took a bit for me to understand what they were up to, but as the soil turned to mud, I smiled. Winking, they pushed the mixture into the keyhole of the door, and I sent a small zap of my magic outward to pull out the moisture with a smile. A clogged mechanism meant they couldn't lock us in, at least not easily, and my lips silently thanked Madison for their astuteness.

We took the stairs slowly, pressed close to the outer wall and crouching as we passed the tiny slits in the structure just large enough for an arrow or a spear or a focused force of power to fling out. My breath was quiet and shallow as we moved. Judging by the size of the tower and the grand height of the ceilings inside, there were three, maybe four floors above us. Learco and Cernun would be at the top. And the others, well, they could be washed with horrors untold.

I felt like it took forever to breach the first landing. As my head crested the liminal space between the ceiling and the floor—that thick slab where it was neither and both simultaneously—I held tight to my breath. The second floor was more open than the first, but carved wooden cabinets and counter tops offered some division of space that centered around the open fire pit and cauldron baked into the center of the room. In actuality, it would have made one hell of a spelling kitchen for an earth witch like me. Though Fae kind didn't really rely on the tinctures and potions we witches often used, I imagined the space still conjured one hell of a feast to sate Balor's "kingly" desires. Damn, I was still hungry. Despite the vision it gave me, I felt my stomach growl for more of Cethlenn's Rowan soup. Luckily, the hunger pangs were short-served, fear and adrenaline kicking into overdrive to quell the rumblings in my gut that weren't being caused by the overactive course of my magic.

The landing stretched about ten feet of open air before the stairwell picked up again along the outer wall of the tower. We'd be utterly exposed. But that was not as concerning as the freshly-stifled fire beneath the still-glowing pot. The embers wafted a silted gray smoke while whatever was in the cauldron pocked and bubbled as it ached to escape the container.

We were definitely not alone.

I held up my hand to slow Madison's advance, and they crouched down to keep an eye on the floor below as I watched for any sign of movement above, ducking quickly when I heard the clatter of metal and glass from behind one of the taller cabinets.

"I do not understand how he expects us to batch enough of this shit for every foot soldier to have a vial."

The gravel-ridden voice of the Fachan was unmistakable. I froze as I watched him amble toward the cauldron, a basket of glass bottles hanging from his arm.

"The Cullen witch is slow, so we will have time," a second

Fachan growled, hopping into place beside the first with a metal funnel. "But he will come. Witches, naive creatures that they are, cannot bear to leave well enough alone. He will attempt to rescue those flesh sacks he calls lovers."

"And we will be ready."

A third Fachan spoke as they took their place in the trio by the cauldron. Except for the odd assortment of limbs and eyes, they looked like Macbeth's witches all hunched and snarling over their bubbling pit. Maybe the Fae were not as adverse to potions as I'd thought. I certainly didn't want to find out what was in the cauldron.

They worked as a team quite well: the first producing a vial, the second steadying the funnel, and the third ladling the thick, tar black ooze into the glass before hanging his spoon to cork up the top.

It was good they hadn't realized Madison and I were on the island yet. We had Cethlenn to thank for that. I did not want to find out what would happen once they realized I'd breached their borders. And I certainly didn't want to know what they'd do if they found us in the tower. As bumbling as they were, I knew they'd be ferocious en mass.

They were distracted by their task though, concentrating hard on not spilling a drop as the ooze slipped from the metal spoon into the glass vial. Perhaps that would give us an opening to pass by unseen. We'd have to move anyway before they'd completed the job and one of them headed out to distribute that goo, and I refused to let retreat become an option while Cernun and Learco withered upstairs.

A finger to my lips, I inched slowly up the steps, hoping our trek across the landing would be mostly obscured by the cabinetry of the kitchen. A part of me thought we could have danced a little jig while singing though. The Fachan were so engrossed in their task, in their bickering, they would not have seen our silhouettes if we'd had broomsticks and a full moon.

We were nearly to the top of the next stairwell when a bloodcurdling wail froze me to my core. My every instinct urged me to run, but my morbid curiosity kept me still. Madison clutched my arm as I slowly lowered into a crouch to witness the bustle below. Our vantage point near the ceiling gave us a perfect view of the carnage. And unless one of them looked up, we'd be okay.

I didn't think they would though. The screaming and the expletives and the foul stench of melting flesh held every eyeline in the room. The ladler trembled, mouth ajar as the Fachan who'd manned the funnel screamed.

"What the fuck did you do?" the vial holder bellowed. "How could you miss the pipe?"

"Because they don't have depth perception," Madison whispered, and I caught the snicker before it could escape my throat.

It didn't matter. The shrieks of pain from the injured Fachan drowned out our noise. My eyes grew wide as the scene unfolded.

The black sludge was powerful. And it didn't stop where it landed. Once it had consumed the Fachan's hand, it traveled—like a living, breathing thing—up his arm to his chest before engulfing his entire body. His screams ceased as quickly as they'd started as the goo covered his mouth, filling inward even as it continued to advance around his head. It turned solid; turned ashy; and the body-that-was disintegrated to a pile of stiffened coal on the ground. Even the stone floor where another drip had fallen sizzled and sparked before the magic in the brew faded.

"Well?" the vial holder huffed. "Go get another! Despite your incompetence, we still have a job to do."

The ladler, still shaking with his spoon held aloft like a shield, kept his eye trained on the pile of stone that was his brother as the obvious leader of the trio commanded him to depart.

They really were idiots, those Fachan. I would have almost felt sorry for them—half a creature under the thumb of a madman like Balor—if they hadn't been trying to kill me and my loved ones. It was horrific to watch, but I couldn't pull my eyes away.

Madison shook their head and pointed as a tiny remnant of the goo dislodged from the ladle and landed on the Fachan.

The first Fachan didn't even wait for his brother to stop screaming and burn to death before he'd dropped his basket and made his way to the stairs, grumbling about duty the whole way.

Madison managed to hold it in until we heard the front door on the ground floor swoop open and slam, but then doubled over in laughter. My breath caught before I realized that if the screams of the dying Fachan hadn't brought any others to the floor, from above or below, we were alone enough to relax. Well, mostly. We still had some witches to save.

"Why was I ever afraid of them?" Madison cried between gasps of laughter.

"Well, I mean, they do pack a punch with those fists," I laughed along, then sobered as I added, "And they managed to take Learco and Cernun."

Madison's face fell. I could see the trauma in their eyes as they remembered the attack, and they nodded.

"Come on," I said, snapping them back to the task at hand as the rank odor of melted flesh began to rise to our position. "The tower's obviously empty. Let's get this done."

I was on my feet and to the third floor without another thought. A bed, slightly more elaborate than the straw-stuffed couch I'd seen at Cethlenn's, floated in the center of the room. The indention of Balor's body on the mattress was heavy and foreboding, showcasing the giant girth of my opponent without him even being present. Jagged, angered scrapes cratered the floor by each of the bedposts to tell me he was restless and violent even in his sleep. An arsenal of weapons clung to the stone walls of the room—spears and maces; scian and swords. It was obvious a warrior lived here. And adding his Fae magic to the mix, it was obvious I was outgunned.

Yet the thing that worried me most was that the stairwell just ended. Cethlenn had assured us the cells were at the top of the tower. Shit. Maybe this really was a trap. Or more of that *enter through the threads of space and time* Fae magic. Either way, we were fucked.

"Do you see anything that might lead to the next floor?" I asked, surprised by the panic evident in my voice which only increased when I got no response.

I spun suddenly. I thought Madison had been right behind me. If they had been captured—or, worse yet, killed—I would never forgive myself. My power churned beneath my stomach, punctuating the core of my being as my agitation and anxiety merged within my mind. I should have had The Mórrígan send them back to our world through the cracks the Changelings had created while we were still near Echo's land. At least then I'd have only been risking my own life to save my lovers.

Their electric blue locs crested the stairwell opening as they bounded upwards, and my entire body quaked as I ran to embrace them.

"Careful!" they called as my arms wrapped them.

I pulled back to stare at their confused but smiling face.

"You don't want to break these," they grinned.

Their hands proudly displayed six corked bottles of the Fachans' vile potion. It pulsed against the glass as if it were begging for freedom, for purchase, for death.

"I figured since the room was empty," they shrugged, "it wouldn't hurt for us to have some of their weapons on hand to turn against them. Speaking of weapons…."

Their voice trailed off as they paced the perimeter of the room, marveling at the glistening, sharp edges of Balor's blades.

"Should we take some of these too?" they asked.

"I'm hoping we don't have to get close enough for hand to hand combat with Balor," I sighed, shivering as I placed the three vials Madison had handed me into the waistband of my pants. The potion was warm against my skin, even through the glass, and I closed my eyes to push the sensation from my head. "We have a bigger problem right now though."

"Oh shit!" Madison said, swirling their head around the circle of the room. "There's no stairs. How the hell are we supposed to get up there?"

I shrugged, the worry evident on my face. There had to be something we were missing. My gut told me we could trust Cethlenn—as much as we could trust any Fae—and, despite the overdramatic telling of her tale, she really did love and want us to rescue her daughter. Though maybe she loved her maniac of a husband more.

"What if there's, like, a lever somewhere or something," Madison suggested. "All those old castles loved their secret passages, right?"

Their fingers traced the edge of a giant silver shield perched upon the wall. Its dented, gashed facade displayed its days of battle proudly, and the crimson, flaming eye of its central crest burned like blood. I jumped as Madison's fingers dislodged it from its hooks, and it fell, crashing and clanging against the stone floor.

"Shit. Sorry," they said, kneeling to the floor to stop the ringing noise of the metal's vibration.

But I was more intrigued by the area of the wall behind where the shield had sat. A small, dark hole—no larger than my fist— had been gouged into the wall, and I crossed the room for a closer look. It was intentional, I could tell. The tunnel was fashioned within the flute angled upward a few inches back. I squinted through the opening, but I couldn't see any light. Still, I knew it led up, and up was where we needed to go.

Pulling down the morning star a few feet away revealed an identical hole behind the spiked ball of its flail. A third tunnel rested behind the hilt of a sword; a fourth, hidden by the flattened head of a spear.

"Well, damn," Madison huffed. "I gotta hand it to his interior decorator. Weapons aren't really my thing, but they do a great job at hiding how badly this tower is falling apart."

"I think it's more than that," I said, trying to wrap my head around whatever patterns the sequence of holes were making as they dotted the room. There had to be a reason for them, a purpose. If we were lucky, they'd show us the way to the next floor.

"Darragh?"

Cernun's voice was weak as it called my name. Caked in cobwebs and dust, he sounded as if it had been days since any water had met his lips. I pressed my ear up to the hole in the wall, hoping my fantasies of reunion weren't conjuring up what I longed most to hear.

"Darragh?" he called again. "Is that really you?"

He sounded tired, but his words were growing stronger as more rushed through the pipe.

"It is me!" I gushed. "Madison is with me. Do you know how we can get to you?"

I held my breath at the silence, then leaned in closer to hear the wheeze and rustle of movement bound down from above.

"We don't," Learco said. Fuck, it was good to hear his voice. "Balor just sort of appears."

"But when he's gone, the stairwell goes with him," Cernun added.

They were both sounding stronger now. Hope could do that for a witch. I just hoped that hope was enough to get us out of this.

"I think there may be some sort of a secret passage," Madison called through another of the holes. "Maybe it has something to do with all these tubes. Like if we played the right song or revealed them in the right order the stairs would appear."

I knew Madison had a love for those historical fantasy novels, but the look on their face told me even they thought their suggestion was far-fetched. Still, it was the only one we had.

Reluctantly, I pulled myself away from the wall—away from my lovers' voices—and studied the patterns of the weapons atop the dug out chambers, but there was no discernible rhyme or reason to them. The shapes were mostly congruent in size, but the placement looked to be dictated by the stones and the mortar of the walls more so than anything else.

"Pay no attention to the holes." A third voice lilted like a song through the tubes. "It just pleases my father to listen to the moans of his prisoners. They are but a lullaby to him as he slumbers."

Ethniu's voice dripped with a resigned indifference, as if centuries trapped in her father's prison had left her both jaded and bored. And yet, it still held the melodic quality of Fae kind in its quiver which only intensified when I said her mother's name.

"Cethlenn has charged us with your rescue also, Ethniu," I yelled back through one of the ducts. "Can you tell us how to reach you?"

My lungs stopped as I waited for an answer. I doubted we had much time before the Fachan returned to their brewing below us. Once they heard us—once they saw us—Balor did too. We needed to move fast.

"His bed," she finally said.

"What are we supposed to do?" Madison whispered sarcastically to me as we rushed to the center of the room. "Jump on it until our heads push through the ceiling?"

I frowned as I moved widdershins around the frame, eyes scanning to search for whatever it was we were missing, whatever Ethniu had wanted us to find.

"I think you may be right," I finally sighed.

"Seriously? I doubt that straw is as bouncy as the springs in our mattresses back home."

"No," I grinned. "I mean your theory about the secret passage. Look at the scrapes on the floor."

The drag lines I'd thought were evidence of Balor's agitated sleep were better patterned than the holes in the wall, the wooden posts scraping to carve out a well-worn semicircle from each leg against the stone.

"Help me," I said as I braced my hands on the side of the frame.

We pushed hard, slowly sliding the foot of the bed along the path, listening for any hint of the Fachans, of Balor, or a magical staircase twinkling into existence. The bed was heavier than it looked—I guessed it would have to be to hold Balor's mass—and it skipped as it made its way forward. I panted as we completed the arc, leaning against the frame to catch my breath but not daring to touch the mattress.

"Now what?" Madison asked. "Is there a magic word?"

As if on cue, an iron stairwell spiraled up from where the bed had been, meeting the ceiling just as the stone shimmered and disappeared. My breath caught heavy in my lungs.

"Here goes nothing," I said as I bounded up the steps.

The dungeon at the top of Balor's tower was flooded with harsh light from the two large, open windows—the only real windows I'd seen in the entire place—with a trio of iron cells that spanned the walls between them on either side. They looked more like kennels than cells, like cages meant to house livestock bound for the slaughter. Barrels of sweet smelling water were placed just out of arm's reach of the occupied enclosures. Cornucopias of fruits and freshly cured meats brimmed with exotic, enticing colors. I was sure it was Balor's twisted idea of temptation and torture as a giddy addition to his magically raised oubliette.

I gasped as I threw myself toward Cernun and Learco, clutching their hands through the bars. Stripped nude, the welts and bruises which covered their skin ached and puckered in the harsh light of the outside world as it streamed through the windows. The haggard stern-set of their eyes softened as they saw me, and I kissed them both through the bars.

The cages themselves were iron—the same thick alloy as the cauldron we'd seen downstairs—and I sent out a wisp of my power to test them. No counter spell met my force with resistance, but the metal itself was insoluble. The locks though, they were a different story.

"Stand back," I said. "You really don't want to get any of this on you."

Madison followed my lead on Ethniu's chamber as I pulled the cork to spill the tiniest drop of the Fachans' potion I could manage onto the locking mechanism. It bubbled as it met the brass that had been molded to make its more intricate pieces, sizzling as it spread to consume the metal until there was nothing left of the lock. As I'd thought from its boiling in the cauldron, it stopped short of consuming the iron of the bars. We gave the mixture time to stall, then die, then ash before my boyfriends pushed open the door.

Feeling their bodies against mine, heaving in the pulse of lust and reunion, invigorated me. I clutched them tight against me as I breathed in them scent of them and forgot about everything Fae or MAW or magic. I wanted there to be only us, to relish in our joining with all the heat and intensity of our love. But this was just the first battle. I knew a war awaited us outside.

Reluctantly, we pulled from our embrace, and I studied the fatigue and hunger beneath the beauty I always saw in their faces. Balor had really done a number on them, but aside from the cuts and scratches that were already healing over, they were solid, and standing, and breathing. It was the terror they were trying to hide behind the softened glow of their eyes that really had me worried. Yet they were doing a good job of hiding it. We all were. The mental ramifications would no doubt come later, but we still had to get home in one piece.

I looked warily to the banquet spread of food standing beneath the windows. Fae knew they needed it, but even the water seemed suspect.

"It's fine. They can drink it," Ethniu said. "Father is too arrogant to believe his captives could ever actually claim the food or water, so he does not bother to enchant it."

My heart ached as Cernun and Learco rushed to drink, to consume, devouring the spread with such hunger I kicked myself for not reaching them sooner.

"Wipe that frown off your face," Learco smirked, his mouth full of the flesh of ripe fruit.

A half smile did its best to subvert the ever-present telecast of my emotions.

"Seriously," Cernun commanded. "If a few bruises and hunger are the worst that's happened, our coven's coming out on top."

"Plus, Ethniu here has been great company," Learco added.

"And she's told us a thing or two about her dad."

I took a moment to take Ethniu in. She had inherited her father's height but her mother's allure, which, especially in this case, was fortunate. Her blonde hair was shorn short and jagged in a way that had probably been meant as punishment yet only served to add an intriguing edge to her soft cheeks, iced eyes, and cherry blossom lips. I smirked at the infatuation evident on Madison's face, but I couldn't blame them. Like all Fae, Ethniu was beautiful. And then some.

"Eat quickly," she commanded. "We must be gone before my father returns."

CHAPTER 20

Light labored over my body as I stepped from the tower, but it wasn't simply the scorching fire of Balor's sun which warmed me. I felt better with my coven at my side, more magical somehow, as if the elements that connected us were reinvigorated in their presence. My heart knew how much I'd missed them, and the wild magic I was connected to leapt to feel the ecstatic pressure of its beating. We couldn't stop smiling although we knew we were far from out of the woods.

Still, we actually had to make it *into* the woods first.

I crouched low to the ground as I studied the open area between the tower and the Rowan trees. There was still no sign of Balor. Even the Fachans we had seen meandering through their duties as we stealthed our way inside were gone. I knew they'd been back though. The cauldron in the second story kitchen was emptied and the remaining basket of vials was gone, which meant there was a hell of a lot of that nasty shit out there somewhere waiting for us. At least we still had four full cylinders of the potion dispersed between us, plus two others that were nearly full. I just really hoped we wouldn't need to use them.

"It's clear," I called, keeping my voice low in case any of

Balor's henchmen were laying somewhere in wait.

Ethniu was the first to exit, head held high as she strode out into the world. The sharp edges of her hair sparked like glinting knives in the sun. She closed her eyes as she let the light wash over her, smiling as she tilted her chin to the sky.

"Of course it is," she grinned. "My father's vanity prevents him from believing any witch could ever penetrate his tower. Or me, for that matter. Though, with your rescue, both instances have proved false. Too, he is smart enough to keep his battlegrounds away from his home."

Her hands were filled with a variety of weapons she'd plundered as we'd passed through her father's bedroom, and I shivered as I remembered the force with which she'd plunged the battle axe through the center of his bed. I was certain she'd imagined her father there; the straw and splinters her blow produced as the innards of the man who'd betrayed her. Now, it hung loosely in her grip, but I knew she could catch it, swing it, or throw it faster than I could bat my eyes.

"I can't believe he kept his own daughter locked in a cage for centuries," Madison purred, still watching Ethniu with an amorous glow in their eyes.

I'd never seen them so captivated, except once or twice as they'd glanced at Angel when they thought no one was looking. And maybe once with Katrina. But even that had been muddled by the will they/won't they agitation of new love. This was pure enchantment. The kind my grandmother had warned me about in her stories about the Fae. It was part of what made them so dangerous for witches to encounter, part of what made our kind so willing to enter into bargains with them, to do their bidding. I felt lucky I hadn't experienced it, even if I'd come close with Cernunnos. Maybe I hadn't met the right Fae yet. Or maybe my grandmother's stories had prepared me to keep my senses.

Or… perhaps the wild magic that slid its way through the power I was used to carrying made me immune. Whatever it was, I didn't think Ethniu would try to use Madison's affection to their advantage, though she did seem delighted by it.

"It was partially due to his madness," Ethniu shrugged. "And partially a game he wanted to play to assuage his boredom. My mother's vision certainly startled him, but it's not like I haven't escaped before. Or mothered children. He has simply managed to murder them all before they could murder him. Well, all but one anyway, who was hidden away in your realm before the worlds were closed. Leading firmly to his new obsession."

So that was why Balor was so determined to gain access to our realm. He wanted to destroy the one thing left in all worlds that had the power to kill him.

I frowned.

"The creatures of our realm," I said, "don't live nearly as long as you do. Surely your child would have passed by now."

"The prognostication claimed 'the red line of the son would claim his life.'"

Learco and Cernun stiffened as the Fae made her appearance from the treeline, and I held up a hand to assure them Cethlenn was safe. The mother and child embraced: one tall and lithe, the other full and rotund, both beautiful.

"He has taken that prediction, as have I, to mean bloodline," Cethlenn explained as she pulled back to look upon her daughter's face. "And as such, with no way of knowing who our descendants may be, he shall find no happiness or tranquility until he has destroyed all lines of magic within your Earthly Realm. It truly is quite trying on a marriage."

It did make sense for "red line" to translate to "blood line," but a scratch at the back of my mind told me it meant something more. I just couldn't quite place it. Yet.

"Mother," Ethniu said, bowing her head slightly, "thank you for facilitating my escape from father's prison."

Her words seemed so forced, so formal to me. But all the Fae spoke that way—even Síl in his supposed nonchalance and authoritarian challenge. I imagined they attributed it to their claims of royalty, but it truly stemmed from their hierarchical structures.

"Allow me to introduce," Ethniu continued, "the witches Learco and Cernun. As more of father's captives, they have kept me in good company for the weeks until our rescue, allowing my mind to recenter, refocus, and find myself once more. As such, they should be celebrated."

"Weeks?" Madison asked. "They were just taken this morning."

"Balor's cells are magicked to make the passing of time seem much greater from within," Cethlenn explained as she turned to take each of my lovers' hands into her own. "It is but one of his methods of torture."

I wanted to cry as I looked upon my boyfriends. They were so strong and beautiful and resilient. I'd felt myself spiraling after twenty minutes behind the MAW's bars, I couldn't even imagine the perception of weeks moving by. Without my magic. Without knowing if anyone was coming to rescue me.

"We knew you'd come," Learco smiled.

The touch of his lips on my neck sent pulses of ecstatic pleasure down my body.

"Reunions are sweet," Cethlenn smiled. "And I thank you all for bringing my daughter back into my arms once again. Yet there are miles to go in your battle. Let us retreat to the Rowans to guide you through to the path of your journey."

Fachans—about forty of them—were milling about a clearing in a semi battle formation, some with spears but most with fists as they awaited our arrival. I imagined the scene of them—twenty angled to a point and facing toward the tower, the others angled toward the bridge—would look a lot like an eyeball from a bird's eye view. I'd yet to see a single crow or any other signal that The Mórrígan was waiting to swoop in to our aid, but something in the way the wild magic rumbled inside of me told me she was nearby. There was still no sign of Balor though, and that worried me more than any number of his lackeys.

A soft rustle in the underbrush behind me drew my attention back, and I clenched my jaw as I turned.

"There's about ten of those things working sentry duty on the bridge," Cernun whispered as he and Learco crouched down from their recon mission.

"And a dozen or so more are hopping the paths along the barrier," Learco added.

So much for slipping out unnoticed. Though I hadn't really figured it as an option, it would have been nice to pop our way out of the barrier—even if we had to swim to the far shore—and be gone before Balor realized I'd freed his prisoners. But hand-to-hand on land versus dodging projectiles in the water was better, even if we were outnumbered and out-magicked.

"How do we want to handle this?" Madison asked, the claws of their former feline form still extended in eager anticipation.

"Directly eye to eye is the only way," Ethniu growled. "Particularly if we can quell those beasts before my father arrives."

Cethlenn had stayed behind claiming she couldn't fight against her husband, though she wouldn't fight *for* him either. Ethniu, on the other hand, was roaring for revenge. And at least her mother had conjured up some clothing for Cernun and Learco so they would not have to battle in the buff. That was a plus, even if the thought of their toned and muscled bodies stretched and sturdy on the field had sent my mind reeling. But I had no clue what the Fae aversion to armor was. I guessed having only one real path to true death kept them from understanding the fragility of our witch lives.

Or maybe they understood it perfectly.

"The Fachans are brutal and strong and aggressive," Ethniu warned us, "but their weaknesses are obvious."

"Peripheral vision and balance," Cernun offered.

"And their magic is sparse," she agreed, then tilted her chin as she considered us. "Though within the Fae Realm, I assume the same may be said of your kind."

I swallowed hard as I looked around the faces of our team. Ethniu was all too right. Although I was figuring out how to use the new power inside of me, my casting wasn't consistent and the spells I had managed had taken a lot out of me. I knew I'd need to reserve it once the fighting started. And I hated that Cernun, Learco, and Madison had only their cunning and fists to rely on.

"At least we'll have The Mórrígan," I winced, trying to bolster confidence in the crew. "She promised she would help once the battle got underway."

Ethniu huffed so loudly I worried she'd draw the attention of the Fachans.

"The promises of Fae leaders amount to river ice in a warm current," she said. "They melt as quickly as the eddy churns. Particularly if they are able to drive spears through any misdeeds they decide muddle the completion of your end of their bargains."

She was speaking my fears, but this wasn't the time for wallowing.

"I believe her," I insisted. "Besides, this is not a bargain with her. She simply gave her word."

Ethniu opened her mouth but paused, tilting her head as she

studied me as if for the first time. I could tell she was wondering the same thing I was: why a Fae leader would make such an assurance to a lowly witch like me. But I'd learned long ago not to pull at sprouts before I was damn sure they were weeds.

"If that is so," she finally said, "then our task is to stave off my father's minions, pushing back the line of battle to the edges of the island, and removing the barrier so that she may enter these lands."

My eyes rolled as the realization struck my brain. So *that* was why The Mórrígan had been so cagey with her promise. The barriers which divided their lands were not constructed to keep out the—as she called us—"lesser beings," they were strongholds against the other leaders with high Fae powers. The Fachans and the Púcas, the Banshees and the crows could pass—bringing the nuisance of their respective leaders in tow—but Fae like Balor or The Mórrígan or Cernunnos were stuck within their own regions. Unless they were willing to brave the Thresh. The Mórrígan had been too proud to admit to what she no doubt deemed a weakness.

"Alright. What do we have to do to drop the barrier?"

Cernun asked the question from the tip of my tongue. Ethniu frowned, her lip trembling slightly as she looked away toward the waiting Fachans.

"There are but two ways," she sighed. "The manageable route is the final death of the Fae leader to which the barrier is tied…."

She faltered, squaring her sights back on us. The blush in her cheeks made the white gold of her hair shine brighter. She truly was beautiful, even through the rage and sadness and worry which swirled behind her features.

"The other requires a magic even I do not possess," she finished. "The barrier spells were tweaked and individualized many eons ago, centuries before even my birth. One must know the power used to reverse it, and only the caster—my father—

would know that. Beyond those options, my father would have to invite her in, and would only do so were she likely to fight by his side."

I understood why she frowned. We could not kill her father without finding the soul of her bloodline and fulfilling the prophetic destiny. And it wasn't like Balor would willingly give us his spell to let us dissolve it. The best we could hope for was fighting well enough—surviving long enough—for escape. Our *dues ex machina* was out. Fuck.

I winced as I looked at the stern resignation passing over my compatriots' faces. Learco's hand reached to clutch my shoulder; Cernun's rested on my bent knee.

"So mote it be," Learco smiled, feigning bravery in his resolve. "We get out swinging or we go out trying."

"Either way, we do it together," Cernun agreed.

This was it, what all our magic, all our power, all our time together came down to. I'd imagined a much longer life with these men. More love. More sex. A lot more sex. And more adventures. Okay, maybe not the type of adventures we'd been having, but trips to the shores of Ireland, or Learco's hometown in the Caribbean, or even just a weekend getaway to the North Georgia mountains from time to time. I hoped the Changelings who'd taking possession of our lives inside our realm went on to do those things so that it was sort of like we did them, in some way. At least for those who loved us whom we left behind. My parents and Uncle Gardner, Learco's cousin and family, Paul and Katrina, and Verne and Stacy back at HEX; they'd get to see our escapades and think we'd led a fulfilling life.

There was still a chance we could make it back to our world, but as soon as the battle started, it would grow slimmer and slimmer until there was nothing left but the memories of war within our dying brains. At least our love would outlast that terror though. Of that I was sure.

"Is there any chance your mom would know the spell?" Madison asked, their young spirit still unwilling to give up hope. I'd been like that too for so much of my life, prided myself on it even, but my new encounters with the Fae had worn that hope so thin. Still, their optimism rallied my own.

"It is possible," Ethniu conceded. "There was a time when they shared everything in their love. A moment, as it were, before the borders of distrust in both our lands and their home. She once held his secrets for him, carried those burdens as she carried me in her womb."

"Okay," Madison smiled. "We go back and ask her."

"You go back and ask her," I said.

Madison's face fell as if I was putting them out to pasture, which, in a way, I was. This was my mess, brought on by my trust in a wannabe witch who'd placed me and my lovers squarely within the Fae's line of fire. It was my fault Madison had gotten tangled up in the chaos in the first place. At least if they went back to Cethlenn's, even if they were unable to find the barrier spell, they'd have a better chance of making it back to our world when the chips and the bodies fell.

They opened their mouth to protest, but Ethniu cut them off.

"He's right," she said.

Madison's pout as they watched her lips still didn't hide the admiration in their eyes.

"The Fachan have not entered the wood at my father's request. But that is only as a courtesy to my mother. If he were to assume any of these three witches were there, that truce would end, and I cannot allow that. While you attend your quest, brave soul, the rest of us must fight our way through so that, when you complete your goal, when the barrier falls, you can all make your escape."

Madison nodded, but I could still sense they were reluctant to leave us on our own. Ethniu felt it too. But damn was she good at the rallying speech. That she'd no doubt inherited from both her parents and perfected during her imprisonment. I imagined her words—poetic and real yet hopeful—were what had kept Learco and Cernun intact.

"Be careful, young witch," she said, bending to press her lips against Madison's forehead. "Go with the light of the wild."

I did my best to quiet the pounding drumbeat in my ears. Even with Ethniu by our side, Balor's stolen weapons in our hands, and the tiny sliver of wild magic arching through my stomach, I felt woefully unprepared. Not for the Fachans. Despite their numbers and their vitriol, I knew we could take them, especially when it wasn't a surprise attack on their part. But I also knew, the moment they saw us, Balor would too. He would appear. And he was the one who had my heart pulsing in fear.

"So, how do we do this?" Cernun asked as we crouched in wait near the clearing.

"Charge!" Ethniu bellowed, bursting into the clearing with her father's axe waving.

"Guess that was the signal," Learco quipped as he moved after her.

Cernun and I were quick on his heels. The daggers I'd grabbed from Balor's wall were short but sharp, and they felt awkward in hands that weren't used to holding weapons. When all this was over, I imagined I'd have a Shakespearean time trying to out the damned spot from my palms. Even with all they'd shown me, I still wasn't quite able to wrap my head around the warlike qualities of Fae kind. But when death in its truest form was rarely on the table, destruction of this type became another way to pass the time.

The Fachans stiffened as they saw us coming, the first line growling as they lifted their spears or fists to advance. The second line adjusted their positions to hold the rear. Ethniu reached them first. Her battle cry sounded like a song as a single swing of her axe decapitated three of our foes in one fell swoop. With their heads severed, the Fachans' bodies burned to ash—as if their souls were made of pure fire—before they'd even met the dirt. But their blood remained, crimson and splattered across the soft white of her dress.

Learco and Cernun were primed for their own blows when my attention was turned to the creatures barreling down on me. The Fachans were quick, I had to give that to them, even with their single leg. A spear hurdled toward my chest, and I shifted just in time for it to glint off my arm, the metal tip shattering in the process as it brushed across the fibers of the tunic The Mórrígan had conjured. Hmmm. Perhaps I was wrong about the Fae aversion to armor. Or the plant based fibers of this world were really fucking strong.

I spun to kick out the leg of the spear-thrower as another Fachan leapt to land a blow against my chin. The impact clanged my teeth together, and I winced at the harsh taste of burnt oak and iron as my lip split and poured my blood over my tongue. It hurt, but it also helped to intensify my resolve. I pushed hard at my attacker as I dove to drive a dagger into the felled Fachan, snatching it away quickly before the fire of his death consumed the weapon too.

From the corner of my eye, I could see Cernun and Learco surrounded in charred remains of our attackers as well. We were winning! Against all odds, we were winning! But no matter how many we took down, there were three others to take their place.

I smiled as I spread my legs hip width apart, taking on the battle stance I'd seen in every superhero movie, and raising my eyebrows at the advancing minions. We could do this! Plus, the sudden murder of crows flapping in from above meant The Mórrígan really was staying true to her word, even if she couldn't cross the barrier herself.

Some of the crows swooped toward the second line of waiting Fachans, while others flushed the rest of the motley crew of monsters from their bridge and shore positions. There were so fucking many of them! But it was better to have them all in one place, to keep the battle contained and free of any surprise attacks later on. Besides, they were falling so easily. Almost too easily.

I felt the presence of the potion vials before I saw them, the dark magic inside of them calling to the one I kept—the one each of us was keeping—hidden in the fabric at our hips. The potion called to itself, begging to become one again almost as loudly as it pleaded for destruction. For death.

Fuck. Now things were getting serious.

I watched in horror as the Fachans uncorked their bottles, spraying the black goo not at us, but at the birds pecking and clawing them. Only a few birds were hit, thankfully, though their screeching was terrifying as they succumbed to the potion. I watched the murder rise upwards, above the reach of the Fachans' throws, as the potion rained back upon the creature's hissing faces.

I shook my head. They were taking themselves out faster than we could. And using up their killing potion in the process.

A second wave of The Mórrígan's reinforcements hurricaned in to caw at the deaths overtaking the field. Their blacked bodies swirled the air above us, the force of their winds guiding the potions directly back toward our enemies. I held up my own vial, happy to get the magic as far away from me as possible, as a crow swooped by. She met my gaze with a lascivious smile as she took it and emptied it over our aggressors. Six more Fachans fell, and I shook my head in amazement. We were winning! Against all odds, the playing field was leveling itself!

An open palm to my chest, thrust at full speed like a battering ram, sent me flying backwards, only stopping when my shoulders hit the rocky soil. I gasped to fill my lungs with the air that had knocked from them. Pain shocked through my akimbo limbs. Maybe I'd celebrated too soon.

My fingers twitched as I realized I'd lost both daggers in my flight. Panting, I turned my head against the soil, craning my neck to try to find either of them in the scuffle of Fachan bodies surrounding us.

It was chaos—complete and total—and yet, the wind knocked out of me, my body pinned to the ground, the harsh red sun bearing down on me, I was overcome with new perspective. The Fachans, in all of their bumbling absurdity, attacked with method. Several at once, yes, but others waiting for their brothers to be dispatched before centering in. Like they were just trying to keep us busy. Like they were offering themselves for death.

And, too, each group seemed stronger than the ones before, as if their power was growing exponentially with each minute that passed. Even still, their blows were glancing. They slipped from my lovers' bodies, hard enough to hurt but never direct enough to do any real damage. Even the Fachans with spears would misdirect their aim, sometimes altering it altogether if Cernun shifted to the left or Learco ducked his head too quickly. I took all this in within seconds, but I saw it all so clearly. I could hear it too, as if the wild magic inside of me was whispering the elements of their plan into my ear.

When the leaping kick of a Fachan sailed my dagger back into my reach only moments before a second one threw himself upon the blade, I knew my theory was sound.

Still reeling from the impact of my back hitting the ground, I pulled myself to my feet and yelled, "Stop killing the Fachans!"

"Did I hear you right?" Cernun bellowed back, the hilt of his sword pressed into the stomach of one creature as the blade passed through another's side behind it.

Learco had already paused the swing of his mace at my words, his head cocking with realization in lieu of understanding, when his intended target threw himself at the spiked ball anyway. I loved that about my boyfriends. Although we didn't always understand each other, we trusted one another implicitly. Especially in these new life or death situations we had somehow found ourselves in.

"Why should we not kill these creatures?" Ethniu asked, axe still high in the air, but her free arm swatting them away instead of killing. I was glad she was listening too. "My father feels the pain of their deaths, and I want him to suffer."

"The Fachans are pieces of Balor, right?" I called, ducking and pulling back on my dagger to prevent another Fachan from impaling himself. "Which means they are also pieces of each other. The more there are, the weaker each individual one is. Physically, magically. All of it. They're getting stronger as we kill them."

Another Fachan blow slammed against my jaw to keep me from speaking, but I'd said enough for my lovers to understand. And to pick up my slack.

"They're a hurdle," Cernun added, sidestepping another advance and tripping him to the ground. "They're here to distract us. To tire us out and keep us occupied."

"They don't even want to kill us!" Learco yelled, and comprehension crept over Ethniu's face.

"My father wants that pleasure," she smirked, dropping her

axe and bringing her heavy fists down on the Fachan nearest her to knock him out. "But the more Fachans there are, the weaker he is, as he is divided amongst them."

She grabbed another Fachan and lifted him, staring into his snarling face to speak directly to her dad.

"Which is why he's yet to show his cowardly face!" she bellowed, then tossed the creature aside like he was garbage.

Even the crows—reluctant to stop the gleeful pillaging they'd long been dreaming of—held back as we figured out how to regroup. Knowing their play may have prevented us from playing their game, but it still kind of left us, as my father was fond of saying, between a rock and a hard place. The Fachans may not have wanted to kill us, but the sheer number of them could easily overpower us all, pinning us to the ground, or throwing us back in Balor's tower cells until he was ready to dole out his own brand of terror on us.

Plus, they really weren't happy with us understanding their plan. As our weapons turned from them, their own turned to each other.

"Maim them, trap them, knock them unconscious," I yelled. "But don't let them burn!"

Cernun's sword cut through the air, striking down a flying spear that wasn't even aimed at him.

"And, I guess, don't let them kill one another," he huffed, panting both from the exhaustion of battle and the absurdity of it all.

"We just need to hold them until our backup arrives," I yelled between blows.

I didn't want to say more in case Balor was listening as well as seeing. If he knew we were attempting to drop his barrier so that The Mórrígan could join the fray, he'd be on us like locusts in Spring before we could blink, even if it meant he had to take out every Fachan himself to regain the full capacity of his strength. And I certainly wanted her here before we took him on directly.

"Um. About that…"

I was surprised to hear Madison's voice call out from the edge of the clearing. I grunted as I pushed a Fachan away, and turned toward them, nodding solemnly as I took in the worried shake of their head. Either Cethlenn hadn't known the spell or had been unwilling to share it. It didn't matter either way. Without the spell, we couldn't take the border down. With the border still standing, we were facing Balor on our own.

I shuddered at the thought. I had come face to face with Balor before, but never like this. My first encounter with him had been in the space between our realms, where all of us had our power, but none of us truly did. After that, he'd been inside Madison's body without all of himself to force upon us. Or, we'd been inside of his mind where the swirl of his madness disguised the violence of his fists. And still, every instance had been terrifying. I did not want to find out what he'd be like in his homelands and at the full intensity of his strength. Even the derangement in his head would be no match for the fury in his eye.

I gasped as a truly horrible idea passed through me, the wild magic within me jumping to clasp its edges and hold it in my second sight.

Shit, I told myself as I kicked another leg from under another henchman. *You are as crazy as the MAW thinks you are.*

I really did not want to do it. But what other choice was there.

"Can you all keep the Fachans off me for a bit?" I asked. "I have something I need to try."

I repositioned myself between the circle of Ethniu, Cernun, and Learco with Madison forming the fourth point as they entered the grove. Their eyes squinted in question as the wince on my face told them everything they needed to know. I was about to do something wild. But hey, wild had gotten us out of a jam or two before.

"We've got this," Learco assured me. "Do what you need to do."

I nodded, closed my eyes, and dropped to the ground.

CHAPTER 21

I tilted my head back, letting the heat of the sun burn my skin as I breathed in deeply to center myself. The wild of my being shivered, sending sparkles of green, untamed power through every cell in my body. It threatened to overwhelm me, to consume me in its quest to be unleashed. It was a powerful, intense magic—greater than any I'd ever felt before—but still a part of me knew it had always been there, twining with what I recognized as mine, waiting to be discovered, to be seen, to be utilized. I hoped I'd be able to control it, or, at the very least, guide it to my intent.

When I opened my eyes, the vast slate gray of an immense abyss stared back at me, vague and empty, yet somehow familiar. The red clay at my feet carried my footsteps right up to the edges of its cliffs. As soft and malleable as if it had just experienced the torrents of a southern storm, the impressions of my bare feet in the clay were evident for only a moment before they eroded away to memories. A distant storm sparked in lightning of red and yellow. I had been here before.

"Clever witch," Balor's voice sounded from the ether. "Attempting to meet me *within* the flesh instead of *in* the flesh."

I scrambled to the center of the plateau as his words pulsed in my ears, as the wild magic pulsed inside of me. I could barely contain it as it leapt to meet like with like, but it seemed willing to do my bidding. At least for now. I just hoped my manifestation was strong enough for the task at hand.

"It makes no difference," Balor cried. "I shall best you in my head before I beat you into the earth."

I gasped as the storm moved closer, gathering in strength and size as its colors began to swirl the cliffside of Balor's mind like the ghosts of every memory, of every thought he'd ever had. It was such an odd materialization, such a distorted view of what made up a being. But completely appropriate for his demented brain.

"I wouldn't be so sure of that," I teased.

The magic which swirled through the vision of me was bold, and a snarky smirk twisted my lips. The courage felt good, even if it was mostly bravado. It seemed to be doing its job in keeping him focused as my eyes scanned the growing strength of his thoughts.

"You think you can defeat me?" His voice echoed through the void. "A simple farmer playing at powers he can never comprehend stands no chance against a god."

I was getting under his skin. And not only literally.

"Says the Faerie whose minions barely have a single leg to stand on," I countered. "Says the leader who hides behind his henchmen instead of placing himself in the line of fire. Who sends his warriors off to die in his name while he sits all comfy and cozy on his metal throne."

My visage was pacing now, hands clasped behind my back without an ounce of the overwhelming fear which actually encased me showing. I definitely had his attention. I felt his unseen eye focus squarely on me.

"Stupid witch," he snarled. "I could smite you where you stand. Trap you here for an eternity of torture. You are but a gnat. A plaything to pleasure my whims—"

"Oh I know," I interrupted with a vicious laugh. "I am a bug to be squashed. A big mass of nothing. And yet, you seem so concerned with me and my coven. So intent on our destruction…. So afraid you can't even show yourself."

"Be careful what you wish for, witch."

Balor's throne, the same one I'd seen in my vision, shifted into being at the edge of the cliff, its metal feet sinking into the red clay as the silver, gold, and single red ray of its great sun pierced the centuries of memories swirling ever faster in his mind. It was beautiful, but the beautifully grotesque Fae who shimmered into existence on it was strangely moreso. I hated thinking Balor was beautiful, but he was. Sexy even.

One thick, muscled leg crossed the other from his perch and my eyes followed them up his majestically muscled nude torso. His abs, so tight and compact, made a ladder to the sea-wide expanse of his pecs, his collarbone, the angry veins of his neck. Even the large, singular eye that raged with every fire that ever burned in any universe was enticing in its danger. He licked his lips, the sharpness of his teeth on display, as he leaned toward me.

"Say it again, clever witch," he purred. "Tell me how I will squash you. It is so nice to hear the truth spill from your feeble mouth. My Fae kin are so adept at twisting it to their will, it becomes almost endearing for a simple witch to state the obvious."

I smirked as I tried to figure out how to respond. I just needed a few more minutes. I needed him centered on me.

"How about you say it?" I commanded. "Tell me exactly how you will punish me."

The fury in Balor's eye was so close to lust, twinning there in dual flames, as he leapt from his seat. He was on me in seconds. His thick fingers, calloused even in his mind's approximation of himself, pressed hard against my throat. His teeth, all sharpened into the tiny bone tips of spears, dripped with thick, glistening saliva as he growled into my face.

"You think you hold any power here, witch?" he moaned, sliding his forked tongued over my cheek. "We both know that is a lie. You taste not of power but of fear. Of regret. Of avoidance. All those witch emotions, batting around inside of you like moths, clogging against each other as swords in a never-ending battle." His tongue swam my other cheek. "It tastes delicious. Like blood and flame and the bitterest of chocolate."

My shaky breath wheezed through his tightening grip, and he bristled at the ecstasy of my agony. But I had found it. I had what I needed. My fingers twitched at my sides.

"You bring these people into your life. These men there only to comfort you as you distract yourself with their carnal pleasures. But truly, you place them in danger, and you are too selfish to let them go. To face your fate without them. You would rather see them dead than apart from you. And trust me when I say you shall."

His grip forced tighter on my neck as he lifted the vision of me from the red clay of his mind's eye. His free hand caressed my chest seductively, pulsing where my heart would be, speeding it up as he attempted to coax every errant anxiety from within it, to sate him until he shattered me.

"It does not matter who or what shall deal the final blow," he purred, "it is you who shall be the cause. And their deaths shall accompany you for an eternity of torment. One that I shall oversee personally. Until I grow tired of you and turn you out. Alone. Forgotten. Powerless and miserable."

"That's a lot of big talk," I gasped through gritted teeth, "for someone who only has the ability to see what's right in front of them."

The confusion on his face was palpable as he turned to see the real me—not the apparition I'd used the wild within me to create—and the phantom in his clutches faded away. The swirling rush of his mind picked up speed as the red and yellow flashes of his storms amplified in his mania.

"Witch!" he howled, leaping toward me in deranged ferocity.

But it didn't matter. At least not yet.

I had what I'd come for.

I smiled and closed my eyes.

A surge of magic swept outward from where I sat, kicking the Fachans my friends were holding at bay onto their asses as I scrambled to my feet. Lightning, splitting and sizzling like fireworks, cascaded around the island's perimeter, shimmering crimson and gold against the turquoise sky. It worked! It actually fucking worked!

"What the hell just happened?" Cernun gasped.

"The barrier fell."

Ethniu's eyes were wide, and the astonishment in her voice filled me with resolve. We could do this. We *had* to do this.

The Fachans broke from their stupor, spears acting as crutches as they pulled themselves back to their feet. Anger—more than they'd shown before if that was possible—clouded their features as they stared us down. It took me a moment to realize it was Balor's ill temper amplified through them all. I guessed I'd really pissed him off. The Fachans sounded like wild beasts as they growled and readied themselves for attack.

"Retreat! Now!" I commanded.

As the five of us ran, a terrifying shriek filled the air. High-pitched and wailing, it wavered like a mix of cawing birds, singing locusts, death. Another and another joined until a chorus of sorrows filled the atmosphere. Panting, I turned my head slightly, refusing to break my stride.

Banshees, white and gaunt and hollow, swooped in hordes from the sky. Their great mouths opened as they fell, growing larger with each inch they descended, stretching to consume the Fachans, swallowing them whole. They didn't burn; they didn't ash. They were just gone, consumed by the death wails of The Mórrígan's Banshee children, unable to fight back, unable to return to their lord.

"What the fuck did you do?"

Learco's question was punctuated by gasps as he ran, but I could tell he was impressed.

"Remember how I found that binding spell inside Balor's memories when we were stuck inside his head?" I asked, picking up the pace slightly as I steered us across the island. "I figured the barrier spell would be somewhere in there too."

"You went inside that crazy fucker's head again?" Cernun smirked. "Remind us to scold you for that later."

Fuck, his muscles looked good as he ran, all covered with sweat and dust. I couldn't wait to get him and Learco home, safe and naked and in my bed. I could tell they felt the same. And even if we hadn't been saving ourselves for the Ostara rites, the pulse raising thump of our battle would have promised an elaborate festival of our own. But that would have to wait. We had one more thing to finish.

"Does this mean we're going home?" Madison asked, leaping debris as the Fachans and Banshees continued their screams behind us.

"Not yet," I admitted. "But we'll get there soon enough. I promise."

The lamentations of the Banshees and their Fachan victims were faint and fading fast as we stopped before the tower to catch our breaths. The air was still and calm as if solace had fallen over the island. No wind moved the limbs of the Rowan trees. No river waves sounded as they pushed back from the shores. It was Death—long-awaited and long-revered—come home.

I was sure that was just the presence of the Banshees billowing out from their rippling gowns though. I had yet to see The Mórrígan herself. Still, I felt the eyes of her crows upon me from the highest branches of the forest. She wanted to see just how far I'd go. And with everything at stake, I couldn't turn back now.

"Do we really have to do this?" Madison asked, searching the horizon with their eyes as we breathed to gather our power. "I mean, wouldn't it be better to just go home rather than test our luck. It's not like Balor can follow us to our world."

I shook my head and sighed.

"We have to end this now," I said, attempting to sound strong.

I'd explained the plan as best I could as we ran, It was a good one. Especially if my interpretation of the prophecy was correct. If we were successful, even if it wasn't a final death, this was our chance to get Balor off our backs. For a while anyway.

"The Cullen witch is right," Ethniu agreed. "My father will not stop until the limits between our realm and yours are destroyed. And, as you four have experienced time in our world, in his mind, his connection to you will ensure he begins with your souls. He will manipulate that connection until the four of you are as mad as he. He will rip everything you have ever loved from your life. Make you watch as your own hands destroy it all. Only then will he allow you to die. Slowly."

Her knuckles whitened as she gripped her battle axe before her chest, craning her neck as she moved her face toward the sunlight. Her eyes squinted as she focused on the top of the tower, on the prison her father had left her in for centuries, allowing the terror of her capture to fuel her for what was to come.

"Besides," Cernun chimed in. "Right now, Balor is weakened."

"And once we get home, I have zero desire to come back here," Learco agreed. The fight was beautiful on him, his muscles twitching as he balled his hands into fists.

I swallowed hard as I winced.

"I need the three of you to stand watch outside," I said, looking away quickly from the protests which erupted from my lovers' throats. "If I fail, The Mórrígan will still lead you back to our world, back to your lives. And somebody's got to stop those fucking Changelings from destroying everything we built."

I couldn't stand to look them in the eyes, even though all I wanted to do was get lost in them, even though it may very well have been my last chance to memorize every fleck in their irises. I knew they would be angry at me, but Balor's warning was reverberating through my head, and—unfortunately—he was right: I was scared shitless of becoming the cause of their deaths. And I'd rather have them mad at me than six feet underground. I braced myself for their opposition. Instead, Cernun's laughter danced through my ears.

"You're crazy as a Faerie—no offense—if you think we're letting you go in there alone," he said.

Ethniu shrugged off the slur and nodded, crossing her arms over her chest in approval of the bravery on display from my coven. A sigh of relief washed over me as I looked to the determination on both my boyfriends' faces.

"If you're going, I'm going," Madison added. "In for a penny and all that. Besides, you slayed the *Ollphéist*. I'm sure you'll make quick work of some cyclops."

"You haven't met my father," Ethniu sighed. "Not directly anyway."

I could see the *if he's anything like you…* in Madison's throat, but the words never made it to their lips.

Ethniu was right. The visions we'd had of Balor—in his head and in ours—would be nothing compared to the Fae in the flesh, no matter how ferocious he tried to make the image of him seem. I was sure of it. The power he wielded alone could overwhelm us in an instant. I'd seen him do far worse in his memories.

But it was now or never. And I couldn't spend my life waiting for the other shoe to drop. We needed this to end, and this was our shot. I had to take it. Even if it killed me.

"I think it's time we all made his acquaintance then," I said, swallowing hard at the dread which coated my throat.

Ethniu's hand settled on my shoulder.

"I must warn you, brave witch," she said, "there are many Fae who support my father. Some out of fear or desperation. But others who believe he is the true one King of our realm. Should he call upon their aid—"

"Then we just won't give him the chance," Learco said, and I pushed to open the door.

Eerie whispers forced circles around the edges of the throne room the same way Balor's own thoughts and memories tornadoed around his mind: always there but disembodied, always found but lost. They were the same voices I'd heard during my first encounter with the Fomóraiġ, all those months ago when Aiden's spell had brought me and my boyfriends face to face with Balor in the space between our realms. He'd insinuated—or perhaps I'd assumed—

they belonged to the whole of Fae kind, sprite-like and watchful and ready to pounce upon our souls for nothing more than their own enjoyment at the behest of their king. Now, thanks to Ethniu and my time inside their world, I knew that wasn't the case. Each Fae monarch had their attendants, those ready and willing to do their bidding, but Balor's acolytes were waning. That knowledge made them no less frightening.

Still, the voices were weaker than I remembered them as if they were less somehow. Perhaps word was already spreading of our victory over the Fachans, of the fall of Balor's barrier, of The Mórrígan's help. Maybe his followers were already abandoning ship, diving from the island to the river to wash up on some other leaders shore where they could trade penance for protection. The whispers that remained swirled the edges of the room like songs in search of their staffs, aching to hold their melodies as the orchestra continued to disband.

Balor's throne was positioned slightly off center of the circular space. It was precisely as I'd seen it in my vision and in his mind: metal and massive with rays beaming out as if the soul who sat upon it had deemed himself the center of the known universe. The stone floor before it—the exact center of the circle; the place where he would force his subjects to bow—was etched with symbols from a language I did not know yet somehow felt familiar. I imagined they were shortcuts to his magic; where a quick call would shift the threads of Fae reality and send those he deemed unworthy straight to his tower dungeon or the center of the *Ollphéist's* lair.

Pennant banners clung to the walls, their weavings depicting great battles in which Balor was always victorious. Threads of orange and gold and brown and black set the scenes. Even with all the blood spilled on the dead earth fields, not a single thread of red found its way into the tapestries. No, the only red inside the room was the apex ray of Balor's throne. The one which pointed like an arrow to his empty seat.

"I was certain he was here," I whispered, taking another apprehensive step forward from the door.

"Oh, he is," Ethniu assured me. "He just enjoys his games."

The cadence of the voices around us grew faster, amplifying in volume and tempo. A pointed gust of air swept by my face like a glancing punch and drew my attention to my right. It spun through my entourage too, and I pulled a tiny bit of my magic through to my palms as a warning.

Balor's harsh, unearthly laughter filled the room, bouncing in from every direction, compounding in upon itself to grow louder and more ferocious with each descending note. I almost didn't hear the growl building in Ethniu's throat as it rumbled through her gnashed teeth. Her fingers trembled with the intensity of her grip on her axe handle, and I ducked just in time to miss the sharp of its edge as she hurled it toward the flickering visage of her father as he appeared on his throne.

His laugh magnified as the axe flew through the airy image of him and clanged against the metal seat, bouncing off to clatter to the floor. Balor leapt from the throne as he solidified, flying across the room—just as he'd done when I was in his mind—to grab his daughter by the throat and force her back against the wall.

"Insolent child," he spat as her hands clawed at his fingers.

There was nothing but fear and determination in her eyes. No love. Barely even any acknowledgment. Feral from captivity, she was refusing to back down.

I gathered Cernun, Learco, and Madison to my side, stepping between them and the Fae as Balor spun to toss Ethniu across the room. Her back slammed against the far wall. She crumpled to a heaving pile on the floor. I pulled hard on my power, manifesting a spitting orb of green before me in one hand as my other urged my friends to keep back.

Balor barely even looked our way as a flick of his hand extinguished my magic and trapped us all where we stood.

"Your time will come, clever witch," he purred as he walked, slowly and sternly toward Ethniu. "I must first bear welcome to the prodigal daughter returned."

I struggled against the unseen binds he'd placed us in, feeling the slither of ropes or vines or serpents as they tightened to hold me in place.

Damn. He truly was a menace. Large and foreboding and just as ripped as he'd shown himself to be, his physical form carried with it a weight that settled onto his shoulders, pressing down against his nearly eight foot stature. Veins swam like rivers across his biceps as he clenched his fists, but the haggard tremble of long life—of the burdens of being real—flicked across his skin in a reminder that he was not nearly as impenetrable as his spirit would have liked us to believe. He licked his lips as he paced before his child.

"I am almost… proud," he said, punctuating the word with the raw rage of one scorned. "My fair child, my little Ethniu, all grown up and as vindictive as her sire."

His foot met her gut in a powerful kick, and she doubled over as she fought to find her breath.

"There is so much of me within you."

His fist landed on her shoulders as she struggled to rise, forcing her back to the stone.

"I knew there would be," he purred. "One day. With the proper upbringing."

A swipe of his leg tripped her arms from under her, and her cheek planted itself against the cold floor.

"That is why I did not kill you when I first learned of the prophecy," he smiled, his face almost reminiscent as it quivered beneath his evil grin. "I promised your mother I would not harm you. 'Less, that is, you rose to do harm to me."

He balled his fist, rearing back to deliver his death blow with a maniacal spark in his eye. I shuddered. If this was how he treated his own flesh and blood, what the fuck did he have in store for us? Still, I was close to breaking the bonds he'd tied us in. I almost had the right counter spell in place.

Cethlenn materialized as he swung, stopping his fist effortlessly in the palm of her own hand, and tossing it back at him as he stumbled from her grip. He hissed as he moved, cocking his head to the side but continuing to step backwards as Cethlenn moved towards him.

"As your wife, I have abided your ways," she snarled. "I have allowed your imprisonment of our child. I have let you claim the glory of our battles when it was truly my spear to mortally wound the gods of the old wild ways. I have been your companion and your confident, but I will not allow you to murder our daughter as you fall prey to your own fits of madness."

Balor was at his throne now, and he sat as elegantly as he could, his large eye squinting at his wife. Its red glower complimented the green of The Mórrígan's amulet around his neck. I hoped she was locked onto it. With the barrier down, I hoped she'd arrive soon.

Cethlenn stared her husband down with an intensity that rivaled his own. I was glad to have her and her daughter on our side even if it was merely out of convenience. Their strength put us in a much better position. And it was nice to see his wife put Balor in his place as her stance dared him to move against her. Finally, he shrugged his shoulders.

"Fine," he huffed, and turned his head to us. "I shall deal with these pests instead."

I broke his binding spell just as a crimson, dripping ball of his energy flew toward us.

"Dive!" I yelled, and the four of us jumped to the floor, barely avoiding the harsh gurgling splatter as his magic landed where we stood.

"We will not let you win!" I bellowed, trying to sound strong as I rose to my feet.

"We?" Balor snickered. "A trio of powerless witches and a fourth who cannot control what little he has and leads his coven into a trap?"

My eyes scanned the room, but Ethniu and Cethlenn were gone. Shit. Her allegiance apparently went only as far as retrieving her daughter. We really were on our own.

"We have The Mórrígan," I countered, hoping her name would give him pause.

It only made him laugh louder. His guffaw reverberated around the room, shaking the tapestries where they hung and making me tremble to my core.

"Lady Lilith?" he said, rising to his feet and stepping slowly toward me. But at least with him centered where I stood, my lovers stood a chance. "Little Anand? She may add a 'the' to one of her names, and yet it makes her no more powerful."

I swallowed hard as he advanced, trying to keep his eye on me, lifting my chin in defiance and refusing to move. I hated putting my friends in this type of danger. I had no desire to bring them this close to Balor. But it was necessary for my plan to work. My fingers worked slowly at my sides, signaling Cernun, Learco, and Madison to their posts, pulling at the threads of the Fae realm.

"The Mórrígan is afraid," Balor howled, spitting her name like it left a vile taste in his mouth. He pulled her amulet from around his neck, holding it aloft and grinning as it melted to lava in his palm. "She dares not ever show her face in my presence. You, clever witch, are alone. Which is just how you shall die!"

But I wasn't alone. I had my coven, my lovers, my friend. And I could see, as my fingers twisted through the Fae magic of the room, the transparent shimmering of The Mórrígan's crow form behind Balor's throne. She was helping. She was guiding my magic where it needed to go. And it seemed she understood what I was intending to do.

"Now!" I screamed.

Madison, Learco, and Cernun leapt forward and grabbed Balor's arms, surprising him enough to throw him off balance, as they pushed him back toward his seat. I gasped as I pulled every ounce of power I could muster from within me. My fingers ripped at the fabric of reality, pushing through the threads of space and time to reach out and ensnare the red ray spear at the top of the throne. Gripping it with all the force of my magic, all the power of the wild that was, I retched the ray free, leaving its jagged edge sharp and waiting. Another burst of adrenaline sang through me to summon forth another burst of magic, this time focused on the center of Balor's rippling chest.

It happened in seconds. It took an eternity.

My coven released his arms as my blast rammed into him, pushing back his wide-eyed, spiteful snarl.

He hit the chair hard, howling as the spear ripped through the back of his skull, pierced his mad, unruly brain, and exited through the thick flames of his eye. The rage which animated his body convulsed as his energy left him, and he slumped against his throne.

"Is he dead?" Madison asked, breaking the silence as we all found our breaths once more.

"That remains to be seen," The Mórrígan laughed.

We spun quickly to see her standing behind us, a wicked smile on her crimson lips as he emerald eyes took in the sight of her fallen kin.

"That is the spear which would kill him," she continued, stepping through the crowd of us to get a closer look at his death.

"Forged eons ago by a smith of your world. He kept it near for safety, like he did his daughter, which, in the end was rather foolish of him."

"You understood what I was trying to do," I gasped, thankful she had been here to help guide my magic when I needed it most.

"My crows have wonderful hearing," The Mórrígan grinned, looking around the throne room as if she were sizing up how she would redecorate once she claimed the lands for herself. "It was a good plan, Darragh Cullen. One which appears to have done its duty quite well."

A flick of her hand sent Balor's body off to parts unknown, and the Fae queen wafted to the edge of the room to remove his tapestries by hand, taking great pleasure as her nails ripped through the battle scenes.

"Is he dead?" Learco echoed Madison's question, stepping forward to bring the Fae queen's attentions back to us.

"If your bloodline were somehow mixed with the earthen child of Ethniu somewhere way back in your history, then yes. He is dead," she smiled. "Or, if Darragh's interpretation of the prophecy is true, if the 'red line of the son' were actually spelt with a 'u,' then there is a permanence to all that occurred here today. Yet, if he is not truly dead, his regeneration shall take some time. So, for now, let us claim him to be."

I sighed, the tension I'd been holding melting with the expulsion of my breath. I'd been counting on the vagueness of visions, of the multitude of meanings inherent in each interpretation, to give us the upper hand—er, spear—in this battle. Maybe there was a little Seer in me after all.

I pulled my lovers to me, meeting their lips with ferocity as Madison hugged us all.

"There will be ample time for your carnality later." The Mórrígan rolled her eyes, but her smile was genuine. "For now, we must send you home."

I didn't want to let go of their hands as we followed her from Balor's tower to beneath the turquoise sky. The island, once so barren save for the Rowan trees, was bristling with bursts of yellow flowers billowing like starbursts across the entirety of the land.

"Is that Silphium?" Learco asked, bending down to take in the sweet aroma of the plant.

"It appears so," The Mórrígan hummed. "This is a good sign. The spell which gave this flower to Balor has been broken." She looked at me intently. "And, as such, all that went with that ritual."

"Holy fuck," I gasped.

That meant our bargains—the ones made under duress by myself, Cernun, and Learco; the ones where we had to bring Balor to our world or become his playthings—were no more. That alone made this entire thing worth it. I'd have to thank those Changelings for trying to take our lives. Once we kicked their asses back to the unknown.

"Let us go," The Mórrígan sighed. "Your window of return is closing."

I wasn't sure if that was true or if she was simply eager to extend her lands to consume Balor's now unkept region, but it didn't matter. I didn't want to spend another minute in the Fae Realm. I was so ready to get home.

I watched closely as her fingers twisted through the air, snipping and parting space and time to create a portal back to Echo's land, back to the small cracks the Changelings had forged to pass through. I supposed with Echo locked inside a bottle, she was no longer worried about entering her barriers. And she had the whole of Balor's island—and its new surplus of Silphium—at her disposal as well. No wonder she seemed so happy.

I wondered what she would do with it all, what battles would ensue as she tried to claim it, but that was a problem for the Faerie Realm. We had issues in our own world to deal with.

CHAPTER 22

I was the last to push through the crack, and I trembled as I felt it close behind me. Though sutured, I could still feel the space where the tear had been, no doubt thanks to the wild that still purred inside of me. I was glad to finally know it was there, even if there was a long road ahead to understanding what it meant. It, alongside the remnants of the rip, hung like weighted air. I was exhausted and hungry and ecstatic we'd made it with all our limbs still attached to our bodies.

"My forty-something bones are too old for this," Cernun groaned.

"Hell, my twenty-something bones are too," Madison smiled.

I laughed along as I embraced them, happy their feline form hadn't returned with our passage from the other world. We had done it! We had survived days within the midst of monsters and were well on our way toward reclaiming our lives!

Magic sizzled from Cernun's fingertips, and I smiled at the closed mouth sigh he exhaled at reconnecting with his power. I gave his aura a slight push with my own, and he winked at me in appreciation and promise.

Learco looked troubled as his hands traced the MAW-packed

boxes of all his worldly belongings stacked in delicate towers throughout Cernun's living room.

"Why is all my stuff here?" he asked, concern clouding his features even though we all wanted to celebrate.

But he was right. We weren't finished yet. There was still one more piece to set right.

"Uh, well…" I hesitated. "Our Changeling selves have done their own share of damage to our lives already. I'll explain it all, as best I can anyway. But we still have to face them so we can get our lives back."

Realization stopped our revelry as we switched back into battle mode. By the Fae, I never thought my life would have a battle mode, but because of the Fae, it did.

"Is it too late?" Madison asked. "Did we miss the deadline?"

They bolted to the living room, winding through the stacks of Learco's life, and clicking on the television as Cernun's eyebrows furrowed.

"I thought we just had to look those fuckers in the eye, and they'd wither back to where they came from," he said.

"That's true," I nodded. "But The Mórrígan told me their place here would become permanent if they existed through a great power shift."

"Ostara," Learco gasped.

Cernun pushed through the boxes on his kitchen island and found his cell phone discarded amongst the debris of the Changelings' presence in his home. Half-eaten food, spilt drinks, soil, and spelling herbs were strewn everywhere. Everything sampled and discarded as the Changelings tried to take in every flavor of our world. We were going to spend weeks cleaning them out of the carpets.

"Today is Ostara," he confirmed, looking through his calendar and checking the clock. "We've got eighteen minutes until the poles align."

Fuck! That would be the power shift they needed. The exact time the vernal equinox struck, when the sun and the Earth's equator were in sync, the shifting of Winter into Spring would also welcome the Changelings to a new home in our lands. Permanently. Eighteen minutes was not a lot of time to stop them.

"Where would they be?" Learco asked, his MAW training taking over as he pushed down his emotions to bring a militaristic strike to the situation. "I'm assuming there is some ritual involved. Where would it be?"

I'd thought the ritual they'd promised me was about bringing Echo through, which wasn't a problem now that she was stuck like a genie in a jar. But apparently, it had another purpose.

"Uh, guys?" Madison called from the living room, but I shook it off as I tried to remember what they'd told me.

"The Botanical Gardens," I sighed. "They said they had something planned at the Botanical Gardens."

"Guys?!?"

"I'll call a Broomer," Cernun said, already punching through to the app on his phone.

"There's no way we'll make it in time," Learco sighed. "Let me contact Leland Hyde…"

"He's already there!" Madison bellowed, and we made our way to join them by the television.

A news report was well underway from outside the front gates of the Botanical Gardens. Cressida Troy, as prim and as proper and as angry as I remembered her, scowled at the camera as she announced the "rogue witches" who'd destroyed the Starry Nights Festival for all of Atlanta's witch-kind. MAW agents, clad in their stealth black gear, lined the background as they ushered frantic guests from the park. Leland Hyde and Rafael Acosta kept their heads down as they made their way inside.

"We have to get there now," I growled. "We have to make this right."

The wild in my gut reached for my intent, grouping with the magic I'd always known as I found the language for both.

I was surprised it worked. Yet somehow, the magic that I'd always known met the wild with a cherished understanding to spread the fibers of our reality and grant us access to the Atlanta Botanical Gardens. I supposed it also helped that I knew the grounds so well, having spent so many hours exploring its vast landscape within Piedmont Park, that I could summon an exit that didn't send us square into a tree or a building.

"I don't think I'll ever get used to that," Cernun smirked, and I smiled sheepishly as he kissed my cheek and the portal closed behind us.

Learco was smirking too, but it was all business behind his eyes.

"There are thirty acres here to cover," he sighed. "We should split up to find those monsters."

I liked watching the fire that burned inside of him when he was on task. I knew it meant mountains of ecstasy when he finally released from his stoic focus once all was said and done.

"They're calling forth their mother, right?" I smiled, tracing my hand along his arm to remind him we were in this together. Even though his doppelgänger had ruined his career at the Moral Authority, we would get through this. "They'll be at the Goddess."

The Earth Goddess exhibit within the Cascade Gardens was

one of my favorite places—amongst a bevy of favorite places—to stop and sit to enjoy the beauty of nature in all of the Botanical Gardens. Rising twenty five feet above a water features, her closed eyes and outstretched hand dripped with moisture and moss and ivy and annuals to create a dynamic tribute to the natural world. Every witch worth their salt—even those of us who did not believe in an anthropomorphized "god"—took time within their visits to the grounds to pay homage to her gorgeous personification of Nature with a capital N. I knew instinctively that's where the Changelings would go.

Unfortunately, we weren't the only ones who knew.

I tugged on Learco's arm to prevent his sudden charge as I scurried us all behind the vast expanse of the nearby hydrangeas, already lush and flowering from the early Spring the Changelings had brought to Atlanta. He looked annoyed at first, but nodded as Leland Hyde's voice bellowed out.

"I don't know how you got out of that cell, Cullen," he yelled, "but this ends here."

The Changelings stood in a circle, hands-clasped by the water's edge. They barely looked up at the intrusion of the MAW agent as they continued their chanting.

It was odd, seeing the four of us performing a ritual ten yards from where we actually stood. They had mimicked us so completely, even if they hadn't mastered our personalities, and I tried not to let my mind wander to the potentialities of having another me, two Learcos, and two Cernuns in my bed.

Fuck.

Ostara was closing in, and the heat of Spring was pulsing through my brain. I shook my head to brush the image from my mind. I could always revisit it later.

"Mister Clarke," a new voice yelled, and it took me a moment to center it with Rafael Acosta as he too stepped forward. Both he and Leland had their palms raised, showing they were not holding a spell but were ready to twist their wrists to produce their own magic if necessary. "Please, just come with us."

The Changelings continued to ignore them, so wrapped within their spell the voices of their adversaries barely even registered.

The anger on Leland's face amused me. Even from this far away, I could see him red and fuming at the blatant disregard for his supposed authority within the Moral Authority of Witches. But those things didn't give a fuck about the MAW. Hell, even if they were "lesser beings," those things held no authority in their lives beyond Echo herself.

"We've got to do this now," Learco warned. "We have less than three minutes before the equinox hits."

Damn. We were going to have a hell of a time explaining the Changelings to the MAW, especially since they'd already fired Learco and wanted me fired at the stake. But those consequences were nothing compared to four Faeries loose in our world with our faces.

I watched as Leland and Rafael approached our doubles, reaching out to sever the connection of their hands in hopes that breaking their circle would circumvent any magics they were working.

Fake Learco growled, his true visage showing only briefly, as he tossed Rafael away, sending him flying through the air before he tumbled, back first, to the ground.

Leland faced off with fake me. Watching the hatred that clouded my face, the pure and utter evil of my snarl, made me grateful my life had never led me to such anguish. I had not even known my features were capable of such bile, and it chilled me to my bones. I watched myself pounce, tossing the MAW fixer to the ground as I growled above him.

Learco was right. We needed to charge.

"Let's move," I whispered, hoping the claws of the Changelings couldn't meet us before our stares met them. "We each have to take our own."

We burst from our hiding space quickly, all the fatigue of our Fae adventure extinguished by the sudden burst of adrenaline in our systems. Learco ran to Rafael's side as Cernun and Madison darted toward their copies still entrenched in completing their ritual.

"Hey there, ugly!" I called.

It wasn't much, but it was enough to distract my Changeling from his pummeling of Leland. He coursed toward me on all fours, barreling across the grass as if, in his rage, he'd forgotten how our witch limbs worked. Maybe this would be easier than I thought. The creatures were more feral than smart. Still, my copy kept his eyes averted as he ran. His sight line followed the ground as he hurdled himself into me.

"What the fuck is happening here?" Leland screamed, shifting against the ground and gasping as he watched me tackle myself.

I rolled as my own hands gripped me, pushing at my chin to keep my sight line from centering on my own eyes. My face pressed against the grass-softened ground, I could see that Madison and Cernun were facing similar odds. Our bodies were equally matched, but the Changelings' Fae strength, magic, and ferocity were overwhelming.

Luckily, I had a little fierceness of my own.

A sudden burst of wild magic sent my doppelgänger off me, flying backwards to splash into the lake beneath the Goddess's hand. I scrambled to help Leland to his feet, smiling timidly as he brushed himself off. He had a few scratches from his fall or the Changeling's nails and a knot on his chin I was sure would become a nasty bruise, but overall he was alright.

"Hey," I smiled weakly. "Um… So, that's not me. And the other guy wasn't Learco. So just stay back, and let us deal with this. After that, I promise we'll explain everything."

Well, almost everything, I added under my breath.

Confusion met the anger in Leland's eyes as I shrugged, but I didn't have time to cater to his MAW need to know. Plus, this would all go a lot smoother if he stayed out of the way. And would potentially give me time to fabricate something close enough to the truth to appease him.

"Darragh," Cernun called as he kicked himself away. "Forty-five seconds!"

Fuck. The Fae truly were chaos goblins. The Mórrígan's assurance all these "lesser beings" needed was a quick moment of eye contact to get rid of them really undersold the situation. This was going to take magic. The kind Leland Hyde would be happy to throw away the key for if he caught me performing. The type I really didn't want the Moral Authority of Witches aware that I could do, especially since I'd just promised them I couldn't before they locked me away. But the seconds were counting down, my coven were losing their fights, and the Changeling pretending to be me was waiting out the clock underwater.

I had to hope the MAW's rule against performing magic on another living soul did not extend to Faeries. And that, whatever happened next, we could keep their existence away from the whole organization. Even with Balor out of commission, temporarily or not, I did not want to even consider what the MAW would do while thinking they could harness Fae magic for themselves. It was bad enough I was about to demonstrate that I had it—though I'd unknowingly done so before and that had put me in their targets to begin with—but, hopefully, they'd just see it as more of the same old trouble from Darragh Cullen. And I was certainly good at trouble in their eyes.

"Thirty seconds!"

I closed my eyes to center myself against the bedlam of the scene, asking the wild within me to twine with and strengthen my earth-bound power. Now that I knew it was there, I also knew I needed to pay respect and homage to both for them to work as I intended. Within me, they whispered at different frequencies, but it only took a moment of acknowledgement for them to find their rhythm, to cling to the language they both shared. I felt them equalize as they flowed through my extremities, awakening parts of myself I never knew were asleep. I brought my hands before me as I reopened my eyes, viewing the scene unfolding with new sight, new understanding.

Magic—my usual kelly green hue tinged and twined now with a brighter, undulating tint that oscillated between new-growth moss and pine—swam around my body. I could see it, even without attempting to manifest it, and it was beautiful!

"No spells!" Leland howled, stepping between me and the battles raging across the lawn. "By order of the Moral Authority of Witches, I demand you lay down hands!"

I didn't have time to argue with Leland Hyde. I had twenty, maybe twenty-three seconds before the Changelings' presence in our world became permanent. And I could get done what needed to be done before he could fish the power-dampening amulet out of his bag of tricks.

"Cullen!" Leland stammered. "I said stop!"

The pulse of my power shot out in four directions, searching for the aberrant entities only the wild within me could recognize. It pushed past Leland, knocking him back on his behind and cultivating a fury in his eyes I did my best to ignore, before finding and swirling around the Changelings.

"*Díluailithe*," I whispered, immobilizing the imps in place, arms prone and eyes focused forward.

It wasn't much, and I could feel their muscles struggling against my magic, but it gave Cernun, Learco, and Madison their opportunity. The Changelings screeched and cursed, taking their mother's name in vain, as their eyes were met. My jaw fell but I kept my focus as the creatures turned, growing black and gaunt and vicious as they took on their natural form before fading within the confines of my power.

But I still had my own Changeling to deal with. Refocusing my energy I called out *"Tarraingt"* to pull him from the water to face me.

"Ten seconds," Cernun warned as he and Madison traversed the yard to my side and attempted to reason with Leland as he sputtered and whined about his lack of control over the situation. But his "I'll have your skin"s and his "by order of my authority"s fell limp as my boyfriend stood his ground between us.

Learco was back on his knees, helping Rafael sit up in his newly regained consciousness. Rafael's eyes were wide as he watched the Changeling wearing my body float to meet me.

The snarl on my face was unnerving. I trembled a bit seeing it, watching my features twist and set in ways I didn't think were possible. Seeing so much evil, so much hatred within myself almost broke my concentration. Almost.

I centered in on my eyes. The Changeling had the green down perfectly. Even the specks of gray and brown spread to the exact same spots within my irises. It would have been impressive if it weren't so damn freakish. I could hear Leland cursing as Cernun physically held him back from stepping between me and myself. But, as the Changeling began his transformation to his true form, Leland stopped, mouth agape, and struggling to make any of this fit within his worldview.

Hell, for what it was worth, I was doing the same.

I watched my skin stretch as talons emerged from my

fingertips, gnashing at the vines of my power like knives as the creature struggled through the bonds. My face peeled back upon itself as the tar thickened skin of the Changeling came to bear, asking to the white-gray of burnt charcoal as quickly as it met the heaving air of spring. It howled, showcasing the knives of its teeth to the setting of our sun. But its eyes—wide and hollow and untamed—stayed locked onto mine.

The seconds were counting down until the equinox leveled the solar and lunar energies of our realm, but I only needed a few more.

I saw its eyes change once more in the moments before its death. They softened, as if they were seeing me truly for the first time instead of the physical manifestations it thought made up my being. It was unnerving, for both me and the Changeling, and I gasped at the untold horrors of the Fae.

How truly miserable it must have been to finally understand the thing it so longed to be for only the mere moments before it ceased to exist. Though, I supposed, that wasn't exclusive to the Faeries.

As the Changeling collapsed, so did I, doubling over on myself as the last remnants of my magic, earth and wild, returned to me. I breathed deeply, letting the power equalize within the recesses of my gut, feeling it calm just as the Earth aligned its equator with the sun. That was the true moment of Ostara. I could feel it within me without even looking at a clock, without the pinpointed timing of the witches and the scientists who'd been studying the planet's motions for ages.

I couldn't help but smile.

But my grin was short-lived. It only took a moment for Leland's shock to wear off and his "get your hands off me, you heathen" to change to "What the fuck just happened? I should throw you all in a cell! You and your blasted coven performing black magic out in the open. Is this the kind of city you ran, Clarke? No wonder I had to can your ass."

The words spewed from him without breath, ringing through the thick, Bostonian accent which only truly emerged when he was flummoxed. Despite his flurry of words, his feet stayed planted firmly where he was, even when I rolled my eyes.

"It would seem, Mister Hyde, that Learco, Darragh, and their friends just saved us both," Rafael asserted as Learco helped him walk across the field.

He was limping a little and favoring his left leg as he balanced himself on Learco's arm, but he was going to be okay. Plus, he seemed remarkably unfazed, particularly in comparison to the MAW's resident fixer who claimed to have seen it all. In all honesty, I had no doubt the man had seen a lot of strange shit in his time, he just got flustered when he wasn't the one in control. Or the most powerful witch in the circle.

"Saved us from demons of their own creation," Leland bellowed. The red of his face was growing pale as his brain worked overtime to make sense of things. "I should lock all of you up right now."

"On what grounds?" Learco asked, his voice measured and sure as his MAW training kicked into overdrive. "You witnessed with your own eyes the entities who bore our faces. The entities who, I would argue, performed each task for which you have charged my coven and myself. The entities whom my coven prevented from wreaking further havoc upon Atlanta and the magical community at large. To charge four witches with crimes committed against the Moral Authority when you have witnessed the actual perpetrators with your own eyes could plunge the entire organization back into the darker days of Salem—a reputation we rightfully earned and have fought so hard to overcome. Do you, Mister Hyde, wish that to be your legacy?"

Leland glowered, but he stopped talking, choosing instead to fume as he considered Learco's words.

"I will give you a complete report," Learco continued, sinking further into his suave control as Leland continued to flounder. "To the best of my abilities, at any rate. A complete explanation and a magical cover-up that will keep the Moral Authority archivists busy and active for years."

His slight glance in my direction calmed the question that was forming on my features. Learco, as tried and true a company man as he was, knew better than to trust the agency with any of the Fae knowledge we had learned. At least not yet anyway. They had miles to go before they could be fully trusted. Learco had been an agent of that change. I hoped his firing wouldn't stick.

"You no longer work for the Moral Authority of Witches," Leland huffed, crossing his arms over his chest to take whatever ground he had left to stand on.

Learco simply shrugged. A quick look to his old assistant asked if he was okay and was met with a nod. Satisfied, he motioned for us to follow as he began to walk away.

"Then I suppose you will never truly know what went on here," he smirked over his shoulder as we moved to follow.

It was a power move, but it worked.

"We can talk," Leland conceded.

"We can," Learco called back. He continued walking as if he were unconcerned, but the relief on his face was obvious. "On Monday. Right now, I have the rites of Ostara to celebrate."

I glanced over my shoulder to see Rafael comforting a flabbergasted Leland, and laughed as I gripped hands with my boyfriends.

"You fellas gonna need any energy for those Ostara rites?" Madison asked, smirking as they watched our fingers pulsing already against one another's skin. "I was thinking maybe a stop by Aunt Paulina's to see Katrina would be in order."

"I mean," Cernun chuckled, "I wouldn't turn down a burger."

His fingers felt delightful as he tickled my wrist, and I shivered as he sent his aura out to tease me. Learco's joined Cernun's, and I bit my lip to stifle my moan. Damn, I had missed them. I couldn't wait to show them just how much.

"So should I call a Broomer or is Darragh just going to portal us there?" Madison asked, trying their best to ignore the sexual energy pulsing around us.

"I'm not about to show off that trick while the MAW's favorite boogeyman can still see us," I laughed.

"But it will make your trip to New Orleans a lot easier," Cernun smirked.

"I need to know the place I'm traveling well," I replied. "Make sure I don't step into a brick wall or something. Besides, I just got y'all back by my side. There's no way in hell I'm leaving so soon."

"We wanted our lives back, right?" Learco argued, his aura trickling down my spine in a warm, erotic massage. "It's only five days. That's less than a week. You should go. I have my own mess to clean up here anyway. And I spent a hell of a lot of money on that mask. Especially considering I'm currently unemployed."

His joke was meant to mock Leland, I knew, but I still sensed a bit of worry in him.

"Besides," Cernun purred, "we'll definitely be making the most out of tonight."

"We could find other ways to make use of the mask," I quipped.

Despite the sexual power exciting every cell in my body, I could still hear Balor's voice echo in my mind. *You place them in danger, and you are too selfish to let them go. To face your fate without them. You would rather see them dead than apart from you. And trust me when I say you shall.* Maybe a few days away from them would be a good thing. At least I wouldn't risk throwing them into danger again. And the reunion sex would be amazing.

But I had until my morning flight to decide. There were other things that needed my immediate attention.

"No offense," Madison laughed, "but could y'all save the sexcapades until after we eat?"

"Sure thing," I teased. "But if I'm not distracted, I might just have to tell Katrina about the googly eyes a certain someone was giving a Fae princess."

"What googly eyes," they started, then switched to, "It's not like we're exclusive," before finally settling on, "Fine. Have your public sex show. See if I care?"

I laughed as I peered back over my shoulder to ensure Leland and Rafael weren't following, then pulled on the wild magic to sort the threads of space I knew so well. It'd be nice to step back into HEX, back into my apartment, and back into my lovers' arms. It was going to be wonderful to step back into normal, though I wondered aloud if I'd ever really know normal again.

"Normal is boring," Cernun winked as he reached to pull me through the portal with him. "The first day I met you inside your shop, I knew I'd never know normal again."

I laughed as I kissed him, the portal closing behind us with a majestic pop.

What was normal anyway? For a witch with wild magic pulsing through him, with two gorgeous and powerful lovers, and a magic shop on his favorite street in Atlanta, normal was whatever I wanted it to be.

HEX BLOOD & RITUAL

**BOOK FOUR
IN THE
HEX'D SERIES**

**COMING SOON
FROM**

PARLYAREE
PRESS

ACKNOWLEDGMENTS

For me, attempting to write acknowledgements—the mere task of trying to encompass all the people, known and unknown; all the places, experienced and dreamt; and all the influences, good and bad which have made up this book—is more daunting than the story itself. Perhaps that's because no matter how large of a world I create in fiction, it will never be vast enough to encompass all its real-life counterparts.

I suppose that makes me lucky. I surely know I'm grateful to all the friends and teachers and parents who stood beside that little kid who didn't say much because he was too busy watching and analyzing and recording everything away into little notebooks. I certainly know I'm thankful that they hung around when he got older and spoke too much and too rashly and too loudly. And I am definitely indebted to their support and encouragement when he grew up and pursued his childhood dream of making these words—these worlds—his life.

You all mean the world to me—you *make* the world in my mind, after all—and I carry you with me always.

Too, I'd be remiss to not name the names necessary to name:

Melissa Tober: one hell of an editor; one angel of a friend; and the most glorious cheerleader I've ever met.

Sean Key: the most fabulous partner-in-life any guy could ask for.

Mom & Alan | Dad & Harriet: who always expected more, never accepted less, but were wise enough to realize the arts were not a dead-end path.

And, of course, to all my fellow witches and faeries out there. You're the ones who make this world magical.

Founded in Atlanta, Georgia in 2023, **PARLYAREE PRESS** is dedicated to publishing writing that expands, reveals, and interrogates the mainstream. We seek out fiction, creative nonfiction, and poetry that exists in the liminal space between what was and what will be.

The cant of circus performers, freaks, queers, and thespians, Parlyaree is the invented language required to tell the stories of those othered, to keep their secrets, to keep them safe. It is a polyglot of experiences that may only be told in one's own voice. Parlyaree—as an invented language—borrows from what was to create something new.

That is what excites us at Parlyaree Press. Stories that transform; essays that reimagine; poetry that takes us behind the stanza to the core of our being and back again; language that plays as much as it conveys.

Writers: tell us your secrets.

Readers: reimagine your worlds.

www.ingramcontent.com/pod-product-compliance
Lightning Source LLC
Chambersburg PA
CBHW011153310726
48973CB00010B/2886